*f*P

WUNDERKIND

A Novel **NIKOLAI GROZNI**

Free Press

New York   London   Toronto   Sydney   New Delhi

Free Press
A Division of Simon & Schuster, Inc.
1230 Avenue of the Americas
New York, NY 10020

First Free Press hardcover edition September 2011

FREE PRESS and colophon are trademarks of Simon & Schuster, Inc.

For information about special discounts for bulk purchases, please contact Simon & Schuster Special Sales at 1-866-506-1949 or business
@simonandschuster.com.

The Simon & Schuster Speakers Bureau can bring authors to your
live event. For more information or to book an event contact the
Simon & Schuster Speakers Bureau at 1-866-248-3049 or
visit our website at www.simonspeakers.com.

Book design by Ellen R. Sasahara

Manufactured in the United States of America

1 3 5 7 9 10 8 6 4 2

Library of Congress Cataloging-in-Publication Data

Grozdinski, Nikolai.
Wunderkind : a novel / Nikolai Grozni.—1st Free Press hardcover ed.
p. cm.
1. Pianists—Fiction. 2. Gifted children—Fiction. 3. Adolescence—
Fiction. 4. Anxiety—Fiction. 5. Soviet Union—Social condi-
tions—1945–1991—Fiction. I. Title.
PS3607.R6787W86 2011
813'.6—dc22
2011002831

ISBN 978-1-4516-1691-0
ISBN 978-1-4516-1698-9 (ebook)

For Iliya

"What is hell? I maintain that it's the suffering of being unable to love."

—The Brothers Karamazov, F. Dostoevsky

WUNDERKIND

PROLOGUE

The sky over Sofia is made of granite. It is gray in the morning, grayer in the afternoon, and black at night; black, but with a faint ruby glow, its hard, grainy surface ignited by blinking traffic lights, brightly lit streetcars, restless apartment buildings, television sets, neon signs, by iridescent Russian soldiers cast in bronze and the red dreams of fat apparatchiks sleepwalking through the collected works of V. I. Lenin.

Airplanes don't fly here. Time can't escape the granite dome. In the afternoon, the sweet smell of *ponichki* laces the chthonic stench of Sofia's ancient sewers, a thousand rivers flowing beneath the city, washing against Byzantine ruins, Thracian tombs, and nuclear shelters, pulling bones out of old Ottoman cemeteries. High above, the chimneys of decrepit apartment buildings spout sulfur; charcoal clouds hang low, tangled in the colossal accretion of TV antennas spread across the endless patchwork of clay-tiled rooftops.

A Gypsy woman selling flowers stands in the traffic circle on Boulevard Zaimov, next to a monument marking the spot where the Ottomans hanged Christian insurgents. "We are inside time, and time is inside us," reads the inscription. An unsolvable paradox offered by a monk hanged for conspiring to overthrow the sultan.

Over the fence, into an alley, across a courtyard littered with cigarette butts and empty beer bottles there is a high brick wall that I must climb before slipping under the wire netting, and I am back at school again. The guy in the sweatpants and thick glasses is Mulberry, the gym teacher. He also happens to be a rapist. The man coming out of the main entrance, in the military uniform and the medals: that's the army instructor; he teaches us how to throw hand grenades, bayonet imperialist soldiers, disassemble Kalashnikovs. His breath smells like shit. The short, frail middle-aged woman with a crooked nose and raven hair is the math teacher. She wears exactly twenty-eight brass and copper bracelets along each wrist because, according to the Pythagoreans, twenty-eight is a perfect number, equaling the sum of its divisors. A curse upon her.

The Sofia Music School for the Gifted is, in many ways, my home. I've been here since the age of seven, when I passed my first piano and ear-training exam. Stepping into the hallway is like being transported to another universe: the stale air, dwarfed inhabitants, and bronze idols fade away, and in their place emerges a boundless, empyreal city where everything—the walls, the colors, the people—is of sound. Dozens of soprano voices collide with the rumble of drums and timpani from the percussion department down in the basement. There's a vibraphone, a tuba, a trumpet; someone practicing a chromatic chord progression on a grand piano bends the boundaries of space, opening up a new dimension: in the city of sound, unlike other places, there's no limit to the number of dimensions one may enter. A string section races through a Brahms concerto, the cellos and upright basses carving out new suns, weaving black holes. An oboe and the faint sound of a flute break the laws of relativity: they roll the city of sound like a tiny glass ball. Space is weightless; a G major scale sets forth an explosion of blues, bottle greens, light ambers.

If you're a student here, pacing the dimly lit corridors day and night, you learn to rely on your ears. The eyes aren't that important here. Streets of sound, bodies of sound: these are far more vivid than the objects of the visual world. Even when we rush to the attic to fuck between classes, we do it with our eyes closed, listening to a clarinet, listening for footsteps, perfecting our pitch.

On the left-hand side of the main entrance, in a windowless cubicle made entirely of welded metal sheets, sits the school's porter, a bald septuagenarian dressed in blue coveralls whose main job is to hand out keys. Some fifty keys hang on a wooden board at the back of the cubicle, each of them numbered. The unusually long and shiny silver key at the bottom right corner of the board is for the Steinway in Chamber Hall No. 1. Next to it hangs an almost equally long but less shiny gold key that unlocks the Yamaha in Chamber Hall No. 2. Only the most privileged piano students get a chance to practice on the concert grands. I happen to be one of them.

It's not difficult to tell the two grands apart. The sound of the Steinway is sharp, cold, austere. Each chord carries a bright white aura that gives Mozart, Liszt, and Scriabin a removed, otherworldly presence. The tone of the Yamaha, on the other hand, is warm and damp, creating a vast space where all sunlight is filtered through a thick velvet curtain: Chopin's chords have a tint of mahogany; Beethoven's militant spirit is drowned in wine; Debussy's high-register flurries shine like black pearls.

The main foyer opens up onto a spacious, dark hallway with high, ornamented ceilings and terrazzo floors. To the left is Chamber Hall No. 3, equipped with a Russian upright and reserved primarily for small ensemble concerts. To the right is Chamber Hall No. 2, which is slightly bigger than No. 3, and used for minor piano recitals. A set of heavy folding doors leads to the stairwell and Chamber Hall No. 1, an acoustically insulated room with three hundred seats, wood paneling, and a stage big enough for a full orchestra. Twice a month, and on special occasions—say, the anniversary of the October Revolution—Chamber Hall No. 1 is transformed into a Communist temple complete with red flags, pentacles, images of Marx and Lenin. Teachers march on stage, perform salutes, exchange occult incantations. The principal and other accomplished proselytizers deliver hourlong lectures filled with messianic fervor. At the end, a dozen sixteen-year-olds walk onstage to be initiated into the body of the Communist Party.

The cylindrical space created by the wide, spiraling staircase rising through the center of the five-story building functions as a kind of damper pedal: here every sound seems louder, longer, less distinct. The echo of a trumpet merges with the echo of a violin. The voice of the history teacher, shouting somewhere on the fourth floor, sounds exaggerated, almost operatic. Walking up the stairs, one cannot help noting the large, ugly bolts screwed into the lacquered wooden handrail at even intervals. These were put in by the janitor after a tenth grader, sliding down the railing sidesaddle, lost his balance somewhere between the second and first floor and plummeted to the ground, breaking his neck.

Most of the school administration's offices are located on the third floor. Before and after classes, the teachers hang out in a large room labeled *Teachers' Headquarters* into which inner sanctum no students may enter. For in the far corner of Teachers' Headquarters, inside a massive wooden cabinet that remains locked during the night and the latter part of the day, rest the school's most valued relics—a series of large, vinyl-bound logs, also known as daybooks, each one a hundred and fifty pages thick, containing the full history of every student. Each class has its own daybook in which teachers mark attendance, grades, reprimands, offenses, as well as promotions and demotions of personal standing. There are four levels of personal standing: Excellent, Good, Satisfactory, and Unsatisfactory. If, for example, a student with Excellent personal standing skips three classes, he is downgraded to Good. If a student is caught smoking, his standing drops two levels. When a student's personal standing reaches Unsatisfactory, he's expelled from the school. The daybooks are the only official record of the school year, so should one miraculously disappear, the students logged in its pages lose all their grades and are automatically cleared of all offenses. Needless to say, miracles do happen at least once or twice a year, and the response of the school administration and the government is always fierce. Detectives take fingerprints and interrogate the usual suspects; teachers use fear tactics to pit model students against rebels. And those found responsible are sent to Labor-Intensive Correctional School which is, in reality, a prison for kids.

The fourth floor is home to the piano instructors. My instructor, Katya G., nicknamed "Ladybug," receives most of her students in room 48, near the very end of the left corridor, though she also has a key to room 49, in a spacious corner of the building, with large windows overlooking the National Library and Doctors' Garden, where she sends her favorite students to practice before and after their lessons. It was here, working on the old but respectable Yamaha baby grand with its browned keys and missing third pedal, that I first cracked the main theme of Prokofiev's *Mercutio,* a syncopated nightmare designed to needle the conventions of time. Room 49 is also the place where, after playing for five hours without access to water or a toilet (Ladybug being in the habit of locking the door from the outside and not letting me out until I've delivered a satisfying performance), I perfected Liszt's "Les Jeux d'eau à la Villa d'Este," perhaps the most beautiful piece of music ever composed for piano. To play something as divine as "Les Jeux d'eau à la Villa d'Este" in room 49 of the Sofia Music School for the Gifted is only fitting, if not ironic, since the school's original inhabitants were servants of God. It is a little-known fact—one that the principal would undoubtedly like erased from the memory of the sixty-year-old cleaning lady who services the fourth floor—that before the Communists confiscated and remodeled every prime piece of real estate in the city, shortly after the end of World War II, this building was a functioning Catholic monastery with prayer rooms, priests, candleholders, and crucifixes. For those with even a grain of imagination, it takes but a moment of readjustment and the old building, defaced by the pedestrian aesthetic of the ruling ideology, emerges from the shadows in its entirety—the dark hallways filled with whispers and faint footsteps; the arching niches on each flight of stairs hosting marble saints and angels; the altar in Chamber Hall No. 1; the confessional, in a wall recess on the altar's right hand side. Passing through the stained-glass windows at the high end of the back wall, a beam of multicolored light falls on the altarpiece. Liszt, who himself spent five years in the Madonna del Rosario monastery outside Rome, would have felt at home here, back in the days when God was still allowed to exist. The niches are empty now. The altar is obscured by a set of timpani, the stained glass painted over with thick beige paint. Can an atheist ever learn to play "Les Jeux d'eau à la Villa d'Este"?

On the fifth floor, past the corridor where the violin instructors receive most of their students, one comes to a straight wooden staircase leading up to the attic—a mysterious place of narrow passageways and triangular rooms with slanted ceilings pocked by porous skylights. In addition to the flutists and oboists who come here to practice their horns, the attic also happens to be a favorite hangout for those of us with lowered personal standing. Only a handful of initiates know that part of the odd-shaped wall at the very end of the attic is actually a small door leading to two additional rooms. Still fewer know that opening one of the wooden panels in the first secret room reveals a crawl space circumventing the entire building. The objects littering the floor of the crawl space—cigarette butts, used condoms, liquor bottles, tiny espresso-stained plastic cups, ripped-up textbooks— speak to the sort of events that take place here. The tenth-grade textbook *Moral Conduct and Citizens' Rights* (famous for its two-page-long, single-sentence, Marxist definition of love) hangs impaled on a nail protruding from a roof beam. A broom and a dustpan, which someone must have stolen from the janitor's room on the fourth floor with the intention of cleaning up the mess, lie next to a heap of ashes and the webbed, black plastic remains of an incinerated daybook. A single chair, lifted from the principal's office, stands beneath a skylight.

At night, when the only people left in school besides the doorman are a half-dozen pianists possessed by the irrational urge to keep on playing—in spite of the hunger and dehydration that accompany five-hour-long practice sessions; in spite of the cramps in their legs and the stinging pain of chronic tendonitis; in spite of the fact that they've never had a childhood and now find themselves entering the battleground of adolescence armed at once with the bitterness of prisoners and the infantile projections of seven-year-olds; in spite of having nothing to look forward to except more practice, more concerts, more competitions, and more humiliating episodes of stage fright—I climb on the chair in my favorite attic practice room, the one with the Chaika upright, and, squeezing through the narrow skylight, pull myself onto the roof to smoke a cigarette. The street that runs alongside Doctors' Garden is lined with chestnut trees, the tallest branches of which brush the edge of the roof. A faint light pulses atop the mountain to the west. To my right lies Sofia's center, defined by the golden dome of Nevski Cathedral, the pentacle-tipped tower of Party Headquarters, the mosque's minaret, and the mausoleum where Georgi Dimitrov, former head of the Comintern, rests embalmed in a glass coffin.

It was from here, on a dark, foggy December morning, that I watched as a black government Volga carrying the body of our principal, Natasha Zimova, a.k.a. the Owl, pulled up at the curb next to the school's art nouveau gate of wrought iron vines and all the students from fourth to twelfth grade, bearing hundreds of flowers, formed ranks and then marched out onto the street. So many flowers and wreaths, and the Owl deserved none of them. The Owl had deserved to die. They said it was cancer, but I knew that Irina had killed her. I saw how she did it. She didn't use a knife, a gun, or some kind of poison. She used words. Irina always had a way with words. She was also the best violinist at school.

People can be very forgetful. One day they're high-ranking apparatchiks, giving salutes, parading their power, spouting formulaic verbiage, and the next they turn into docile chickens, grateful for the crumbs their former enemies have tossed their way. But forgetfulness doesn't close the past, and neither does death. For there is time within time, a present within the past. Those who have died will die again, and those who have been doomed will be doomed again. And the system that has manufactured crippled beings will work again, until its predicted collapse.

"Read Nietzsche!" my chamber music teacher, Igor the Swan, told me after giving me an F for allegedly sodomizing Beethoven's "Spring" Sonata, for violin and piano. Now he roams the streets of Sofia in a ripped-up old sweater and pajama bottoms, talking to himself, hugging trees, kicking pigeons, throwing his hands about as if he is still on stage, conducting. And if he doesn't recognize me, it is not because of his madness, but, rather, because he has returned to a point in time when he and I were still mere acquaintances.

Others have gone back as well. Natasha Zimova is already at school, giving orders, saluting, teaching Russian to eighth, ninth, and tenth graders. The sixty-seven-year-old history teacher is climbing the stairs to the fifth floor, whistling the "Ode to Joy" and tapping his long pointer against the railing. Mouseface, the literature teacher, stands by the main entrance with a pair of scissors: she's been ordered to give an instant haircut to all boys with long hair. Bankoff, the physics and acoustics teacher, is on his way to Doctors' Garden to check if there are any students smoking. It's 1987, I'm fifteen, and there are still two years until the fall of the Berlin Wall.

November 3, 1987

Russian midgets are the tallest and Russian watches are the fastest, went the joke, and my watch—a Sputnik, which I had bought in Moscow after my recital at the National Conservatory—lived up to its reputation. On average it gained about two extra hours a week, which, considering my incurable habit of arriving late for every class or meeting, was quite helpful. I kept it in the front pocket of my brown leather shoulder bag, as I couldn't bear having anything on my wrist.

"It's somewhere between ten thirty and eleven," I told Irina, who was rubbing the hair of her violin bow with a piece of dark-red rosin. She was leaning up against the window, her right foot pointing away, toward the door, looking at me with her turbid green eyes in a manner at once provocative and inviting. We'd locked ourselves up in room 59, on the fifth floor, skipping classes as we usually did every other Tuesday. Below and around us, the diligent hierodules in red, blue, or Komsomol ties were memorizing Mendeleyev's periodic table, singing hymns to the gods of dialectical materialism, transcribing four-part inventions, reciting Mayakovsky. Occasionally, the voice of Negodnik, the history teacher, echoed up into the stairwell outside like a stray bassoon.

"I'm going to get you this time," Irina said, and she tried pulling my shirt out of my blue uniform pants with her bow. "Before this is over, you'll be running naked through the whole school."

"That's what you said last time," I reminded her, and I emptied the contents of my bag on top of the piano: Chopin's Préludes, Études, Ballades, and Scherzos; Prokofiev's *Romeo and Juliet*; Scriabin's sonatas; Liszt's transcendental études.

"You start first," Irina said, and she opened to Eugène Ysaÿe's Sonata no. 4 for solo violin. "Play the opening seven lines of the Allemande in real tempo, using only your right hand."

"And if I make a mistake?"

"You're going to run to the west-wing bathroom wearing nothing but your underwear!"

Irina laughed like a child, tossing her long black hair back and holding her stomach. I sat at the piano and scanned the chromatic zigzags of sixty-fourth notes, an army of angry ants taking the opening page by storm. Playing violin partitas *a prima vista* on the piano was quite tricky, since notes that seemed nearby on the violin fingerboard were often miles apart on the keyboard. But I wasn't scared. I just wanted her.

"This is stupid, Irina," I said, standing up and moving closer toward her. "You're going to get me kicked out of school. Let's just skip the duel, and the striptease, and move on to other things."

She raised her leg and stopped me where I was, her boot digging into my ribs. "Play the Allemande!"

I sat back down at the piano and took another look at the score, noting the double sharp, the triplets, quintuplets, and septuplets, the high B, B flat, and A flat perched four and five lines above the staff, the hazardous string of sixths running up and down, the stretched-out chords. Then I played the entire page, fast and confident, like a well-rehearsed étude, even finding time to observe the accents.

"You're such a dork!" Irina exploded, in irritation. "God, do you *ever* make a mistake?"

I could barely contain my joy. I was good, damn it. Really good. Plus, I had the perfect thing for Irina: "Juliet as a Young Girl," from Prokofiev's *Romeo and Juliet*.

"Well, honey, I think you better start undressing. You're not going to get through this one."

"Watch how you talk to adults!" Irina said, pointing her bow at me.

"You are just a year older."

"Yeah, but that's just in human years. I am talking about my soul, stupid!"

She set the score on her violin stand and studied the whimsical scales ridden with accidentals, biting her lips. "And if I screw it up?"

I closed my eyes, savoring all the things that I could have her do. "Then I want to see you walk, slowly, across the third floor, past Teachers' Headquarters, barefoot, wearing your uniform dress unbuttoned, with nothing underneath."

I tapped my foot, giving her the tempo at which "Juliet as a Young Girl" is played. Irina looked as if she was going to kill me. She was prettiest when she was angry, the passion and sorcerous impulses of her Gypsy ancestors turning her skin darker, her eyes quicker, her muscles tighter.

She began phenomenally, demonstrating the best bow work I'd ever seen, but then, in bar six, she suddenly let all the notes drop and collapsed in the chair by the piano.

"I have a better idea," she said, resting the violin in her lap.

"Don't try to get out of it."

"No, *listen!* I'm raising the stakes—I'm going to play something that will make you cry."

"No chance."

"If I don't succeed, I'll walk through the entire school completely naked. How about that? But if I do succeed, you're going to—let me think . . . take your pants off and enter your classroom through the window, like some kind of lunatic." She giggled with abandon, and I detected a few violet notes that reminded me of the fire with which she craved the secret pleasure.

"And how exactly am I going to enter my classroom through the window?"

"You'll have to go out this window and walk around the ledge."

"Walk! That ledge isn't even wide enough for my toes! Not to mention that there's nothing to hold on to."

I knew the ledge in question, because not long ago I'd had to stand on it in order to retrieve my report card, which someone had tossed behind the drainpipe on the fifth floor.

"Well?"

"You're crazy, Irina. Really. But that's OK, because you will never make me cry."

Smiling, Irina adjusted the pegs of her violin, drawing a long *sol, re, la,* and *mi* with her bow, tucked away her hair on both sides with bobby pins, unfastened the top three buttons of her navy blue uniform dress, and then, legs astride, began playing Rachmaninov's "Vocalise."

I couldn't look at her, because she made me terribly horny. Instead, I looked out the window and thought about the frozen rain that had fallen overnight, leaving everything coated with a thin film of ice. The chestnut trees, still bearing a few yellow-brown leaves, glistened in the dull November sun like fragile glass sculptures. Across the street, the dog-rose bush by the pond in Doctors' Garden resembled a crystal broach, its scarlet fruits shining like rubies. The gray stucco facades of the apartment buildings were wrapped in silver foil; silver tears ornamented the window sills. Irina was weaving funeral wreaths, honoring each descending note like a fallen hero. The grasping, then the sudden release—wasn't that the fundamental trait of the Slavic soul? The downward spiral, the darkness, the melancholy, but then also the letting go of all of it, the opening of the great gates of St. Basil's Cathedral on Red Square. I had been clutching to my miserable existence for too long; playing the piano like a machine, obsessing about things that only made me weaker, fighting with others to be number one. I knew that one day I would let go of everything that I cared about. I would rise above it, and I would be happier, for a moment. Si-do-mi-sol-la; going up, like a bird.

I thought about our first kiss, in seventh grade, when Irina and I had rented a small rowboat by the pond at Eagle Bridge; I thought about the cities I'd visited during my performances in Italy—Bologna,

Venice, Naples, Rome. Perhaps the difference between me and the other kids in school was that I knew for a fact that we were all imprisoned in a counterfeit reality. I had peeked over the wall and seen what lay beyond. I had proof: a silver Parker pen given to me as a gift by a southern Italian family that had wanted to adopt me after one of my concerts.

Irina returned to the beginning, repeating the main theme. It hadn't occurred to me before just how painful the F natural was, coming right after the firebird ascent from the underworld, as E minor moved into F major; how sobering it was, how disheartening. I suddenly remembered what Igor the Swan had said to me last time I'd met him on the street, in front of the school. "We've all been created idealists!" he had announced with his habitual bravado, shaking his finger at the sky.

Now my eyes were stinging, but this didn't have much to do with Irina's rendition of the "Vocalise." At least not entirely. There was something devastating about my chamber music teacher's pronouncement. Because if we were all created idealists, then life was bound to be one relentless disappointment. But then, there was also music. We unlearned the lies with one hand and repeated them with the other.

I turned to Irina. She had stopped playing and was looking at me with a mixture of amusement and pity. Would she really send me off to do something that stupid? She would, of course. A deal was a deal. One way or another, she'd made me cry.

I took my shoes off, then my ugly uniform pants and socks. Luckily, the ledge wasn't icy. I tied the shoes together and hung them over one shoulder, my pants over the other. Then I stepped out the window and, facing the stucco wall, extended my right foot onto the ledge. Irina giggled behind me, a hand over her mouth. She found the whole thing amusing! Or maybe she thought I'd give up. Two sidesteps to the right, and there was no longer anything to hold on to. The distance to the corner of the building was about ten meters. Then another ten meters from the corner to my classroom window. And what if it was closed?

I looked over my shoulder and down at the tin roof extending over Chamber Hall No. 1, littered with textbooks, brooms, and sponges. What an absurd way to die! Yet not so much more absurd than my life in Tartarus, under the granite skies, during the reign of the red midgets. But I couldn't afford to panic now, tiptoeing sideways five stories aboveground, bearing my white underwear to the elderly *devushki* next door. I knew the feeling of becoming suddenly self-aware while playing in front of a large audience; the halfway panic that seizes your mind and body when you realize that you've been playing a Chopin ballad for what seems like ages, and you've yet to go through the coda. To forget oneself again, once you've woken up in the middle: that's the hardest thing to do onstage, and perhaps in life. I would make a mistake one day, that much I knew for sure. One day I would fall. Just not today.

From where I stood, I could hear the high-register notes of the Yamaha in Chamber Hall No. 2, five stories below. Someone was rehearsing Chopin's Prélude in A Minor with unabashed barbarism, exaggerating the inherent ugliness in the chord progression. Balancing on the ledge of the building with nothing to hold on to except my will, I thought back to my twelfth birthday, when Ladybug had given me the sheet music of the complete preludes and instructed me to spend a night reading the A-minor prelude, without touching the piano. In this way, before I ever heard this prelude played, I'd heard it in my mind. I'd heard the raw chromaticism in the left hand and the bleak, determined voice in the right. I'd heard the voice and the accompaniment drifting apart until the voice was completely alone, a quiet monologue going nowhere, saying nothing. What I hadn't heard while reading the sheet music was the left-hand groove, evoking the sound of a broken barrel organ played in the streets of Paris, or Warsaw, in the middle of winter, an eternal winter with gray skies and chandeliers of ice and stray dogs sleeping on steaming manhole covers. On the bottom staff—the taste of earth, worms, and dust; the smell of dead leaves and frankincense. On the top—the luminosity of awareness making sense of transience and predestination. Three quiet major chords marked the moment of death, because death was sweet. It was our true home, the home we'd left and been trying to get back to. It's what we had passed through before and would pass through again, a moment of truth that suspended the weight of thought, the weight of the will to inhabit a dead universe.

The third bell rang just as I reached the corner and edged myself toward the window of my classroom, which, fortunately, was open. "Here she comes," I heard Lilly announce inside. "All students rise!"

Six more meters, maybe seven. I moved slowly sideways, imagining that my fingers were magnets that snapped onto the stucco wall with great force. I felt the frightened eyes of passersby on Oborishte Street, but I refused to look down or behind me. One last step and I was safe. I sat comfortably inside the wide window frame and put on my shoes and pants. The fear was gone now, along with the nausea.

I peeked in through the curtains just as the Raven, flanked by Angel and Ligav and shaking all fifty-six bracelets, entered the door and toddled to the middle of the classroom, placing a triangle, a pair of compasses, a daybook, and her purse on the large teacher's desk. It deserves to be pointed out that the teacher's desk—in itself an instrument of power—was marred by five white horizontal lines that stood as a permanent reminder of the laborious task of sanding down graffiti that had been etched into the wood with a knife and then filled in with ink, an anonymous five-line manifesto articulating the reality of dating girls who are also professional musicians. The manifesto read: "Lesbians play the piano. Whores play the violin. Airheads play the flute. Bears play the cello. Singers have no brain." Even the girls in our class had to admit that the manifesto contained some incontrovertible truths, though they were quick to point out that all boy musicians, for their part, were socially retarded, total imbeciles, pussies in love with their mothers, or all of the above—which was pretty much true as well.

Angel had volunteered to be on duty again. Being on duty meant that you were responsible for making sure that the blackboard was spotless, the water in the bucket was clean, the sponge was sitting on the board sill, and there was enough chalk to last until the Americans dropped the bomb on us.

I glanced at the exemplary students in the middle file—Lilly, the violinist; Dora, the cellist; the two Marias; and the twins, Ligav and Mazen, both untalented French horn players who always acted like sixty-year-old pedants—nodding while holding their chins, contemplating the life-altering wisdom of arithmetic with furrowed brows, ever ready with an *Aha!* were, for example, our history teacher to announce that the French Revolution had actually started in 72 B.C. in southern Italy and had been led by Spartacus, a natural Communist who well understood the works of Marx and Engels without even having to read them.

Normally, I sat alone at the second-to-last desk in the right row, behind Bianka and Isabel. Bianka's parents were Hungarian Jews, but that wasn't something you talked about. She wasn't a particularly good pianist, which was kind of hard for me to swallow because I'd had a mild crush on her since seventh grade. Even now, in ninth grade, with everything that had happened between me and Irina, I was still curious about Bianka, not least because she was an aspiring young apparatchik and it was fun to imagine what it'd feel like to do it with the enemy. Once in a while we met before school or hung out in the afternoon. We sat together during the evening recitals and walked in Doctors' Garden. We'd been doing all of this for two years and we hadn't ever touched hands. My friend Alexander—last desk in the left row—claimed it all had to do with the fact that Bianka had no tits. Girls with no tits, he once told me as we smoked in the attic during long recess, have zero passion. Not that I believed him. He'd never had a relationship with a girl beyond fucking tenth graders in a school bathroom.

The Raven was incredibly short—though not short enough to qualify as a midget—and wore a black skirt, stiletto heels, and a woolen cardigan the sleeves of which were rolled up above her elbows. Her wavy, black-dyed hair seemed to be styled after a lion's mane. She had a triangular chin and an excessive, permanently inflamed triangular nose which created the impression that she was always on the brink of bursting into hysterics.

"Dear Teacher and Comrade," Angel began the mandatory report joyfully, "the students from grade nine, section B, are fully prepared to begin geometry class. Absent today are students number two, ten, and fourteen. This report is presented by student number one."

"I'm not absent!" I said as I slipped through the open window and stood behind the teacher's back, causing a ripple of suppressed laughter to pass through the room.

The Raven turned around abruptly and examined me from head to toe. I looked ridiculous in my school uniform. The blue polyester jacket and matching pants were too tight for me, while my white shirt was always stained and wrinkled. I had ripped the school's badge (an improbable, poorly executed fusion of a harpsichord and an open book) off my sleeve, tearing a hole in the jacket. I kept the badge in my pocket so that I could show it to the government agents patrolling the streets.

"Where were you when I came in?" the Raven asked me wrathfully, testing the sharp end of her compasses against her thumb.

"There," I answered, pointing at the gunmetal sky hanging low above the sea of rooftops.

Lilly raised her hand and stepped forward. "I'd like to explain that Konstantin just came in through the window. And he has brought nothing to write on!"

She glanced back at me and then at Bianka, with a what-are-you-going-to-do-about-it grimace.

"Greetings, students!" the Raven shouted, ignoring Lilly's comment.

"Long live the teacher!" everyone shouted back.

"Sit down! That doesn't apply to number fourteen, however. Number fourteen is going to prove the theorem that we discussed last time. Go on, pick up a stick of chalk."

"I had a recital last night," I said. "I didn't have time to study."

The Raven let out a laugh in her heavy smoker's baritone. "So what? Everyone in—"

"The Communist Party, and the higher echelons of power, including the National Institute for Gnomics and the Ministry of Forests and Heavy Metals!" barked Alexander, jumping from his seat to perform a military salute. Short and beefy, Alexander had a doughy face and angelic blue eyes that concealed a cruel streak. He played the piano but was training to become an opera singer. We'd been friends since the fourth grade.

"Sit *down*!" the Raven commanded, her face flushed with anger. "Interrupt me one more time, Alexander, and you're out! As I was saying, everyone in this school plays an instrument and performs in public, and that cannot diminish their ability to study all the subjects that are going to teach them how to become respectable members of the working class. Without physics, biology, chemistry, *math*—without math, you're nothing! You're half human, despite the fact that everyone may treat you as if you're somehow special."

The Raven, ever the staunch empiricist, was perpetually irritated by the fact that students of the Sofia Music School for the Gifted were taught physics, biology, chemistry, algebra, and geometry only through the ninth grade. She couldn't bear the thought that one day we'd all immerse ourselves in the sorcery of sound, perfectly free to forget that the sciences ever existed.

"All Bach and Chopin did was transpose basic mathematical principles to the field of music," the Raven went on. "Anything you can think of is explained by math. Even—"

"The unanimous declaration of the Fourteenth Congress of the Communist Party expressed the view that our immediate and long-term goals are—"

"*Alexander!*"

"Disarmament, stabilization, and the abolishment of the Cult of the Person, without saying who the Person was, since naming the Person would also mean creating a Cult of the Person, which—"

"Hand me your report book and leave the classroom!" the Raven screamed, pounding the table with a clenched fist. At any moment, Angel would offer to bring her a glass of water.

Alexander marched past the Raven, right hand raised in salute, head turned to the left, face twisted in a vacuous smile—just like the cretinous soldiers from the Military Academy one would see marching in front of the mausoleum on days of national celebration. As he passed me, I nodded my thanks. Thanks, *kopeleh,* for mocking the bitch.

Just before exiting, Alexander turned around and took a bow. Then he slammed the door with enough force that the soprano and pianist practicing down the hall fell silent and an angered teacher inquired loudly whether this was a school of music or a circus.

Standing close to the Raven, one could never resist the urge to examine the enormous hairy mole at the base of her nose, and her bushy eyebrows, thick enough to hide a small pencil in, and perhaps a few paper clips, for good measure.

"Give me an F," I said and headed for my desk. I wanted to slap Lilly on the neck and knock all her stuff on the floor, but then I remembered that day when I had decided to sit in on one of the regular after-school orchestra sessions in Chamber Hall No. 1 attended by all the string students—they were playing Schubert, I think—and the conductor told everyone to stop so that he could hear Lilly play her part alone. The toxicity of her playing—the radiation—made everyone absolutely sick. Then again, it wasn't her fault that she had been born a peasant, with the musical proclivities of a crocodile, and—with the help of her daddy, a Party member, and a system that championed mediocrity—ended up enrolled in a music school for the *gifted.* If you've ever competed with other musicians for a prize, you know that achieving perfection can cost your life. One wrong note, one convoluted melodic phrase, and you could end up in an insane asylum—or worse, in a bathtub with slit wrists. To see mediocrity thrive in a place where perfection was the norm, then, was not just offensive; it was torture. Still, I felt sorry for Lilly. She knew she was useless. The untalented always know what they're worth. That's their tragedy.

"Get back to the blackboard and start working on the theorem," the Raven said calmly to me now, flipping through the daybook. "You're going to have to earn your F, number fourteen. And if you decide to ignore me, I'll kick you out and put you down with an absence—I see here that one more absence is just what you need to have your personal standing lowered to Satisfactory. And we all know what a slippery slope it is from there. I wonder what kind of pianist you'll be once you're kicked out of the Sofia Music School for the Gifted!"

Most of the sheep—Ligav, Mazen, Angel, Lilly, and Emile (a befreckled pianist with thin blond hair)—burst into laughter. Which was absolutely fine. After nine years of school and four years of government day care, where the bad kids were sent home with black stickers on their blue uniforms, I was virtually immune to every form of humiliation, except the kind that occurred while performing onstage. In the end, it was who you were onstage that really counted. The Raven and the sheep could never hurt Konstantin the pianist. Even standing idle here, beside the blackboard, a piece of chalk in my hand, I still made them feel small. When I laughed with them, I laughed at their pedestrian imagination. As for the Raven, shaking her fifty-six bracelets, she was just a cursed old spirit with an insatiable appetite for revenge and not a single blessing. I could see it in her eyes. These lands were infested with old, conniving, fallen spirits: the spirits of Thracian and Mongol warriors, of Roman slaves, of blinded and beheaded Serbs and Bulgarians, of exiled Greek philosophers, of Turks and Illyrians; they say that everyone born here is cursed, and it's true that I, too, carried the shadow of the curse in my soul.

I couldn't remember exactly how the feud between the Raven and me had started. Had she hated me from the moment we met five years before? Or had she only begun to hate me a few years later, when her niece, a second-rate piano player with waist-long hair and incredibly short fingers, was admitted to the school under dubious circumstances? Or did it all start in sixth grade, when my father, during his last appearance at a parent-teacher conference, told the Raven he'd given up on me?

"Draw an acute triangle and label the angles," the Raven said, without turning around to look at me.

"Excuse me . . ." said Slav, sitting at the front desk near the door, as he held his pen and pointed at his lips and tongue, which were stained with black ink. Slav—a violinist who looked remarkably like Paganini—was known around the school for his habit of sucking the ink out of his pens. He claimed that he did this in order to earn a trip to the bathroom and get away from the teachers, if only for a few minutes. On any given day of the week, Slav might be seen walking around the building, carrying his cracked, hundred-year-old violin case, ink smeared all over his face, hands, shirt, and jacket. Both he and Ivan—another violinist who sat next to Slav in class—were very talented, especially Ivan, and were often cited as proof of the widespread view that gifted musicians were invariably messed up in one way or another. Ivan, for instance, was capable of transcribing the first ten bars of a four-voice fugue upon a single hearing—a feat of genius bordering on sickness, for even the best trained ears in the school could transcribe only seven or eight bars of monophonic melody after a single hearing. Ivan was also the kid who famously walked onstage to give a recital (a bow in his right hand and a violin in his left), tripped, and fell to the ground, his hands stretched behind his back like a pair of wings, in defiance of every self-preservation instinct known to man. He broke his nose and split an eyebrow, but hadn't let his bow and violin touch the floor, which, as he later explained, would have been a "major faux pas."

Slav returned from his trip to the bathroom with water dripping from his face and hair, his lips still black from the ink. I had been standing in front of the blackboard for ten minutes now and was prepared to stand another thirty. The Raven wanted me to feel humiliated, to feel as if I had walked onstage and suddenly forgotten every note from my repertoire.

"Just write anything!" Lilly complained.

"He's wasting everyone's time," the twins murmured, dusting the sleeves of their jackets. I wasn't embarrassed to look at the faces of my classmates. They had all stabbed me in the back, at one time or another. Except Bianka and Alexander. But none of this really mattered to me. This wasn't a stage, and geometry had nothing to do with life. Life was so much larger than the Raven and her dreadful mole, her Pythagorean bracelets, her meaningless numbers; larger than the glaring faces of my classmates, the mustard-colored classroom, the ripped linoleum floor, the Chaika upright with dented lacquer and missing lid; it was larger than the seven-foot-tall windows with their century-old locking mechanisms and brass handles, the clay-tiled rooftops, the golden dome of Nevski Cathedral, the tree limbs weighed down with ice, and the rules that governed traffic and made little people get on and off trams and buses and go to work; larger still than the yellow cobblestone streets, the government Volgas occupied by fat, greasy apparatchiks eating fresh cherries in the middle of winter, and the mummy of Georgi D. lying in its glass coffin—a sleeping beauty stuffed with cotton—than the banners announcing the abolishment of the Cult of the Person, even though no one dared to say who the Person was, and the third graders in blue ties, and the fifth graders in red ties, and the ninth graders in Komsomol ties, and the policemen with pentacles on their hats, and the military generals who came to our school every year and made us strip naked and then examined our bodies to determine if they were sweet enough to be fed to the insatiable imperialist enemy.

Life was larger than all that. Life was about walking out of the Sofia Music School for the Gifted after dark—at the end of a long day of classes, ensemble sessions, piano lessons, and additional practice—and wandering downtown toward Tsar Shishman Street, past the National Assembly and the Russian High School, past pastry shops and old apartment buildings with dimly lit staircases and cramped kitchens dressed in cheap curtains, past the dirty fish store with a giant tank full of dead fish and crabs floating on its surface, crossing the street to avoid the National Security Headquarters and its cretinous soldier guards hugging their Kalashnikovs like newborn babies, over the grass and the sign that read "Don't Walk on the Grass!" and around the stinking underground public lavatories, into the little park with the pond and the weeping willow and the miserable-looking pigeons, and the drunks, and the cancer patients in their pajamas, and the mentally ill, and the stray dogs, and the head-scarved widows; and then sitting down under the weeping willow to light a cigarette, aware of time, and gravity, and the unstoppable process of metamorphosis; aware also of the warm, golden light beaming from the door of the ancient Seven Saints Church at the park's periphery and the black-robed orthodox clergymen tending to their tiny god—their deaf, mute, blind, limbless, powerless god, which had been banished from the Kingdom of Scientists, Proletarians, and Empirical Thinkers for bad behavior. A tiny god with a lowered personal standing.

Life was about playing Chopin's preludes to yourself; about anticipating and surviving the stretched-out, capricious Sofia spring when cherry trees blossomed, when boys and girls walked hand in hand and made love at night on a bench in Doctors' Garden or at the back of an empty, unlit street car; when so many adolescents decided to get ahead of the pack and hanged themselves in their grandmother's attic, or drained their blood in a bathtub, or jumped from the top floor of their high school, most often without leaving a note, for suicide notes were rather tasteless and presumptuous: they always underestimated the intelligence of those who'd opted to wait for their natural end.

Life was, finally, about understanding the great perfection, about placing it in time, tasting it, dissolving in it. And the great perfection was death. Death, the final abode. Death, the sweet cure. Death, the only truth. Three major chords—tonic, dominant, and tonic again—at the end of Chopin's Prélude in A Minor.

It was 11:05 a.m., according to Angel's watch, which meant that there were still twenty minutes until the end of the period. Bianka looked so cute, three rows back, resting her head in the palm of her hand, staring gloomily out the window. Her eyes were prettiest when she was sad. Was she disappointed in me? Perhaps. I couldn't even prove a simple theorem. I had D's and F's in every subject except piano, solfège, chamber music, and counterpoint. I didn't even have the dignity to tell the Raven to go fuck herself.

I was tired of playing this game of teachers and students. Even my piano playing, which people said was on par with the very best, was by now an act of desperation. I knew I could never win. Not against the onslaught of mediocrity; not against the robots who played ten hours a day, had perfect grades, and did everything exactly as they were told; not against the protégés of the proletarian nobility who had the hands and sensibility of pigheaded weight lifters. Yet I kept on playing, kept on perfecting my chromatic and diatonic scales, my arpeggios and chord progressions, my voice—for voice was everything. Out of a thousand players, only one or two pianists had a voice. Even a ten-year-old could learn to play Rachmaninov. It was the slow pieces that were the hardest—the nocturnes, the preludes, the quiet passages of the ballads and the scherzos—for they required only voice. In the morning, in the afternoon, even in the middle of the night, I searched for the secret source of the *voice,* pressing a single key and listening to its sound with every cell in my body, tuning my inner being to the resonance of the ether.

It had started raining again, and, standing there with my useless stick of chalk at the blackboard, I wondered if my cigarettes were getting wet. Every morning before walking into school, I snuck through the narrow gate adjacent to the school's main entrance and hid my cigarettes in the *pushkom,* a spacious backyard enclosed on all sides by a tall, mossy brick wall. Hiding one's cigarettes outside school was essential for students with lowered personal standing as we were searched every time we approached the main entrance. Once, when Alexander was stopped by the two gym teachers and Bankoff for a routine check at the end of long recess, he kneeled down and instantly ate all six of the cigarettes he was hiding in his sleeve. We were at war with the state, and cigarettes, booze, and diazepam were our weapons of choice. The Communist pigs owned our lives; they owned our hands and fingers, our talent; they owned our childhoods and our minds, which they never ceased cramming full of occult incantations and slogans foreshadowing the dawn of the Supreme Social Order. "In a solid body, a solid spirit!" "Love is the responsibility of single working entities to form healthy proletarian cells." "Exercise is the principal duty of every son and daughter of the working class." "Youth is the fertile soil of the Communist Ideal." They wanted healthy, work-loving entities who would march, salute, and procreate with the sole purpose of filling the Bright Future with yet more healthy, work-loving enti-ties. Well, we weren't going to give them any of it. We were going to destroy their most cherished property: in a rotten body, an eternally dead spirit. Love is fucking in public places and aborting all accidental progenies. Exercise is smoking two packs a day, drinking eight pints of beer at the Dondukov Boulevard tavern during long recess, and steal-ing painkillers from the nurse's office. Youth is feeling seventy years old, misanthropic, and ready to die at fifteen.

At their desks, the sheep were hard at work on a quiz that the Raven had given them if only to make them stop yawning. Maybe Ladybug would come and rescue me from this nightmare. She had done it before. She would knock on the door, apologize for interrupt-ing, then ask the Raven if she would be kind enough to let me attend a rehearsal. Ah, the electricity that would pass between the two! My beautiful, thirty-one-year-old piano teacher never missed an occasion to demonstrate her superiority over the musically retarded inhabitants of the school. In an instant I would change from a hunted pariah to a kid with a unique gift that warranted unsurpassed privileges. Wasn't it the *gift* that bothered them the most? How unfair, how un-Marxist and unproletarian it was to be born with a gift! If we were all born equal, and talent were merely the outcome of hard work, why was it that some—Vadim, for instance—achieved perfection spontaneously, without having to practice at all? And what empirical materialist the-ory could explain why some kids *learned* to play the piano, while others simply *remembered*?

"Excuse me," Slav said, standing up clumsily and knocking the violin case propped up against his desk. He walked toward the Raven's table, ink dripping from his hands and nose. "I'm afraid that I . . . again . . ."

"What is wrong with you?" the Raven shouted, and she pointed at the door. "Get out of my sight! *Out!* Snorting ink in my class! Like an *animal!*"

Someone in the corridor burst out laughing and we all heard Alexan-der distinctly say that animals don't, as a rule, snort ink.

Now the Raven's voice shifted to bass baritone. "Worthless brats! You all deserve to be sent to Labor-Intensive Correctional School! Number fourteen—very well—you've earned your F. And I'm going to do everything in my power to fail you this semester. That's a promise!"

I placed the chalk on the blackboard sill and walked leisurely back to my desk. Never had getting an F felt so good.

Chopin,
Scherzo in B Minor, op. 20, no. 1
(Presto con fuoco)

December 14, 1987

Room 49 was tiny. A chair, a piano bench, a baby grand, a metal wastebasket. A skewed hat stand in the corner completed the setting. The door was wrapped in a burgundy vinyl sheet fastened around the edges with oversized black thumbtacks. Some curious soul had made a slit in the vinyl to investigate the composition of the sound-proofing foam inside. The Yamaha filled up the entire room, its keyboard facing the six-foot-tall double-pane window and its rear pressed right up to the permanently padlocked closet where Ladybug kept her extensive personal collection of sheet music. The silver radiator underneath the window emitted syncopated hissing noises: half its ribs were cold, the other half but a few degrees warmer, not even body temperature. Two small black circles on the beige carpet marked the spot where every apprentice dug his heels in while pressing the loud and soft pedals.

I leaned on the windowsill and stared at the students crossing the street four flights below. A steady traffic of violin cases, viola cases, cello cases, guitar cases, French horn cases, trumpet and oboe cases. Flute cases were the smallest. Stand-up bass cases couldn't even fit in a car. Loading a stand-up bass onto a bus required superhuman effort. The kids who played stand-up bass had the constitutions of giants long before they reached puberty. Igor, for example, was six foot six at just sixteen. Getting off the tram at the National Library stop, his stand-up bass strapped to his back, he looked like an enormous turtle.

Vadim was still at the piano, paging through a tattered edition of Chopin's Scherzi. His dark-blue Komsomol tie was lying on the floor, on top of his uniform jacket and leather case. His pre–World War II watch and silver band had been set on the left corner of the keyboard. Vadim was a much better pianist than I. This was quite clear to me, notwithstanding Ladybug's insistence that we were her two top students. Yet I didn't feel even the slightest degree of envy toward him. Vadim was different. He played with the purity and naïveté of a composer who has just stumbled upon a melodic phrase that sums up his entire experience of looking into the glass of time. He wasn't afraid of hitting a few wrong notes or blurring a finger-breaking passage because, in his playing mode, he *was* the composer: What he cared about was following the melodic breath passionately, unwaveringly, inhaling at bar one and exhaling only at bar five hundred, tracing the thread through chromatic falls and cadenzas, through explosions and moments of silence, like a fakir able to cut an apple peel into a string thin enough to cover the surface of the Earth. Vadim didn't care if he forgot a chord: he invented a new one on the spot, and then composed a transition to connect it to the rest of the piece. Whereas even the most insignificant faux pas committed by other musicians produced exasperated coughing, the squeaking of chairs, and loud whispers that swept across performance halls like a torrent of humiliation, Vadim's rare missteps were greeted with sighs of awe. So incredible were his improvisational skills that Ladybug could not bring herself to express any disapproval. She would just shake her head and purse her lips, holding back a smile.

I wasn't envious of Vadim's talent; I was envious of his sideburns. Vadim was two years older than me, and his long, loosely trimmed sideburns suggested a degree of maturity that compelled even the most aggressive guardians of the school's order to treat him with deference and caution. He didn't talk much. Even when he and I happened to be standing alone in the attic or in the backyard of the building next door, our communication amounted to lighting each other's cigarettes and counting the days to our next joint performance at Chamber Hall No. 1. Still, if we weren't exactly friends, I was nonetheless one of the very few people in school who knew him well, and I always felt a tinge of pride when, during her semiannual bashing-of-the-social-parasites speech, the Owl read my name after his over the short-range radio.

Vadim wrestled with the opening sequence of Scherzo no. 1 in slow tempo, trying different fingerings and practicing the sporadic jumps in the left hand. It was obvious that he hadn't yet begun to study the piece, though Ladybug must have assigned it to him back in September. But this was typical of Vadim—he'd procrastinate for weeks and then learn his repertoire overnight, right before he was expected to give a performance.

"She's going to kill me," Vadim said, squeezing his head with his hands as the door to the fourth floor's west-wing corridor slammed shut and the tapping of high heels, at first muffled and drifting, grew louder and louder, and then suddenly stopped a few feet outside the door. Vadim played a few chords and began working again on the scherzo's explosive opening sequence. If Ladybug was standing outside, listening, he had to show her that he wasn't wasting his time.

"I can't wait to hear how you've prepared this piece," Ladybug said as she opened the door and walked in, greeting both of us with a warm smile. She hung her purse on the hat stand and sat on the only chair, placing her plastic cup of chamomile tea on the floor. She was dressed in a black skirt, black tights, and a faded pink sweater. I noticed immediately the fresh coat of lipstick, the mascara, the soft glimmer of blue-green eye shadow. She always returned from the buffet, located in the school's basement, wearing more makeup than usual. Could it be that she had a crush on one of the young teachers? The new counterpoint instructor who had just completed his internship at the conservatory was certainly handsome. But it was also entirely possible that she made up only for us, me and Vadim. Perhaps she wanted us to find her attractive.

She leaned back and crossed her legs clumsily, exposing the inner sides of her thighs. How did she feel, seeing her two favorite boys waiting impatiently for her to come back from the buffet? Her gifted protégés, smelling of sweat and cologne, desperate to earn her approval? Did she secretly take pleasure in sitting close to us, in touching our hands and leaning over our shoulders to show us the subtle nuances of some melodic movement? Did she detect the traces of cigarettes, espresso, or pine needles on our breath? Did she examine my neck for love bites? Or notice that sometimes my lips were redder and fuller than normal, that my shirt smelled of cheap, flowery perfume? And if she did notice, did she feel any jealousy? I knew that, at thirty-one, she was still a virgin.

Vadim straightened his back, took a deep breath, and moved his hands to the high register, preparing to strike the first chord. Scherzo no. 1 opens with a scream of total desperation: you've woken from a nightmare to discover that everything you were dreaming is real. The last grains of sand, attracted by the immense pull of the beyond, fall onto the meaningless heap of memories. There's no exit, no horizon. There's only *now,* and even that is an illusion.

The second chord is simultaneously wiser and angrier: in the hourglass prison, you can only wait. Trapped in time, out of time, remembering the end of time. Then comes madness, breaking every window, knocking down every wall, a whirlwind of consciousness looking for a way out. Can there be no secret exit? No hidden trapdoor? If this is a nightmare within a nightmare, then there's still the possibility that you may be dreaming, that there's a higher state of wakefulness. Perhaps there's a trick, some counterintuitive solution. If you could only remember what your *real* hands feel like, where your final body resides.

Ten minutes ago, Vadim had been limping through the piece *a prima vista,* molding his fingers into the shapes of unfamiliar note clusters. Now he flew through the virtuosic passages with the confidence of someone who could control not only the color and oscillation pattern of each piano string, but the charge of every particle in the universe.

What he lacked in tonal clarity—something achieved only after count-less hours of painful practice—he compensated for with his vision of the interconnectedness of every melody, leitmotif, and memory knot scattered throughout the scherzo. Clutching the side of her chair, Ladybug watched Vadim work himself into a fury, playing faster and faster, his shoulders expanding as if pressed by the immense weight of the sound, his right foot feeding the damper pedal hungrily, unevenly, each stroke opening a wider tear in the veil separating our world from the world of Chopin, where the air smelled of ink, linen napkins, mold, and old furniture, where the sound of the piano blended with the echo of carriages and horseshoes receding into the distance.

Standing next to Vadim as he played was like hurtling through space at immense speed. His playing changed the quality of our surround-ings—the floor seemed to tilt to one side, the ceiling retreated beyond reach, the windows darkened, as if obscured by rain clouds. There isn't a recording that can approximate the experience of being in the pres-ence of a great musician. Even if a microphone could capture every overtone, every resonance and reverberation in the room, what you'd get on tape would be mere sound—sound minus the actual experience of music. "A melody is a sequence of notes that unravels in time," my fifth-grade ear training teacher once proclaimed. You can smell a rose in an instant. An image is grasped at once. Music, on the other hand, is experienced only in time. Not now, not after. *In time.* But who has the power to transport you *in time*? Not the robots, certainly. Not the ambitious either. Ladybug had warned me: first to fall out of the race are the talented; second to leave are the ambitious. Only the robots stay till the very end—which is why most piano recordings are so insufferably bad. You can't be both talented and ambitious, Ladybug had told me. That's why Vadim and I needed her to push us forward, to protect us from ourselves. The ambitious were fakes—they faked it by being ambitious. Vadim and I were different. We each had a voice and an instinct to resist the external world. It was our stubbornness and inherent apathy that kept us pure and uncorrupted, she had said. But if our instincts dictated that we must fail, Ladybug was there to keep us afloat. She would never let me give up. You are not a loser, Konstantin, she had said when, in seventh grade, during a weekend lesson at her house, I froze halfway through Debussy's Prélude no. 1, and refused to speak or move for an entire hour.

Because what was the point of continuing? What was the meaning of all this? The gray sky, the somber mountains in the distance, the relentless celebration of the coming social order, the pamphlets and the slogans, the banners depicting the bearded Soviet midget with his syphiloid brain, the marching of retarded soldiers, the ban on thinking, the sickening fascination with war, the triumph of the fat apparatchiks, the glee of the mediocre man, the rusted red pentacles guarding the graves of the dead like demonic seals. What was the point in perpetuating this doomed reality? Indeed, what was the reason for playing other people's music, for reliving others' thoughts and fears and exposing oneself in the process? If it was about developing empathy, about learning to love others and forgetting oneself, then why did every note make the ugliness in everyone and everything around me all the more impossible to bear?

You can't give up now, Ladybug had said that day, sitting beside me on the piano bench and putting her arm around my shoulder. They can never hurt you, she had said. Even if they kick you out of school, you'll still have to go on. No one likes the talented. It's only natural that they are trying to suffocate you. You have to keep playing, she had said.

But I would not look at her, just stared up at the pencil drawing of our disheveled, tubercular god, Frédéric François Chopin, with his huge, protruding eyes and slightly crooked nose. It was one of four small framed images—a drawing of St. Thomas's Church in Leipzig, where Bach was buried; a portrait of Beethoven conducting; a reproduction of Delacroix's unfinished portrait of Chopin; and a lithograph of Chopin's left-hand death cast—hung on the wall above the century-old Bösendorfer, its yellow-brown keys weighted with extra lead. How strange that they had made a bronze replica of Chopin's hands. As if by preserving the precise measurements of his wrists, fingers, palms, and nails they might guard the secret of his genius.

Now Vadim entered the slow middle section of the scherzo and Ladybug, having held her breath throughout the entire first part, exhaled with a shudder. It was magical: the monotonous high F sharp, coming on the offbeats, transformed from a static echo—accompanying the melody an octave below—into a melodic line of its own. This was the special thing about Chopin: he could create tension in even the simplest setting by weaving in two or three voices, each striving for its own unique conclusion. Then came the aside, *the explanation*. There was always a moment in his pieces where Chopin put his fountain pen down, walked over to the window, and, handkerchief in hand, explained everything as it was, without ambivalence, embellishment, or deception. A moment of unexpected honesty that in an instant laid bare the human condition. A wordless answer to all the old questions. My eyes were stinging. Ladybug was on the verge of crying as well. What had Vadim touched upon? How could a mere intonation pacify all existential quandaries, disentangle every paradox? It was what made Chopin's asides so devastating and at the same time so thoroughly cathartic. A moment of truth in music demonstrated that the battles between being and dying, between the corporeal and the eternal, were nothing more than intonation, a melodic expression of tension. Perhaps the dilemmas underpinning existence contained no words and didn't strive for higher meaning. They were pure movement, a caprice of harmonic gravity. The voices echoing through the school's stairwell, the female opera singer reaching for a high note, the intermittent eruption of a tuba—all of these were erased by Chopin. The Raven and her mole, the chalk dust on my fingers, the pointless math riddles, the smugness of the A students, Bianka's black stockings and charmingly condescending smile, the chilling baritone of Principal Zimova spelling out the latest Party directives over the short-range radio, the pay phone on the first floor that would ring for hours, adding a tinge of desperation to the general cacophony—they all dissolved in Chopin. There was no more hunger, no need to fear the messengers of the crooked reality. I listened to the wordless answer, lukewarm water pouring over an open wound. Vadim—pale, stone-faced, barely breathing. The soft hammers stroking the strings. Chopin was our god, our supreme reality. His compositions were our prayers, and we recited them without pause. They were in our minds, in our fingers, in our dreams. Day after day we reached back in time and dissolved into him, we relived his life, we walked the dark halls of his consciousness.

Even as Vadim played, I was mapping the scherzo in my mind—noting all the ritardandos and accelerandos, the internal logic of the phrases, the accents that gave the fast passages a necessary punch, the lyrical out-of-rhythm moments, the places requiring superhuman precision (like the final high E in the transposition of the opening sequence, which demanded a leap over ten white keys in a hundredth of a second, and which Vadim, possessed by a streak of diabolical luck, hit on the head each and every time, with a smile, no less)—for I knew that before long I, too, would have to study the scherzo, just as I had studied all the other pieces Vadim had mastered: the mazurkas, the polonaises, the waltzes, the nocturnes, the études, the ballads. Much as a younger brother inherits his older brother's faded, stretched-out shoes and clothes and, while admiring their legacy and uniqueness, tries to make them his own, I took Vadim's already sculpted repertoire and reinvented it to fit my dimensions: the length of my fingers, the pattern of my breathing, the weight of my desperation and anger, the depth of my pain. Vadim played Andante Spianato with the satin-cloaked longing of a teenager who has fallen in love for the first time; I played it with the lust and grief of someone already familiar with the sins of youth. He crafted sweet and whispery scenes, exquisite in their reach for what is yet to be tasted; I conjured dark moods, transforming innocence into disillusionment. He played the Prélude in E Minor like a lullaby to a dying friend—soft, sedate, each note a step toward the silvered shore, a drop of memory falling into the Lethe; I played it with the angst and restlessness of the eternally damned, shouting out the old question again and again and then mocking the obvious answer. He played the Revolutionary étude in one sweep, single-mindedly, like a wind that enters a room through an open window, ruffles the sheet music on the piano, lifts the loose pages into the air, and then exits, slamming the door; I played it at a maddening speed, with the intensity of someone hanging from the edge of a precipice.

During concerts, I always played last, while Vadim played right before me. It was the way Ladybug wanted it: smoke and water followed by earth and fire. First the spontaneous, introverted intoning of a dying romantic; then the raw pain and the failed transcendence of corporeal beauty. Ah, Ladybug certainly loved us. But how would she save us from ourselves? Would she hold our hands until we grew old? Would she talk to us about the sheep and the rose in *The Little Prince*? Would she strip for us and lead us to the place no one had ever been? I had caught something in her eyes, once, when she had taken off all of her clothes and sat at the edge of the bed in an old hotel with enormous chandeliers and chipped ceilings where she and I stayed after my performance at one of the many musical festivals I used to attend each year. "Don't look!" she had said to me, but of course I had looked the entire time—from the moment she'd stepped behind the screen, dropped her panties to her ankles, and walked out, naked, her white silk gown in her hand. Why hadn't she put on the gown behind the screen? When she finally turned off the night light and slipped under the blanket, her legs touching mine, I almost expected her to reach out for me. She and I alone in some godforsaken town on the Danube filled with crows, in the middle of a rainy winter. She had been twenty-eight and I twelve. Nothing wrong with that. She could've given me a little warmth. It only made sense. A piano teacher and her student. That's what music was about. A little warmth in a world of stone and metal, of faded colors, walking skeletons, and stuffy performance halls.

The grand piano that I played at the festival had been atrocious, the high register buzzing and crackling like a loudspeaker of tin cans, the low register hoarse and shallow, like the barking of the black and gray crows guarding every windowsill in town. On the second night of our stay, after my final performance, she and I had gone out to a restaurant. I wore my tuxedo, over a white shirt and a black velvet bow tie. Ladybug wore a green dress and high heels. At one point, as I struggled to halve my schnitzel, my fork slipped and I sent the entire contents of my plate over the table and into Ladybug's lap. "The tomato sauce will never wash off," she observed after the initial surprise. "Well, I only know how to play the piano," I responded. "I never said I can cut a fucking schnitzel!" She laughed. Later that night she had stripped for me again, but this time looked sad and frightened. Before getting into bed, she placed her medicine and a glass of water on the night table, in case she should get sick in the middle of the night. "Promise me that you'll never play like an older man," she said to me as we lay quietly, the spotlight on top of the opera house across the street shining on the screen standing next to the window. "Promise me you're not going to be like those pathetic, arrhythmic men who wipe their tears on the keyboard and cry for their mommies. There's no place for self-pity in music. You have to play as if you've just written your will. You have to play as if you've reached your final hour and you've got nothing to prove, nothing to win or lose. You should play with the conviction that when all is said and done, your heart will be ripped out of your body and buried separately, in a glass jar." She paused. "Do you know why Chopin requested to have his heart removed after his death? It wasn't because he was afraid of being accidentally buried alive, as his biographers have suggested. He wanted to make sure that the strings between ugliness and beauty had been cut forever." "I don't understand," I told her, and she said, "You will, one day."

Vadim swept the keyboard with an ascending chromatic scale and banged out the concluding cadenza. He knew he had pulled off an exceptional performance, though he was too modest to expect applause.

"I spent a lot of time working on it," he said, wiping his hands on his pants.

"Liar!" Ladybug shouted, pretending to be angry, and then punched him playfully on his back. "You haven't practiced at all, have you? I can bet my head on it, you were playing *a prima vista* the whole time. And where was your left hand throughout the exposition—all the staccato jumps, the bass line . . . I didn't hear any of it."

Outside, in the corridor, the bell announced the end of first period. It was 2:15. This was another thing I envied Vadim for. As an eleventh grader, he attended school in the afternoon, from 1:30 to 7:00, while students from the fourth through ninth grades went to school in the morning, from 7:45 to 1:15. This was known as "doing first shift," while first, second, third, tenth, eleventh, and twelfth graders did "second shift." For them, the final period ended at seven o'clock. Seven o'clock! I couldn't get over it. The things that happened in the dark. The dark was our friend. That's why those of us with lowered personal standing had smashed all the streetlights in the vicinity. By five o'clock, in the middle of winter, it was so dark you could walk out of school and light a cigarette, just like that, without worrying about any teacher, or a policeman who might stop you and demand to see your ID and report card. You could hug your girlfriend, pin her against a wall, unbutton her dress, lift her undershirt, and kiss her naked breasts. What could anyone say to you? You could burn your history book and spit on the photographs of the Soviet midgets. Even if things got out of hand and some exemplary citizen started chasing you, all you had to do was jump over a few fences, and you were in a different part of town—a little out of breath, true, but free. This endless maze of neglected, overgrown backyards was the soul of the old city of Sofia. Every nineteenth-century apartment building had a backyard or enclosed playground connected to the backyard and playground of the next. After years of practice and exploration, I had learned all of the city's secrets. I could have escaped an army of national security agents if I'd had to. I had trained myself to take on a two-meter-high wall on the run—jump, grab onto the top, swing to the side, one foot over, two feet over, and down on the ground again. I could run for miles in my mind: I knew the trees, the benches, the sheds with gardening tools, the rosebushes, the rusting skeletons of busted Russian cars, the frozen fountains, the empty ponds, the broken swings and toppled slides, the clotheslines. I knew the height of every brick wall, I knew every shortcut, every dead end, every tear in a wire fence, every building with side doors that opened up onto different backyards. I'd been chased by dozens of citizens and policemen with a reputable proletarian conscience who had seen me break a window, rip off the receiver from a public phone, or smash the marble tablets bemoaning the murder of Communist guerrillas fighting the Nazi-allied government in the early forties. And, thanks to the hidden territory locked between the old buildings, I was never caught. Some of my friends objected to my fondness for vandalizing the marble tablets hung across town. "Don't crack those," they'd say to me. "The Communists were fighting the Nazis back then." "Whoever fights evil, becomes evil," I'd reply to them. "The victors always inherit the sins of the defeated."

For my thirteenth birthday, Ladybug gave me a copy of Saint-Exupéry's *The Little Prince*. Inside it she'd written: *To my most talented student, may you never stop worrying about the danger of the sheep eating the flower*. In teaching piano, Ladybug demanded nothing less than a pure, virginal mind. It's why she constantly lectured me about my sexual exploits, my smoking, my affiliation with the bad crowd. "You're going to forget about the flower," she'd say to me, holding my hand. "You're going to lose track of the paper sheep. You're going to get used to the corruption all around you. And then you'll never be able to play again."

She was right. No matter how hard they tried, adults couldn't play the nocturnes. And try they did. The rubatos, the choked-up resolutions, the make-believe defeats, the staged acrimony—it made you want to puke. Whenever I went to one of the year-round mandatory concerts given by the faculty and saw "Nocturne in B-flat Minor" or "Prélude no. 4" written in the program notes, I burst into a sweat. For God's sake, leave the nocturnes alone! Dumb robots. That's what they were. Most of them, anyway. Ladybug was an exception. She was the best musician I'd ever heard. But she was also a virgin. She had to stay a virgin, I guess. Her two favorite books were *The Little Prince* and *Madame Bovary*. It wasn't hard for me to understand why she liked the boy prince. Everybody liked him. Emma Bovary, on the other hand, was an entirely different creature. If Ladybug identified with Emma, it certainly wasn't because she—like Emma—was bored with her life in the country and was cheating on her husband. Ladybug lived the life of a nun. Her dark house, tucked away in a quiet corner below Dondukov Boulevard, had the feel of a medieval nunnery. I knew for a fact that the first and last time Ladybug had invited a man she liked over for tea at her house, her mother slapped him on the face and kicked him out the door, warning him never to talk to her daughter again. The Old Lady, a retired piano teacher, was six feet tall, temperamental, and strong as a bull. She believed that all men were detestable weaklings who relied on women to survive. I'd heard it all a million times. I'd heard about Ladybug's father, how he'd spent the family inheritance and drunk himself to death. Ladybug had been born after her father died, so any memories she had of him were borrowed from her mother and her older sister, Maya—a watery-eyed, blond kindergarten teacher who, at six feet two inches, seemed to me like one of those Thracian forest apparitions, a *samodiva,* known for seducing and then killing her victims.

The Dark House of the Three Giant Women—that's how I had thought of Ladybug's home when I first visited it, at the age of seven. Everything about the place spooked me: the stale air smelling of unwashed curtains, moth balls, animals, and burnt wood; the cats, passing through the rooms like blurry shadows; the black silence of the baroque furniture; the enormous doors and the gray, funereal wallpaper; the labored tick-tock of the grandfather clock. Having adapted themselves to living in near-perfect darkness, the three giant women navigated their way like moles, touching the surface of a cabinet, grabbing hold of the spiral finial of a chair, circumventing a tea table, brushing past a tall porcelain vase. And then there were the shoes. The sister's boots were a terrifying size eleven. I couldn't help feeling that if I didn't manage to impress the giant women with my piano playing, they might stick me into a large cauldron and boil me for dinner.

Vadim slipped his silver band back on the index finger of his left hand, strapped on his wristwatch, and reached for his tie.

"How is the étude coming along?" Ladybug asked. Vadim raised his shoulders and said nothing. He stuffed the scherzi in his leather case and put on his uniform jacket. He looked disheveled and fatigued, as if he'd just fought in a boxing match. Now the bell sounded, announcing the beginning of second period. "You should hurry, or they will put you down with an absence. Can you drop by and play the etude for me tomorrow at two fifteen, right after the end of first period?" Ladybug tapped her watch, indicating that he had to be absolutely on time. Vadim nodded and smiled. Then he looked at me and nodded again, as if to say, *Hey, kopeleh, what's going on*. Vadim was cool. Cool and secretive, and without any friends.

I lowered the piano bench significantly and began warming up with a series of chromatic exercises. The keys were absolutely dry, one of the advantages of playing after Vadim. His fingers never got sweaty. He had the touch of a surgeon—steady, precise. There are piano players who literally douse the keyboard with their sweat. The girl with whom I played Ravel's *Ma Mère l'oye,* for piano duet, in my ensemble class perspired so heavily, I often felt as if I were ice skating. I couldn't strike a simple chord without slipping.

"Start directly from the fast section," Ladybug instructed me, pulling a small bottle of pills from her purse. She opened it and placed a white pill under her tongue, then took a drink of her tea. Sitting in the faint December afternoon light coming from the window, she looked like a sixteenth-century Italian model, with her classical chin, high cheekbones, reddish curly hair, and incredibly long, sculpted fingers. I worried about her. At the age of twenty-one, a week before she had been scheduled to play at the Tchaikovsky Competition, she had suffered a heart attack that left her incapacitated for three months. Her career had ended. And so had her youth.

Alone at night in the attic, unfolding the majestic, full-bodied arpeggios in the first Chopin étude on a crappy old Chaika upright whose keys felt shallow and much too soft for my liking; pounding the melodic line in the left hand with gusto, the prophetic *sol-fa-mi-re!* sinking into the very core of my being, delving into my heart like a wedge, making me blissfully dizzy and disoriented, hungry for air, for life, for more illusions, more lies and heroic dead ends. After countless repetitions, the mold of each arpeggio had begun to set around my fingers like a plaster cast; the piano keys appeared larger and fatter, my hands became infinitely long, the corners of the piano receded in opposite directions. Suddenly there was so much open space, it was virtually impossible for me to hit a wrong note or to break the perfectly aligned string of pearls stretching across the entire keyboard. And I played faster and faster, the heat from my wrists—especially my right wrist—spreading into my arms, my chest and shoulders, engulfing my heart, setting my stomach afire, and as soon as I reached the end of the étude, I started again from the beginning without so much as missing a beat, I just couldn't stop, could not disentangle myself from these diabolical arpeggios, I craved the magisterial sound of the chords rippling through the lower and upper registers, I craved the pleasure of conquering each octave at an inhuman speed, I craved even the stinging pain racing just behind me, trying to paralyze my fingers before they could climb the ladder of perfection and take me out of this miserable world. I had this sense that if only I could keep on playing, keep on pushing the boundaries of the ether, every earthly bondage would eventually fall away and I would emerge on the other side incorporeal, a child of music and light.

When I played Chopin, I wasn't; there was only music, the illusion of music, the illusion of the illusion of music, a river of remembered sounds, motifs, and tonal brushstrokes floating past and morphing into other motifs, other harmonies, and as soon as I crafted something beautiful with my fingers—a shape, a contour—it crumbled and disappeared. Surely if there was a reason to stay alive, to endure the diurnal torrent of stupidity, sorrow, insult, and indignity, it was to spend time in this state of rapture, in which my breath was synchronized with Chopin's, and the secret code revealing the divine was written in the air. All I had to do was move my fingers over the keyboard and I was in, the gates swung open. If listening to a piano recording was like watching people drink wine; if attending a live performance was like smelling the wine; and if playing the piano by yourself was actually drinking the wine—then drink and stay drunk, I thought. Leave the ghost world behind.

The reprise of the étude always killed me with its bombastic flare, its triumphant hopelessness, the thundering *do* all the way at the bottom, a *do* whose immolating flames burned through my material body, annihilating every atom, every memory, every moment of the foretold future. Strange that Ladybug never agreed to include this étude in my repertoire, though I asked her to do so countless times. Perhaps she thought it rather emotionally unchallenging and monochromatic. God, the sound of a shotgun going off is simple, too, but it can certainly stop your heart.

I stood up, lit the half-smoked cigarette I had left at the edge of the piano lid, and poked my head up through the skylight, breathing in the cold air. One drag for Bankoff, the physics teacher. One drag for Zimova, the principal. One drag for Alexander, who was probably back at his dad's place, finishing dinner. The neon-lit letters on top of the Hotel Balkan, across from the National Assembly building, blinked on and off. A tram screeched to a stop outside the library and a few passengers climbed into its unlit body. *I'm going to be sixteen next month and I'm still not dead,* I thought. *This must be some kind of conspiracy.* I flicked the cigarette out of the skylight and watched its tiny red cinder disappear into the night. Checked my watch: the concert would begin in fifteen minutes. Before switching the lights off I turned around and examined the room, making sure I hadn't left anything behind. In the hallway, I walked over to the room where someone was playing violin and stood for a moment outside, listening. Then I opened the door and peeked in. I knew the girl. She was in the same class as Vadim. A pretty one, with a mysterious freckle just under her left eye. I wanted to tell her I liked her tone, but somehow couldn't. It was only the two of us up in the attic tonight. Everyone else had gone home. Everyone, that is, who had normal parents and a life outside the music school.

In some respects, all young professional musicians are de facto orphans, raised by their piano, violin, cello teachers. But whereas most other kids had mothers and fathers who at least tried to act like parents once in a while, I was blessed with two monsters who conspired day and night to crush the very individuality I'd worked so hard to create in my piano training. They hated me for being different and yet expected me to become the greatest pianist in the world before I turned eighteen. They seemed unable to understand that I couldn't be both a genius and an average kid who went to school and brought home straight A's; that my tendency to sabotage my own achievements was perhaps a direct consequence of being born with a gift. I couldn't give a damn about all those awards I had won at international piano competitions in Italy and Germany—starting at age nine, and then again at eleven, thirteen, and fourteen. Competitions, as anyone with half a brain could see, had nothing to do with music and everything to do with the art of taxidermy. And there were enough stuffed, vacuous, perfectly stitched-up creatures around to keep every jury member busy for a thousand years.

Tonight, my parents were celebrating their sixteenth wedding anniversary. They'd warned me that if I didn't come home to see them, I'd better not come home at all. As if I cared. I could always find a place to crash—on the floor of a practice room, or at my grandmother's on Rakovski Street; at one of Peppy the Thief's hideouts, or, if worse came to worst, in the catacombs, the city's maze of underground tunnels and decrepit nuclear shelters that served as a refuge for the truly wretched. I was returning to my parents' only a couple of nights a week by now, and, almost invariably, spent the entire night fighting with them about my grades, my behavior at school, the length of my hair, or my understanding of the notion of freedom. My father, a philosophy professor at the university, knew everything about freedom, while my mother, a chemist who conducted experiments on mice, specialized in control. Between the two of them, they had everything figured out. Only I refused to be a laboratory mouse endowed with the exceptional wisdom to understand the conditional nature of freedom.

The violinist with the freckle didn't even pause to look at me, just kept playing. Was it Scarlatti? Paganini? Elgar? One of these days I would go to the library on the second floor and ask the nice lady who worked there to give me the recordings of all the great violin concertos, and then I would sit by the window, headphones on, and listen to each record ten times so that I would never again feel like a fool when talking to violinists. Every time I was with Irina, I had to pretend to understand things I didn't know a thing about. Alexander, on the other hand, was brilliant at such fakery, I thought, as I descended the narrow wooden spiral staircase, which shook and squeaked beneath me. Alexander could talk for an hour about a book he'd never read or a composer he'd never studied. Perhaps this was why he received better grades than I did and why he was able to get along so well with Irina. Had Alexander and Irina slept together? Most definitely, if fucking on a desk chair in the attic constituted sleeping together. I didn't care. Irina was a genius; she was allowed to act crazy and dangerous. Sometimes she flirted openly with me, whispering dirty things in my ear, playing with my hair, taking drags from my cigarette, searching my pockets for money. At times she even acted as if we were in love. Most often, though, she walked past me on the street looking the other way, like some mysterious stranger I would never be lucky enough to meet.

I entered the south wing of the third floor to see if Teachers' Headquarters was locked. If it wasn't, I could steal a few daybooks, go to the concert like an exemplary student, clap enthusiastically, and later burn the damn things in a trash can out in the park. Certainly wouldn't hurt to get rid of all the absences, reprimands, and late notices I'd been collecting lately. From the way the double doors stirred and rattled with the draft wheezing through the corridor, it was safe to conclude that they were unlocked. I pressed my foot against the left one and looked through the tiny gap between the doors. I could only see the latch bolt. The dead bolt was withdrawn. I was just about to walk in, when the bathroom door at the end of the corridor opened and out rushed the south-wing janitor lady wearing a dark blue apron, brown knee socks, and a pair of black galoshes. I froze with my hand on the doorknob, but didn't panic.

"I'm going to report you to the principal!" she shouted in her shrill voice, shaking her index finger at me. So that's where the draft's coming from, I thought. The septuagenarian witch had probably left the bathroom window open after she finished cleaning. The third floor, south-wing janitor was the eyes and ears of the Owl. Having presided for decades over this most strategically important area—in addition to Teachers' Headquarters, the south wing also contained Archives, Payroll, the offices of the principal and the deputy principal, and Admissions—she acted as if she were an elected member of the central committee of the Communist Party itself. I didn't doubt that she had the power to bring someone's personal standing down, or even to get him kicked out of school. Yet I wasn't scared of her. For the south-wing janitor had at least two considerable weaknesses: one, she drank during work; and two, her granddaughter, a pianist, was an eighth grader at the school. It was Alexander who had first discovered her bottle, hidden in the south-wing bathroom locker. Alexander had a police picklock he'd bought on the black market and used on a regular basis—to steal painkillers from the nurse, to get into various lockers and closets, to visit the principal's office in the off hours.

"How was the vodka today, Maria?" I asked the janitor calmly. "And how is your granddaughter doing? She hasn't slipped on the ice and broken her hand, has she?"

I made two steps toward the old witch, who, I was pleased to see, appeared suddenly overcome with fear. She wasn't going to report me, I was certain of it. She was a coward. Not that I would ever have considered breaking one of her granddaughter's precious fingers. There had been incidents of violence, true, but I'd never been involved in any of them. Stepping closer, I tried to meet her eyes but couldn't. It was as if they were buried in her skull. Or perhaps the light was too dim. Or perhaps she was a vampire, feeding off the souls of the talented. Just to think of the different ways in which she had hurt me over the years, and Ivan and Slav and Irina and Vadim, and all the others. I remembered all her conniving little schemes. But she couldn't scare me any longer. I knew her secret.

Down the stairs I went again, second floor, first floor, through the folding doors, across the corridor to the left, past the porter's cubicle—"Why in such a rush again?" he yelled after me—careful on the ice-coated exterior stairs, and then I was out in the school yard. I could hear the students who would be playing at the concert rehearsing furiously on the second floor. I liked the school like this, at night, when all the nonmusic teachers went home and Chamber Hall No. 1 and No. 2 filled up with people eager to experience something beautiful. There were all kinds of people at these nightly concerts. Some were friends or relatives of the players; some were music teachers. But there were many who had no connection to the music school at all: old people who had nothing better to do; strangers who had walked past the school and seen a poster by chance; widows with sophisticated hats; mothers accompanying their grown-up Down syndrome children; balding bachelors with fastidiously ironed shirts; alcoholics; philosophy graduate students with messy hairdos and an assortment of nervous ticks; retired military men bedecked with medals;

apparatchiks with comb-overs, self-important in their gray suits and detestable shoes; young couples holding hands. It was incredible how, with the fall of the night, the school transformed itself from an insane asylum packed with lilliputian dictators, retarded ideologues, and brainwashed students to a temple of music and perfection. Even the foyer, its walls covered with slogans and framed photographs of the entire Soviet politburo, seemed unreal, benignly anachronistic, like a museum hall exhibiting the paraphernalia of some bygone proto-Egyptian dynasty. The curse of the red pentacle was significantly weaker at night, I could see that with my own eyes. People looked different, talked different. Trees came to life, whispering secrets, remembering things that hadn't yet happened; ravens spoke in tongues; stray dogs barked at invisible passersby; the street lights went out of order; the wind carried the sound of distant human voices; the Sofia Music School for the Gifted became once again a place of worship and divine contemplation. There was something mysterious and inviting about this massive old five-story building towering in the dark like a gate into another dimension—a dimension of formless beings and infinite space filled with music. Even the metal bars girding the back entrance door appeared less sinister, I thought, as I slipped through a tear in the wire netting surrounding the school yard and then jumped onto the sidewalk two meters below. It was freezing but my hands and arms were still burning from the études. I raised the collar of my father's old military-style greatcoat that I wore over my uniform jacket and hurried down the back alley, toward the broad, poorly lit boulevard. The clock on the building facing the Levski Monument traffic circle read 8:35, which meant that my Sputnik watch must have died on me again. I was already late for the concert.

"Three red roses," I said to the scrawny Gypsy woman standing on the stairs leading to the modest marble-plated monument. I pointed to the metal bucket with the youngest-looking roses and handed the woman my entire daily allowance. I'd gone hungry all day so that I'd have enough money to buy these flowers.

"For a girlfriend?" the woman asked, grabbing onto my hand as we exchanged money and flowers. Then, taking me in, her eyes grew wider, and she pulled me closer to her. "You've got a curse, my boy. You've been marked. Come near. Two women: a mother and daughter. Let me look into you, *baba*. I will try to lift the curse. I know some *murafeti,* I can even cast a bullet against *uroki*."

"I don't have any more money," I said, disentangling my hand from hers. "And I'm running late."

"But that girl is no good, *baba*. Come near, now, and let me look *into* you. You have to give something to get something back, see? That's just how the world works. I'm not asking for a lot. You're not a ghost, I can see that. You're not like them—look over there, that man getting out of the car. A ghost. They're not real, *baba,* they're just filler. But they're going to drag you down. Come, let me look into you."

"Good night," I said.

"Watch for the moon, *baba*. When the tips of the crescent moon point down, the devil has returned."

But the crescent moon never points down, I thought, as I crossed the street and veered into the dark backyard connected to the school premises. A mother and daughter. Strange, because I had heard the very same verdict from another Gypsy woman who stopped me in the park, just a week before. Perhaps I should've offered the flower lady my cigarettes in exchange for a little more information, and, possibly, a counterspell. Not that I really cared if I was cursed at this point, so long as the curse wasn't severe tendonitis. My hands were all I had, my only weapon against the progenies of mediocrity, my first and last refuge. Without my hands I was nothing.

"Back again," the porter greeted me in the foyer. There were five or six people standing outside Chamber Hall No. 2, waiting to sneak in during the next applause. It was a busy night for the porter, signing in all the guests, monitoring the stairs, locking up the grand pianos, cleaning, sweeping, switching off the lights. These night concerts could go on for hours. A piano teacher might have fifteen students, and with each student playing for ten or fifteen minutes, the concert would end around midnight. Which meant that before you got to hear the best performers—and the best always played last—you had to endure an avalanche of Czerny, Mozart, Mendelssohn, and early Beethoven drivel, executed by third-tier musicians frightened by the thunder of the grand piano's lower register and able to convey their emotions only by jerking their shoulders, tossing their heads, and performing theatrical hand pirouettes, as if they had been cast in a production of *Swan Lake*.

I walked over to the stage entrance of Chamber Hall No. 1 and pushed the heavy double doors open just a crack, to get a better sense of what the student on the Steinway was playing. A twelve-year-old boy dressed in a suit and a bow tie approached from behind and poked his head through the crack as well. The stage entrance opened onto a small wooden chamber separated from the podium by two burgundy velvet curtains. The podium was exactly four steps above the ground floor, which meant that in order to land on the fourth step on your right foot (the only way to enter a podium without incurring bad luck) you had to begin climbing the stairs with your left: a rule that every musician in the school followed with religious zeal. When I was in the third and fourth grade, I would march up and down the corridors before each performance, calculating how many steps it would take me to walk straight to the Steinway from every imaginable signpost on the first floor. I knew, for example, that if my turn to get on stage came while I was standing by the swinging doors, near the main stairway, I would need to make eleven steps to reach the stage door, two to pass the wooden chamber, four to climb the stairs, and another four to arrive at the piano bench.

"You came to see Bianka, right?" said the boy with the bow tie, smiling omnisciently. I ignored him. Sixth graders didn't talk to ninth graders about girls. Period. I turned around and walked to the arching patchwork of small windows, some of them round, others rectangular and triangular, with leaded ornamental branches running through them. *I shouldn't have bothered to buy flowers,* I thought, and hid the bouquet inside my greatcoat. Now everyone's going to tease me about it.

At last, the applause! I snuck into the hall, trailing two elderly ladies in massive fur coats, and made my way quickly toward the back. I recognized Bianka's mother, sitting in the second row, behind a somber delegation of piano instructors. I also spotted the Hyena, seated inconspicuously in the middle of the left section of rows. The Hyena—Antoaneta Gesheva—was the supervisor of class 9B, and thus my chief tormentor. Every class in school had an appointed supervisor whose responsibility was to monitor the behavior and learning development of her or his students, to write reports and make recommendations to the principal as to appropriate punishments. Ever since my first day in the fourth grade when, after introducing herself and speaking at length about the benefits of being an exemplary student, she had asked me to stand in front of the class and recite a page or two from the Young Communist's manual—which I hadn't even read—the Hyena had made my life hell. The fact that the Hyena's own daughter, Luba, also happened to be in 9B, only made things worse. Was the Hyena terrified I might corrupt her timid, large-breasted daughter? That I might teach her to smoke and drink double-distilled rakia, introduce her to illegal contraceptives and impromptu fucking during the long recess? The truth was, Luba was too vacuous to be corrupted by anyone. She was right on the border of having no personality at all, a nonperson, some sort of liminal, violin-playing nonentity, a machine. Yet even a machine like Luba knew that her mother was fundamentally evil. After her mother had succeeded in lowering my personal standing in seventh grade, Luba came up to me and told me that she didn't understand her mother's actions. "What is there to understand?" I had asked her. "Your mother is fucked. She's not even human anymore."

I sat down in the very last row, a few seats away from the best piano tuner in town, whose daughter had just finished playing a Haydn sonata. The twelve-year-old boy who'd asked me about Bianka walked out on the stage and took a bow. No one clapped. I placed the flowers on the floor and slouched down into my chair, anticipating torture. The boy played well, however—first a Czerny étude for the left hand, and then a piece by Schumann. I knew the Hyena was looking at me, I could see her face in the corner of my eye, but I kept staring straight ahead, at the stage, with its great Steinway and the gigantic crystal chandelier dangling above it. I loved how high the ceiling was. I felt as if I were sitting in a cathedral, a cathedral filled with ghosts. The Hyena was a ghost, I thought. There was something alien about her, a coldness, a rationality of a different order. Why did she have to keep looking at me? What was so important that it must be conveyed to me right now from the other side of the concert hall? I didn't want to be poisoned by her eyes, by the pattern and frequency of her logic. That's how they conquered the world, after all—by staring people down. Transmitting their coldness, spreading the parasites of obedience. "Obedience is excellence of the highest order!" The Hyena had actually said that one day in class. It was all a part of an alchemical formula designed to turn humans into shadows, to erase the individual. The Nazis, the Communists, the capitalists—they were all possessed, as far as I was concerned, hypnotized. How fitting that the *Communist Manifesto* opened with the proclamation that a ghost is haunting Europe, the ghost of communism.

Boris Negodnik, our history teacher, knew the *Communist Manifesto* by heart; every now and then he would walk into class and start reciting it passionately, banging his pointer against the teacher's desk, stamping his foot, waving his fists in the air. He had a miserable combover, cemented with sugar water, and owned two suits: one light gray; the other, dark. Negodnik loved to remind us that, after forty-three years of teaching, he'd missed but one class, because he'd been admitted to the hospital with a ruptured appendix. We imagined that even after the Americans dropped the bomb on us, he'd still make his way to school, covered with a white bedsheet to repel the radiation, stand in the smoldering ruins of Chamber Hall No. 1, and denounce the imperialist enemy by quoting fiery passages from *Das Kapital*. In the fifth grade, Ivan, Slav, and I had gotten into the habit of showing our appreciation for Negodnik's tirades by performing loud and extremely violent hara-kiri. Negodnik would walk into the classroom—his neck jerking forward with each step like a camel, his body stiff as a stick insect—and say something like, "On this day eighty-six years ago, V. I.

Lenin was sitting in his hut in the Siberian village of Shushenskoye,"
whereupon Ivan, Slav, and I would pull out our broken radio antennas
and, plunging their telescoping lengths into our abdomens, fall dramatically on the floor, kicking and drooling and shouting, "Down with
the imperialists!" and "Long live the red pentacle!" Quickly confiscat-
ing our ceremonial weapons, Negodnik would drag us into the hallway and down the stairs to the principal's office, so that we could tell
the Almighty Owl just what we'd been up to. In fifth grade, we were
still treated like kids, though. The teachers attributed our fascination
with Japanese-style suicide simply to artistic temperament and curiosity about foreign cultures. But we grew up fast. By the sixth grade
we were already treated as adolescents, and by the seventh, we were
adults capable of overthrowing the government.

Now my ugly duckling appeared onstage, blushing and insecure
in her black long-sleeved dress, black stockings, and black shoes. No
bow from her. She went straight to the Steinway. Why was there a barrier between us? What had made her stop short of asking me to come
upstairs that afternoon when her parents and brother were out of town
and she and I had met in the dreary enclosed courtyard of her apartment building and had sat down on the bench by the metal gate and
the tall brick wall overgrown with ivy? Who was she saving herself for?
I knew she was curious. And I knew that she loved me, in a secretive,
forbidden-fruit sort of way. All those nights I had waited for her at the
corner of the French High School and the old bakery, just to see her
for ten minutes during her routine piano break, from 7:20 to 7:30; ten
minutes of silent and painful expectation as we walked the narrow,
cobbled streets crisscrossing her neighborhood, our shadows growing closer and closer and then merging into one each time we passed
under a working streetlight. But even when, on occasion, we stopped
to look into each other's eyes, standing just an inch from the magnetic
pull of a first kiss, she remained unreachable, an ephemeral creature
filled with sadness and disappointment. Once, during one of our more
intense moments, I told her that I loved her. I thought that if I just said
it, casually, the way I might say that I'm running late or feeling sleepy,

I would be able break the invisible barrier. She just responded that I'd watched too many movies. She knew I was a liar.

Do-do! Do-si-do-si! Do-mi-re-do-do! In Bianka's interpretation, the opening of Liszt's Hungarian Rhapsody no. 2 sounded like a lame valse. I'd always thought the difference between Chopin and other composers was that Chopin wrote in the first person, and everyone else in the third. Beethoven, Mozart, Liszt, Ravel, Schumann, Debussy—they all told you what happened to *other* people, to countries, to societies. Only Chopin talked about himself. It was the naked, burning honesty of his phrases that set him apart from all the rest. But, God, how hard it was to be honest in music! To sit down at the piano, toy around with a few chords, a few progressions, and then lay it down without any pretense or hesitation, as if, rather than being something external, the keys and one's fingers *were* the innermost essence of one's soul, that secret place from which every thought and emotion sprang. What had to happen for someone to achieve this immediacy of expression? Did one need to be dying of tuberculosis before he could be rid of the pretense, the demagoguery, the self-vindication?

The slow section of the Rhapsody in C-sharp Minor is one of the most beautiful things Liszt ever wrote, but it's still in the third person. It tells a story of two anonymous people who have loved, fought, and broken up; it describes the sea, and the sound of seagulls in the distance. But it says nothing true. It only skims the periphery of the gorge of sorrow; avoids the gaze of death; stands motionless by the gates of bliss, refusing to read the names of the soon-to-be-dead already engraved on the tombstones; refusing to take pleasure in the smell of fresh soil and brushwood. It lies—beautifully, grandly, the way a mother lies to her child and the sky lies at sunset. "A good little Christian" is how George Sand had described Liszt in her intimate diary, which I'd read as part of my immersion in nineteenth-century French literature. Ladybug made me read all the big ones—Hugo, Balzac, George Sand, and Flaubert—so that I'd get a taste of what life had been like during Chopin's time. She believed that the nineteenth century had been the peak of human civilization. Everything that came after had been fanned by the flames of the apocalypse. People lost the ability to think and create, forgot God. She'd told me she would readily give up all the stuff of modernity for a life in France before the February Revolution of 1848, before the invention of the telephone, the internal combustion engine, before dynamite. She would trade movies, trams, and airplanes for a small house in the country with an upright, a fountain pen, a fireplace, and some candles. She would trade the radio and the record player for the sound of a carriage receding slowly down a winding road and the hourly chiming of church bells. She would trade modern medicine for the smell of cherry blossoms in spring, the taste of science-free fruit, and an early death by consumption.

Perhaps Bianka will let me unbutton her dress after the performance, I thought. *She'll be confused and disoriented, and she'll let me do anything I want.* Sand once wrote to one of Chopin's best friends that women who make men feel ashamed of their sexual desires ought to be hanged. Both Bianka and Ladybug seemed to be this kind of woman. Unlike Irina, who was made of passion. Sand also said that the separation of the mind and the body has led to the creation of monasteries and the rise of prostitution. But while probably true, this observation failed to answer why spiritual beings like Chopin were always suspicious of the wants of the body. Could it be that the mind-body separation occurred because the mind was cheated by the body in everything—in happiness, in the supreme embrace, and, finally, in death? Could it be that Chopin refused to sleep with Sand after their first kiss because he didn't want to be cheated again, to be disappointed—again—by the mediocrity of the senses?

Bianka's sluggish and unenthusiastic rendition of the rhapsody's fast section triggered an outbreak of yawns and coughs that spread through the hall like an infection. The hunger that had been clenching my stomach since six o'clock in the morning finally subsided and, cocooned in my father's warm greatcoat—my legs stretched under the chair in front of me—I began drifting away, the sweet paralysis of sleep numbing my limbs, anesthetizing my senses. Sounds turned into echoes and then blurred into a single experience of space. The Hyena was far away now; her eyes could no longer reach me. In this state—half-awake, half-asleep—I could sense the hidden side of things. Bass notes were bolts of sound that sank into the ground and amplified the drone of the earth; melodies were secret messages that slipped into people's dreaming minds undetected and began transmitting the seeds of future thoughts, of future dream colors. I could sense the ghosts around me, too. There were two types of ghosts, it occurred to me: those with souls but no bodies, and those with bodies but no souls. It was the latter type that made the human experiment possible, that made countries and national anthems and wars and gods and tyrants and mausoleums; it was these spiritless machines that spread the disease of subservience and false order. But they weren't scary just now, they really weren't. The Hyena's eyes were but two hollow orbs leading into the void, and I could look inside them now without fear. The Hyena was nothing more than the husk of a person. She could harm no one.

Woken by the applause, I picked up the flowers from the floor, hid them inside my coat, and rushed toward the door just as Bianka was doing a second curtsy. I exited the school through the main entrance and placed myself by the metal gates, shivering in the windless February night. It wasn't really that cold, yet I couldn't stop shaking. The sky was red again, red and glowing like the surface of a lake lit by a blood-stained moon. "It's just a cloud of red dust blown over from Africa," our seventh-grade geography teacher once said of Sofia's strangely colored night sky.

Bianka appeared on the top of the exterior flight of stairs, a beige raincoat over her dress, and instantly burst out laughing.

"Why were you sprinting through the hallway in the middle of my curtsy? It was so embarrassing!"

She walked down the stairs and stood just a few inches away from me. I could feel her warm breath on my cheek. I could smell her hair. This was one of those moments, I quickly realized, when anything was allowed. She was happy and lightheaded. Had I had the courage, I would've kissed her. The headlights of a passing car revealed her lovely long neck, then her mouth and her eyes, and suddenly she recoiled, as if taken aback by my disheveled appearance. She must have known full well I was just a thief after her treasure, that sweet, heavily guarded treasure she was determined to save for some proletarian intellectual.

"I don't want these," Bianka said quickly. "You know I don't like it when you buy me flowers."

"I didn't." I stuck the bouquet between the bars of the gate and noticed, in the faint light coming down from the windows of Chamber Hall No. 2, a new, not yet ripped up necrology glued to the stucco wall behind the gate. Looking closely I recognized the face of the boy—fifteen—who had died over the winter from meningitis. "He went out with that girl in ninth grade who plays the harp, right?"

Bianka turned around and crossed the street. I followed her, past the barrier and the pond and into Doctors' Garden. She climbed the small mound at the center of the park, strewn with ancient marble slabs and broken Thracian columns, and entered the summerhouse, where all the students with lowered personal standing usually gathered in late spring to smoke and drink, shielded by a tangled curtain of ivy and wild grapevines.

"I don't know why you do this. What do you want from me?" Bianka sat on the back of the bench, crossing her legs. I sat beside her, on the seat, and lit a cigarette.

"And what do *you* want? You want to make your parents happy? Go back to your fucking parents, then."

"I don't know why you think you're so brave. You always act like you're above everybody else. It's why nobody likes you."

"They don't like me because I'm not willing to play along. All of you are just playing along! You salute when you're told to. Kiss the flag when you're told to. You recite all the bullshit when you're told to. You're bullshit people."

"And what's smarter? To stand in the way of the steamroller and get crushed, or step aside and let it roll past you?"

"Get crushed, of course! Any day. I'd rather get out of here dead, but with a grain of dignity."

I stared at the sweetshop across the street, adjacent to the National Art Gallery, where Alexander and I bought our cigarettes after school. A neon light blinked inside, right above the cash register. I had no dignity, I thought. If I had, I would have kicked the gym teacher in the balls as hard as I could, so that he'd never come on to a fourteen-year-old girl again. I'd have punched the music history teacher in the face for saying that jazz isn't music because it was invented by impe-rialist monkeys. I would've painted swastikas on the door of Teachers' Headquarters to point them out as the Nazis they were. I would have defended Irina when Negodnik called her a stupid whore in front of everyone. I would interrupt the Owl's annual soliloquy and shout out that all the Soviet midgets are murderers, that all people with power are murderers, for that matter—the Russians and the Americans, too; they all wanted to unload their damn bombs on our heads. I would wrestle the 9 mm Makarov pistol from the colonel who, at the end of each school year, inspected our bodies and private parts for signs of homosexuality and other diseases that would render us unfit for military service; I'd force him at gunpoint to take off his shit-colored uniform, and then parade his fat apparatchik ass down the school's corridors and out onto the street. I would do all this and more, if I had dignity. I would tell Bianka that I hated her far more than I liked her. I hated her because she was one of them, she was the commander of our unit and on important occasions she would strut, with all the other pubescent commanders, up onto the stage of Chamber Hall No. 1, or across the school yard, dressed in that ridiculous uniform—a pleated indigo skirt and matching vest, a white shirt and red scarf. In those moments I watched her with contempt, hating myself all the more for the fact that seeing her in the role of a Party servant, a well-greased cogwheel in the system, only made me desire her more, made me want to take her into a bathroom and fuck her standing up, ripping her com-mander's costume in the process, tearing her young apparatchik's silky red scarf with my teeth, shredding it into long, narrow strips that I would then tie around her thighs like bandages, and I would spread that pristine white button-up shirt on the floor and make her kneel on it, and then I would fuck her more, *con fuoco,* I would corrupt that subservient mind of hers through fucking, contaminate her with shame and remorse and indignation and depression, with a debilitating sense of futility and a romantic vision of suicide, and in the end I'd render her unfit to function in the system. I would make her human again.

"You didn't like my playing," she said sullenly. "I just can't play fast enough for you, right? Or I'm *untalented,* whatever that means."

"I did like your playing," I lied. "You're great. No, I'm serious! Who cares about speed?"

Bianka scooted closer and looked at me. This wasn't a give-me-a-kiss kind of look, though. It was a look that conveyed strength and superiority. She seemed to find my interest in her amusing. It was how she killed me, day after day—by acting like a cold-blooded anthropologist. She was always the sober one; I was the drunk.

"Yesterday I heard your friend, Vadim, play the second ballad. You were right, he's pretty exceptional. I just don't think he'll get anywhere with his kind of playing. He does whatever he wants! And he's messy."

"He's a genius. Of course he's going to do whatever the fuck he wants. He never plays a piece the same way twice."

"There's no such thing as a genius, Konstantin. I don't even know what that word means. You keep saying it as if it explains anything."

"A genius is someone who's born with a knowledge of certain things. Look—Vadim doesn't need to practice. He remembers things he's never ever heard or played before. He can sight-read an étude in real tempo. Hell, he could finish the *Unfinished Symphony* if he wanted to. This isn't a joke. He can come up with a different reprise for a nocturne on the spot. He's like someone who's traveled here from a different era."

"That's what *you* think. In reality he's no more talented than you or me. He just happens to play differently."

"But you're so wrong! So wrong! We're not at *all* the same. What Negodnik says is bullshit. Everyone comes to the world alone, naked, and nameless; therefore we are all equal. That's just retarded Marxist bullshit! It might appear that we're part of the same species, and we inhabit the same planet, but the fact is, we live on completely different planes of existence. We come from different times, we've arrived here from other places. What's amazing is that we can say 'Pass me the water!' for example, and, most of the time, understand it to mean the same thing."

"Pass me the water!" Bianka ordered and burst out giggling. I lit a cigarette and moved an inch closer to her, so that I could feel her breath on my face. "Pass me the water," she repeated, lowering her voice.

"Very funny."

"Who fills your head with this stuff?"

"I met a madman once."

"I don't want to hear about it. And please don't come to pick me up tomorrow morning before school, OK? My dad saw us the other day and lectured me for an hour on the perils of teenage pregnancy."

"Fine."

"Pass me the water!"

Brahms,
Intermezzo in E flat, op. 117

March 6, 1988

It was a sunny Saturday, and the sound of melting icicles made me want to go for a walk in Boris Garden, which, I imagined, was filled with kids on bicycles, and mothers pushing strollers, and boys and girls kissing on the benches and smoking and playing Kino songs on their guitars. But I was stuck inside the Dark House of the Three Giant Women, listening to a boy of seven play the Intermezzo in E flat again and again, each time making the exact same mistake in the middle. I had already practiced for three hours, under Ladybug's stern guidance, and was waiting for my turn to begin practicing again. Then suddenly, as the boy played the sinister octaves in both hands at the end of the exposition, I was transported back ten years, to the precise moment when the doors of the yellow tram opened and everyone descended the stairs in pairs, girls first, and then the boys. It was a special day: my kindergarten class was going to the mausoleum to pay homage to the Father of the Nation. I held hands with Peppy the Thief, who had a huge Band-Aid on top of his head from the time I'd thrown a brick at him in the sandbox. His name wasn't really Peppy the Thief, but we all called him that because every time one of us brought something nice to kindergarten, it always disappeared, somehow ending up in the side pocket of Peppy's navy blue uniform. Peppy was horrible to most of the kids in our class, and he and I fought all the time. Still, I considered him a friend, if only because I felt sorry for him: his father had died and then his mother had found another family, leaving Peppy and his German shepherd at his grandmother's small apartment not far from our school. The kindergarten was located at 13 Charles Darwin Street and had an enormous playground with slides and swings and truck tires and bronze deer statues and two dried-up water fountains. There were eighteen kids in our class, and we had two teachers—Ivanova, who liked to mete out punishments, and Mechkova, a purple-haired behemoth who had a hard time squeezing through a tram door. Every day Ivanova made us sit at the art table and cut circles out of paper of various colors. These she later attached to the lapels of our uniforms with a pin. The best-behaved went home wearing a blue circle on their lapel. The not-so-good kids wore red circles, and the worst wore black. I usually went home with a black circle on my lapel, and once, on my mother's birthday, I got not one but two black circles at the same time because I had stolen the blue paper and made myself some blue circles while Ivanova wasn't paying attention.

We marched past the Russian church, which looked like a vanilla and strawberry birthday cake, and made our way across Central Square toward the mausoleum. Central Square was paved with shiny yellow cobblestones that tended to get quite slippery when it rained, and today was no exception. Ivanova had brought only one umbrella, which she was sharing with Mechkova. The rest of us had to walk in the rain, getting thoroughly wet. Peppy the Thief said that the dead man in the mausoleum had a giant mustache that kept on growing, and every month the soldiers with pentacles on their hats and silver bayonets on their rifles had to open the glass coffin and trim his giant mustache with a pair of scissors. I'd never seen a dead man before, whereas Peppy the Thief had seen lots of them and so knew what he was talking about. He warned me, in particular, to avoid looking in a dead man's eyes, because I might get trapped in the world of the dead and travel there before my time had come.

We climbed the marble stairs up to the mausoleum's main entrance and gathered in the foyer. Inside it was unusually cold and smelled of rotten flowers and a dentist's office. Everything was of marble—the floor, the walls, the ceiling. There wasn't a single window. Apparently there was a problem, because the lady behind the desk kept shaking her head and repeating that they were doing maintenance on the body and we had to try again some other day. Ivanova was insistent. We'd come all the way from Kindergarten No. 165, she said; we were wet, and we'd be terribly disappointed if we didn't get a chance to catch a glimpse of the Father of the Nation. After some debate, Ivanova wrote our names in the visitor's archive and handed her coat to the lady behind the desk. Mechkova did the same. Two soldiers with bayoneted rifles and feathers in their hats led us up a dark, sloping corridor into the mausoleum's inner chamber. We clung to the railing of a wide balcony that encircled the glass coffin below. The Father of the Nation was wearing a gray suit, a gray tie, and a plate of red medals. Lying on a reclining white platform, he looked very much like a real person, except that his skin seemed fake, as if made of rubber. The smell, on the other hand, was real. It was so bad, Peppy the Thief pinched his nose and started making funny faces. I pinched my nose and started making funny faces, too. The Father of the Nation smelled like rotten eggs! The soldiers with the bayoneted rifles didn't seem particularly impressed with the monkey faces we were making at them. But then, you could never make a soldier stationed in Central Square laugh. They just stared at the tip of their noses and pretended not to see anything. "Why is his stomach covered with a blanket?" asked one of the girls—whispering, so as not to offend the Father of the Nation. "Because they're doing some maintenance on the body, what do you think," Ivanova said.

Dead people needed to see doctors, too, apparently, for just then two men dressed in white aprons approached the glass coffin, set their black briefcases on the floor, and took the lid off. "Step along!" the soldiers ordered us, but Peppy the Thief and I couldn't move. We held hands and stared at the doctors as they lifted the blanket from the dead man's stomach and then began to unbutton his shirt. "Move along!" the soldiers ordered us again, and now we heard Ivanova calling our names from the corridor that branched off the balcony. All of our classmates had left, and Peppy the Thief and I were alone with the doctors and the soldiers and the dead man who had a giant mustache and a gaping hole in his stomach filled with fluffy white stuff that looked awfully like cotton candy. All of a sudden, I had the terrifying sensation that the dead man knew I was watching him. He was dead, but he was alive as well, alive in his death, and he was secretly keeping an eye on me from every corner and nook of his eternal house.

Outside, we formed ranks and Ivanova walked up and down, inspecting our postures. The rain had stopped, leaving Central Square dotted with puddles reflecting the slow march of the gray clouds above. Opposite the mausoleum was a yellow three-story building that had once been the home of the king. Now it was a museum filled with paintings. To the left was the National Bank and Party Headquarters, with its pentacle-tipped tower. To the right, on a quiet street across a park, was the Grand Music Hall, where my mother and I went to hear pianists perform every Sunday.

"I want everyone to tell me what they've learned today after paying homage to the Father of the Nation," said Ivanova, clutching her hands behind her back. "Maya, let's start with you. Today was a most important day in your life. What did you learn?"

"I learned that the Father of the Nation is a kind man who will live in our hearts forever."

"Good. Who's next? Rada?"

"I learned that if you help others and fight the imperialists, people will remember you and bring you flowers even when you are no longer alive."

"Do you think this is funny, Peppy? Tell your classmates what you've learned."

"I learned that they have to stuff the Father of the Nation with cotton candy so that he won't smell so bad."

Wading carefully through a puddle, Ivanova stepped in front of

Peppy and lowered her head as if to examine his big brown eyes and his pink lips and his black eyebrows, which looked really strange because Peppy's long wavy hair was not black at all, but a dark gold. The slap came unexpectedly and with such force that Peppy fell sideways, clutching in vain at Rada's uniform as he hit the ground. I didn't need to look at him to know that Ivanova's hand would be imprinted across his face like a nasty burn.

"Konstantin, what have you learned? Or do you think, like your little criminal of a friend, who is headed for a correctional school, that coming here to pay homage to the Father of the Nation is something to joke about?"

"I just want to go home," I said, and looked down at my feet, already anticipating what would come next—the sting of a slap on my face, the ringing in my ears, and the moment of lightheadedness, blurring the lines between inside and outside, between the conviction that your cheek was you and the realization that your body was nothing but a disposable object in the external world, not much different from a table or a chair; an object that other people could poke and kick and ridicule and lock up in a room. Maybe Ivanova would be satisfied with just pulling my ears. There were three different ways in which she could pull my ears. The first was to pull my ears straight up. The second was to twist them until something in my head cracked. The third was to pinch them between her nails and then squeeze hard until she broke the skin.

But she simply walked away from me and I suddenly wished she had slapped me and pulled my ears and screamed at me and called me a criminal, so that Peppy the Thief wouldn't be the only kid to walk across Central Square—in front of the soldiers and all the people in suits—with a red hand print across his face and tears in his eyes.

I just wanted to go home and play my piano. I had started studying the Intermezzi by Johannes Brahms on the blond August Forster my grandfather had bought for my mother when she was a child. The nicest thing about the August Forster was that it had a key, and after I finished practicing at night I could lock it up and put the key in my pocket. I usually brought the key to school, and when Ivanova ordered me to stand facing the wall for an hour, I played with the key in my pocket and thought of the smooth ivory keys and the universe of sounds they could unlock. Peppy the Thief had sworn that he'd never steal the key from me. He really didn't care about keys.

Chopin,
Étude in E flat, op. 10, no. 6

March 23, 1988

We stopped before we even began. We didn't say a word or look at each other. We just stopped and everything that had been building up to this moment—the white cherry blossoms brushing against the cracked window, the cold hug of the terrazzo stairway, the overpowering smell of geraniums and old roof boards, the aftertaste of the pink lipstick she had put on to kiss me, the hint of tobacco on her skin, her sweaty thighs and burning breath, my arms around her waist, the torrent of thoughts propelled by our racing hearts, all the stupid stuff I'd said in defense of the Romantics—zoomed past us like a train, leaving us dry-mouthed, empty-headed, and a trifle dizzy. We could hear the old midget moving about in his attic, crinkling plastic bags, folding newspapers. There was always the possibility that he would walk out and catch us in the middle of it, me sitting at the top of the stairs, between two large pots exploding with red blossoms, and Stella in my lap, dress hiked up above her hips, panties clutched tight in her fist. Not that he would do anything. He would probably just stand there and watch. He'd seen us on previous Wednesdays, when Stella's classes ended at 11:25 and she walked over from the Classics High School to wait for me in the apartment building behind the music school. But perhaps it wasn't the midget that made us stop, or his mother, who lived on the second floor and was probably getting ready to go to the mineral spring downtown to fill up her glass bottles, or the hurried steps and strange noises haunting the apartment building, or the knowledge that Peppy the Thief was standing outside the main door—smoking and keeping an eye on the narrow alley's street entrance—or even the fact that Stella and I had done it too many times already and were getting bored with each other. We had fun, certainly, when it came to it, and we were even passionate at times, but not enough to make the whole thing seem less fake. I didn't even like this girl. I hated how arrogant she was, quoting Ovid in Latin, reciting Homer in Greek; this whole obsession with dead languages drove me mad. I couldn't stand another conversation about how she'd slept with her "amazing" Latin professor, and how great it had been. Not that I was jealous; we never said we were together for anything but the sex. That and music, for she aspired to become a classical singer. The first time we'd done it—in Peppy's bedroom, while he was out in the kitchen punching his stepfather and calling his mother a whore—she sang quietly in my ear, something by Puccini, and I told her that her voice was amazing, which was true. She'd always wanted to date one of the boys from the Music School for the Gifted, she told me, to which I responded that I'd always wanted to date a girl from the Classics High School because they were the prettiest and weren't fucked up from playing a musical instrument eight hours a day—which, of course, was a total lie. Stella and her twin sister, Anna, who also attended the Classics High School, were extremely pretty, prettier than any of the girls at my school, but they both had a screw loose. The night Stella and I had gotten together in Peppy's mom's apartment, Anna had refused to leave the room and lay on the other bed, smoking and listening to us and her mad boyfriend, who was breaking glasses in the kitchen.

Ah, I couldn't stand it. Me, Peppy the Thief, and the Evil Twins. I had no idea how I'd ended up as part of this strange quartet. It was Peppy who first introduced me to the twins. He'd had a lot of time on his hands ever since he was kicked out of the Bastille (or High School No. 7, the last place where kids with criminal behavior were sent before being transferred to a correctional camp) for urinating on the national flag. All he did now was drink and hunt for pretty girls at the elite high schools downtown. The truth was, from the very beginning both Stella and Anna had been in love with Peppy. I was just someone who was supposed to make their cozy love triangle a little more interesting, but it wasn't working. When Stella began sleeping with Peppy, and Anna suddenly started acting like my girlfriend, I got out. Then they switched roles yet again, and now we all pretended we were great friends.

Stella stuffed her panties under my shirt and got up to open the small window. When we didn't know what to say or how to act, we smoked. Even now, as I watched her reach for the window lever—one foot planted in a flower pot, the other stretched out and balanced on a shallow ledge, her left hand playfully hiking up her uniform dress so that I could take a good look at her ass (she knew I'd be looking)—I wondered why it was I'd never cared about her. Wasn't it enough that we wanted each other, that we played the game and helped each other reach that moment of unconsciousness? But sex was just a chemical intervention, an aspirin that only briefly alleviated the chronic pain, its effects wearing off quickly and forgettably. And now I was under the spell of a strange longing, a nostalgia for a desperately awaited spring that had never arrived, the chromatic left-hand accompaniment in Chopin's sixth étude running endlessly through my mind, scattering fall leaves the color of wine and gold and amber. Time was up and the end had already administered a powerful anesthetic: a mix of resignation and indifference. From the top of the stairs I could see over the tall brick wall behind the music school. I could even see inside Zimova's office on the fourth floor. But she couldn't see me.

Stella finally succeeded in opening the small window and the stairway instantly filled up with the sounds of violins, pianos, and oboes. She smoked standing underneath the window, looking down at me with desire and resentment. It was all an act—her provocative posture, the way she propped the elbow of her cigarette-holding hand with her wrist, letting her wavy ash-blond hair cover half of her face. Still, it was an act that, even after four months, amused me.

"Are you afraid that Peppy will steal me from you again?" She giggled and flicked the ashes from her cigarette in a flower pot.

"Peppy the Thief steal my girlfriend! That's a novel idea."

"You know he killed his dog."

"The German shepherd?"

"He's only got one dog."

"No, I didn't know."

"He got home drunk the other night and when his dog jumped to greet him, Peppy kicked him in the head with his boot."

The image of Peppy in his greatcoat, inebriated, walking over his dead dog and collapsing on the couch in his grandmother's apartment made me sick. But then again, I needed him. He was an important asset, as Alexander liked to remind me. Peppy could do and procure things we simply couldn't. He had no conscience and wasn't afraid of getting caught. He would happily break someone's fingers or beat him up, if Alexander and I asked him to. But this lack of an intuitive discrimination between right and wrong also made him unpredictable. At any moment he could turn on me, or report me to the snoops.

"The lovebirds!" Peppy called out to us as we walked out of the apartment building. "Some marathon fucking, if you'll excuse the language. You were up there an hour! Did you tickle the ivories? Ti-ti-ti-ti-ri, tam-tam-tam!"

"No, as a matter of fact."

Peppy looked at Stella and then at me again, amazed. "You didn't? Not at all? My dear, you aren't still pissed about our little, how should I say, rendezvous? Our little, er, get-together? Stella and I are just really good friends, you know, and good friends, sometimes, you know, have a tête-à-tête, right, Stella? It's only natural."

"God, he's never opened a book in his life," Stella said with a derisive smile. "And all of a sudden, he's speaking French?"

"Nothing wrong with that," Peppy said. "Been taking lessons from a friend of mine at the French High School."

I pulled a bunch of blank, officially stamped medical slips from the inside pocket of my jacket and handed them to Peppy. They were a valuable commodity that Peppy sold to students all over town. A properly filled-out slip with a convincing diagnosis and competently forged doctor's signature could excuse a student for up to five days of missed classes, and that—in a system where three absences automatically led to a lower personal standing—was nothing short of a life saver. Before a medical slip could be approved, however, it had to be examined and signed by the school nurse and the class supervisor (in my case, the Hyena), which meant that the risk of getting caught was always high.

"Only ten?" Peppy exploded. "I told you I'll do it for *fifteen*."

"I could only get ten this time," I said. "I'll get you the other five by Sunday."

"What's the problem? Your grandmother's a fucking doctor. You can get as many slips as you want."

"I told you, you'll have them on Sunday. Here's the plan. You'll need a watch, a flashlight, and a screwdriver. The first recital starts at eight o'clock. You should get here by quarter of and sneak into the school along with the crowd. Go up to the attic and stay there until two o'clock in the morning. By that time the doorman will be asleep. Make your way to the third floor and take the locking mechanism apart with the screwdriver—or you can push the left door off its hinges with a lever. Once you're inside, take the daybooks, and really, you have to take *all* of them, from fourth to twelfth grade; then go down to the second floor. Room twelve is on your left, and it has a balcony that isn't too high off the ground, so you can easily jump down from it. Just make sure no one's watching you from this building. The guy on the second floor works in the police department."

"Fuck me over, and I'll fuck you over double, all right?" Peppy said, pointing his finger in my face.

I pretended that I wasn't scared of him, but I was. Every time I saw him I studied his handsome face, trying to determine what it was that made him look so broken, so devious and mercenary. Was it the deathly color of his bloodless lips, or the way they curled up when he smiled? The tiny mole on the right side of his mouth? The strange combination of copper-colored hair, washed-out hazel eyes, and swarthy complexion? But of course it wasn't any one of these characteristics. It was his presence, his stance, the timing of his condescending smile, the cool way in which he moved his long hands, his unwavering ring finger.

At the end of the alley, I turned around and looked back. Peppy had his hand wrapped around Stella's waist and was speaking into her ear. She stared at the ground, distant, indifferent.

"Heard you killed your dog," I shouted and lingered to see his reaction. There was none. I kept walking.

A silhouette of a man standing by the pond in Doctors' Garden caught my attention and I crossed the street to get a better look at him. I recognized the stained beige raincoat, the worn leather briefcase, the tattered shoes, the gray bowler hat. "Uncle Iliya?" I said quietly, though by now I was certain that the man could be none other than my distant relative, mentor, private English teacher, and guardian angel, the man I'd always called uncle.

"Let's take a walk," he said and, without waiting for a response, started down the graveled path away from the torrent of sounds emitting from the music school. When I was with Iliya, I felt like the luckiest person in the world. He was a treasury of secrets, and I his only initiate. I always found it hard to believe that there weren't crowds of people trailing behind him wherever he went, crowds of people filled with anguish and anticipation, desperate for answers. But, of course, no one knew who he was. Not the Hyena, not the Owl, not Alexander or Irina, not the passersby or the plainclothes agents patrolling the streets, not even my parents. Iliya was here incognito, a dignified translator working for the American Embassy in downtown Sofia, who had accidentally slipped into the tunnel of time and emerged at the other end, forty-four years later—disheveled, wrinkled, unemployed, yet unbent, the same stoic spark in his eyes. He was an older, agnostic Dante who'd toured the hells and returned home without ever catching a glimpse of the gardens of paradise.

Iliya was born in 1911. In 1944, when the Communists staged a coup and arrested him on charges of espionage, he was thirty-three. By the time he was released from the Lovech concentration camp, in

1966, he was fifty-five. Eleven years later, in 1977, released on parole from another camp, he was sixty-six. Now it was 1988 and he was seventy-seven. These numbers seemed magical to me: 11, 33, 44, 55, 66, 77, 88. It was as if Iliya's life were governed by a series of powerful eleven-year-long cosmic cycles, closing old wounds even as they opened new ones. Or perhaps there was just one cycle, one perfectly circular path, exactly eleven years in diameter, and Iliya traveled upon it again and again, and each time his journey ended and began at the same place, and he was always thirty-three, and the city had just been rebuilt after the American bombing of 1943, and the king was dead and the German-allied government had just been ousted, and it was autumn, with the last russet leaves falling from the chestnut trees lining Stamboliiski Boulevard to lie strewn about the sidewalk, and Iliya was going home with a bar of dark chocolate wrapped in brown paper which he'd bought for his two daughters from the candy store across from Saint Nedelya, and the city was oddly quiet, as if caught by surprise, the warm caress of Helios seeming to promise better days, days without the thought of war, and Iliya was going home, but he wasn't in a rush, the day was still young and there was so much time—time for a Turkish coffee and a newspaper on the corner of Stamboliiski and Botev, time for a shave and a haircut on Alabin Street, time to visit his high school friend in the Jewish quarter, time to buy some fruit at the market outside the mosque; kids were playing with marbles on the sidewalk, the milkman was still doing his rounds, the church bells had just sounded eleven, and the plainclothes men who were about to wrap their elbows around Iliya's and whisk him off to a dungeon beneath the cobbled streets were still a block away.

"How long have you been waiting for me?" I asked.

"About forty minutes, I think," Iliya said, checking his watch. "I took the seven thirty, as usual."

We headed toward the edge of the park and sat on a bench, under the canopy of a young oak tree.

"I don't think I've ever told you about the Maestro, and you're too young to remember who he was. He came to the Lovech camp in

1957, after the second big wave of political prisoners. We all knew him from before the Communists took over the country. He used to play for the Royal Symphony Orchestra in the early forties. First violin. A true virtuoso. After 1944, when the red government disbanded the orchestra, he took to playing in bars and restaurants. They arrested him for his habit of telling dirty jokes about the prime minister during performances. He was a man of existential makeup, you see, unlike any I've seen. Even after his first extended stay in solitary confinement—a cell narrow as a chimney; couldn't even bend your knees or elbows, so you were forced to sleep standing up, kissing the concrete wall and skinning your back—he continued to tell jokes and make people laugh. At the quarry, where we sometimes had to work for two days and two nights without a break, he would just drop his sack of stones and sit on the ground, waiting for the blows. His hands weren't made for this kind of work, and yet they forced him to carry *twice* as much as the other prisoners, just to see him suffer. In the beginning we all tried to help him when the guards weren't looking. But they really hated him. They wanted him crushed. One minute, a graduate of the Paris Conservatory, first violin in the Royal Symphony Orchestra, the next, a restaurant clown, and now, a slave in a labor camp: they wanted to write the final chapter of his life."

Iliya stopped talking and checked his watch, allowing for a curious middle-aged woman all in black to walk past. But the woman didn't pass. She stood for a brief moment in the middle of the path, hesitating, and then sat on the adjacent bench. Iliya cleared his throat and looked sternly in the direction of the pyramidal monument built to commemorate the doctors who had lost their lives during the Russo-Turkish war. It was impossible to read Iliya, a man without laugh lines, a man who never asked any questions. He'd never asked me anything. Never bothered with *how are you, how is school, what are you planning to do with your life,* or any of the other conventions. When he bought a newspaper or got a shoeshine, he never asked for the price. Even when his train was canceled, he refused to ask the station clerk when the next train to Lukovo was scheduled to depart. He got by only on the information that others volunteered. And he never laughed. The only time I'd ever seen him smile was when I'd asked him if he believed in God; a question he did not answer.

Was this some kind of defense mechanism he'd developed in the camps? Don't ask questions and you'll stay alive. Was it a sign of his deep distrust of humans? Or was it, perhaps, another state of being, where one no longer sought answers or feared the unknown? Even in old age, his face looked refined, almost noble. There was so much dignity in his strong jaw and pointed chin, in his thin lips and pronounced cheekbones; at times he reminded me of a photograph of Beckett I had seen on the poster for *Waiting for Godot* shortly before the government banned the play for its unintended commentary on the mass anticipation of the final phase of the utopian Communist order. I couldn't imagine Iliya treading the marshes on Persin Island with a sixty-kilogram sack of stones on his back, the icy wind bruising his face, the black waters of the Danube thrashing on the shore; I couldn't imagine him suspended upside down, with broken teeth, smashed nose, mouth full of blood; submerged in a barrel filled with feces, holding his breath until the crumbling of the last levee of hope. And I felt ashamed to sit beside him, dressed in a uniform designed by his torturers, stitched up by the progeny of pigheaded peasants and proletarian halfwits, a pair of panties stuffed into my jacket pocket.

I zeroed in on Iliya's enormous lizard-skinned hands, which had carved out whole quarries, moved mountains of stones, dug graves, and fed human bodies to the rabid pigs of Persin Island; which had emptied marshes and caressed the faces of his dying friends; which had been tied with ropes and wrung with metal rods; which had written countless letters that would never reach their destination. Why was he burdening me with all these stories? Was it because he wanted me one day to take revenge on his behalf, or because the horrors from his past lost some of their power each time he talked about them?

"They hated him for having seen Paris," Iliya continued now. I turned around to look for the woman who had interrupted him just a minute before, but she was gone and in her place were perched two ravens. "He didn't last long. Ten days, maybe twelve. They accused him of being a womanizer, of setting up the Egyptian ambassador with the best prostitutes in Sofia. The Maestro was a worldly man, I should say. He enjoyed certain things, nurtured his indulgence. But was that a crime? To the Communists, it was. Evil always comes with a golden system of ethics. Who would've guessed that the reds would become the new puritans, with a perverse appetite for classical music, solid forms, decadent ballroom kitsch? But I shouldn't have been surprised. Nobody should've been surprised. There aren't different systems of control. There's only one. It just keeps changing names."

"So how did the Maestro die?"

"The usual way. Gazdov, the camp's security chief, ordered us to form ranks, then walked to the middle of the square and drew a circle in the dirt with his boot. This was a signal that one of us had been chosen to die. It is strange when you expect to hear your name and suddenly realize that your name isn't necessarily yours and that your body isn't you. Names, bodies—they belong to time, but the still time. Then Gazdov asked if there was someone among us who could play the violin. 'I think I can try,' the Maestro called out from the back. He knew he'd been sentenced to death, and he was going to remain himself until the end. Perhaps he was ready to go. There are times when you can feel the coming fall at the beginning of the summer; in your fingertips, under your tongue. There are times when fate lowers a ladder and lets you take a peek at the other side. Times when you know just how easy it is to shake off this burden—with all its geography, chemistry, its rules of gravity—and dip into the lukewarm waters of eternity. Ah! Another moment has slipped by, unnoticed!"

Iliya checked his watch and stood up, holding his briefcase under his arm. He had to hurry to catch the 1:30 train to Lukovo, the tiny, mostly abandoned mountain village about forty minutes outside Sofia where he lived in a small house and looked after a modest apiary. I often wondered whether Iliya's routine twenty-minute morning walk from his house to the train station wasn't in a way a transposition, a reenactment of his early morning walks from the barracks to the quarry during his life in the camps. Did his daily train rides and his aimless wanderings around the old part of Sofia restore, even partially, his sense of freedom? And how much freedom did one need in order to feel free? Was mixing a spoon of his own amber-colored honey in a glass of cold mountain water, or cutting a bunch of grapes from the pendulous vines shading his patio, enough to compensate for the decades that had been stolen from him?

"Gazdov was a man of rituals," Iliya said as we approached the library and began hearing the sounds of pianos, clarinets, and human voices coming from the music school. "He had a small mirror that he kept in the inside pocket of his military coat. When a condemned prisoner was called to step out of the ranks and enter the circle drawn on the ground, Gazdov would hand him his mirror and tell him to look inside, for the very last time. Of course, to Gazdov this ritual was but another perverse joke, a final mockery of human dignity. But to the condemned, the mirror held—how should I say—a metaphysical significance. Different people saw different things. Some were surprised. Some were crushed. Some were relieved. Others saw the divine. One of the Catholic priests who was sent with me to Persin Island, in the early years, when Gazdov first began his career as the Lord of Flies, told me, after looking in the mirror, that he'd seen the truth. Birth is the beginning of dualism, he'd said. And death, the end. The inner eye looking out, the body and nonbody, time within and time without, the face of the I and the faceless eternal—they are all a nightmare in the minds of those who have forgotten the source. So he said. They shot him in the neck on our way back to the barracks. I carried him to the latrine, where the bodies of the recently dead were usually left overnight before being thrown to the pigs. In the death certificate they usually wrote down pneumonia, heart attack, or tuberculosis."

"And what about the Maestro? What did he see in the mirror?"

"The Maestro, true to his nature, took the mirror and put on a little act. He styled his hair back, licked his ring finger and smoothed out

the outer ends of his eyebrows, twisted his thin mustache, smiled . . .
It was his last performance and he wasn't going to let anyone walk
away disappointed. They knocked him down on the way to the quarry.
One of Gazdov's lapdogs swooped by on his horse and whacked the
Maestro on the back of his head with a club. One blow was all it took.
Others came and beat him while he was on the ground, but by that
time he was a goner. When I saw him outside the latrines that night he
was still breathing, if barely; his head had ballooned and he could no
longer open his eyes. The next morning he was fed to the pigs."

It was the end of March, a cold gray spring, and as we walked
underneath the shy chestnut trees I kept searching the crowded sidewalks for familiar faces, someone from school who might, seeing Iliya,
realize that everything had been a nightmare: all they had to do was
look at Iliya and they would understand—the interrupted memory,
the geography of time, the itinerary of the robots, the secret world of
ghosts. But no one ever saw my uncle. He was a shadow, a blind spot
in people's eyes.

Ask him! I wanted to shout at the passersby. He *knows*! He remembers the nuns who once walked the dark corridors of the music school!
He remembers the king, and the Nazis, and the anarchists, and the
reds; he remembers the devastation of Sofia and the American bomb-
ers wedged into the leaden sky: the B-24 Liberators, the B-17 Flying
Fortresses, the B-25 Mitchells; he remembers Peter Deunov's sun
worshippers, the Theosophists, the Catholics, and the chief rabbi
of Sofia who became a sun worshipper himself and received a vision
of Jesus descending upon a sunbeam; the German soldiers and the
industrialists dining at the Rotary Club. He remembers what happened before, during, and after the new megalomaniacs switched on
this amnesia-inducing machine and everyone forgot who they'd been
and what they'd worked for.

But how comfortable it is to live in a country where everyone is a
prisoner. The sweet burden of being told what to do and how to do it
twenty-four hours a day, seven days a week. To live for the common
good, to eat and work for the common good, to fuck for the common

good, and then to lie compliantly in the friable soil. And when it all comes to an end—with the clouds of cold neon light—it will be the robots who have led us there, those who make sure that the system works, who observe the law and believe all the lies they've been fed, year after year, one smile at a time, one subservient act, one docile nod, until, at last, the leaden zeppelins arrive, just like in my dreams, and the enormous granite dome bearing down upon the earth with the weight of the whole universe fills everyone's head with a quiet thought-stopping bass drone, the sound of the iron gates of Tartarus opening up to swallow the tribe of liars back into the primordial vacuum.

Iliya's tram hugged the corner of Tolbuhin and Dondukov Boulevard, disappearing amid much screeching and grumbling behind the dilapidated mustard-colored agrarian bank. Nowhere to go but back to school, my only home, my accursed home of pubescent smells and pure musical forms, back to the attic, where I could be alone and smoke and play the études into the night, fighting off the acid of hunger burning my insides; fighting off the yearning to cease, once and for all.

So long as I was up in the attic, facing the piano, my right foot feeding the damper pedal, the poisons of the body could not reach me. I knew at five, and then again at nine, and ever since, that the visible world was but a small part of the whole thing. There was something else beyond the misery, that much was clear. It was as if we had fallen here from a place of beauty and pure forms, and had forgotten the way back. Awake or asleep, we never tired of searching our impoverished memory for a trace of our origin. Desperate to unlock the forbidden memory, we designed ourselves doors, formulas, keys, haunted spaces. We dreamed of vehicles that could take us beyond the horizon. But only a few of these had the ability to escape the gravity of the human condition. The piano was perhaps the best one ever made. Even the beat-up Chaika in my attic room was powerful enough to take me at least halfway to the place that can't be reached while one has a self. One more leap toward the sun and I might catch fire and begin to burn—first my wax wings, then my fingers and my hands, my face and

neck, my heart and my memories—until every part of me was incinerated in the all-purifying fire and I emerged on the other side, complete
at last.

But who could take that last step? Ordinary beings, the sons of Ica-
rus, invariably fell into the sea. I fell every time, after hours of playing, and I felt wretched and worthless, like a ghost who grows darker,
baser, whenever he steps closer to the light.

Chopin,
Sonata no. 2 in B-flat Minor, op. 35,
Scherzo

March 24, 1988

C louds came to Sofia to die. They arrived from the northeast, from the direction of Belgrade and the Danube, and queued up above the Central Cemetery, on the outskirts of the city, like a fleet of grace-less, rotten ships covered with soot and verdigris; they teetered over Luvov Most and Women's Market, over the mosque and the synagogue and the Turkish Baths, snagging on the multipronged antennas atop all the old apartment buildings and wrapping themselves around the patinated domes of the taller churches. By the time they approached Doctors' Garden and the music school, they were tattered, flying low, the smell of sulfur and charcoal presaging their end. One by one they collapsed over the remains of the Thracian cemetery scattered on the periphery of Doctors' Garden. I could see it all from the fenced-in backyard near school where I awaited the first bell with a cigarette, shivering in the damp morning air and blowing into my scorching hot plastic cup of espresso. Coffee and cigarettes on an empty stomach left me feeling sick, but then, I was used to it. I had already spent my lunch money on the espresso and probably wouldn't eat until I got back to my parents' place, later that night. I could always go to eat at the crowded, foul-smelling cafeteria at the University of Sofia, of course, but I didn't want to run into my father, and, besides, the food there was pure, unadulterated shit.

I was a little surprised to see Pirozhkin, our army instructor, turning the corner of the National Library at twenty to eight, five minutes before classes began, if my Sputnik was to be trusted. Pirozhkin, who was a retired colonel, taught third period every Thursday and was convinced that going to the shooting range was an educational activity. Thanks to him I'd learned how to disassemble and reassemble a Kalashnikov in fifteen seconds, how to throw hand grenades and aim RPG's at imperialist tanks. I had to give it to him—he was as dimwitted as a blind pig, the bastard, but he could salute like no one else, bending backward, his tendons and facial muscles stretched to the point of snapping, his chin jutting forth, his eyes vacuous, devoid of any personality. Like many military men serving the state, he existed on the fringes of human intelligence, barely conscious, struggling to prove that he was, in fact, alive. "The only difference between war and music," he once proclaimed, in a flurry of unexpected brain activity, "is that war is a lot louder." Brilliant! He was an expert.

Sensing trouble, not least because he was carrying his government-issued 9 mm Makarov strapped to his belt, I put out my cigarette and waited for him to cross the street. There was the bell.

It seemed I was the only student to come to school that day. The corridors and stairs were deserted, the usual bacchanalia of sounds and voices reduced to the distant echo of an oboe. Had Peppy the Thief broken into Teachers' Headquarters and stolen the daybooks last night, as Alexander and I asked him to, there would've been students and teachers crowding outside every classroom, anticipating an official statement by the Owl. This was different. Something was very wrong; I knew it by the way Maria, the south-wing janitor, greeted me on the third floor.

"They're all in the basement, waiting for you," she said, unable to contain her excitement. Were the moral police to hang me over the stairwell one day, I had no doubt that Maria would be right there, to spit and throw stones at me.

I weighed my options. I could just walk out of school and skip classes. Perhaps I would even succeed in pushing a forged doctor's notice through the school's labyrinthine bureaucracy. But what would Iliya do in my place? How would the Maestro have acted? They'd never run. They would face their tormentors, accept their fate. Life is what it is. You can fight it, only to die of futility and exhaustion.

The pay phone on the first floor was ringing again. It had been ringing, on and off, as long as I could remember. There was no point in picking up the receiver—there was never anyone on the line. Outside, the branches of the chestnut tree stirred violently, spraying the window with raindrops. I had been walking these hallways for ten years now—at sixteen, practically my whole life.

God, my shirt and my jacket and my pants, my underwear even, stank of communism. The windows and the wide wooden ledge and the doors to Chamber Hall No. 1 and the terrazzo floors all reeked of it, too. The whole city reeked, for that matter, the trams and the streets and the parks, and the colors were all shit as well, they had chosen shitty colors for their shitty little social order.

I reached the basement. They were all waiting for me at the bottom of the stairs, the entire class of 9B lined up against the wall, and the Hyena standing in front of the heavy vault door leading to the underground nuclear shelter, notepad and a pencil in hand. There's a certain smirk that shows up on people's faces, a predatory glee, when they realize that they have total power over you. The oldest, most primitive tickle of the ego, it is also deadly contagious. The chickens of the world, the brainless vertebrates with stunted wings, want part of the action; they, too, would like to smirk. Just the sight of someone yielding the wand of power makes them drool. The Hyena said something that caused the chickens to tremble with anticipation. I didn't hear it, but could tell that it wasn't exactly well-intended. Lilly, the large-breasted and crushingly untalented violinist, was standing by the Hyena's side, staring at me coldly. The bitch had been promoted to the rank of personal advisor. I headed to the end of the row and took a position next to Alexander, who avoided looking me in the eye. He was furious. I could hear him grinding his teeth.

"The police inspector will be coming later this afternoon to question you and take your fingerprints," the Hyena announced, tapping her pencil against the notepad. "Unless we find the perpetrator of this revolting crime ourselves."

Somehow, in the early morning haze of cigarettes, caffeine, and dream detritus, I had to admit to myself that Antoaneta G. was probably a decent fuck, so long as she was on her knees and kept her mouth shut. Her face had the grotesque quality of an unfinished sculpture, her voice sounded like a duck's, her brown hair was thin and fluffy— a twisted lock always dangling out over her forehead, between her vapid eyes—but her ass and legs, especially when suited up in tights, were quite agreeable. It occurred to me just then that the door to the nuclear shelter was slightly ajar; a faint flicker of light from the underground passageway cast shadows on the door frame. Perhaps today would be one of those days when the authorities turned on the air-defense sirens and the teachers, armed with Geiger counters, led us to the nuclear shelter, where we would enact the end of the world— with great somnolence and heroism—wearing weird pajamas and gas masks. The Americans wanted us all dead, it was fantastic! The world was ruled by raving lunatics. I could see it, the merest glitch in communications, some mistranslated Russian word or phrase—for the Western tribes, of course, lacked the passion to learn proper Russian; even if they memorized *Eugene Onegin* and all of Pushkin, they still wouldn't get a feel for it in their bones—and the whole thing would blow up, a beautiful neon cloud descending upon Sofia, ionizing every evil idea established by the First International. Maybe, when we were all settled underground and everything aboveground was dead, we would start digging tunnels and meet the Americans halfway under the Atlantic, whereupon we would create a new language, something removed from Russian—for Westerners are scared shitless by the sound of Slavic, the lingua of black magic—and something different from English—for Easterners detest the scientific coldness of the Germanic tongues—and we'd all be friends, in the end.

I'd always been curious, I couldn't help it. I'd study the expressions on people's faces, look into their eyes, eager to determine just how removed they were from the reality that I'd inhabited since birth. It was a spectacle. The twins, Ligav and Mazen, with their smart-ass glasses and professorial posture; giant Dora, the cellist; Emile, Georgi, and Luba, all huddled together, wringing their hands; Ivan and Slav staring at their feet with an air of deep-rooted, almost genetic culpability; Angel and Dodo, the drummer, blinking with fear; melancholy Bianka and Isabel; Nadia, Tanya, and the two Marias, on the verge of crying; the five well-connected boys at the far end—all twenty of them, dressed in the mandatory navy-blue costumes, looking petrified, awaiting their sentence. They took everything so seriously, it made me doubt whether I had all my wits about me. For them, the reality defined by reds and navy blues, by pentacles and proletarian kitsch, by somnambulant demagogues and deflated revolutionary slogans, by a culture of frigid anti-imperialism and fake memories—this was the reality that they actually lived in, *they were inside it*. Unbelievable as it was, they seemed unable to realize that it was all a show, that we were all pretending. Playing students and teachers, governments and countries, playing humans. Then again, how was I any different from them? Knowing as well as I did the ins and outs of our macabre little carnival, the decor and the props and the slimy clichés, I still played their stupid game, trembled at the thought of losing my spot in the hierarchy of gifted pianists; I smiled and nodded, I waited for my cues to recite the insipid bullshit that passed here for communication. I was a jerk, really, lacking the integrity, the true madness required to write a brilliant manifesto and then off myself. To tell them what I really thought, for once. Violence only perpetuates the reign of the robots, of the soulless ghosts, but a good slap on the Hyena's face—that would be something to see, a role worth playing. Nothing too excessive, just a hearty slap humiliating enough to interrupt her relentless masturbation. The bitch! She wanted to play games! You could see it in her eyes. Wasn't this why she had brought us all to the basement? To have a little fun.

"Perhaps Konstantin can save us all the trouble by simply explaining how he broke into Teachers' Headquarters, stole the daybook of class 9B—just that one, strangely enough!—and then managed somehow to unlock the door to the nuclear shelter and take off with six Kalashnikovs and a case of live ammunition, which had been stored by our brave military for the use of self-defense in the event of war. Do you understand what this means? It means that you'll be brought to a court-martial! What do you have to say to us?"

"Well, I've been known to do crazier things sleepwalking."

I thought it was funny, but no one laughed, not even Alexander, who had the look of a bull entering a slaughterhouse.

"You're laughing now, but we'll see you when they read your sentence and your mother starts squealing from the back of the court hall. Parasite! You . . . parasite!"

She was screaming at the top of her lungs and trembling the way people do when they're about to squash a disgusting insect with their bare hands. Her veins were pumped full of venom and she was breathing heavily, aroused by the image of my timely demise.

The fact of the matter was, she had no proof of my involvement in the whole scheme. None. And Peppy the Thief was impossible to catch. Even with fingerprints and a detailed description from a witness, they would never find him. He had made himself invisible. He slept in basements, on park benches, in abandoned attics, at his many girlfriends' apartments, at schools, in nuclear shelters. I couldn't just call him and meet him somewhere. I had to wait for him to show up. The bastard! He had fucked Alexander and me over royally. Clearly he'd stolen only our daybook on purpose, to incriminate us. We were the obvious suspects. Nikolai D., the violist, was wild, too, but he wasn't the type that would plot to destroy the school's vital records and steal the arms cache from the basement. Besides, Nikolai D. had no motive. His grades were good, and his dad—who taught choral singing to the ninth, tenth, and eleventh grades—always took care of his absences. Alexander and me, on the other hand, they wouldn't put anything past us.

What was Peppy going to do with those Kalashnikovs anyway? Start a revolution? And why was he trying to get me kicked out of school? Could it have been that our threesome had finally started to get to his head? Maybe after Stella stopped giving him any, he realized he wanted her for himself. That was probably it—he was jealous of me, his pathetic male pride was hurting. Little did he know that Stella had lost interest in both of us completely. She was sleeping with her Latin professor, a bachelor with a flat and money for wine, who was working on a new translation of St. Augustine's *Confessions*. Peppy and I couldn't compete with that. Understandably, she had grown weary of the hassles of sporadic adolescent intercourse in public places and had opted for the real thing—bed sheets, long, sophisticated dinner conversations, lots of showers. She was looking after herself, I couldn't blame her.

"Here is what I've decided to do," Antoaneta G. announced as she paced up and down, triumphant, like a general inspecting his troops. "Since the perpetrators of the crime are obviously among us, and since all of you know their names, I'm going to give everyone a chance to come clean and avoid any administrative penalty. One by one, I want you to take a step forward and tell me the names of the perpetrators. Those who comply will be allowed to return to our classroom. The rest will see their personal standing drop by two whole levels. Any questions?"

Lilly raised her hand and glanced at me with undisguised contempt. "Excuse me, Comrade, but what if the perpetrators decide to name one of us and walk away with impunity? How would that be fair?"

The Hyena laughed. She had an evil, vulturine laugh—hence her nickname. "Oh, don't worry about that, Lilly. You see, that wouldn't work at all."

"We have to be united!" Bianka suddenly cried out. "If none of us takes a step forward, they can't do anything to us!"

The Hyena seemed amused. "You're inciting your fellow students to rebel against me? I'm surprised to see you—an exemplary student, an honorary commander of our unit—defending the criminals who are trying to destroy the creative forces that propel our great school into the future! We all know that you're in love, but love is fickle and unrewarding. The future belongs to those who have sound judgment, obey the law, and never tire of working for the common good. If you want to be part of the legion of parasites, be my guest. There are hundreds—thousands!—of talented musicians all over the country waiting to fill your spot at the Sofia Music School for the Gifted."

For the first time that morning, Alexander turned to look at me. I knew what he was thinking: Bianka deserved a medal for bravery. She had risked her future to save us. Had she finally come to see that the world we inhabited was nothing but a sick puppet show, written and directed by an invisible grand puppet? Or maybe she had finally decided that it was time to lose her virginity and taste the forbidden fruit, the substance that had created time and death, pleasure and pain, white asphodel blossoms in spring and blood-red pomegranate seeds in the fall. She and I would taste the cyclic nature of things together; we would remember scents and states of being from a mythical past; we would sneak into the French High School at night and make love in a classroom on the third floor; we would meet early in the morning before school and walk hand-in-hand across the park; we would practice piano in adjacent rooms and run to the attic every two hours—sweaty, out of breath, our hands burning and our senses overloaded with endless, cascading cadences—to reaffirm our knowledge of the saccharine secret.

But why was I lying to myself? Bianka was no rebel. She had been one of the robots from the start. Since the moment she walked into class, back in the fourth grade, she had been ready to recite slogans, salute, wave the flag, and sing songs of servitude. How could she ever change? It took a certain kind of spiritual depletion, of time blindness, for someone to prance about with a giant flag and spout mind-numbing platitudes on demand. People don't change. They only get more accustomed to being who they are.

Lilly was the first to go. She pointed at me and Alexander and said our full names. Then she excused herself and walked into the neon-lit basement buffet located near the stairs. Briefly, as Lilly squeezed through the double door, I caught a glimpse of the linoleum floor, the tables and chairs, and the disproportionately large vitrine exhibiting no more than four items at any given time—a grilled cheese sandwich, a grilled ground pork sandwich, a box of waffles, and a tray of marzipan brownies; the red-haired lady behind the register was pouring yellow and purple chemicals into the transparent juice cooler; a whiff of cigarettes escaped the back room where teachers went to smoke. Then the door to the buffet closed, reinstating the inquisitorial feel of the dimly lit basement hall. We could all hear Lilly talking to the red-haired lady, ordering lots of food. After carrying out her duty as a mindless cow, she went to pig out on grilled ground-pork sandwiches and marzipan brownies. That's freedom for you.

The others followed suit. The twins, Ligav and Mazen, didn't say my name or Alexander's out loud. Instead, they gave us a little lecture: "You shouldn't feel angry at your fellow students for turning you in. We are all doing this for your own good," said Ligav. "That's right!" Mazen concurred. "Perhaps after this episode is over, you'll finally take notice and heed the right path. You can't take everyone hostage just because you lack the discipline and moral conviction to get good grades and follow the established rules! It's not fair!"

This went on for a while. Everyone took a turn—Dora, Ivan, Slav, Isabel, and, in the end, Bianka, though she didn't dare to point at me. She named only Alexander. She wasn't blushing anymore. Her face was cold and unexpressive, the face of reason and pragmatism. Pragmatism always wins. Nikolai D., the violist, was the only one who refused to name either me or Alexander. He laid the blame on Santa Claus.

When Alexander and I were the only ones left, Antoaneta G. gave us a choice: turn each other in, and she would plead with the police to show some lenience.

"Are you done?" Alexander asked her in his thunderous, operatic voice. He was only seventeen (he had missed a year of school due to kidney disease) but he was already being compared to titans like Chaliapin and Boris Christoff. It was pleasant to see the Hyena recoil at the sound of his bass timbre, no longer quite so confident without her little soldiers cheering in the background. Playing a despot is a lot easier when there's an audience that believes every word you say. How would the Hyena behave if she were to run into us in the park and there was no one around to validate her authority? But, of course, she'd be very polite! She might even inquire after the health of our parents. Powermongers are all cowards. The more they act out onstage, the more cowardly they grow inside, the delusion eating away their fragile reality like woodworm.

It was entirely predictable that a day like this would end on the third floor, in the office of the Owl, the school principal. The only rooms in the school that didn't have pianos were Teachers' Headquarters, the buffet, the Owl's office, the colonel's classroom, and the bathrooms. The absence of a piano in the principal's office demonstrated to every teacher and student that, at its foundation, the Music School for the Gifted remained purely a secular institution. Never mind the hundreds of musicians immersed in single-minded contemplation, dissolving into the invisible; never mind the constant resonance of harmonic spheres, mirroring the dimensions and internal makeup of our forgotten, eternal abode; never mind the urgent reach for that elusive high note which promised a transporting climax, and then closure. Here, in the office of Zimova, reigned the spirit of the Twenty-fourth Congress of the Communist Party of the Soviet Union, embodied in the bronze bust of Leonid Brezhnev, that hairy old gnome, towering over the principal's cherrywood desk, next to an obtuse crystal triangle commemorating the agrarian directives adapted in 1971. On the wall opposite the westward-looking windows hung medals, plaques, flags, and framed certificates. An oil painting of Georgi D., the nationalized mummy, occupied the wall behind the desk. A massive bookcase with golden edges sported two dozen trophies, a steel relief of Lenin, and the entire thirty-eight volumes of the party chairman's collected works.

This was the temple of the robots, of science and reason, of empirical hallucinations and ideological hemorrhaging. This was where the smell of embalmed corpses and pickled contempt came from. The smell of never-ending war. The fact of the matter was, we were all still at war—only by now the battlefield had moved from the fields and the streets into our brains. We had been forced to dig trenches around ideas and big words. We had built fortifications to protect the permitted centers of thought. We had isolated our subversive tendencies with barbed wire. What a great time to be alive! Lunatics to the west, lunatics to the east. On both sides of the thought divide, people hid in shelters, clinging to their meager rations of reality. What should it be? The champions of greed or the harlequins of misery? The priests of selfishness or the heralds of the disposable soul? The grateful slaves of plentitude or the conniving experts of government-sanctioned kitsch? Take your pick.

And yet, there was no doubt that, though I detested the whole experiment, I, too, had grown up with deep trenches running right through the center of my psyche. How else to explain the fact that I felt so sinfully comfortable in the monolithic grayness of this eternal dusk, caressed by the dying clouds, surrounded by Sofia's crumbling buildings and human shadows, protected by the indestructible cobblestones, loved by the flickering streetlights. This was the taste of existence stripped down to its essence, without the gloss of money or faith in promises or lingering expectations of a different future. There wasn't much to do here but endure. And people endured—working, standing in lines outside bakeries and bookstores, staying up all night at their kitchen tables, rereading their old books, staring out their windows, growing their cancers, their cirrhosis and dementias, quietly, perseveringly, like good soldiers, without complaints.

But you've got to dig your trenches while you're young; there's no time to waste! Zimova, in her long black skirt and turtleneck, was of the opinion that Alexander and I had a lot more digging to do. She gave me a heavy, newspaper-bound book and asked me to read aloud a passage underlined with red pencil. I began reading with fervor, enunciating the long words, pausing after each comma and slowing down at the end of each sentence. I might as well have been reading Latin. I heard the words as pure sound, a distant recitative set against the ascending barrage of octaves and overflowing chords at the beginning of the Scherzo in Sonata no. 2, which I had been rehearsing in my head relentlessly throughout the day, as I waited in line to be fingerprinted and then as I was questioned by the stone-faced police inspector in a small room on the second floor. I didn't care that I hadn't eaten breakfast or lunch; I just wanted to get to a piano and lay down the entire Scherzo with its sprawling harmonic structure, six flats, heart-racing build-ups, polonaise flurries, waltzing temperament, and Mozartian cadences; I wanted to feel the immense power of these chords rush from my hands into my head, to hear the colossal pile-up of overtones, to disappear into the *piu lento* and emerge at the fish market, near the harbor, in the city I've known only in my dreams, an old city set on a hill overlooking the sea, where strangely clothed men walk the steep cobbled streets pulling small carts or donkeys, where women stay indoors, where the coffee shops are dark and quiet, where the houses are surrounded by walls ten meters high and the wooden doors are small and heavy with enormous keyholes, and where the girl working in the tin shop by the ancient fortress on top of the hill knows who I am, but won't tell me the name of the city, even after I buy some nails and scraps of metal.

"Only the rich are allowed near the arts!" Zimova was screaming at the top of her voice. "And the rich are untalented by birth! It's genetic! This has been proven a thousand times, in music, in everything!"

What on earth was the fossilized bird ranting about? I looked at Alexander but he seemed as clueless as I. With her furry eyebrows, round glasses, wide unblinking eyes, and swollen lips, the Owl had a fixed expression of revulsion. But nothing spoke as much about her soul as her clawed hands, the hands of someone who has never known music. She went on:

"Not here! Here we have neither rich nor poor, neither privileged classes nor beggars. No beggars! Ask the stinking capitalists if they have beggars. Ask them! Ask them if they teach the arts to the poor. Well, they don't! They let the poor rot and die in the streets. And look at you, sniveling brats! We've given you Mozart and Beethoven on a plate! We shove culture down your throats like pigs! We've given you counterpoint, harmony, accompaniment, chamber music, sight reading, orchestration, solfège, history of music, theory of music and private lessons. . . . We've bought you grand pianos and uprights, violins, cellos and flutes, we've arranged for you to give concerts in order to prove your mastery over your instruments. . . . And what do we get in return? Vandalism, theft, subversive acts, cigarette butts and condoms in the bathrooms, disrespect and disobedience. You act like imperialist agents implanted in our midst to wage war. Vladimir Ilich, the great thinker, said that war is the absolute expression of capitalism. Who in this room can dispute that?"

Alexander and I weren't disputing it. We were nodding approvingly.

"Every lightbulb in this school, every chair, every door knob, has been paid for by the brotherhood of socialist workers, by workers in factories, by the workers who collect your garbage, by doctors and machinists . . . Look at this lightbulb! Behold it in its wholeness! It's a miracle of the highest order—everyone according to their needs, as they said . . . this is the culmination of billions of years of evolution . . . it's the moment when matter looks back at itself and sees its own beauty, at first wanting to possess it, and then, later—after evolving from the primitive cotton fields of capitalism to the rose gardens of socialism—wanting to share the vision with every living being. . . . The great socialist revolution and its fruits are the true meaning of what we call dialectical materialism, materialism taken flight like a bird, like a seagull! Communism is inevitable!"

The old hag had lost it completely! She was off her rocker, spit foaming at the corners of her mouth. If only I could rise to the occasion and whack her on the back of the head with something heavy, like the bronze bust of Leonid Brezhnev sitting on her desk, to finish her off once and for all. My father used to say that in a lifetime, every man is once a poet, and once a murderer. But that was certainly a romantic notion, for most men, including myself, lacked the passion to become either.

"Ah, the day will come when our government will pronounce you irrelevant. That, fellow citizens, is the harshest sentence a man can receive. Do you understand what that means? Irrelevant! Useless! Cast away from the brotherhood of men. You're nothing but a few specks of dust that we'll brush off with the flick of a finger . . . two bourgeois leeches who have been sucking the blood of our workers! I will personally sign your death sentence with my favorite pen, a gift from Tovarich Andropov himself!"

This was great news, I thought. One must always take heart when the threats leveled at him are set in the future tense. If the Owl was still so keen on filling our head with her slimy delusions, we weren't headed for the gallows, not yet. The miserable fuckers! They didn't have anything on us, no proof, no clues. Hours of torturous interrogations, coupled with fingerprinting, and in the end they still had nothing. Alexander knew it, too, there was a hint of a smirk forming on his face. Another day, another trial, and I was going to walk free again. Of course, I would have to lay low for a few weeks, attend classes with the rest of the robots, the *otlichniks*, listen to their endless drivel . . .

The night, my savior, was beginning to set in, and already I could see the long shadows of the ghosts with sneering faces slipping past the window on their way back to the catacombs of Tartarus after a day's work at the centers for thought control. Irina, I suddenly remembered, would be performing in Chamber Hall No. 1 at 8:30. The poster had been hanging in the hallway for a month. A sexy young genius playing the violin, that was something to see. Maybe after the concert she and I might scrape together enough change to buy a cheap bottle of wine and go to the small cemetery behind Seven Saints Church to smoke and drink and huddle together—this year's spring had proved strangely chilly—and talk about life and school, which were mutually exclusive. Irina was a tough girl—two abortions in two years, personal standing at Satisfactory, concerts in Berlin and Dresden, gigs with the National Orchestra, first violin in the Schubert ensemble.

But first I had to escape this prison cell, and the unwavering gaze of the Owl. The old bird was finally getting tired. She had lost her dramatism, her toxins, and the dark circles under her eyes seemed larger than before. Another minute or two and she would stop, mid-sentence, beckoned by the voice of her master. Her robot body would make its way home, under the blossoming chestnut trees and the moonless sky, to await the dawn in its designated resting place. The puppets are much easier to spot at night, you can see them riding in trams, waiting for the bus, buying tickets at the rusty kiosks, hiding their expressionless faces behind newspapers and textbooks. Try to talk to them! There's no one there. Automatic replies. Empty eyes. Mechanical voices. You could push them down a cliff, and they would plummet obediently, like drunken sheep. Yet somewhere, in the midst of a hundred—nay, a thousand, ten thousand—puppets, you might find a real human being, watching, awake, more awake at night than during the day, with enough sorrow packed under his chest to make the gods cry.

I t began with a distant bell with a silky, tempting ring that opened the doors to a spacious F major promenade. White clouds glided against the charcoal sky, the *other* sky; a deep, nacreous *fa* served as a pedal point that breathed life into the opening theme. Contained within all this was the serenity of the end, the sound of eternity. The clouds dispersed, the silver sea retreated, and from the depths of the blackness came forth the sun, fireless, a cool amber that introduced the countersubject atop a magisterial cadence, the harmonic blueprint of a divine imperative, reaching deeper, and deeper, until it untangled the ingrained, false fear of death. Wasn't every cadence, every movement from the dominant to the tonic but a preparation for the final journey, a reenactment of our death and rebirth, a reminder that, rather than something to be feared, the end was what we'd always been reaching for, after a lifetime of building tension, after taking upon ourselves the colossal weight of existence?

The keys were dry and cold and I tried to draw the texture out, to will those overtones into an open space where I could bend and reshape the arrow of time to mirror my inner makeup, but the timpani and the cymbals and the muffled trumpets of the marching band rehearsing for the May Day parade down in the schoolyard kept throwing me off, messing up my conjuring act. The second ballad was in six-eight, a succession of alternating long and short notes, the rhythm of a human heart. No surprise that there was no meaningful recording of the second ballad. Perhaps it just couldn't be recorded. It was too elusive, too impossible to measure. Everything was about rhythm, I knew, but the art of keeping rhythm wasn't about being on time so much as breaking free of time, creating the illusion of time without being bound by it; it was a magic act on par with stuffing elephants into a bottle or catching the milky way in your hand like a firefly.

If I could hear all this in its entirety—the bass and the melody and the middle voice lines; the spaces between the notes; the inhalation and exhalation of each phrase; the past still resounding and the future constantly pulling the present farther from the shore, like an undertow; the sotto voce; the clear, unmelancholy quality of sound, sound as knowledge, as a sense rather than a sense object; the pulse of the heart, long and short, long and short, where each beat was its own eternity; the statement and the conclusion, the aside, the epiphany and the resignation—if I could experience all this, then Ladybug, sitting on the chair to my left, and Vadim, stretched out on the floor behind me, might experience it as well. But I could see out of the corner of my eye that my piano teacher wanted more; her hands moved agitatedly, her breathing flowed against the tide of the music. *Silence!* I tried to silence the drums and the shouting of the demented crowd, the honking and the orders spouted through loudspeakers, and then to play out of that silence, sculpting silent forms in empty space, wresting intoxicating colors from the night. A minor, the key of twilight: ashen, lavender-tinted clouds gliding across a darkened sky washed in turmeric, the chestnut trees shuddering, awakened by the wind, and then that old question about the end; a *why,* a passing note stretching the distance between two chords. The dominant, and then F major again, back to the opening theme, back to that spring day in sixth grade when, after the end of classes, I had rushed into an empty practice room and begun reading the ballads, ravenously, desperately, like a mortally poisoned man in search of a cure. I had finally been permitted to advance to the next level. Everything I'd ever needed to know—

about gravity, time, girls, sex, power, death, reality, truth, delusion, the absolute—was in this hardbound edition of the four ballads, written in the language of passion, punctuated by accents, pedal marks, fingering numbers, and footnotes in Italian. For years, Katya had talked to me about the ballads as a forbidden drug, as a source of power granted only to the chosen few. And then she had given me her own copy, a sign that I had passed the test of maturity. Striking the opening chords of the second ballad, I had been seized by a profound sense of recognition, an awareness of who I had always been in contrast to who I was being instructed to become. In an instant my childhood ended, and with it all the lies that had codified my existence. I found myself standing on the outside and looking in at the grotesquerie that was my life at the Music School for the Gifted, in the City of Ruins, on the outskirts of Tartarus. I didn't know these people. I felt no desire to take part in their hallucinations. I had no use for math and geometry, for catalogues of meaningless facts, for histories and ideologies. I was just passing through.

Katya grabbed my left hand and placed it on her thigh. "Come back," she said softly. "You're wandering again, and it shows in your playing." She looked at me with her searching eyes and, sensing that I wanted to disentangle myself from her and return to my private catacombs, pressed my hand harder against her thigh. I could smell the perfume on her neck, the traces of shampoo in her hair, and, in the weave of her pale pink sweater, the tobacco and grilled sandwiches of the school buffet. She expected an explanation. I said nothing. It should've been obvious that all the rehearsing marching bands, which were about to explode into a full-scale orgy of automatic exaltation, made me feel poisoned. The streets were already clogged with the troops of thoughtlessness, waving red flags, holding banners, pentacles, and giant portraits of the bearded midgets. Soon the young soldiers from the music school would march out to join their comrades from the other elite high schools. I would march at the very back, in the company of the boys with lowered personal standing. It was the same thing, year after year. And then there would be speeches.

"Please, get up," Ladybug said suddenly and pushed my hand away. "Vadim, would you mind playing the ballad for us?"

Vadim looked terribly embarrassed. "I haven't played it in two years. So . . . frankly . . . no, I'd rather not."

"Sit down, Vadim, come on. I know you can do it." Ladybug tapped the leather piano bench.

Before beginning, Vadim sat motionless for two or three minutes, staring unblinkingly at the strings of the grand piano. I knew what he was doing: sharpening his focus, amplifying the present, inviting the healing properties of sound to purify him.

Katya was right. He played the ballad like no one else. His tone, his breathing, triggered the intense experience of déjà vu that so often accompanies a truly genuine performance: So that's how this was played! It didn't even sound like the same composition!

Vadim had entered the theme in A minor, and I hadn't even become aware of it. Velvet sound, time moving unusually slowly, the present hanging in the air like a sustained note. How strange, to walk the streets of your town and see everything for what seemed the first time. Hidden alleys you'd never noticed, secluded gardens with fountains, dark buildings with spacious courtyards, cobbled streets that go on and on without end. How was this possible? Like an oracle speaking in tongues, Vadim delivered the second ballad as a prophecy. His thought followed a higher, superhuman logic.

It's easy to pronounce the words, to parrot the curve of each sentence, to mimic the intonation of human speech. All the ambitious ones do it, they compete with one another to perfect the expression of the universal puppet. But to mean the words, to be the words, to follow them to the abyss—that demands nothing short of martyrdom. You can't lie in music and get away with it. In music, each deceit translates into a melodic banality. Greed and self-indulgence take the shape of harmonic poverty, anger and nihilism become noise and dissonance. The shallow mind is a rhythmically stifled tune; it's time blind.

La-mi-si-do! The crashing octaves in the lower register opened a chasm in the ether, but Vadim kept his cool—standing in the center of

the fury, he was a force of tranquillity and silence. This was not apocalypse; *presto con fuoco* didn't mean tragedy. Rather, it was the ushering
in of a grand dance of metamorphosis—first the ecstasy of destruc-
tion, then the climax, a shuddering E flat in the seventh octave, and
in the end, after a long, winding descent, the resolution: an E flat
major chord, the first complete major chord since the beginning of the
fast section. Chopin knew how to make you beg for the sound of a
major triad, and Vadim understood the game better than anyone. He
revealed the resolution with unadorned solemnity, like a long-guarded
secret. Slowing down, he articulated the chromatic runs in the right
hand, spiraling from E flat down to the dominant; a visionary *sol-si* led
back to the main theme, this time a variation.

"That's enough, Vadim. Take your things and go, please." Ladybug
stood up and walked to the window. "I don't think I'm going to have
time to hear you today. Come to see me tomorrow, around noon." She
didn't turn around to look at him as he exited the room. I knew what
was coming—a talk, garnished with handpicked memories and dramatic premonitions.

"You've been playing since you were five, Konstantin, when an old
Gypsy man stopped your mother on the street and told her that you'd
been blessed with the gift of music. The moment you touched the
piano, doors started opening for you. Everyone wanted to help you, to
put you on the path of the great masters. This path was chosen for you
before you were born." She walked over to me, and bent forward to
look into my eyes. "You have no other choice now; you're going to be
a musician for the rest of your life. Unless you destroy yourself along
the way, like all the others. Do you remember the old man who came
to shake your hand, crying, after your second performance in Italy?
You didn't understand what he said to you because he was speaking
Italian, but you knew that you had communicated with him, that you
had given him something precious. How did that make you feel? Ful-
filled? No? Still, the piano is your only ticket out of this nightmare!
One day you can go wherever you want—France, America. Musicians are excused from participating in the madness of governments

and countries; musicians can pretend that they don't understand the language of the common people. They can hide from the ugliness of the world. Isn't that what you want? All you have to do is practice, and practice more, and give your schoolteachers what they want, which is, Konstantin, obedience. No more stolen daybooks. No more absences. Just three more years, and school will be over! You'll never have to see or listen to these people again. This is not the time for friends and girlfriends, for adolescent games. You're older than that, in your heart. The Chopin audition is just twenty months away, and you're nowhere near ready! What happens if you fail? Just think of Warsaw, of Paris!"

"Yes," I said.

"You will change, then? Promise me, you'll get on the right track."

"Yes."

"Promise!"

God, the Iron Virgin made me cry. I hated her for that. I hated her for making me weak and vulnerable. She knew me too well, knew that if she hugged me tight and pressed her head against mine I would break down and surrender my solitude, knew how to whisk me away from the gods of self-destruction, if only for a brief moment. But it was all a short-lived romance; that was my solace. The moment I left her room, my tears would dry, just as if I had walked out of a stupid movie. Tears are nothing but lies, they are little hooks attached to the command center, that mysterious organ everyone is born with. One lever brings a smile; another starts the tears; yet another triggers a pledge of allegiance and the automatic suspension of thought. But if the levers were something external, something available for anyone to play with, what did that say about free will? Could free will be anything other than a force of pure resistance against reality? Whenever I cried, I had made it a rule to repeat to myself, *Either someone's telling me stories, or I'm telling stories to myself.* It is so easy to take a grain of truth and turn it, like an alchemist, into a self-appeasing delusion. But watch for the tears, they will give it away. The hardest truths in life are taken in with dry eyes.

I found Vadim waiting for me in the corridor, one shoulder leaning into the wall. He looked tired and depressed, his uniform jacket twisted over his arm. "Did she give you the usual lecture? The whole thing?"

I dropped my leather case and slumped to the floor. Vadim sat beside me, his legs stretching all the way to the opposite wall. The fourth-floor corridors formed a narrow, zigzagging labyrinth divided by many doors. This last section, where Ladybug gave lessons, was the quietest. The school babble couldn't reach this far. The only thing breaking the silence was the muffled sweeps of rapturous black-ultra-marine-auburn dissonance in Debussy's "Feux d'artifice" prelude seeping through the soundproof door of room 49. Ladybug was practicing her repertoire.

"I'm sorry I had to take your place at the piano and give you a lesson, as it were. I actually think you play the ballad much better than me, technically, and presence-wise. She's just pitting us against each other, trying to get us to practice like maniacs. You know what she told me the other day? That, ideally, one should practice from four in the morning till noon—eight hours nonstop!—then take a break before going back for another six hours, from four in the afternoon till ten in the evening. I mean, what's the goal of playing the piano? To become a musician, or a maniacal imbecile?"

"Clearly an imbecile," I said. "She told me a while back that she wants me to move in with her and her mom at the beginning of November next year—a month before the Chopin audition—so that she can wake me up in the middle of the night, at two or three in the morning, and say, 'Scherzo number three, bar fifty-seven, go!'"

"See! It's you that's her racehorse. It's you she's grooming for the big prize. She has no faith in me, which is fine because I don't play to compete with anyone. I'm not cut out for this. If I continue down this path, after I graduate from the conservatory I'll just be another player for hire, a slave. I'll have to play what other people ask me—Prokofiev, Scriabin, Ravel, Debussy, or some atonal shit."

"How come you've never liked the Impressionists?"

"They're fakes, man. Their music doesn't create life; it mimics it. I want music to tell me something true. I don't want fantasies and science fiction. And I don't care about fancy chords and the whole extravaganza of the grotesque. I don't get this obsession with newness. It's got to be new, fancy, weird, somehow broken and distorted, never thought of before. But there's no such thing! If you have something true to say, *say* it. Otherwise you're just faking it. Look at Brahms—four chords, total simplicity. But he gets to the point. And he breathes new life into you."

"I don't know. What about this?"

We listened as Ladybug struck the *do* pedal point that comes at the end of Debussy's "Brouillards" prelude: the enormous weight of another impenetrable, unfathomable day mired in wisps of glistening fog, clusters of five thirty-second notes splashing drops of mercury and silver.

Vadim smiled. He'd played both the fog and fireworks preludes at dozens of recitals. "You'll get tired of it."

We parted ways at the stairwell: he went down to meet his girlfriend from the English High School, and I headed up to smoke a cigarette in the attic. I still had five minutes to decide if I should be a good boy and join the parade or just say fuck it, like Vadim, and watch the whole farce from a practice room on the fifth floor. But I was too curious to miss the march of the puppets. And the scraggly little note Bianka had handed me as I walked into school at eight o'clock that morning was burning a hole through the inside pocket of my uniform jacket. I took the note out and read it for the tenth time, going over each word, analyzing the curves of her cursive for clues that might reveal her state of mind. Had she written this in a hurry, yielding to a momentary impulse of boldness, or had she finally decided to make a confession? *If we get lost at the parade, I'll wait for you at my place.* And then she'd drawn a small heart. I couldn't believe it. I knew that her parents had left town for two days, and that her older brother was probably going to crash every party in the neighborhood. But was this really an invitation? And what would happen if we didn't lose track of each other at the parade?

Would Bianka still take me to her place afterward or just suggest we take one of our usual long walks? But the heart . . . The heart did offer a hint of promise. In a school famous for wild and indiscriminate fucking, she had the courage to draw a heart! A true romantic, perhaps.

The thought of going up to Bianka's apartment, of entering her intimate world, made me forget about Ladybug and her advice at once. On this cloudy day, with the streets of the city littered with flags, pamphlets, and balloons, with exuberant crowds clogging traffic, Bianka and I would sit at her kitchen table and silently have our tea, looking out the window at the dreary facades of the adjacent apartment buildings, at the high overgrown brick walls separating backyards, patios, and neglected gardens, at the bright future exemplified by infinitely long laundry lines stretching above the trees and exhibiting every size and type of underwear. Bianka's old Steinway upright with its empty candleholders would be standing next to a baroque china closet in the living room, but we would resist the temptation to play it. There would be no études and Hungarian rhapsodies. Instead, we would go to her dad's gramophone and put on something terminally beautiful, like Bach's sonatas for violin and harpsichord: the fourth, in C minor; or the one in F minor, the Adagio; or the Largo in the sixth. Then we would lock the door and walk hand in hand to her bedroom. We'd do it the old-fashioned way, like virgins, like god-fearing peasants or exemplary proletarians fulfilling their duties. We'd do it distractedly, thinking about other things. We'd be thinking about the music and the pigeons fluttering on the ledge of the kitchen balcony. Might there still be time to save my innocence? Was it even worth it? And was I really attracted to Bianka or was I simply fascinated by her expertly cultivated melancholy? It was quite obvious that whatever there was between us could never grow into passion. And yet it was this dysfunctional, broken quality of our relationship that I cherished the most; the stifled emotions, the locked-up demons, the aborted rapture.

The tiny trapezoid door, which looked indistinguishable from the other wooden panels covering the unlit wall at the very end of the attic, was for some reason locked. Had the school administration finally discovered our secret lair? This entrance had never been locked before. Where was I going to go smoke now? Where would I hide from the world? I pressed my foot against the door and pushed hard. The boards were solid and very thick. I was just about to leave when I heard something that sounded like a choked-up chuckle. "Anyone there?" I demanded and knocked insistently. Silence. Finally, a high-pitched voice said, "The password, please!" I realized right away it was Alexander. His falsetto was as familiar to me as his bass roar. "You are a genius," I shouted. The deadbolt clicked twice and the door swung open. I was surprised to see Irina, her raven hair falling in waves over her shoulders and reaching two-thirds of the way down her back. I had never really noticed her hair before. My God, it was like a mythical weapon that could cast spells and trap souls. She was clearly in a flirting mood, throwing fiery glances and secret smiles, moving across the room with the lightness and elegance of a cat. Alexander stood under the skylight, smoking, his neck wrapped in a cream-colored silk scarf. Irina's violin case was propped up against the wall, in the corner.

"Well, good morning and welcome to our special private gathering," Alexander announced grandly, as Irina locked the door behind me. "On this important day, the day of the slaves, when our Gorgonian Mother, the Owl, endowed with a heavy Russian accent and a womb filled with snake oil, leads the pigeon-brained peasantry to the tomb of our Idiot Father, the Great Mummy, formerly known as General Secretary of the Comintern, we have heeded the call to gather here and perform a small Dionysian rite, complete with dance, music, fire, and prophetic visions, the way it was performed for thousands of years in the mountains just to the north of Sofia. Irina, show our guest the sacramental objects."

After a moment of hesitation, Irina unfastened the middle button of her obligatory school dress, slipped her hand inside, and took out a lighter, a tiny round mirror, and a condom, which she then arranged on the decrepit writing desk in the center of the room, together with the long silver key for the deadbolt. Alexander, for his part, opened Irina's violin case and brought out two bottles of red wine. Apparently, the whole thing had been planned in advance; Irina had left her violin at home.

"May I inquire as to the method by which you obtained the key to this sacramental chamber?" I asked, joining in the act.

"Seduction," Alexander replied, extending his hand toward Irina, who did a half-assed curtsy and then quickly lit a cigarette. There was something rough and uncompromising in the way she inhaled the smoke and flicked the ashes on the floor; an air of daring that contrasted with her gracious stride and sweet voice.

"The doorman's all right," she said. "A little old for my taste, but charming nevertheless."

A tight drum roll, at first distant, then suddenly very near and loud, ushered in an attack of splashing cymbals and heart-stopping bass drums just outside the building—one, two, three, four bars, and then the brass section kicked in with full might, sending a loop of whiz-bang echoes through the maze of courtyards and buildings all around us. Naturally, the Music School for the Gifted had the best brass section in town. I pulled myself up through the skylight and peered down as all the students, from first to twelfth grade, marshaled in stiff units and led by teachers, marched out onto the street through the main gate and headed toward Nevski Cathedral. At the intersection of Oborishte and Tolbuhin, the procession stopped to allow the English High School, coming up from the Levski Monument, to pass in front. There were endless rows of people from assorted schools, universities, hospitals, newspaper presses, and institutions grouped in rectangular formations, draped in red flags and massive slogans, inching across the main arteries in the direction of the mausoleum at the city center, where the chief puppet, standing behind a wall of bulletproof glass, waved mechanically at the masses. Sofia was under siege.

"I have to go," I announced, calculating that I still had time to catch up with my class. "They stopped at the light."

"You're not going anywhere," Alexander said. "They're not writing absences; I already talked to our friend Maria, the third-floor janitor. You'll get a reprimand, that's it—if they even notice that you're miss-

ing. You know how it is. The Hyena will be too busy singing and ordering people around to take attendance."

"Well, it's not like—you know. It's Bianka. I think I have an invitation to visit her private quarters."

"Bianka! I don't believe it! *Kopeleh,* when are you going to give up on
her? Man, she's untalented and a complete square!"

"And she has no tits," Irina noted matter-of-factly.

"You said it," Alexander commended her. "Come on! We've got wine,
cigarettes . . . The school is empty, no one's going to come and bother
us. With the insanity taking place outside, what normal man would
reject our company?"

"She gave me a note . . . A rather special one, I have to say."

"Let's see it, then! Produce the note for inspection, come on! Number fourteen! Irina, please search him and retrieve the note. Hell, this
is getting really interesting!"

Persuading me to skip classes, stand friends up, and renege on my
daily responsibilities seemed to be one of Alexander's chief amuse-
ments, and he'd go through no small trouble to get me to abandon my
routine in favor of spending a long afternoon with him, listening to
his evil schemes, drinking, picking up girls, or taking exhausting walks
through the park. It gave him immense pleasure to see me dissuaded
and resigned, surrendering my will to his boorish charm.

"I don't have it," I told Irina, who put out her cigarette and came
close to me—and even closer—until her body pushed against mine
and I felt her cheek brushing my neck. Hugging me tight, she searched
the back pockets of my pants, then the front, and then, after confis-
cating the little money I had, the inside pocket of my uniform jacket,
where the note was.

Stepping away from me, Irina unfolded the small piece of paper
and instantly burst out laughing, her laugh radiant and ringing,
devoid of any self-pretense. "A heart! The little bitch has drawn him
a heart, how sweet! It's like they're in the nineteenth century. They're
in love!"

She handed the note to Alexander, who examined it with the gravity of an inspector collecting evidence at a crime scene. "My question to you is: What could you possibly hope to learn about Bianka after sleeping with her? Think about it. Because if you know everything about her, and you know what's going to happen, you're just wasting your time."

"Alexander, don't be stupid. We already know everything that's going to happen to us. Life is just a grand rehearsal."

"He's getting all philosophical, like his father!" Alexander squealed and reached for the bottle of wine. "I love it! I'm telling you, Irina, this guy can come up with some great nonsense. . . . But we forgot the wine opener."

Irina took the bottle from him and pushed the cork in with a key. Then she took a few swigs and handed it back to Alexander, who halved it in one chug. The snare drums started up again and I looked down at the street through the skylight to see if the music school contingent had marched ahead. They were still at the stoplight, holding their slogans and portraits and raising hell. I quickly finished the bottle. Irina opened the second one.

"Hey, Button, do you remember the time when I found you, asleep, on the bathroom floor at the stinking tavern on the corner of Dondukov and Paris?" Button was the nickname that Alexander had given me in fifth grade. Of course I remembered passing out in the tavern bathroom, in the middle of the school day. It was the previous spring, and I had just turned fifteen.

"I walked in and asked the redhead at the bar if she had seen Button. She said, well, check in the bathroom; he drank twelve pitchers of light beer, and I told him he'll get sick. Twelve pitchers! During long recess! What an idiot!"

"My personal record," I said, not without pride. "I'd never peed so long in my life. Felt like I was draining the Black Sea."

"So I dragged him back to school, just in time for fifth period, which was history of music, with the Gnome, and the bastard fell asleep and dropped on the floor in the middle of Schubert's Eighth. The Gnome told him to go home, and didn't even give him an absence."

"The Gnome is all right," Irina confirmed, and she drank to his health.

But I was drifting away, with the dying clouds passing overhead on their way to the far corner of Doctors' Garden, as the sound of drums and horns receded in the direction of the mausoleum. We were each alone in this. There was no love, except in music. I smoked, filling my lungs and veins with fire; fire was what I needed, and there was never enough. I would walk barefoot through a field of burning embers, like the *nestinarki* of old, and I would walk slowly, absorbing the heat and the pain, incinerating the dualistic mind. Fire was what was missing. It was cold and dark here, the sun too far away. How could I ever forget the time when Igor the Swan stormed out of Chamber Hall No. 2, in the middle of our lesson, and started dancing through the school corridors, shouting, "Bring back the fire, Prometheus, and burn this goddamn place down!" What did the other teachers think of him? Did they see him as a fat, benign lunatic—once a promising concert pianist—or did they think him a dangerous parasite threatening to corrupt the public order?

Off they went, Irina and Alexander, to do their little thing in the crawl space behind the wooden boards covering the inner wall of the room, still talking about Alexander's plan to shut off the school power from the main switch on the third floor and, in the ensuing darkness, push the math teacher, the Raven, down the stairs—triangle, bag, compasses, and all. Irina was curious to hear the sound that the Raven's fifty-six bracelets would make as the red-nosed vampire rolled to the bottom of the stairs. "I'm sorry, Comrade Raven," Alexander said, pretending to be one of the school nurses who'd arrive at the scene, "but we'll have to place you in brackets until we determine all the variables at the front of the equation." Irina laughed, and then they both fell silent.

I finished the second bottle of wine and looked out through the skylight, at the long rows of chestnut trees lining both sides of the street below. Without the trees Sofia would be nothing more than a dreary necropolis. It was only the trees and the plants that fought to bring the city back to life, to wrest it from the grip of the God of Schaden-freude and Common Curses. A mighty web of creepers had taken over the macabre stucco buildings, wrapping their vines around down-spouts and balconies, digging their tendrils under the mossy roof tiles; birch trees kept vigil outside hospital windows; weeping willows grew around ancient churches; apple and cherry trees—the messengers of the divine—blossomed outside cancer wards and mental clinics; wild grapevines hung from the walls of shady courtyards, teaching the kids playing there about the mystery of life. The trees outside the music school were an ever-present audience; in the morning, in the after-noon, in the dead of the night, they listened. Even when I stayed late, practicing a single passage ad nauseam, they were there, touching the windows of my practice room, stirring with anticipation, absorb-ing every note. In the autumn, I filled my pockets with their smooth fruits whose oils healed my aching hands. In late October, I rolled in the mounds of red-brown leaves piled high on the sidewalk and spill-ing onto the street. In the winter, I broke off crystal icicles from their branches and melted them in my mouth. Then, in the spring, their tiny blossoms renewed my zest for life, for practicing even harder than before. I listened to their music at night, I read the recital posters and necrologies pinned to their trunks. Every two or three years, a team of workers from the agency for the preservation of parks and green areas arrived in a beat-up cherry picker and cut the long branches arching over the street, to keep them from leaning against the trolleybus wires.

Once, a pair of storks built a large nest in one of the trees across the street from the school, causing teachers, students, and passersby to pause and look up in astonishment. Where had these pure crea-tures come from? What were they doing all the way down here, at the bottom of the cosmos? Had they possibly been lured by the music? Some said that the storks' arrival presaged the commencement of a new cycle, because everything happened in cycles—moon cycles, sun cycles, life cycles. The birds didn't last long. Soon they started to look weak and dirty, as if they had been bathed in a pool of spilled pet-rol. Then one disappeared. The other was run over by a trolleybus. It was predictable. This place was for ghosts. The only birds scouring the hard skies were black ravens, gray-and-black crows—millions of them—and cadaverous pigeons.

Alexander squeezed through the narrow opening in the wall and returned to his spot under the skylight, chewing gum, adjusting his scarf. "Irina said that she would like to have a word with you."

"About what?" I asked. Alexander shrugged his shoulders and gestured for me to go and find out for myself. Wondering what was going on, I entered the crawl space and, after fitting the removable board back in its place, walked hunched toward the open area where the initiated usually hung out, and which, after the latest additions, featured a beautiful chair—stolen from the Owl's office—a desk, a coat hanger, and a trash can. Someone had even had the prudence to bring in a fire extinguisher, in case the ceremonial burning of textbooks and report cards was to get out of hand. It was much darker here than in the previous room. The skylight was tiny. I found Irina bent over the desk, writing vigorously in a thick, clothbound notebook. She held her hair with her left hand. "What?" she asked, without pausing or turning to look at me. As I sat in the chair, I noticed that she was barefoot, standing on tiptoe. Her black stockings were suspended from the coat hanger; her gray Clark's were on the floor, by the desk.

"Alexander said you wanted to talk to me."

"Never said that."

I wasn't surprised. Alexander loved playing little games. Good manners demanded that I leave, but instead I lit a cigarette and played on, impertinently. "Do you write in your diary every day?" It was a dumb question, not least because Irina had zero tolerance for bullshit.

"Get out," she said. "Don't you know when you're unwelcome?"

God, what passion! I waited for her to turn around and look at me. Her dark aura, the intensity of her gaze, the contempt and the cold, green flames in her eyes, the silent wind that seemed to swirl around her—I suddenly felt as if I were being pulled into the mouth of a powerful vortex. Irina had a kind of hypnotic presence I had seen in only a handful of musicians. She had achieved, through her mastery of the

violin, what the ancient sorcerers had once acquired through the practice of alchemy and sacrifice. There was a famous story of how she
had brought the gym teacher to his knees, after he'd attempted to feel
her breasts in the basement. She had grabbed his hand and whispered
in his ear. She had drained the blood from his face, made his knees
tremble. I believed it.

"Actually . . . wait." Irina opened her notebook at the very end and
scratched something down with her pen. "What are your Wednesdays
like? Do you have anything at three o'clock?"

"No."

"Do you want to be my accompanist? I'm joining Igor's chamber
music class and I need a new partner."

Of course I wanted to be her accompanist. She was the best violinist in the whole school.

"But that means that we'll have to set up a time to practice before
or after class," Irina said, looking at her schedule. "And you have to
promise me that you're going to take it seriously. I can't afford to get an
F from Igor at this point. Everyone's out to get me, the Owl wants me
kicked out of school, I know it."

She closed her notebook and stood beside me, staring into the dusty,
tenebrous space that surrounded us. Her lips were stained with wine,
her hair smelled of cigarettes and something sweet, a trace of vanilla,
perhaps. I wanted to touch and kiss the nut-brown pigmentation on
the left side of her neck, just below her chin, but she wouldn't let me.
Violinists were marked for life, the seal of the Moirai imprinted on
their necks. Did the boatman, that old lethean smuggler, take notice of
the violin burn on the pale skin of recently departed virtuosos? Were
musicians entitled to a free ride, or did they too have to bite the silver
obolus, just like the plebs and the wealthy pigs, in order to cross to the
other shore?

"Sometimes I feel that all of this is for nothing," Irina said and took a
drag from my cigarette. "All the practicing, hundreds of pages of memorized music, the performances. It's just a way to keep the demons
away. When I play, the nightmare fades a little. But how long am I

supposed to keep it all up? I don't think I'm going to make it to my twentieth birthday. I've experienced everything, I've tasted everything. I'm old and tired."

"Old!" I cried. "You're seventeen!"

"Yeah, which is about thirty years older than you. I'd say you're a little over forty." Irina giggled and tucked her hair behind her ear. I noticed her hands again, confident, powerful. More than anything else, it was her hands that made me desire her. I wanted to know their secrets, their wisdom and sorrow. "Haven't you noticed? Time moves differently here, a year sometimes feels like a decade, and even more. My childhood ended when I was nine. I was done with puberty at fourteen. I've married, had kids, traveled . . . in a way. I've already lost everyone who's been dear to me. And all of it happened while I was practicing that damned violin. I didn't even notice."

"You're probably feeling tired because you still have two more years to graduate. True, two years here is an eternity. Concerts, absences, demerits, auditions. And the biannual proficiency tests where the satraps on the committee can just sign your death sentence and finish your career. We live in a constant state of stage fright."

"Not me. I'm not afraid of anything."

Another marching band drew near, this one blasting "The Quiet, White Danube" with such profanity that it could only be the geeks from the Mathematics High School down the street. A thin ray of light passing through the crawl space revealed an animate, swirling column of dust, with a snake of smoke in its center. Outside it was euphoric spring, and the crisp, delicious air seeping in through the roof tiles was just another reminder that we were prisoners, we'd been sentenced to spend our lives in seclusion, breathing the stale air of the music labyrinth. Irina looked at me now for the first time. Was she sad? Where was the fire in her eyes, the promiscuous flare, the disarming hauteur with which she looked down upon the mortals? She seemed suddenly weak, almost needy, childlike. I took her hand.

"Did you come here for something else?" she asked.

"Of course not," I said. I was a pathological liar. I wondered what it would taste like this time. Was it going to be warm and sheltering like a summer night, or heart-racing and jolting like a dive in the cold sea? Or was it going to be distant, crepuscular, and autumnal, with a pinch of pomegranates? It was pomegranates. We held hands. We didn't kiss. This wasn't love. We were just good friends. Or perhaps I was deluding myself. Wasn't she the one I truly loved? There was the old rhythm again, the uneven heart pulse, six-eight, and Irina knew more than anyone about time, about keeping rhythm, the importance of every odd beat. She pressed her cheek against mine and wrapped her hands around my neck, tightly, as if she were afraid of what we were doing and wanted me to help her forget the words and the names. We had done it before, but this time we couldn't hide behind the head rush of passion.

Was I angry at her for sleeping with Alexander? Of course I was, I was burning with pain about the whole thing, but the worst part was that this burning only made Irina's movements sweeter and more intoxicating, the way a cigarette burn or a razor cut only intensifies the sensation of being inebriated.

Finally, my mind was silent. There was no more music. No more Chopin ballads, chamber ensembles, strings, brass bands, piano duets, and timpani. No more counterpoint, no more harmony. No more keeping rhythm. At last it was quiet. The crowd of puppets was gone, too.

"I just ruined your date with Bianka, didn't I?" Irina ruffled my hair and pinched my nose.

"I wasn't going to go anyway," I said.

J. S. Bach,
Sonata in C Minor, BWV 1017,
Allegro

August 23, 1988

Igor the Swan and Irina were already an hour late for our final extracurricular ensemble session. I sat on a bench outside school, looking at the water flowing lazily in the small fountain, and thought about the events of the last two months. My plans for a carefree summer spent in dirty trains and wild beaches on the Black Sea, subsisting on stale bread from the local restaurants, cheap wine, beer, and filterless cigarettes had been ruined. Instead I'd spent July and August at school, digging into my new piano repertoire and studying for my correctional exams. I'd gotten Fs in algebra, literature, and, yes, chamber music. Igor the Swan had kept his promise and failed both Irina and me for not showing up for his class. To be precise, I'd shown up every time, eager to build a castle where Irina would reside at ease and let her hypnotic voice flow. But Irina hadn't even bothered. She probably had better things to do.

Fixing my F in literature was the hardest. The proletarian poets, those plebeian jerk-offs, turned my stomach. Their fervent psalms about factories, science, and progress were so toxic they could kill a mouse from five hundred miles. Algebra, on the other hand, was a breeze. I had actually studied this time, and the Raven conceded defeat without putting up much of a fight. It was a joy to see the feath-

ered demon scribble down a crooked C in the daybook with her left
hand, on account of the fact that her right arm was still in a plaster
cast. Still! She must've broken it a second time, there was no other
explanation. Her clinking bracelets were reduced now to fourteen,
down from twenty-eight. Her mathematical powers had taken a direct
hit, her Pythagorean spell broken. I almost felt sorry for her. She
could've broken her neck—those school stairs were truly vicious, each
flight twice as long as most, and far steeper. I would've felt terrible if
she had gotten really hurt, as it was I who flipped the main electric
switch on the third floor, outside Teachers' Headquarters, throwing
the entire windowless stairway into total darkness. It had happened
very quickly—"Go for the switch!" Alexander had whispered, and I
had acted instantly, thinking that he'd positioned himself to give the
Raven a little scare. I hadn't expected that he would actually send her
flying with a kick in the ass. Joking about doing something and actually
doing it are two different things, though in Alexander's case, as I ought
to have learned, it was generally wiser to proceed with caution. The
Raven hadn't made a sound as she reached the middle landing. When
the lights came back on, she stood up and walked away, unperturbed.
She was an old spirit, there was no doubt about it. But it was all over
now, my dealings with her were a thing of the past. Come September
15, I would never have to study her subject again.

It had started raining and I had retreated inside the school when
Igor the Swan, carrying a violin case, finally arrived. He blasted into
Chamber Hall No. 2, throwing the static left door off its hinges, and,
gesticulating wildly and twirling with the grace of a whale, declared
that Plato cannot be trusted. "The demons of joy! The demons of
joy! Plato, you see, Konstantin, cannot be trusted; bring in the horns,
the trumpets, here's the cadence—hop!—a glissando, and now: violins! The river flows again. The whole school has been turned into a
factory for fucking; the stairs are covered with sticky stuff, condoms
hang on the walls, and the janitors can't even clean up the orgy litter
fast enough. And the smells! Sixteen-year-old girls with no underwear
walking through the dark corridors, touching themselves, squeezing

their nipples. I can see the ghosts of the Catholic nuns masturbating in heaven. Jesus' little squirrels. It goes up, with a crescendo, a swoop of brilliance . . . The demons of joy! The doorman is getting sucked off as we speak, it's madness, I can't take it anymore. I should've joined the eunuch choir, back in the day. Perhaps you and Irina should just get naked, under the grand piano, and fuck, *presto,* one minuet, maybe even a saraband, and I will watch from the back . . . Discreetly! I won't say a word. It's an offer, take it or leave it, I'll give you both As. It's a good deal! You can't play an instrument anyway. . . . Worthless shits! In my time we played ten, fourteen hours a day, we played through the night, we played to stay alive. I was heading to the top, I was almost there. Perhaps you've heard. The Tchaikovsky Competition. And then, my little incident. I was banished from the conservatory, forced to accept a job in this rat hole, that was my punishment. To be tormented by my appetites for eternity. But Plato cannot be trusted. Who could've known that the petite, mousy, talentless opera singer teaching on the third floor of the conservatory was blowing the secretary general of the Party on the weekends! You haven't heard it from me, I haven't said a word. Boom! It's buried under the thunder of a hundred timpani and stand-up basses. Gone! The chorus sings in unison, the cellos burn through the sixteen notes like a comet crashing into the Earth's atmosphere at the speed of sound. In life, just as in music, one wrong note, one wrong move, could end it all. That's all it takes, one wrong note . . . and you think that if you practice enough, you'd be spared the humiliation. The demise! At least I went down in flames. One should never go quietly, that would be distasteful. Yes, I laid my hands on Lady Cassandra's nymphic behind, I admit it. I squeezed her buttocks ravenously, like a clawed vulture, right in the middle of the conservatory staircase, she was walking in front of me, a pendulum of carnal delight, what a catch! I wanted to devour her, to lick her up and down. The demons of joy! You haven't heard it from me—plop!—it's forgotten, strange fog descends upon us, the sun is eclipsed by a foreign body. . . . Where are we? What is this room? Why am I holding a violin? Hm . . . I wanted her to slap me in the face, that was my hope, to be honest. There's no greater turn-on than to be humiliated by a pretty nymph. Give it to me. Come on! One slap, two slaps, three slaps, and I will wet myself. Instead she went and reported me to her midget general, she turned out to be a Party concubine. Who could've known? Snuggling with the chief clown! I didn't say it. Did you hear me say clown? You must've misunderstood me. Comrade Zimova, I protest! In the name of the red pentacle, the student was clearly hallucinating. It is self-evident that he is not all together on the upper floors, if I may be so bold to suggest. . . . An offer was extended to me almost immediately—to join a labor camp, or to accept a job at the Music School for the Gifted and stop performing. Labor, you see, wasn't for me. My hands are not made to dig out stones, in the mines, and my fragile persona isn't built to withstand the vagaries of radiation. Uranium, I've found, isn't something you want to include in your diet. I may be too fat to fit into a Trabant, but I'm still a gentle spirit, with a weak heart and sore testicles."

So Igor the Swan and I played the Allegro in Bach's Sonata no. 4—Igor filling in for Irina, who never showed up. We played it fast, at a hundred and twenty, with zest, and it was the best, most satisfying experience I'd ever had as an accompanist and musician. Igor played the violin incredibly well—especially considering that he'd picked it up in the eleventh grade, when students in the Music School for the Gifted were required to choose a second instrument—but what made our rainy, late afternoon session special was his understanding of Bach and his skill at leading me into his secret world, a world that had its own rules, dimensions, and rationale. Igor the Musician was profoundly different from Igor the Swan, or Igor the Barbarian. With the violin under his chin, he transformed into a refined Renaissance man whose palette of expressions consisted only of honesty, love, yearning for enlightenment, and selfless introspection. His intoning was pure and sacred, devoid of the profanity, cynicism, and flamboyance that defined his everyday persona. Perhaps one could detect a touch of eccentricity around the edges of his phrases, or a spark of luciferous insight in the way he drew the bow and sculpted each note, but that was just added brilliance.

It was strange how we understood each other without words or gestures. Standing to my right on the stage of Chamber Hall No. 2, he
was no longer the giant bespectacled vagabond with greasy hair and a
Pandora's box of manias, and I, for my part, no longer the emaciated,
insomniac sixteen-year-old in a tattered uniform with cigarette-stained
nails. You could say that the first thing that disappears when we play
music is our bodies.

We played for hours, we played the Adagio and the second Allegro,
we traveled through the other violin sonatas, the fifth and the sixth,
without a memory of who we were and who we had been. We traveled fast, unburdened, exculpated, forgotten. At times, after the sun
had crept behind the apartment buildings on the periphery of Doctors' Garden and Chamber Hall No. 2 became alive with the shadows and whispers of Erebus, I would catch Igor waltzing across the
stage, carried by the ecstatic flow of the sixteenth notes, or doing slow
pirouettes during those long, oscillating violin colors that illuminated
the immaculate counterpoint of the piano cadences spiraling rapidly
down into the tonic. Bach was the law that set us afloat in the great
weightlessness. We craved the law, the logos, the final way of things—
but this wasn't the vindictive, blind law that only chained humans to
their inherent shortcomings and defects. Here, there were no rules;
just symmetry and unadorned beauty. Did Igor live alone, or perhaps
with his mother? I knew that his apartment was just a few blocks from
school, but I didn't know anything about his personal life. I suspected
that he didn't have any friends. He was a lone freak with a profound
sense of symmetry.

"Your playing wasn't entirely pathetic this time," he complemented
me at the end of our exhausting session, as he wiped his violin with a
cloth and tucked it gently into its case. "For which I'm awarding you
a C. I will mark it in the daybook when school resumes next month."

"Only a C!" I protested. "And what about Irina?"

"Irina will get a C, too, though she doesn't deserve it. I expected a
small performance, Konstantin. I would've given my left ear to hear you
two play in Chamber Hall Number One. The chemistry! And Irina,

with her wanting bosoms, in a skirt . . . The heavenly birds are upon me again, covering my wounds with their cold wings. Bach isn't for imbeciles! Take it from me. Who could understand how it's all intertwined, this and that, the demons of joy! A school full of imbeciles, each and every one, teachers and students, the janitors, too. . . . Oh, where are you, Prometheus, to set things right, to glass this nightmare!"

Off Igor went, across the atrium, through the swinging doors, and out the school gate, dancing and shouting, the violin case tucked under his arm, his moth-eaten white shirt flapping in the gentle breeze, loose shoestrings bouncing up and down. The doorman and I followed him a short distance, to see if he would get run over by a car or a silent trolleybus. Igor evaded traffic heroically, like a buffalo caught in a strong current, and then continued prancing on the sidewalk across the street. "I've been buggered!" he called out to a group of elderly black-veiled widows carrying jugs with mineral water. "Who will catch the perpetrators now?"

The doorman looked at me and shook his head. He didn't understand, didn't know what music did to people. I thought the doorman was all right, even though he was a Communist, even if he did actually believe that people could one day live in harmony, without jealousy, distrust, or competition. Such an egregious misconception regarding the spiritual propensity of the tribe of liars was astonishing, if not beautiful. We had become friends over the summer, the doorman and I, and he'd begun letting me spend time with Her Majesty, the concert Steinway in Chamber Hall No. 1, without the principal's permission. I had the key all to myself; the school was deserted. There was no one who could hear me play or interrupt me. I loved the smell of the Steinway, the smell of shiny black lacquer, of velvet hammers, of dust gathered on the soundboard and the gold-stained iron frame; the smell of fear and stage fright, but also of elation and transcendence. Alone in the dimly lit hall, I caressed the red lining that separated the lid from the keys and studied my reflection in the black mirror. Everything sounded different on the Steinway—Bach, Beethoven, Mozart, Liszt, Chopin, Brahms, Debussy, Prokofiev, Scriabin, Rachmaninov. I played everything I'd ever studied; I played until my tendons caught on fire and I started to feel dizzy with hunger and dehydration. I imagined that the school was my private medieval castle and I lived in it alone, except for the silly old doorman, my butler and confidant. My private quarters, where I spent my evenings smoking and contemplating the breathtaking view of the misty mountains and the crumbling edifices of the ancient city, were located in the attic, while the other floors housed my extensive collection of uprights and antique grands of various sizes. For I was a renowned piano collector, a reclusive virtuoso, and in order to keep my prized items in good shape, I took daily tours through all the rooms of the castle and dusted the pianos by performing Chopin études—a daunting task that kept me busy for most of the morning and afternoon. The gems of my collection—two concert grands of exquisite substance, Her Majesty and the Velvet Widow— were staged on the first floor, in a great hall that had once functioned as a cathedral. Generally, I accepted my guests in the atrium, though few, in fact, sought my friendship.

Stella came to visit me in the beginning of August, all distressed and morose, her ash-blond hair a spectacular mess, her blue-green eyes puffed up and lifeless. Still, she wore a miniskirt, and we fucked for old times' sake, with the cordial resentment of old enemies forced to shake hands at an awkward social gathering. Peppy had left her and her Latin professor avoided her as if she were pregnant. "I am all yours!" she proclaimed and jumped in my arms like a suicidal maniac leaping out of a fast-moving car. I pleaded with her to give her Latin professor another chance. What if he loved her? I wanted her off my back.

Iliya was finally beginning to recover from a monthlong bout of pneumonia, and he looked paler, weaker than usual. Being deathly ill didn't affect his routine. He still woke up at four, bathed with icy water in the stone basin outside his house, and then took the six o'clock train from Lukovo to Sofia.

At dusk, following my last session with Igor the Swan—my whole being resonating with Bach's inevitable cadences and winding counterpoint—Iliya and I sat on a bench in Doctors' Garden and traveled

back to the forties, to a time when the sun seemed obscured by a
strange shadow and the stinging smell of dynamite still hung in the
air, months after the last unexploded ordnance had been cleared from
the bombed-out buildings. We walked on the newly paved streets in
the city center, down Tsar Shishman, Patriarch Evtimii, and Solun-
ska. I held on to Iliya's tattered raincoat, he led the way, keeping one
hand on his hat, for the tunnels of time tended to be rather windy. We
snuck into the prison with the metal lions out front, where Iliya had
been detained in 1945 on charges of espionage and aiding American
interests, and stopped in front of cell 32, on the fourth floor. Inside,
lying on the ground, was a bearded man in his forties, his body covered
with a black robe worn by members of the Orthodox clergy, his head
bruised and bleeding. I wanted to ask Iliya again if he believed in God,
but I knew that he wouldn't answer. It was a flawed question. Even I
could understand that. The word *god* invited duality; the word *believe*
forfeited direct knowledge.

"Why is it that, throughout your peregrinations," I asked Iliya
instead, "you've been surrounded by priests?" He replied that it probably had to do with his upbringing. His father had been a priest and
always wanted him to join the seminary. But there had been something else. In the months leading up to Iliya's passage to the labor
camp on Persin Island, he had gotten to know the priest in cell 32
and had heard him expound an esoteric teaching called the *thresholds
of knowledge*. The priest had died of natural causes one hour before
he was due to appear in front of the firing squad, exactly as he had
predicted when he'd first been interrogated. Iliya said that the priest's
example—his foreknowledge of the exact time of his own death, the
calm with which he had accepted his fate, and the wisdom he'd shared
with the prisoners in the neighboring cells—had given him strength to
survive the camps and the transmogrification of his being.

"My dear," Iliya told me, "I do hope that you realize how lucky you
are. To live in the temple of music—that is a gift. Music can heal,
it can grant a new life. I'll tell you a little story. The first time I was
released from the camps was in the fall of 1966. The night before, at

the Lovech concentration camp, I had been ordered to climb into the back of a military jeep with blackened windows and handcuff myself to the railing. No one told me where I was going. After traveling for hours, I was taken blindfolded into a building and left alone in an empty room for what seemed like a whole day. I thought my hour had finally come. At one point a military officer walked in and gave me a set of civilian clothes, my old clothes, which I had worn when I was first arrested in 1944. Still no one told me what was going on. And then, just like that, the officer opened a heavily fortified metal door and pushed me out onto a narrow cobblestone street flanked on both sides with old apartment buildings. I had no money or documents. I took a cautious step forward, looking back at the metal door, which was now closed behind me. What if this was a setup? I took another step, and another, and suddenly, like a somnambulist awakened mid-step, I knew exactly where I was—in the middle of Tsar Shishman Street, heading down toward Parliament. Sofia had changed, though not as significantly as it might have. Some of the old stores were still there—the fishery, the pharmacy, the newspaper booth—only now they looked decrepit and uninviting. An old cousin of mine lived nearby, and I headed straight to his apartment. At first he didn't open the door. He didn't recognize me. When he finally let me in, after I had been standing in the stairway for hours, he seemed fearful, as if he'd invited in a ghost. He told me I would bring him bad luck. I kept my mouth shut.

"First thing I did was to take a hot shower. Twenty-two years without a hot shower, practically without a shower of any kind, sleeping on the bare concrete floor without a blanket, digging holes into the rocks, a human worm. Now, under the hot water, my skin fell off. Completely. From my forehead all the way down to my toes. It bubbled up and peeled off in large sheets, heaping up at my feet. My outer skin; a thick, dead layer of protective coating. I had been dead so many years.

"I borrowed a pair of pants, a hat, and a shirt from my cousin. I put on my old raincoat, too, though it was quite warm outside. The Grand Music Hall was close by, and I immediately set out to see if someone was playing. That was the second thing I did. The big hall was closed, but there was a concert under way in the smaller hall, on the first floor. The lady selling tickets let me in for free, as I'd already missed half of the performance. I sat in the very back. It was quite dark; a single spotlight on the grand piano. Almost instantly, something in me broke apart, and I started crying uncontrollably. I didn't want to cry, nor was I experiencing pain or remorse. But the tears flowed freely, they flowed through me. Just as it had happened before with my skin, the music and the chords ripped away the dead substance at the core of my being. These tears carried the salt and debris that had encrusted my soul for decades. Suddenly I felt vulnerable again. I felt. And I felt love."

"What did you hear?" I asked him. We'd just come to the end of Tsar Shishman Street, and Iliya was still looking for the metal door he'd exited from back in 1966. Doors are strange things, however; sometimes they appear in the most unlikely places and then disappear, never to be found again.

"Of course you'd ask. Brahms, it was, the ballads and the intermezzos."

After we parted I returned to school and bummed a few filterless cigarettes off the doorman; I needed something strong. Iliya was right. I was lucky. The key to my escape was at my fingertips. But this wasn't an escape from the real into the imagined; quite the opposite, in fact. The world was unreal, without substance. The lies and the liars, the robots with their numbers and calculations, the imposed memories, time's gravity, the concave mountain suspended from the sky, the drone of the exhausted summer, the crushing inevitability of the future, the drudgery of answering to an assigned name, the commands, the forced communications—they were but a reverie, a silting of shapes and colors at the bottom of one's eyes. The chords and the wordless sentences, on the other hand, mirrored a primordial template that we'd forgotten. There was plenty of love here, more than one person would ever need.

I opened the windows in room 43, on the fourth floor, to let some air in. The last dark pink strokes above the mountain were quickly dissolving into the black dome. The summer was almost over. Soon I would have to surrender my castle, along with the majority of my private collection of pianos, to the vandals. I felt so tired. Nothing ever changed. It didn't seem like I was growing older anymore. I had reached an age past which adding numbers was just a conventional trifle.

Chopin,
Scherzo no. 3 in C-sharp Minor, op. 39
(Presto con fuoco)

September 15, 1988

The noise was back. Hundreds of screaming pubescent and pre-pubescent students, running, pushing, lugging basses, cellos, violas, trombones, and tubas up and down the stairs, opera singers vying for the highest notes, vibraphonists and drummers speed-racing in the basement, a somber bass clarinet drilling triplets into the foundation of the school, the janitors shouting, the bell ringing louder, longer, more asphyxiating than ever before. The chief gorgon was strutting in and out of her office on the third floor, her glasses suspended from her neck by a silver chain. Boris Negodnik was climbing slowly up the stairs, whistling the "Ode to Joy" and tapping his pointer against the railing, arrhythmic as ever. He was going to tell us again that he'd missed only one class in his forty-four-year-long teaching career, and that he wouldn't miss another anytime soon. Like most old-school proletarians, he planned to live forever by eating fruits, vegetables, and certain grains. No smokes, no alcohol. He bragged in class that his sex life was getting better by the day. Good for him! The Raven was back, too, tottering down the long corridors with her plastered arm and her compasses. The gym teacher and Bankoff stood by the main entrance searching the usual suspects for banned substances and making lascivious comments whenever a pretty girl passed by. Mouseface, one of the literature teachers, was pacing nervously in the atrium, waiting for word on the status of her stolen purse. "When I catch the perpetrator, I'll kill him!" she was shouting, pinching her own nipples with the ferocity of a deranged masochist. Every time she got angry in class, she would fold her arms over her chest and start playing with her breasts. It was a tic that she was most probably not aware of but which was truly painful to watch, for she exuded near-lethal doses of pedantry and had all the sexual appeal of a frozen mastodon. But what was this hideous, Tartarean sound coming from the librarian's office, on the second floor? A sound that passed over your skin like a death chill and made your blood curdle . . . Well, of course, it was the baritone, nearly human laugh of the Hyena, entertaining a clique of menial solfège teachers. The excitement! It was a grand mythological circus. There were medusas, chimeras, satyrs, centaurs, gorgons. There were vampires, cretins, midgets, butterflies, nymphs, giants, and ghosts. And no reopening of school was complete without garlands, flags, and banners promising a bright future to the bovine masses. March onward! The fatherland is our sun! Through the study of the arts, the Communist ideal is achieved at last! *Boom!* went the timpani in Chamber Hall No. 1, in preparation for the upcoming speeches. I slipped through security and, leaping three and even four stairs at a time, made my way to my classroom on the fifth floor to get a copy of the fall class schedule. Then I exited the building and headed for the *pushkom,* or smokers' committee, as it was known, in an adjacent backyard, away from the ideological reactor and the herd of willing mutants.

"Konstantin!"

I turned around. It was my father, in a brown raincoat and a leninesque beard, a small briefcase under his arm.

"Look at you, all disheveled and unkempt, one would think you are returning from a party! I haven't seen you in a week, and you made your grandmother lie that you had slept over at her apartment, and I know for a fact that you didn't. I've told your grandmother that you're not allowed to visit her anymore, not until you change."

I laughed. "Is your lecture going to take long? Because I have other things to do."

"Take that vulgar smirk off your face, will you? Your mother and I are expecting to see you tonight around seven. There are important things we need to discuss. The summer is over, as I'm sure you've noticed. You're starting a new school year, you have responsibilities, the Chopin competition is looming: in fact, I just got a note from your piano teacher about that. . . . Also, your charming supervisor came today to my office to inform me that your school absences will no longer be tolerated. You will be kicked out. It pains me to say this, Konstantin, but it's becoming increasingly evident that I must have failed you. I seem to have raised a perfect savage—"

"I don't have time for this," I told him and pointed across the street, toward the university. "Why don't you just go back to your classroom, where you can lecture your students until they drop dead of boredom."

"Now you listen to me, Konstantin: if you don't start respecting the rules in our family, you're not going to be part of it! Is that clear? I have the power to take you out of this school and stick you in a mediocre but strict high school out in the country, far away from here, where no one would tolerate your posturing. As a matter of fact, I've already begun making preparations, if you really want to know!"

"Maybe you should start planning my funeral as well."

"Do not try your paranoid . . . extortionist rhetoric on me, you ungrateful little psychopath!" He tried to hit me on the face, but I ducked backwards and his nails only grazed my chin.

"The tragedy of small philosophers like you," I said, walking away from him, "is that you are destined to be forgotten."

"Come back, you little shit! You act tough now, but wait until the system grinds you down and your girlfriends marry the *otlichniks* and the aspiring apparatchiks! I'd like to see you then, a prodigious boozer with a bright future *behind* him!"

I walked back to him so I didn't have to shout what I wanted to tell him in front of all the teachers and students passing by. "Has it ever occurred to you that if there were a civil war, you and I would be on the opposite sites of the barricades? I would be shooting at you."

I left him standing there, in front of school, clutching his miserable briefcase and trying desperately to think of some appropriate come-back.

In the *pushkom* I found the usual crowd: Irina, Vadim, and Alexander, as well as a bunch of new faces, some of them likely spies. A blond fifteen-year-old boy, an oboist, was asking too many questions about the best way to unlock the door to Teachers' Headquarters at night, while his friend, a mousy, bespectacled violinist, was professing to have bedded a tenth grader from the English High School. A fifteen-year-old cello player, her uniform dress unbuttoned up to her crotch, was smoking and taking big swigs from a small bottle of rakia.

"You should take her home," I said to Alexander.

"They're all in a terrible hurry to get to the place we've just escaped," he said, checking her out. "They are too brave for their own good! They want to get hurt, and they will." Vadim said nothing, even though it was he Alexander was talking to.

Irina, morose as usual, came over to ask me for some change. "Come on!" she whined, punching me on the shoulder. "Don't be such an asshole!" But I kept my hands in my pockets. I didn't feel like giving her any money.

"Why didn't you show up for the chamber music rehearsals all summer?" I asked her. "Why did you leave me alone with Igor, week after week, even though you promised? *You* asked me to be your accompanist!"

Irina stuck her tongue out and closed her eyes halfway, as if taken by some mind-numbing erotic fantasy, then stepped closer and closer until her tongue was nearly in my mouth. Then she shoved me suddenly away and retreated, alert and contemptuous, a predator waiting to attack.

"I was giving concerts in Vienna and Salzburg, you fucking jerk!" she shouted. "That's why! You think I give a damn about this shithole?

Well, I don't, and don't get any ideas about me, either; a fuck is a fuck, I never promised you anything!" She was drunk, it was clear by the way she swallowed her consonants and struggled for her balance, but that wasn't why I let her anger and contempt pass through me as if I were an apparition: I forgave her because she was right. She did have a genuine talent, she was special, and every time she thought that she'd escaped, she had to come back here, to the swamp, like a god condemned to share the fate of mortals.

I understood her. Indeed, I shared her contempt. I had been perfecting my own version since the day I was born. Contempt was the vaccine that kept me immune from transmogrification. It was part of what made me different from the rest. And this fall, like a long-held diminished seventh chord, my contempt had reached a cathartic momentum. And though it was just another September—chestnuts strewn about the sidewalks, sun-soaked leaves falling over the cars and trolleybuses on Oborishte Street, dead cats floating on the surface of the pond in Doctors' Garden, freshly printed necrologies of smiling teenagers thumbtacked to trees and stucco walls, old chimneys spewing sulfur, new conscripts armed with shiny lances staring vacuously at the world from the back of military trucks, the steam of hot *pirozhki* enveloping the Levski Monument and making the street dogs howl—everything felt different. I was meaner, more arrogant, more detached then ever before. I felt it in my veins; something big was going to happen, something was going to change the course of my life. I was prepared to take on the monsters and fight one last war, a little war perhaps, and I was prepared to lose.

A silver wind blew through us. It ruffled Irina's hair and slipped behind her irises, turning them into tiny mirrors. I saw my own reflection, my messy long hair and the cigarette ember waning between my lips. The silver wind was everywhere and in everything. It passed through my heart, penetrating my flesh tenderly, bloodlessly, leaving neither scars nor memories; it resounded in the burdened clotheslines stretched between buildings like harp strings; it whistled through the crack of the basement window where we tossed the stubs of our cigarettes; it whispered in the trees and let out pained howls as it possessed the tall, cylindrical garbage bins lined up against the brick wall; it even found its way into Chopin's third scherzo, where it filled the gaps between the four resignations with the sound of descending tubular bell glissandos.

The four resignations were my predicament, the lifeline on the palm of my hand and the spell that the Gypsy woman selling flowers at the Levski Monument had cast upon me. The first resignation began with a lonely A flat sounding three times and then went on to reiterate the oldest decree: accept the death of the self. The second resignation began where the first left off, and, with the hint of the tonic bearing down from the top—an enormous, existential weight, a D-flat major over E-flat minor—resolved into the dominant. As resignations went, this was perhaps the ultimate. Life was sweetest when you no longer resisted its conclusion. The third resignation was a step into the beyond, the fourth—a final moment of reckoning. Then the gates closed quickly.

Everyone heard the warning signal at once: three whistles, followed by low-pitched hooting. The gendarmes were afoot and we had to clear the area. The only escape route was through the adjacent backyard, which ultimately led to Zaimov Boulevard, but the fifteen-year-old cello player slowed everyone down. Too drunk to open the tear in the chain-link fence wide enough, she got caught in its sharp metal claws and Irina had to practically kick her through, ripping the girl's uniform dress in the process. By the time Vadim and Irina had squeezed through the fence, I could already hear the footsteps of the gendarmes echoing in the narrow pathways on the left and on the right side of the apartment building behind which we were hiding. Alexander and I looked at each other and, without saying a word, agreed to stand our ground and face the enemy, come what may. We didn't even bother to put out our cigarettes. If you're going to get caught for sure, at least act as if you don't give a damn.

First to turn the corner was Bankoff, the acoustics and physics teacher, ambitiously bald, with thick, tar-black eyebrows, pronounced cheekbones, and tiny eyes, dressed in his usual dark green apron, gray proletarian trousers, and moccasins. Then the gym teacher, Mulberry, in his black-and-red-striped tracksuit, popped out from the left side of the building. With his oleaginous hair and beard, dirty little mouth, and narrow forehead, he looked like an Eastern Orthodox priest who'd had too much lamb and wine for breakfast. If they were shocked to see me and Alexander standing there and smoking so nonchalantly—and on the first day of school, no less—they didn't show it. Bankoff walked over to the tear in the fence and, assuming the professional manner of a forensic specialist, removed a piece of the fifteen-year-old cellist's uniform dress from one of the rusty wire prongs sticking out.

"Who else was here?" Bankoff asked in his weak, husky voice ravaged by chronic pharyngitis. When he spoke in class none but those sitting in the very first row could hear anything he said. Consequently, his drawn-out lectures on acoustics always bordered on the surreal. "I just want some names," he said. "What kind of cigarettes are you two smoking, anyway? Camels? Imported? Where did you get the money?" He extended his hand, demanding the whole pack. Alexander gave it to him with a smile. He knew as well as I did that we had just bribed our way out of trouble. Bankoff waved his forefinger in the direction of Doctors' Garden: "Get lost."

"Wait a minute," Mulberry disagreed, twisting his hands. "Why don't we beat them up, they're all ours! Who's even going to see?"

"It's the first day of school," Bankoff replied. "Let the boys go. We'll catch them again."

"Let the boys go," Alexander grumbled as we walked out onto Oborishte Street and headed toward Parliament. "They're setting us up, I'm sure of it. You know, if I had fifty deutsche marks, I would pay Peppy the Thief to cut that fucking gym teacher's balls off. Just the balls; he could keep his little pecker. Did Irina ever tell you? Last May he tried to lock her in his basement office, just the way he did with Sonya when he raped her two years ago."

"Fucker," I said, dizzy from the adrenaline rush that had suddenly swept away all logic and common sense. "Let's go back and kick the bastard in the groin! And his boss, Baron Frankenstein, as well. God, I hate that cunning little mug!"

"Can't do anything to Mulberry, he's a national judo champion," Alexander reminded me. "Peppy, on the other hand, can take him out—no problem. Peppy's a psychopath, and there are no martial arts designed to neutralize psychopaths. If only we had enough money to pay him."

This was the coldest September 15 I could remember. It felt weird coming to school at 1:30 in the afternoon, rather than 7:45 in the morning. Second period began at 2:25, long recess was at 4:05, and sixth period ended at 7:00. Growing up within the confines of the Music School for the Gifted, I had always been envious of the tenth, eleventh, and twelfth graders who got to go to school in the afternoon and the evening. From the point of view of a budding adolescent, the life of a tenth grader was one of dark pleasures and delicious misery. A tenth grader had access to vast and exhilarating stores of despair. He was always fatigued and severely deprived of sunlight and basic existential logic. A tenth grader got to watch the sun drop behind the mountain while sitting in a neon-lit classroom as an orchestration teacher sight-read a student piece on a dilapidated piano with a shallow lower register and plastic highs. Now that was real misery. The yearning for the unreachable sunlit eternity waiting beyond the ever-closing horizon, the orange rings of refracted twilight moving across the linoleum floor, the nagging fear of the upcoming graduation exams, the tunnel vision of a prolonged stint at the conservatory and then a lifetime of brain-shrinking pedagogical toil and meagerly attended concerts, the specter of the red pentacle hanging in the leaden Sofia sky, the prospect of more ideology—anything would do—more lies, more wars, more celebrations and synchronized acts of marching-band puppetry, more crushing triumphs of mediocrity, more disappointments and deeply satisfying little tortures, more illusory time, more emotional atrophy and less recollection, less contempt but also less love, less faith in the advent of the promised revelation, less thirst for truth, less awareness of the ever-present tinkling of the untuned piano down the hallway, the sound of the transmundane slipping quietly into the sulfurous waters, one pedestrian phrase at a time. The secrets of the night would never lose their allure.

I wasn't planning on returning to school until the third period, which happened to be military conduct and preparation with the stinking Colonel Pirozhkin. Alexander and I split outside the Russian High School, on Tsar Shishman Street. He went to visit a friend of his who lived in a furbished storage cell in the basement of an old apartment building nearby. I had been there before, once with Alexander, and once with a girl, and the thought of going underground into the kingdom of giant cockroaches and pathogenic rivers, for the sake of listening to bad music, drinking vodka, and, at best, getting blown by some confused girl, seemed utterly unappealing. Besides, I had a serious decision to make, and I needed some time to walk alone in the light autumnal drizzle.

That morning, after my piano lesson, Ladybug had asked me to consider signing up for the national Chopin competition organized by the Sofia Music School for the Gifted and the Polish Cultural Center, which was going to take place in the middle of November, exactly two months away. Originally, Ladybug had advised me to stay away from the music school's little piano war because it was obvious even at the outset that it was just another ploy by the deputy principal, Kurtswine, to legitimize her incontinent protégés, and that the possibility of my getting a first or any other prize was close to zero. But now Ladybug had changed her mind. She had learned that Kurtswine had arranged for the head of the big Chopin competition in Warsaw to attend all the performances, and that had made her wonder whether the benefits of introducing myself to one of the most important people in the world of classical piano outweighed the potential damage to my career by an all but certain defeat at the hands of the nepotistic midgets. "The choice is yours," Ladybug had told me, but by the way she had squeezed my hand and pressed her head against mine, it was clear she expected me to take on the challenge, if only for the sake of honing my repertoire and getting some stage exposure ahead of the real tests lying ahead.

But how was I going to swallow the humiliation of losing to a bunch of monkeys and dimwitted charlatans for whom playing Chopin was no different than throwing discus or studying algebra? For whom, moreover, Chopin was just another mortal with minor obsessions and old-fashioned tastes? How would I face my rivals on the stairs and in the corridors of the music school after the competition was over and my reputation had been demoted to that of a pigheaded peasant? And how could I commit to sharing my private meditations on Chopin's esoteric texts with the multitudes of myopic players who were trained to repeat rather than improvise?

I had certainly changed. There was a time when I'd enjoyed going into battle and demonstrating my skill, laying it all out without any degree of self-consciousness. But my long piano peregrinations had led me away from the pomposity of the concert hall and into a world of colors and visions and quiet ecstasy. I had grown secretive about my playing. I had discovered that the piano, just like God, is a solitary path that leads to the death of the self. There is no one you can take along, no one else who can partake in the mystery of disappearing.

The cataclysmic octaves from the opening of the third scherzo were upon me again, tearing at the silence of the rainy street and the soaked buildings and the marching raincoats and the bobbling umbrellas and the fogged-up windows of the baklava shop and the cobblestones reflecting the firefly glow of the ashen sun. I stopped to admire the cream, orange, and purple carnations sold by the flower woman at the corner of Tsar Shishman and Venelin, outside the old pharmacy with the large brass bell attached to its door. I had no money for flowers and no money for a cup of Turkish coffee, preferably with lots of sugar, which is what I really needed. I walked ahead, hands in my pockets, my wet hair falling over my eyes. At times like these, I didn't mind wearing the ugly school uniform that much. True: aside from being a prime example of aesthetic retardation, the uniform was prone to insurmountable wrinkles, rips, and frayed threads; but, on the other hand, it was also a magical garment that made me invisible. Once I put on the white shirt, the sport jacket, and the pants, I instantly became an anonymous manifestation of the ubiquitous student.

The small park in front of Seven Saints Church, with the green rectangular patch in the middle and the benches lined up along its periphery, had been constructed in the 1930s, in the place of an ancient madrasa. Seven Saints Church, for its part, had been built on top of a mosque with a lead dome and a minaret of black granite, the so-called Black Mosque, commissioned in the sixteenth century by Suleiman the Magnificent. Underneath the Black Mosque lay the ruins of a fourth-century Christian temple, and underneath that, the stones of a pagan temple dedicated to the worship of Asclepius, the Greek god of medicine and healing. At night, the sick and the wretched would flock to the sanctuary, driven by the belief that if they slept within its walls, the logos would enter their dreams and dream bodies and heal them, a practice known as incubation. An alkaline hot spring had bubbled nearby, providing respite from Erebus's cold embrace.

I sat on the wet stairs of Seven Saints Church looking at an old man with a cane standing under a weeping willow, presumably waiting for the rain to subside. The tree, with its crooked trunk and limp branches, hadn't changed much since the days when I used to come here with my mother to run around and chase pigeons. The water fountain still worked, too. Back then my parents and I had lived around the corner in a small rented studio without a bathroom or running water. Early in the morning, while it was still dark, my mother would walk me to the neighborhood day care, located next to a somber five-story printing house with darkened windows. In my mind, books were something mythical that came to life in the darkest hours of the night, amid heat, bitter smoke, and loud banging rising from beneath the cobbled streets.

A flock of black ravens descended on the park, their urgent, sinister cries blending with the octaves from the third scherzo reverberating through my body. I wasn't afraid. I was going to sign up for the music school's corrupt little competition, and I was going to play like the devil. It didn't matter what anyone said about me in the end. I wouldn't be playing for them. I would play for Iliya, Ladybug, Irina, and Vadim. And even though I would lose the competition, I would dismount the stage with dignity, for I would've played truthfully. Kurtswine, her honorary guest from Poland, and the rest would jerk and twitch in their chairs, terrified by my combustible tempos, my brazen intoning, my paroxysms of abandonment, and my raw, unpolished phrases. Flying close to the sun, I would catch fire, and the octaves in the third scherzo would spread the flames throughout the recital hall, knocking the wigs off the puppets' heads and incinerating their Bakelite irises.

The church bell sounded two o'clock. Some places have a center-of-the-universe feel about them. The small Seven Saints park, enclosed by buildings, had a magnetic pull that not many passersby could resist. You could see them wavering for a moment on the park's periphery, uncertain of the direction in which they should head, then suddenly swerving in. Did they want to pass through the cloud of pigeons, or did they just crave to brush against the old church, the way stray cats wrap themselves around trees and telegraph polls? Perhaps there was something underground—a river or a stone blessed by the healing powers of Asclepius—that altered the way the clouds glided over the park's surface; perhaps it was the solar wind spinning dust devils and charging the ether with a hidden luminosity. The blind accordionist who played all day at Slaveikov Square knew the secret of the park, since he often napped here after lunch. One can only access the mythical undercurrents through the medium of dreams. But listen! The slow, wistful buildup to the coda in the third scherzo—a lake stirred by a warm wind—and then the gasping charge upward, a cardiac accelerando to the lonely peak, to the naked, abandoned E in the fourth octave, which triumphed over memory and pain, over time's bloody clockwork, and which collapsed gratefully into the grumbling final cadence.

The head priest of Seven Saints, his long black robe scented with the smell of frankincense and recycled candle wax, stepped out of the church and invited me to come inside, to take shelter from the rain. I thanked him but remained seated at the top of the stairs, just outside the main entrance. I had no place in his temple.

Chopin,
"Heroique" Polonaise in A flat, op. 53

September 29, 1988

Room 34, on the third floor, looked out north, in the direction of the mausoleum and Nevski Cathedral. The blackboard was covered with a white screen on which the colonel projected his scratched-up slides of Soviet-made weapons and military equipment. It was Thursday, and I was appearing alone before the colonel, at his request. Standing with his back toward the window, Pirozhkin looked even grayer and deader than usual. The skin on his face resembled dried-up parchment that had started to crack around his ears; his eyes were mummy holes; his lips indistinguishable from his gums. He smelled like a corpse.

"Ah, you finally came," he said, looking both wound-up and disoriented. "There's something urgent I need to discuss with you."

"Certainly, sir," I replied.

The colonel pointed at the half-zipped rucksack filled with Kalashnikovs in the back of the room. "How quick can you disassemble and reassemble a standard assault rifle?"

"Fifteen seconds."

"Make it ten. Are you good with grenades?"

"Naturally."

The colonel licked his lips with the indifference and speed of a lizard and walked over to the rucksack. "Do you know what is the beauty of a Kalashnikov? This is a question!"

"Well, it's light and lasts forever."

"No. The beauty is that you could take on a whole army with just a single weapon. How does that make you feel?"

"Good."

"Are you ready to take on the imperialist enemy? Stand straight when you are speaking to a superior! How will you take on the imperialist enemy?"

"With a pocketknife, sir."

The colonel was taken aback. "Do you have a pocketknife?"

"No, sir."

"Are you mocking me? To mock a colonel, awarded twice for exceptional bravery, and once for . . . other things, is like mocking a lame duck. A lame duck isn't what one thinks it is. Moreover, I'm not a lame duck. This is a plain observation. Is that clear, number eleven?"

"Number fourteen, sir."

"Have you been to the shooting range with me before?"

"Many times, sir. I'm the best shooter in the class."

"Very well. I'm assigning you to the task of recruiting two students and delivering this cache of weapons to the central police station, down the street. I don't want any incidents! Is that clear?"

"Yes, sir!"

"And the others? Where are all the others?"

"The entire class is waiting for you in the school yard. They are ready and excited to practice their formations in the rain."

"Excellent. Here is the key to the classroom. When you're done, lock the door and bring the key to the doorman."

The colonel stormed out of the room and headed downstairs. I zipped the rucksack and peeked into the corridor. Straight ahead was Teachers' Headquarters and the exit to the stairwell. To the right was the Owl's office and, farther down, the office of Kurtswine, the deputy principal, where some comatose little brat was meandering through

Beethoven's "Pastorale" sonata in D major. To the left were a half-dozen classrooms packed with first, second, and third graders studying solfège and music notation. Their angelic voices seemed in perfect harmony with the enraptured faces of Mary and Jesus—depicted in gold-stained relief—looking down on the cursed shadows walking in and out of Teachers' Headquarters. I was all alone, with the key to the colonel's classroom and a rucksack packed with grenades and Kalashnikovs.

"Alexander!" I shouted, noticing a shadow at the end of the east-wing corridor. Alexander emerged in the neon light and hurried my way, a finger pressed over his lips.

"Keep it down, you bastard, I almost got cornered by Bankoff and the Owl. Where is the lousing gnome?" I showed him the key and the rucksack and told him about my mission. He loved it. I could see in his eyes, as he leaned over the open window to smoke a cigarette, the merciless flames of the Erinyes. I left him in the colonel's room and went to look for one more student willing to come with me to the central police station.

On the ground floor I ran into Ladybug, who was returning from the buffet in the basement with a cup of mint tea. Beaming, she took me by the elbow and dragged me toward the double-door entrance to Chamber Hall No. 1. She didn't want to hear anything about colonels, rucksacks with ammunition, and a trip to the police station. "You are all mine now," she said, unlocking the doors and then climbing onstage to unlock the Steinway. The whiff of her perfume hung about long after she had taken a seat in the center of the right rows of chairs. "Well?" I began with a series of technical exercises, then a few Chopin preludes, and then proceeded with the first scherzo. She interrupted me immediately, clapping.

"It all sounds like a big muddle over here. I want to hear it without the right pedal." I started again, without any pedal, and put in all my strength to make the triplets tight and crisp, like a hundred marbles bouncing on the terrazzo floor out in the foyer. This time she stopped me by stomping her high heels. "You're doing your crazy thing with the fingering again. Just find the best position and stick to it. God! I don't even know how you manage to play a whole piece without messing it up!"

She was right. I'd always had a hard time choosing a single set of fingerings for each piece. It all had to do with my insane mode of sight-reading. Since I detested the idea of limping and crawling through the foreign lands of a new repertoire, I had developed the unfortunate habit of sight-reading in real tempo, very much in the manner of a blind man who runs wildly down the street until he collides with a passerby or a tree, or is run over by a truck. I would take a short passage and play it as fast as I could, changing the fingering haphazardly and starting over whenever I got stuck and ran out of available fingers. By the time I learned a piece well, I had access to at least three or four sets of fingerings, which added a degree of unpredictability to my playing because I could never really know for certain how my fingers would fall when I walked onstage and faced the grand piano. Consequently, my performances varied—albeit subtly—depending on my mood, my will, my passion, the height of the piano bench, the distance between my torso and the keyboard, the yield of the damper pedal, or even the lighting. Ladybug didn't interrupt me after that. She sat quietly, invisibly, holding her breath. I banged out a few études, keeping my wrists tension-free and placing my entire weight on the tips of my fingers, then slowed down on the preludes and finished with the second ballad. The bell sounded. I ran upstairs. Maybe I still had time to fulfill my mission and deliver the rucksack to the police station before the beginning of next period. But the door to the colonel's classroom was locked. I knocked and waited.

"Password!" It was the voice of Nikolai D., the son of the choirmaster.

"It's me," I shouted, keeping an eye on the teachers that had started pouring into the third floor's west-wing corridor from every nook and crevice in the building, like cockroaches on the run. The door opened just a crack and Nikolai D. quickly pulled me in. He was holding a Kalashnikov and had a lighted cigarette between his teeth and three grenades hanging from his belt. Lined up against the blackboard, with their hands up, were Piggy, Ilarionova, and Redhorse, the queens of literature, Russian, and geography, respectively. Alexander was sitting in the back, smoking as well, with his feet propped up over the desk and an assault rifle in his lap.

"Everything's going according to plan," said Alexander. "We're going to shoot the bitches and go snatch three more teachers. Sergeant, give our comrade his AK, so he doesn't feel left out. I think we're going to start with Piggy. Aim for the knees." Nikolai D. handed me a rifle and bent over Alexander's head, as if to receive instructions.

"Please!" pleaded Piggy with a raspy voice. It was strange how calm the teachers seemed. They were pale, for certain, but they weren't crying or panting. If you told them to live, they would live; if you told them to die, they would die. They awaited our orders. The truth was, they were too automatized to realize that this was all a prank. The grenades used in our military conduct and preparation class were hollowed out, while each of the Kalashnikovs had a hole drilled in the lower end of its barrel, rendering it completely useless for combat. Still, I was scared to death. Suddenly the thought of practicing on the Steinway, in Ladybug's presence, seemed incredibly inviting. This would absolutely be the end of my career. Once the prank was over and the queens had turned us in, we'd never be allowed into the school again. We'd all be sent to a correctional camp.

I should've stayed in Chamber Hall No. 1 until the evening. I should've performed for Ladybug until my wrists had become numb. I could've just sat there, going through my long list of problematic passages and studying the hypnotic ceiling fresco of collapsing squares. Instead, now I was holding an assault rifle and listening to someone terrorize Chopin's "Heroique" polonaise in the next room. Soon the bell would ring again and the Owl would start looking for her missing teachers, her little docile chickens who stared thankfully at the barrel of my Kalashnikov. There will never be peace on this earth as long as there are people programmed to follow orders and accept authority. Look at them! They wanted to get killed, I swear. And yet, if our positions were reversed, they would've happily hanged all three of us, in front of the whole school. The geography teacher, with her heavy brass ring that she used to inflict extra pain when punching her least favorite students on the head, from behind, so they wouldn't expect it; the Russian teacher, who lectured us about the superiority of the Russian mind; the literature greaseball who had famously exclaimed that the school principal doesn't like blood on the sidewalk. (The blood she had referred to had actually been red ink that Iskander, whose father had been from Mozambique, had spilled around his head as he'd lain prostrate on the sidewalk after sneaking unnoticed out of Piggy's class, on the fourth floor, with the intention to create the illusion that he'd jumped out the window. He had been kicked out shortly after the incident, never to be heard from again.)

I released the magazine and then, after pretending to admire its contents, snapped it back onto the rifle. Would I have killed the witches if the magazine had been full and my Kalashnikov was capable of firing live ammunition? Of course not. The Kalashnikov was *their* weapon, a stygian artifact that they had brought into this world along with their ideologies and aesthetic deformity.

"I'm going to blow their brains out!" Alexander bellowed suddenly, jumping off his seat and charging toward the teachers like a maniac, his hair sticking straight up and strings of sweat running down his swollen face. Nikolai D. and I intercepted him halfway and pushed the barrel of his rifle away from the teachers' heads. "I want to see them spouting blood like fucking watering cans! Communism is inevitable! In the name of the bearded German midget and the red pentacle, let me break their necks!"

If one thing was certain, it was that Alexander was born to be an opera singer. He expended more energy in just a few seconds than most people did in a year. He just needed a stage. Ilarionova's chin was trembling. Piggy and the geography queen seemed dizzy and out of breath. Anger and passion are contagious. Even Nikolai D. had started acting panicky.

"*Malchiki!*" Ilarionova beseeched us. "*Malchiki*, let us be humans, just this time!" Alexander burst out in Mephistophelian laughter. What was this purple-haired matryoshka talking about in her quacking voice, her washed-out blue eyes darting frantically behind her enormous glasses? Was she going to invoke Tolstoy's humanism or Chekhov's idealism? *Human—that sounds dignified!* If you were a human, that is. And we weren't all humans. Humans can't kill and lie and follow orders, and we had killed, and lied and followed orders, and would kill again, because we were Tartarean mutts—part shadows, part automatons, with a splash of the Erinyes and maybe one tiny drop of human conscience, just enough to make us crave the light.

The bell sounded. Fourth period had begun. The colonel or the janitor might walk in at any moment. There always comes a time when one has to choose between saving his skin or letting himself be swept away by the wild currents. I, personally, was a firm believer in fleeing. The key was in the door. Perhaps I could tell Alexander that I was going to check if someone was looking for us. I knew he would never believe me. Then again, he never asked me whether I wanted to take part in his suicidal prank. And in the end, it was I who would be facing the great tormentors. Alexander and Nikolai, who were connected, would most likely walk away free. Alexander was prancing about the room with his Kalashnikov under his arm and a cigarette in his mouth, a restless Che Guevara searching for a way to end his poetic constipation. But it's easy to act out when you know that your daddy is going to save your ass, I thought. It always comes to that—my daddy versus your daddy—and I was smart enough at least to know I didn't stand a chance. If I walked away now, I could tell the Owl that I had taken part in Alexander's prank against my will.

Isn't that the most fundamental excuse? Everyone acts against their will, and hence the human tribe escapes culpability. Would I betray Alexander to save my piano career? I was pathetic, the whole thing was pathetic, and the kid in the next room was definitely getting on my nerves. He needed to tighten those tremolos in the left hand and stop slowing down dramatically before the transposition of the main theme. This wasn't some trashy chanson!

If it had been me on the piano, and Ladybug had been sitting beside me, she would've slapped me on the face with the back of her hand and told me to stop faking it. This was how she'd taught me to come out in the open and show my face, even if my face turned out to be that of a crying clown. Before you can play even a simple scale, you need to have temperament. And temperament isn't learned or acquired; temperament is the salt from the past before this past, the quality that separates the awake from the sleeping.

That's the tragedy of classical music: everyone *aspires* to be temperamental. Everyone except Vadim. You'd never see him performing at Carnegie Hall. In time, his temperament would ruin all his chances of playing in front of a large audience. *Mi-re-do-si, mi-re-do-si,* the incendiary bass ostinato in the middle of the polonaise—a barrage of sinking left-hand octaves with a flare of insanity—if played correctly, with the right proportion of hunger, vindictiveness, and imperturbability, can easily bring down a building or a bridge. Ah, the student next door had ruined it. I threw my Kalashnikov on the floor and walked out of the room.

Let them finish what they'd started. I had no time for pranks. I was in so much trouble already, I didn't need to help the committee expel me. What would I tell Ladybug when she found out that I had taken the three teachers hostage and threatened to kill them? She had just pleaded with me to stay away from Alexander and focus on the upcoming Chopin competition in November, and the audition for the big Chopin competition at the end of next year. What pained me, more than the thought of my own failure, was the image of Ladybug looking at me with reproach and profound disappointment. She believed in me as if I were some kind of messiah or savior who could make the crippled walk and the blind see. How much better it would've been to be nobody, never in danger of disappointing anyone. Failure would've been mine alone to savor.

I walked past room 35, where the poor bastard was abusing the polonaise, and knocked on the door of the neighboring room, 36. As I had hoped, the room was empty and the piano was positioned against the wall of room 35. I took the chair from the teacher's desk and sat at the piano, a mahogany Petrof with brand-new keys, hammers, and dampers; the piano tuner must have done some serious work on it since the last time I was here. I started the polonaise quite a bit faster than I should've; in fact, I was flying over the keys at an immense speed long before I had even reached the theme, steamrolling through the opening scales, drilling the squiggly repetitions into the piano frame, delivering each placeholder chord like a heart attack. "Start loud and fast and you won't have anywhere to go," the shriveled piano demagogues would say to their students time and again. Well, it was bullshit. There was always somewhere to go. Chopin's singular and unbroken phrases would lead you along.

How I detested those players who waited until the second or even third appearance of the main theme before they began drawing some sound out of the piano! How many recordings, how many live performances began with some inaudible mumbling, as if the piano player had been forcefully sedated beforehand.

Three-four was the rhythm of knowledge, of possibility and transcendence. Two-four and four-four represented the binary world where life was set against death, truth against illusion, beginning against end. But in three-four there was the extra beat, a door, a force, that allowed you to go beyond the twofold prison . . . and three . . . At the end of the middle section with the furious octaves in the left hand, one unexpectedly came to a musky cobbled street where a blind man stood under a net of intersecting clotheslines and played a barrel organ, sweetly, sedately, the notes falling like bright silver splinters into the dark spaces between the buildings. Chopin was a master of creating melodies that tied time's loose ends and continued further, and further, in a circle. If pieces written in three-four sometimes sounded playful and dancelike, it was because breathing in that third beat brought a sense of freedom; one might even say that it opened the possibility for eternal life.

It was over. Complete silence. The student next door must have stopped playing as soon as I'd begun. I closed the lid and tiptoed to the door. If my intuition was correct, my rival would be standing just outside my room, his ear pressed against the wooden frame. I opened the door suddenly, and . . . There he was, a twelfth grader with stubby fingers and the posture of a drunken *kolkhoznik* who had just jumped off a tractor. It felt good to see him humbled. Each small victory over mediocrity counts.

Everything was in its place—bookcase weighed down by trophies, cherrywood desk, bronze bust of Leonid Brezhnev, crystal triangle, pen holder commemorating the Eleventh Congress of the Party, Georgi D. staring down from the wall, and the Owl in her chair, vulturine hands locked together in her lap. It occurred to me that I had never seen the bird dial her beige apparatchik telephone before. Did the line even work, or was it a prop for the show?

"Number fourteen, the pianist . . . I'm curious to find out what you thought when you heard your name called out on the radio. Did you think I was taking you out of music theory class to give you a present? Do you think you deserve a present? For exemplary behavior? For contributing to our society? For leading your fellow students in the right direction? Or do you feel like a parasite who's gotten a free ride for too long? Arrogant bourgeois brat! Do you really think I'll let you get away with this?"

The Owl rose to her feet and leaned over her desk, ready to swallow me. I wasn't planning to say anything. I knew the game. I was just going to sit there and watch her play the role of the Gorgon Medusa. Granted, she was creepy and poisonous, but she was still only a bird.

"Ah, you probably think I don't know about your sweetheart, Irina, the violinist, and how she is all enamored of you, the two of you holding hands, kissing in the corridors, doesn't that make a great love story? Two gifted musicians . . . Then the boy is kicked out of school and the girl finds someone else right away; with the amount of sex that goes on in this wretched school, she won't be bored even for a day. No? You think she won't forget about you, the onetime wunderkind who ended up in the gutter, disgraced and cast out of society forever? I know. You think that the Owl is just ranting, that she isn't going to use her power. It was you who gave me that apt nickname, wasn't it? Oh, I don't mind it. Let me tell you a few things about owls. Yes, they are nocturnal birds of prey. But what's truly beautiful about them is that they swallow their prey whole—rats, little squirmy nothings—and then they spit their remains in the form of dry, compact balls. I'm going to rid the school of rats like you. I'm going to crush you and turn you to dust. And I really hope you had fun with your friends, playing games and pointing Kalashnikovs at the very teachers who have raised you. Because from now on, you'll be living in hell. You've shown your true nature, and you've surprised no one. We've known all along that, one day, you'll become an enemy of the state. One day, hopefully, you'll be shot. But today, you're in my hands. Your friend, Nikolai, I've already dealt with him. He'll be arriving shortly at the appropriate institution. You'll be following him soon, but not today. I might keep you around for a few more weeks, or maybe just a few more days, to make sure you really feel the sting. I might even let you give another concert. But you have to kiss the bust of Leonid Brezhnev and say thank you. I think that would please me. Come on. Let's see how tough you are."

I stood up and leaned over the desk to kiss the midget's bronze skull. Having transferred my entire weight onto my hands, I was in no position to defend myself from the Owl's left uppercut, which landed on my temple and sent me flying back into the chair. A solid punch, too. Who would've ever thought the wretched bitch knew how to throw punches?

"You forgot to say thank you."

"Thank you," I said and smiled at her. I should've strangled her a long time ago.

"Get out."

The Owl didn't look up at me as I got up and edged toward the door.

She was writing manically in her calendar, trying to fend off the violent tics passing through her body like electric shocks. The bird was being eaten by her own poison.

It was fall, the sidewalks covered with shiny ripe chestnuts, and Erebus, the seductive guardian, was taking too long to arrive. I kept looking west, expecting to see the leaden birds carrying the torch of the End, a torch radiating soft neon light, just like in my dreams, when everything stops—the birds stop mid-flight, the sky stops spinning, memory stops, and, as I lie on the ground drowning in light, I think that we deserved it. We deserved it, and they deserved it, too. I walked down the boulevard, past the chess club, the theater, Levski Monument, the *pirozhki* stand. I was starving. I lit a cigarette and continued walking downhill in the direction of Stochna Gara, staring at the sleazy apparatchiks in gray suits and the old ladies with purple hair and the *otlichniks* returning home to their mommies, and the promiscuous girls who lived to acquire, and the male apes missing half their chromosomes, and the professorial types and the bootlickers and the liars . . . I stared at them with all the bitterness I had stored inside. "You can't hate, you can only love," Ladybug had told me once, holding my hand as she often did, like a girlfriend. But I wanted to hate, I wanted to hate them all, to curse them with my discontent, to condemn them, to incinerate them with my eyes. I always imagined that my eyes were red and on fire but in the mirror they appeared green, light green in the sunlight, hazel-green at night. I took the first street on the right and headed toward Ladybug's house, mechanically, just as I had done since I was seven and started taking the tram across town by myself, carrying the heavy, cloth-bound book of Mozart's complete sonatas, printed by Edition Peters, in my backpack. My feet knew only a few routes—to the music school, to Ladybug's house, to the park by Seven Saints Church, to my parents' apartment.

Ladybug's house was at least a hundred years old, with two arch-shaped windows jutting over the street and a slanted roof covered with clay tiles of various types and sizes that seemed piled up randomly on top of one another by a tornado or some other natural force. In many places the original yellow paint of the stucco walls had chipped in large blocks together with the plaster, exposing the red-and-orange bricks underneath. Inside, an enclosed wooden staircase lead to the second floor, where the three giant fairies lived. I never figured out what was on the ground floor. Was there a trap door through which Ladybug and her older sister descended to some kind of cellar where they kept the blood they'd drained from their victims? There was no denying it, Ladybug's sister was a *samodiva* who flew over the streets of Sofia at night, naked beneath a transparent white gown, her blond hair flapping in the wind, a pack of Hecate's dogs at her feet, in search of sweet-blooded boys she could bring home. The Old Lady would never refuse a liver or a healthy heart.

I stood under the windows expecting to hear the sound of the ancient but well-kept Bösendorfer in the bedroom or the decomposing Steingraeber & Söhne, with its gelatinous, yellow-tinted sound, in the guest room. I craved the notes of something painfully familiar, like Mozart's Sonata no. 5 in G or the "Dürnitz" Sonata no. 6 in D, or, even better, the no. 8 in A Minor. As long as there was someone playing the Allegro Maestoso from the eighth sonata on a piano somewhere, the world would never end. That was absolutely certain. The opening theme of the Allegro Maestoso and its variations were simply more important, more fundamental than the vagaries of time and all the laws that governed the physical world. The fatalistic cadences! The accelerated pulse of the chords in the left hand, the way the eighth notes doubled into sixteenths and passed from the right hand into the left like thunder, the long buildup in the transition with timpani and basses and snare drums charging in the background; it was pure rock'n'roll, the best ever made.

I opened the rickety wooden gate, attached to the fence with two rusty wires, and proceeded down the tiled path to the brown double door with a golden handle and oval panels of veined glass. I could smell all the smells contained in the house from here—the black cabinets, the dusty Austrian porcelain dishes and tea sets, the white screen unfolded along the wall next to the Bösendorfer, the carpets coated with cat and dog hair, the wooden stove in the bedroom, the peeling wallpaper, the parquet, the stale air inside Bach's fugues, the rose petals floating in Mozart's sonatas, the heavy curtains covering the windows of Beethoven's private quarters. I could even smell the rain-soaked dirt and dead flowers on Chopin's grave and the air inside St. Thomas church in Leipzig.

But the three giant fairies weren't home. Or Ladybug and the Old Lady were out, and the blond *samodiva* didn't want to let me in. She was jealous of me, it was very obvious. I was the third and most loved child in the family and she had to put up with my two- and three-hour lessons, my perennial problems at school, my recitals, my drinking, my paranoias and idiosyncrasies, my incessant appetite for attention.

Could Ladybug protect me now, could she stop the storm, could she sacrifice herself for me? Or would she succumb to the power of the Owl and return home glossy-eyed and stiff, repeating again and again that she wasn't my teacher and I wasn't her student? Would she forget about me? I wouldn't put it past her. In time, I would forget about her, too. Perhaps. Tomorrow, or next week, after they announced my expulsion, I would be no one. Again. But I didn't remember a time when I had been no one, a kid without a gift and a grand mission, just passing through life like a shadow. A gift! I didn't have any gifts, I was just another pretentious mediocre brat, like all the others. I only thought I was different, wanted to prove I was different. They'd made me believe I carried the light within me. And now I was groping in the dark. It was rather cruel.

I should find a way to get in the house, I thought, perhaps through the back door, so that when they returned they would find me playing the "Heroique," taking pleasure in the way the leaded keys of the

Bösendorfer resisted my fingers and fought with me over every phrase and scale. I would have quite a workout. But the back door was locked as well and there was a terrible smell coming from a large tin can in the corner of the backyard. I approached it, remembering what the Old Lady had said last Sunday, when Ladybug had walked into the guest room where I was practicing and announced that Lucy, her half-adopted street cat, had given birth to five kittens. "I will drown them while they are blind, before they can miss the world," the Old Lady had declared. She had never understood the Romantics.

What are you going to play on Thursday?" I asked her as we sat down on the piano bench to catch our breath. I was still wearing my white button-up shirt and uniform jacket, and Stephanie her school dress. Our underwear, shoes, and socks were scattered all over the floor of the slanted attic room. My pants had fallen behind the piano, a respectable black Blüthner upright.

"Beethoven's twenty-third in F minor," she said, placing her thin, ghostly white hands over her crotch. Her fingers were so long and thin, they gave her hands the appearance of two giant spiders. Something about the way she'd turned her head before she answered—a tic of haughtiness and smugness—made me burst out laughing. In fact, I fell off the bench. How the hell was Stephanie going to play the "Appassionata," the cruelest, most diabolical sonata of all? And, on top of everything, she thought she had the temperament for it! I had nothing against blonds. But come on! If Irina learned to play the piano, she could play the twenty-third. Vadim had played it in seventh grade, and he'd played it the only way one should—by letting himself be possessed by the devil. I'll never forget his performance in Chamber Hall No. 1 on that windy, September night filled with static electricity, when Vadim had walked onstage with bloodshot eyes and, refusing to acknowledge the audience even with a nod, had unloaded the scales and the arpeggios and the chords and the ostinati and the cadences and the devastating rests—those Beethoven rests!—unleashing a hurricane that had swooped us up and transported us to a wilderness at the periphery of Tartarus, where the music seemed to come from every direction and yet had but one source. Outside the school, tongues of light had passed through the clouds and, at one point, right in the middle of the Allegro ma non troppo—which, I swear, he took in less than six minutes, perhaps even five, without necessarily giving the impression that he was speeding; he was too big, too powerful of a hurricane to be concerned with breaking speeding records; he was just naturally faster than anything human—the huge crystal chandelier above the Steinway had flickered menacingly and briefly gone out, prompting the Old Lady, sitting in the first row between her daughters, to cry out in her gravelly bass voice, *"Light!"* It was a riot.

Naturally, Stephanie was offended. I calmed her down, and even had the indecency to beg her to play a little bit of the first section for me. I guess she liked me a lot, because she agreed without much fuss. But the poor girl didn't have an original thought in her head. Every phrase, every bar had been prepared and rehearsed to the point where, rather than communicating, she was just telegraphing her teacher's instructions. Even her breathing had been programmed beforehand to ensure maximum automatism. It was quite obvious to me, now that I was sitting next to her on the bench and watching her work her determined little fingers, that dating another piano player had been a horrible idea, the well-tempered fucking sessions notwithstanding. What was I supposed to say to her when she was done playing? And how could I ever tell her to stop without hurting her professional pride? If she wasn't biting her lower lip on the faster passages and her school dress wasn't unbuttoned, revealing her breasts and navel, I would've been bored out of my mind.

"A truly cruel sonata," I said as she turned her head toward me, a cute duckling with long eyelashes seeking approval.

"Why? I haven't had a hard time getting it tight and crisp." She put her hands back on the keyboard and played the opening bars of the Allegro ma non troppo as fast as she could.

"I didn't mean that it's technically challenging. If you have ten fingers you can play everything. You might even do fine with nine."

"Then what's cruel about it? Is it the mood?"

The mood! She was going to kill me. Even if her mother's screeching voice hadn't rung across the attic floor at that moment, I still wouldn't have answered her question. I should never have said anything about music. We should've used the old Blüthner upright, with its opportune height, strictly for fucking.

"Stephanie!" Her mother was right outside our room, pushing frantically on the door handle. The door, of course, was locked from the inside. I had borrowed the key from the doorman in exchange for five cigarettes. "Stephanie!" *Bang-bang-bang-bang*. "If you are inside with that punk, I swear I'm going to kill you!" The banging stopped and we heard footsteps receding down the corridor. Her mother appeared to have given up.

"How did she know which room you're in?" I asked Stephanie as I walked calmly across the room to retrieve my underwear. I thought that the storm had passed and we were safe. How mistaken I was! You should always expect everything from everyone.

"I told her," Stephanie said remorsefully. "I called her from the pay phone downstairs."

"Why on earth would you do that? Don't you know there are things you shouldn't tell your parents?"

That's exactly when the door fell on the floor, together with the hinges, and Stephanie's mom entered the room, armed with a giant, four-legged wooden coatrack, which she had probably found in one of the practice rooms on the fourth floor. Still holding my underwear in my hands, I ran behind the piano to get my pants, leaped to the right to grab one shoe, bent over to get the other . . . and lost tempo. Stephanie's mom came from behind and, shouting "I am not impressed!," dropped the coatrack on my back with such force that I collapsed facedown on the floor. It's a miracle she didn't break my spine. *I am not impressed!* At least she had a sense of humor. And to think that Stephanie's mother had once been a famous ballerina! What did they teach them at the ballet school? *The Nutcracker?* She must've doubled on the weekends as a Soviet shot-putter, hence the muscles and the mustache.

But there was no time to think. I scooped up all the scores lying on the floor into my bag, crawled out into the corridor, and ran for it. I wished I could save Stephanie but, under the circumstances, I couldn't do much, short of punching her beastly mother in the face. Halfway down the spiral staircase I bumped into Maria, the third-floor janitor. It was to be expected. She had heard the banging and the screaming. It was nine o'clock in the evening, after all. The school was almost empty. I was actually glad to see her. Perhaps she could save Stephanie from a painful death. I pointed to the source of the commotion and pushed her upstairs. What? You haven't seen naked boys before? I put my pants on and hid behind her back because, at that moment, Stephanie's mother appeared at the top of the stairs shouting, "Whore! Dirty juvenile whore! If you get pregnant, I will kill your baby with my own hands!"

I found the whole scene rather arousing. The former ballerina dragging her half-naked daughter down the stairs by the hair, and Stephanie's hair was really long and straight, like a rope. That's the kind of mother you need if you want to become a professional concert pianist, I thought. Forget about talent and temperament. You need a bodyguard, someone who can wipe out your entire competition with a coatrack.

The "Appassionata" was a labyrinth where Beethoven had been imprisoned for hundreds of years. The hammers went up and down, the puppets marched onward, and Beethoven's angry shouting, coming from somewhere deep underground, was instantly transformed into stylized passion. What's cruel about the piece? Every gem, every vision of beauty invariably turned out to have been essentially flawed, eaten through by worms, and condemned to the world of shadows. The short, sonorous theme that ran through the first movement, at times in a major key, at times in minor, appeared soothing only on first hearing. It was actually a song of eternal damnation, masquerading as a harbinger of victory, with a subtle pull that breathed life into the old and long-forgotten temptations. But Vadim hadn't fallen for it. He'd seen it perfectly, back in seventh grade, when Ladybug had interrupted him during a rehearsal in Chamber Hall No. 1. "Let us hear it!" she had said with a clenched fist. *"Do-mi la do-la sol si-sol la mi,* savor it, it's a new day and you have won!" "You're wrong," Vadim had responded, quietly, terminally, with a conviction that made him sound like an old man even at twelve. "It's a new day. And *they* have won, again."

It's dark, demonic stuff, the kind that can warp your brain forever. That was Beethoven's genius—he showed you the rivers, the asphodel fields, and the gates of Hades without ever letting you hope for escape. It was what it was. It would never change. Even the Andante con molto, with its vast, sweetly scented gardens and the white sunbeam coming in through the skylight, never, not for a second, allowed you to dream of a different world. Was that wisdom, or the final verdict of a deaf man? Regardless, it was cruel. And the Old Lady, in the front row, had shouted, *"Bravo!"* and had stood up to demand that Vadim play again, a prelude, an étude, anything. The blond *samodiva,* sitting as usual on her mother's left-hand side, had offered her a handkerchief. The Old Lady had never cried at a concert before. She had clearly seen something beyond the music. There are two kinds of grief: the grief of knowing, and the grief of forgetting. Most people were spared the former, the grief that precedes a loss or a tragic event that lies in the distant future. But the Old Lady had known.

I ran downstairs, the Allegro ma non troppo blowing at my back and the syncopated *si-Fa-fa, fa-Sol-sol, sol-Fa-fa, fa do re mi, re* ringing across the stairwell like a verdict that set the cogwheels of fate in motion and spelled the names of the future dead. I wasn't afraid. All I had to do was hand the key back to the doorman and disappear into the night. Stephanie's mother could scream all she wanted. It wasn't my fault that her daughter had reached maturity with her ass glued to the piano bench and her head stuffed full of cotton, like a doll. I could see them coming down the stairs two floors above me. Stephanie had reclaimed her hair and now the former ballerina was chasing after her, trying to slap her on the face. There. What a slap! The girl tripped and fell on the floor. Should I interfere at this point? No, certainly not. Stephanie and her mother deserved each other. They would make up and turn against me. That was how things worked. Stephanie was docile and automatized: she needed her mother as much as her mother needed her. I was just someone who helped her get a breath of fresh air after she was done playing the piano. Besides, this was the good stuff: family feuds, passion, punches, burning words—they should both thank me, actually. At the end of the day, Stephanie might start playing less like a robot, at least for a short while.

"Didn't you realize that he is the devil who's come to drink your blood?" The echo of the fat ballerina's paroxysmal shouting resounded through the empty school like a prehomicidal high-pitched recitative. The orchestra would come in any second, first the basses, in a hurried ascending sixteenth-note scale, then the cellos, bassoons, and clarinets, and finally the violins, oboes, trumpets, tubas, French horns, and all the rest. There she was, rolling down the stairs like a cannonball, pulling Stephanie violently by the arm. Me—the devil! It was perhaps the best compliment I'd ever gotten. Drink her blood I certainly would have, given the opportunity.

My back didn't hurt that badly. It could've been much worse, considering the weight of the coatrack and the force with which she'd swung it. The doorman, standing by the entrance, winked at me knowingly and withdrew into his cabin. The old Commie was all right. He let me keep the attic room key for the night. He probably knew that I had nowhere to go. Thank God I had managed to save some money for a greasy slice of *banitsa* with feta cheese, at around seven that evening, before Stephanie and I had absconded to the attic. Now I just needed an espresso and another pack of cigarettes. Smoking on the external staircase of the long and narrow two-story building opposite the music school, where most violinists and cellists went for their private lessons, I watched Stephanie and her mom walk around the schoolyard and exit onto the street. Wouldn't it have been better if we had all been friends? We would've gone back to Stephanie's apartment to take showers and have tea, and in the morning we would've woken up really early, at five or six, and Stephanie would've gone to school—because she was in ninth grade and went to school in the morning, and I would've stayed in the apartment with her mom, and we would've had breakfast and discussed *Heart of a Dog,* and then I would've practiced until it was time for me to go to school. But it was impossible. The ballerina wanted me dead and I couldn't stand her either. Last week I had bumped into her on the street, and she had greeted me with a huge smile. She had thought the Kalashnikov incident would get me kicked out of school for sure. It was so easy to see inside her monochrome reptilian imagination—the schadenfreude, the thirst for blood, the acidic vision of my demise and Stephanie's return to the world of ten-hour practice sessions and total obedience. Oh, well.

True, it was rather shocking that Alexander could pull such titanic connections and have the whole incident dead and buried in less then twenty-four hours. Well, not exactly buried. Nikolai D. had been expelled and sent to a correctional school. The colonel, for his part, had gotten a dressing-down. Alexander and I had escaped the debacle with only a reprimand. Was it fair? Of course it wasn't. It was an evil, dastardly thing of Alexander to put the blame on our friend and have his dad make some calls to people in high places. But I couldn't feel too bad about it. Someone had to go down. I was just glad it wasn't me this time.

It was ten o'clock in the evening. Where was I supposed to go? I couldn't go to my parents' apartment. Not tonight. I didn't have the energy to spend the entire night fighting—me, alone, against the two of them—only to return to school in the morning to drool on my desk and sleepwalk through Chopin's études. My parents were too damaged to see beyond their small world of working hours and hierarchical posturing. My parents were puppets of the first order, their sole purpose in life to ensure that I, too, grew up respecting the pull of the strings. That was their idea of morality. Never mind who was pulling the strings, so long as they were all intact and securely attached to my limbs, my senses, my very soul. My parents' greatest nightmare was that I'd cut all the strings one day and float up into the open Cosmos, in spite of my leaden feet, my wooden heart, and my porcelain eyes, in contravention of every Euclidean law.

But what was I going to do then? The one thing, of course. When you can't play even one more note, when your head is so overloaded with sounds that you feel dizzy and begin to crave silence, just a moment of quiet to regain your footing; when you just can't take another sonata, another étude, another judgment, another cadence, another diminished chord and resolution, another arpeggio, scale, tremolo, or repetitive accompaniment; when the thought of keeping rhythm for even a single bar or injecting another dose of burning venom into your wrists makes you want to throw up and crawl into a dark, soundproof cellar and sleep, dreamlessly, for a long, long time, then you have no other choice but to rush back to the piano and start playing again, as if you've never played before.

"Her mother . . . seemed a bit out of control," the doorman said, ironing his comb-over with the palm of his hand. I ran upstairs, taking two or three steps at a time and sliding across each landing as if I were on roller skates: I'd suddenly remembered an urgent appointment with a certain coachman sent by Count Ferdinand Ernst Gabriel von Waldstein from Vienna to take me across the mountains, the plains, and the rivers, to a distant land where the motorcar and the radio hadn't yet been invented, where people lived quietly, without grand ideas and stygian symbols adorning their streets and graves. But how was it possible, one might object, for an arrogant bastard like me to hop onto a two-horse carriage, stationed in the attic of the Sofia Music School for the Gifted, and then tear into the night, amid much hoof-beating and dust-throwing, exiting presumably through the narrow skylight, without even requesting written permission from the local authorities? Well, it was very simple. All I had to do, really, was sit facing the desecrated old Blüthner (the things the poor upright had seen!), open

Stephanie's Beethoven sonatas—which I had inadvertently picked up during my hastily arranged departure earlier in the evening—to page 117, and then begin reading Sonata no. 21 in C, "Waldstein," in real tempo, with a greedy damper pedal and an acute sense of the metaphysical nature of each offbeat. Such a pity how few people knew about these back roads that passed through the attic and continued north, across the Danube and into the valleys of Transylvania. Here was the coachman, waiting eagerly to hear the feisty ticking of the shiny black C major chords at the opening of the Allegro con brio— this was the sound of movement, of speeding incognito down ancient dirt roads flanked on both sides by endless rows of poplars, of linden, of birches and fruit trees. What style, riding in the Waldstein carriage, what luxury! The bench was upholstered in ruby-colored leather, the walls and the ceiling pressed in dark golden leaf, the windows set in blue and yellow stained-glass frames. The pulse of the chords collided with the clapping of the horseshoes, the scenery changed with the chord progression. C moved up to D and down to G. We passed a sleepy village, a pond, an abandoned well. B flat moved up to C and then down to F. We plunged into a musty declivity, made a sharp turn, and entered a dark forest. Far away now were the demonically twisted trees in Doctors' Garden and far away the underground rivers carrying the nutrients of our warped reality. The farther we traveled, the less crooked the trees and their branches seemed. By the time we approached the gates of Count Waldstein's Bohemian estate, the trees had become solid and majestic, their humanlike hands reaching confidently for the sky.

Beethoven,
"Appassionata" Sonata no. 23 in F Minor, op. 57

October 14, 1988

I t seemed like just another Friday, when long recess began with a sweeping hurrah and everyone stormed out of their classrooms in a rush to get to the school's buffet, or the *pirozhki* stand at Levski Monument, or the *pushkom*. I waited for my classmates to leave room 59, on the fifth floor, so that I could talk to the Gnome, the history of music teacher, about fixing the C that I'd received on the Haydn exam the week before. The Gnome didn't seem in the mood to talk. He kept walking back and forth between his desk and the massive wooden cabinet in the corner of the room, where he kept his record player and his impressive collection of classical records.

"Concerning Haydn, is there a way . . ."

"No!" he interrupted me, wrapping the cord of one of the speakers around his hand. "There was a time to study for the exam, and you didn't. What am I supposed to do with you now? I said it in class so many times: *Learn the themes and you'll do fine.*"

"But the guy wrote a hundred and six symphonies! And they're all terribly boring, I'm afraid."

I was trying to get on the Gnome's better side. I knew for a fact that he wasn't very fond of Haydn either. But the Gnome didn't answer. He stopped putting his equipment away and froze, hands in the air. It was then I noticed that the school had suddenly fallen silent, save for the ominous voice of Comrade Negodnik, which echoed loudly in the stairwell.

I ran out of the classroom and pushed my way through the crowd of students and teachers who'd besieged the staircase. When I finally reached the banister and looked down, I saw Vadim walking slowly across the landing between the fourth and third floors, sliding his hand over the railing. The top three buttons of his white shirt were missing, while his Komsomol tie was hanging from the pocket of his uniform jacket. His eyes seemed incredibly dark, darker than charcoal. But he appeared to be smiling.

"People like you have no place in our school and our society!" Negodnik, the history teacher, was shouting after him. Vadim didn't turn around. He kept going, passing his terrified classmates, and the *otlichniks,* standing with their backs glued to the walls, and the math teacher, and the ear-training witches—*Look at him! A disgrace!* —and the brats, and the serfs, and the nymphs—*Don't be a stranger!*—and the piano instructors, who were all gleaming. Only Ladybug was missing.

"What the hell is going on?" I whispered to Alexander, who was leaning casually over the railing next to me, chewing gum.

"Can't you see? They gave him the boot."

Alexander's response filled me with contempt. I wanted to punch him in the face, push him down the stairs. I still hadn't gotten back at him for the Kalashnikov prank, and for his sleeping with Irina.

"You are a fucking coward," I hissed in his face. "You can stay here and enjoy the spectacle. I'm going to go with him."

"I wouldn't do that if I were you!" Alexander replied, amused. "You've got to choose sides."

I ran downstairs, shoving everyone out of my way. I couldn't let Vadim walk out of the building alone. He needed a friend to escort him to the door.

When I caught up with him on the second floor, he acknowledged me with a nod and held his hand over mine, as if he wanted to give me something. I opened my palm and he placed in it his silver band, which he always put in the corner of the keyboard before playing. It was his talisman. He never went onstage without it.

Irina joined us on the first floor, ready for a fight. But I knew that Vadim was too proud to fight them. Fighting was beneath him, as was begging. I just couldn't believe that he was really leaving. There wasn't a single pianist anywhere in the world who could play like Vadim. Why were they kicking him out, just a month into the school year? What crime had he committed? Unlike me, he'd always had good grades.

We passed through the swinging doors on the first floor, Vadim and I walking side by side, Irina following behind. Chamber Hall No. 1 was to our right, and Vadim turned around to take one last look at the massive mahogany doors whose intricate carvings—flowers rimmed by circles within larger circles within squares—mirrored the decoration of the concert hall's ceiling. How many times he and I had stared at these doors, waiting for our turn to go onstage! I always played last, so I listened to Vadim's performances glued to the mahogany doors, absorbing every note with my skin. And then I had to walk onstage and say something, even though Vadim had already said it all.

I saw now that the Hyena was standing in the entranceway, dressed in an apparatchik-gray suit, her hair clasped pedantically behind her ears, with a daybook in one hand and an espresso cup in the other. I swear she opened her mouth to say something evil, to give Vadim a final slap on the face, but she caught Irina's eyes and her tongue seemed to shrivel up. I loved Irina, what fire, that girl could have turned the puppets to ashes, incinerated their strings and wigs and porcelain eyes.

Was I delusional to think that Vadim, Irina, and I were the only people alive in the whole damn place? We could take on the town, we could torch the government Volgas with the pigs inside, we could storm into the mausoleum, bayonet the guards and burn the mummy—we wouldn't bury it, because, even buried, it would hold the curse. God! The smell of His rotten body was everywhere.

The three of us walked past the marble wall bearing the inscription *Opera Italiana Pro Oriente* (one of the few preserved testaments to the

Vatican's role in constructing the building before the war), past the round fountain with fish carved on the outside, and then through the metal gates. The street seemed to swing gently under our feet, caught in the webbed, late afternoon shadows of the trees. The school building, towering behind us, expanded and contracted, letting out explosions of ghastly and heavenly sounds, like a dragon who'd swallowed the National Symphony Orchestra.

"What happened, Vadim?" I said with tears in my eyes. "Why are they kicking you out?"

"It's all right," he replied, downplaying everything as he always did.

"Is it because of smoking?" Irina demanded. "Missing classes? Was it the Owl?"

Vadim nodded goodbye, then turned around and walked away.

"What about the piano?" I yelled after him. He slowed down but didn't stop.

"I will forget about it." There was a mysterious smile on his face as he looked back at me. Did he know something that I didn't? Had he discovered some secret that had liberated him from the burden of preparing for the future? Or was it simply that, for the first time in his life, he felt truly free, walking away from it all, from the cursed building, and the ghosts, and the catacombs of the ambitious, and the concerts, and the pursuit of perfection?

Irina and I didn't even make it to the attic of the building across from school. We did it standing up, behind the entrance door, and we did it *affretando* and *con forza,* unbuttoning and unzipping our uniforms and biting each other's nipples and staggering from wall to wall and getting caught in the spiderwebs and the hanging telephone cables and scratching our sides on the protruding metal mailboxes, and the whole time, as I listened to the rhythm of her breathing, I kept hearing in my head the voice of the obsessive baron, Hans von Bülow, who had stated in a footnote in the third movement of the "Appassionata," *as the great composer renders all art in thematic work and imitative coun-*

terpoint continually subservient to his aim in the increase of poetic feel-ing, the performer of his works should make this his rule: the more mixed and complicated the work, the more animated and dramatic the render-ing, and I also couldn't stop thinking of the baron's wife, Cosima—daughter of his piano teacher, Franz Liszt—who had ditched him for Wagner, the baron's hero. Ah, the good old days!

Then we smoked. Would I ever see Vadim again? He was hardly someone you could just call on the telephone or meet for a coffee. Too serious for that sort of thing. And what about Irina? What was she thinking as she sucked nervously on her cigarette and turned her head to blow the smoke away from my face?

"This was a public assassination," she said, staring at the framed printout of the city ordinance concerning living spaces, hung high up on the wall behind me. *No person shall make noise between 2 p.m. and 4 p.m., and between 9 p.m. and 7 a.m.,* the ordinance stipulated. *Cats shall be admitted after a unanimous vote of all householders.*

"We are next," I added gloomily.

"God, I just remembered," Irina said, irritated. "I have to go pick up my dry cleaning today. I hope that the wine stains on my concert shirt have come out. It's all your fault."

"Can I come with you?"

"Absolutely not!" Irina said and stubbed out her cigarette. "I have a concert tomorrow. I need to go home and practice."

"Come on, I'm not going to distract you, I promise!"

"Last time you said that, I woke up in the kitchen at your grand-mother's, and I was so drunk, even the day after, I had to miss school and my private lesson. Ugh, and the soup that your grandmother made for lunch—I swear there were boiled cockroaches floating in it. Plus, I'm going to see you Wednesday, at Igor's."

The door on the second floor opened and closed and the old lady—the midget's mother—started down the stairs, clanking her empty glass bottles. She wasn't surprised to see us smoking by the door.

"You are from the music school," she announced, setting her bag full of bottles on the ground. "Let me remember your faces! I will go straight to the principal and tell her what you're up to, shameless vermin! Feeling each other in my building! Is this what your mothers taught you? How many letters of complaint I've sent, called the police, too, and no one does anything! Shame on you! You tarnish the work of our wholesome boys and girls who have sacrificed themselves to bring about a brighter future!"

"Brighter future!" Irina giggled. "Fuck off and die, Communist cow."

That shut her up.

I pressed my ear against the vinyl-wrapped door to room 49 and listened. Grieg. How boring. I knocked twice and opened the door. Ladybug didn't notice me immediately. She was in the process of helping a young girl with a ponytail and thick glasses carry a long phrase to its logical conclusion. "Bring out the left hand," Ladybug said and began singing the hidden melody, all the while gesticulating like a conductor.

"May I speak with you?" I asked.

"Come in," Ladybug said, writing on the piano score with a pencil.

"In private."

I could see Ladybug didn't like the tone of my voice. She dropped the pencil and instructed the girl how to practice the section that they'd been working on.

"What is it?" she said, irritated, as she shut the door behind her.

"I was wondering if you'd heard anything about Vadim's expulsion."

"And?"

"And . . . I'd like to know what you know."

"He deserved what he got. As do you. You're about to get kicked out the door after that stupid Kalashnikov prank. I hope you're happy."

"But what did Vadim do?"

"Well, if you really care to know, he told Zimova, in her Russian literature class, that Mayakovsky is just another sleazy chauvinist without any talent."

"But he's right!"

"That's none of your business!" Ladybug yelled at me. "You're here to become musicians. Everything else is filler. Math, Russian, Communist theory—who cares! Just shut up and do your work. How hard can it be? Aren't you supposed to be in class right now?"

"I've already missed most of it. Can you ask your friend, the orchestration teacher, not to give me an absence? Just tell him that you needed me for a rehearsal . . . And can I have the key to room forty-eight? I need to get some practice."

"You can't blame me for what happened to Vadim," she said, grabbing my hand. "You don't understand."

"Of course I do," I shouted angrily and pulled my hand away. "You're all the same. Servile little bees."

"You really don't understand, my boy," Ladybug repeated, tears in her eyes, as I turned to go. "Look at me! No, look at me! I couldn't save you both. Understand? I had to choose."

J. S. Bach,
Sonata in B Minor, BWV 1014
Adagio, Allegro

October 19, 1988

Octyour is in the key of B minor, everyone knows that, except you two, for you are just a pair of receptacles filled with hormones, cigarette smoke, and knowledge, that meaningless fluff that humans regard so highly. . . . Or was it caviar and blini, with sour cream. . . . Anyway, that's neither here nor there . . ." Igor the Swan rolled up the sleeves of his sweater and began pacing up and down the stage of Chamber Hall No. 2, rubbing his hands and shooting nervous glances at Irina and me. He was getting warmed up.

"But B minor is red, an autumnal red with brown and mahogany overtones, and a stripe of white, an off-white, ashen, like the sun before winter, listen . . . the D and F sharp, that's what makes it bleed, and hence the red dye, you can't avoid cutting your fingers on that D and F sharp, on the C sharp, too . . . ah, it's inevitable and it hurts . . . yet you also have a B on the bottom, and a B is austere, a B makes the blood thicker, darker—but please go on, procreate, copulate, don't let me stop you, don't mind me at all, I'm just here to fail you in baroque music, the demons of joy! If I was twenty years younger and two hundred kilograms thinner, I would join in the orgy, I would hop from practice room to practice room, begging the girls to let me lick them . . . Quick, open the windows and give her a *la,* and a *re,* and a *sol,* hurry, we will be traveling to a faraway land, don't mind me at all, I'm just stretching, all these kilograms, where do they come from? I don't even eat anymore, it must be Wagner! Ha! I'm getting fat on augmented and diminished chords, on rich dramatic expressions and rapturous smells, there's no denying it, I just want to taste it with my tongue, not too much to ask. Thunder and lightning! Zeus, of all gods . . . Listen to the Nevski's church bell! The most beautifully apocalyptic sound there is, just one bell, struck once every ten—no—eleven seconds, but how it fills the ether, how it cuts through the bone marrow and separates the darkness from the light, and what light that is, cold and distant— Konstantin, move away, at once, let me see where it is on the piano, this is it, no, pretty close, you can't capture the overtones perfectly, that's given. There! First you hear a *la* in the fourth octave, then a *mi* overtone right below, and then a deathly *re diese* overtone in the third octave emerges like a sentence pronounced somewhere deep underground; and then—listen!—there is a belated *do* overtone in the fourth octave that isn't here to complete the A minor triad: it is the messenger of the beyond, pure, patient, uncompromising . . . it has come to lead the way. Beyond, there's nothing, and nothing is glorious and eternal. But we should get going, take positions, strip naked—well, that would be too good—one, two, from the Adagio, yes, and *adagio* doesn't mean that you're dead or that you have to asphyxiate your partner, not at all, breathe in, breathe out, take in the sounds, let them heal you, behold their completeness, their fullness, the secret about Bach is that every note he's put down is final, every note stands at the very end of time, it is as if he's written the closing movement of the Cosmos, in a way, he came after humanity, after the wars, after Schoenberg and the rest of the jerk-offs—five and six . . . breathe!"

And so we began. The statement of suppressed consternation in the left hand at the beginning of the Adagio—distant footsteps, a heavy metal gate shutting somewhere in some courtyard inhabited only by the silver wind—was answered by three descending thirds, each repeated twice, in the right hand: *sol sol-fa fa-mi mi*. This was the central motif, the nucleus of the whole piece, its code moving from bar to bar, at times undetected, at times disguised as a passing stranger, a sigh, a yearning, a cry, or a consolation. Irina's first note, an F sharp lasting ten eternally long beats, appeared magically in the ether, like a glow that had become perceptible only after Nyx had cast her shadow on the earth. Ten beats, and then some. Irina's tone was composed, naked, pervading, at times almost chilly, completely unlike the sleazy, wildly oscillating, vibrato-drenched howling of the other violinists at school.

Irina stood behind my right shoulder, but I could see her face reflected in the shiny fallboard, and she was smiling. It was funny how Igor the Swan had walked in on Irina and me wrestling on top of the grand in Chamber Hall No. 2, Irina's hand in my pants, as was customary in these lands before a scheduled performance of baroque music. Igor was right. Bach's compositions were a light that came to us from the end of time. Rather than a thing of the past, the Adagio was futuristic and surreal, the violin line seemed to defy all expectations, it lingered on the high notes and then escaped through a hidden door, emancipated of the harmonic traps and spheres of gravity gathering strength in the piano accompaniment. There was nothing baroque, nothing classical or formulaic, about this sonata. If you listened very carefully, you'd discover that the movement of simple harmonic forms like dominant chords and minor triads wasn't at all routine or given: the shape and colors of a G-minor triad, for example, were as miraculous as a blue-orange orb flashing in a starless night sky; a resolution into the tonic was as strange and inexplicable as a twelve-note melody. If you listened carefully, you could hear the fine line that separated chaos from order, darkness from light, oblivion from being. Spaces, spheres, doors, windows, courtyards overgrown with creeping vines, corridors and hallways, we walked slowly, hand in hand, like lovers bound by the vows of the perfect intervals, of fourths and fifths and octaves. Hours turned to days, heartbeats stretched infinitely; and in the empty space another, subtle pulse had become audible, the pulse that continued through the long sleep. I counted the stairs, Irina looked into the leaden sky; I stepped firmly, faithfully, scattering the autumn leaves piled up on the ground; Irina followed, gliding like a shadow. This is how Orpheus and Eurydice must have walked through Hades, on their way to the light—solemnly, without hope, but also without pain and sadness, aware of the inevitable, acknowledging the wretched souls and the petrified creatures crowding the narrow pathway leading to the gate. Even if there's no exit, you must still walk to the end, pay your dues, say your lines, build your phrases, and think each note through. I didn't need to look back at Irina. I felt the warmth of her body, I tasted the salt of her skin on my lips.

Farther down the path, toward the middle of the Adagio, we came to a crossroads—asphodel fields to the left, lilac groves to the right, ahead were the rivers, the memory eaters—and then Irina asked the question, the one question, using the words from the main motif, and I answered her by repeating the motif because in music questions were often also answers, and by striking the very first major chord in the piece, I let in the lie. Ah, but the lie was beautiful, it was exquisite and supernatural, it explained everything; it was the sustain pedal that prolonged the majestic chord of existence for another moment. What would we do without the lie, how would the flowers bloom? How would Helios ride his chariot across the sky? How would we breathe in again after exhaling? But the lie mustn't be abused—one chord, one drop in a glass of water was enough.

"Pardon me!" yelled a red-haired woman, probably a violin teacher, after swinging into the chamber hall with the door and nearly dropping on the floor from curiosity; there was always some member of the school faculty, or a student, who walked in at the most crucial point of a piece and ruined your concentration.

Out!" Igor the Swan said quietly, so as not to disturb us even further, and tossed his hands at the intruder as if shooing a fly. But the red-haired woman didn't retreat right away; she lingered for another moment, sizing up the length of our phrases, measuring our synchronicity, our tonal chemistry. An open door, of course, is an invitation, and soon the lower end of the room began filling up with students drawn in by our sound. Our chamber music lesson was quickly turning into a concert. Though just a blue blur in the right corner of my eye, I instantly recognized Bianka as she stepped in to see who was playing. It's not difficult to know people by their postures, their shadows, the way they deal with their hands. The pay phone was ringing again, out in the foyer. It was as if the whole school, this giant intrusive monster, were trying to rupture the protective layers of the ethereal realm where Irina and I and even Igor the Swan had absconded to savor the fruits of the beyond. The school was attacking us with everything at its disposal. A trumpet player was hurling lightning bolts at us from the basement; a drummer walking by with a snare drum peppered us with automatic gunfire; the gym teacher, in charge of the moral police squad, pursued a group of fugitives, slapping and punching those he caught and pushing the bystanders down to the ground. And then the third-floor janitor, Maria, accurate as a Swiss watch, pressed the black button on the wall opposite Teachers' Headquarters and released the hordes of sex-starved, obsessive, tic-ridden adolescent musicians from their prison cells with the deafening cry of the bell.

Irina was asking the question again, for the second and last time, in the native key of B minor. I answered Irina in G major, promising her the first light of day, the purest, but I did it quietly, so that the spirits wouldn't hear. Farther down the road we went, through meadows of white daffodils. We were not ascending. There was no road or ladder that could take us beyond the echoes and the shadows and the dreams in which we had once fallen asleep gratefully and contentedly, after cleansing our tired souls in the river. Irina's sudden cry of anguish, an accordioned diminished chord reaching for the opalescent orb of Eos, was quickly pacified and put back to sleep by the tonic. We knew what awaited us ahead, but we continued walking, if only to hear the beautiful lie one more time. We ended where we had begun.

By now Igor had finally sealed Chamber Hall No. 2 off to all outsiders, and Irina nodded for me to start the Allegro. What a dance! We flew across the floor, holding each other tight, and the school spun around us, a blur of colors and echoes. The stairwell spiraled into the sky, pinning janitors and teachers to the walls and sending all the uprights and grands rolling out of their rooms and into the long hallways and corridors, their fallboards and ivory keys glistening in the rainbow flurries hurled by the spinning crystal chandelier; and to think that Irina was fresh from history with Negodnik, and before that, harmony with the Hyena, fresh with the smells of classrooms and chalk and learning; I wanted to lick the wars and the pacts and the treaties off her fingers, to taste those damned forbidden parallel fourths and fifths and octaves hidden under her uniform dress, to initiate a long line of vertiginous counterpoint.

"Stop!" Igor the Swan shouted just as we entered the middle section of the Allegro, where the main theme appeared clad in the white and purple empyrean blossoms of D major, and where the joyous repetition of the same note in the bass line beckoned the opening of the gates above. Igor would have none of it. "This is a travesty! What do you think you're doing? Where are all these festivities coming from? All this strutting and leaping into the air? Tell me what it says here, my eyes are too weak to see, I'm probably dying of diabetes. . . . What is the significance of this tiny symbol, really, just a squiggle on the page . . . *Piano!* And what is the meaning of the abbreviation that precedes it . . . *Diminuendo!* Well, I must be losing my mind, then, because I don't see any indication for rendering this transposition with the abandon of a tenth graders' orgy; moreover, if you two think that this is your special moment where you join hands and have a blast, well, I will not allow it, not at the expense of Johann Sebastian, who wrote things like *Ach bleib bei uns, Herr Jesu Christ,* and *Es Danke, Gott, und lobe dich.* Let's not forget that once, not very long ago, people believed. But what am I saying? The demons of joy! I clearly must be kidding myself, for there's no such thing as chastity in music. Why not, bring it on, flesh it out, draw some blood, only keep in mind that these sonatas were originally written for harpsichord and violin, not for piano, and the peculiar thing about harpsichords—as you certainly must know from your acoustics and music theory classes—is that they have no ability to express dynamics! Their sound is even and gentle, the notes shine like golden grapes, soft and transparent, plucked from the celestial vine. Minor or major, climax or fall, the sound remains even, a metaphysical constant like the earth and the sky, which enable the miracle of creation. That said . . . Forget everything, empty your minds, and start from the beginning of the Allegro . . . and four . . ."

After our lesson was finally over, and Igor had lectured us for nearly an hour on the importance of reading Hesiod's *Theogony* to yourself aloud while taking a bath and blasting Wagner, we left school and started walking under the crooked trees, hand in hand, Irina carrying her violin case over her shoulder, and I clutching my leather bag stuffed with scores.

"One more baroque cadence and I would end up in the seminary, praying on my knees," I said.

"We never got to play the Andante. The Andante's the best part of the sonata. I played it once with my father, before his surgery."

"Want to get a bottle of wine from the Artists' Club, next to the gallery on the other side of the park? And some cigarettes?"

She looked at me with a sad smile.

"What?" I stopped. "Did I miss my opportunity to kiss you? In front of the soldiers, and the headscarfed *babas,* and the drunks, and the delegation of librarians heading to the coffee stand?"

I put my arms around her waist and pressed my lips against hers, aware of the crunching sound of leaves under my shoes and the prickling gaze of the literature teacher, Piggy, a peasant meatball with a crushingly mediocre understanding of poetry, who was heading back to school, and the wounded granite clouds, those exquisite Tartarean zeppelins hovering above the ancient graveyard spilling premonitions and flooding Doctors' Garden with a dark neon glow.

"I don't love you," Irina said softly, burying her fingers in my hair and looking straight into my eyes.

After we procured a bottle of red wine and cigarettes, we sat in the old summerhouse overlooking the National Library and smoked. I pushed the cork in with my thumb and poured some wine on the ground, for the ghosts.

"I don't love you either," I said and handed Irina the bottle. "But I have no one else but you." She rested her head on my shoulder and remained silent. Wasn't this enough? How much more could we ask for in these lands? We'd grown up too fast. We understood too much and too little. We'd seen a thousand autumns like this one, with the black-and-gray crows moving into the emptied nests of the migrating birds and the petrified trees shedding their letters and memories, and the hordes of *otlichniks* marching to and from school, gravely motivated by the precious new writings on the blackboard, and the ordinary men and women returning to their ordinary diurnal routine after an ordinary, government-sanctioned vacation at the Black Sea, or in the mountains—hundreds, thousands of raincoats and suits and long skirts and insipid dresses and high heels and socialized oxfords and military boots reestablishing the rhythm of the city without vigor or hope, full only of resentment and despondence; and the trams squeaked again at night like improperly handled violins, leaning heavily at each turn and scarring the cobblestones with fountains of crackling sparks, their eyes peeking into TV-lit living rooms and smoky kitchens. We'd heard the Nevski's bell ringing into the sunset no less than a million times, especially in the fall, sitting together in the summerhouse just as we did now, the *la, mi,* and *re diese* cutting through the layers of the ether. Why didn't I know more about Irina's father and his surgery? Was he alive? I knew her mother, had seen her around school, mostly at night when she dropped by to attend some performance. But why did I know so little about Irina's personal life, how she lived, what she did on weekends and holidays, where she liked to walk after practicing at night, whether she ever confided in her mother, whether she ever went to the movies, whether she ever thought about me when she was away from school? Why didn't she ever tell me her secrets? And why didn't I share mine? Perhaps our interior life was the only space that hadn't yet been nationalized and so we guarded it maniacally, shielding it even from our lovers' eyes. We hoarded our demons privately, in the darkest corners of our souls.

This year the festivities began early, thanks to the Owl's brand-new, Party-line agenda. It was only the beginning of November, and we'd already taken an elementary theory of music exam and a major solfège transcribing test, had an outing at the shooting range near the Military Academy with the colonel, completed a midterm project in orchestration and an overview of the fundamental definitions in *Moral Conduct and Citizens' Rights,* and today we were scheduled to take the "Maturity Exam in Literature," a two-hour-long essay-writing spree where one had to eke out at least a B; a C automatically meant repeating tenth grade. We had all gathered at the *pushkom,* Alexander and Irina and Yavor, the tall, baby-faced oboist, and Maria, a twelfth-grade violinist who charged younger boys ten leva for a quick bathroom lesson in personal hygiene and who used to teach Alexander for free, and Rada, who was nearly kicked out of school for wearing the holy Pioneer red scarf tied to her ankle, and Peter, a chubby and very funny piano player with whom I had played in chamber music back in the eighth grade, under the tutelage of Villainova, a Russian-trained keyboard artillerist who ended up punching Peter in the face for improvising on Mozart. A bunch of eighth and ninth graders, still lingering after their morning shift, huddled in one corner of the backyard, eyeing us, the older students, with envy. They, too, wanted to go to school in the afternoon, to travel home at night on empty trams and buses, to have undefined relationships with older girls, to talk about things that could happen only after dark, to face the exam of all exams, "Maturity in Literature." Alexander was chain-smoking and taking sips from everyone else's coffee, preoccupied with finding a way to access his giant accordion in the most inconspicuous way possible. An accordion, a gun, or tattoo—all were slang for *cheat sheet,* and in these parts cheat sheets came in many shapes and sizes. A gun, for instance, was something small, a piece of paper hidden in one's pen, in one's shoe or pocket, under the desk, or simply held between one's fingers. A tattoo was usually an inscription inked on one's arm, wrist, or ankle (you could always drop your pen and take a peek) or written on the inside of one's cuffs. An accordion, the most elaborate of cheat sheets, was a long and narrow strip of paper filled with nearly microscopic handwriting and folded to the size of a matchbox. A double-sided accordion of average length could condense the information from an entire textbook. There were only a few people in school who had the skills to write microscopically and legibly, and their services were quite expensive.

"*Kopeleh,* this thing is longer than *War and Peace!*" Irina exclaimed as Alexander demonstrated slinging his accordion out of his sleeve. Peter took out a pocket tape measure and measured the accordion.

"Two meters!" he said, laughing. "Two fucking meters long! You've never even read a whole book in your life, what are you going to do with this papyrus during the exam? You won't have enough time to read it!"

"Oh, I will, it's easy," Alexander said, folding back the accordion and flipping through its tiny pages. "Every page contains a full-length essay on one of the topics that we could get on the exam. I just have to modify it a little bit, answer the question that they put up on the blackboard, and I'm done! Unless I get caught, or one of my wonderful classmates turns me in, in exchange for their lives, of course, for I will strangle anyone who dares to cross me! The twins, especially, how they bug me! Royally! Someone has to show them what good manners are for and why we talk about respect and order and the rule of

law. They've been seriously misguided, I think. And I keep telling Button, let's bring them to the bathroom and have them drink toilet water,
the way we did with that drummer in eighth grade last year when he
refused to cough up some change when we asked him to. Now he's our
best friend. A drink of pure water is certainly healthy."

"That's why they build sanatoriums," Peter agreed.

"If it's not a secret," Rada said, "can you tell us who made your
accordion and how much you paid for it?"

"Guess! Come on, three tries, anyone, say a name . . . what? No, it
wasn't the Fat Waldhorn. No, it wasn't Annie the Harp. You'd never
guess. It was Luba, our own big-breasted Luba, and for free, too. I
think she's got a crush on me."

"The little bitch!" Irina laughed. "She's going to grow up a traitor!
I hope she takes revenge on her mother for all of us. That would be
sweet. The other day, the Hyena said to me in class, she said, *If I were
you, I would start making other plans at this point*. What the fuck is that
supposed to mean? Seriously? *At this point*. I'm leaving for Rome, you
stupid, untalented bigot, and I'm going to give six concerts in a row—
that's what I wanted to say back to her. God, she makes me feel like an
animal."

"We should throw her down the stairs, like we did with the math
witch," Alexander suggested gleefully. "Button will turn the lights off
and I'll trip her, by accident, naturally. A broken leg would do her tons
of good. If I'm not mistaken, a fractured tailbone qualifies for three
months of bed rest. Three months! That's February!"

"She won't do anything to you." Rada turned to Irina. "She's just
parading her power, they all want to rule the world."

I listened to the others, smoking ravenously. *Shit*, I thought, *I haven't
read a thing!* Not a single thing, and I felt great.

"Look at Button!" Alexander squealed and pointed at me. "A classic
idiot! He's going to fail the exam and he's dancing! This is what happens to people who play eight hours a day. I'm not going to be able to
help you once we're in class. You'll be on your own, I swear. You should
go immediately into school and beg one of the girls to slip you a gun

near the end of the exam. You have to beg them: open your green eyes wide and promise them something special."

I shrugged. A strange sense of optimism had clouded my mind, the kind of optimism that looks forward to an impending defeat with a perverse sense of relief. When I fail the maturity exam, and then fail to win an award at the stupid Chopin competition later in the month, I will just quit the whole thing. I will stay home, or I will take to the mountains and wander about like a wolf, or I will sneak onto the slow train to Varna and find some abandoned villa by the sea where I will squat for months, subsisting on nettles and wild apples. Why struggle to keep my head above water, why spend countless hours trying to tame the mythical creatures in Chopin's opus 10 and opus 25, why bow down to the masters of mediocrity? If music was the knowledge that helped us heal our atrophied inner senses so that we could, once again, touch, see and hear the primordial presence, then we should keep it in the temples, or hide it at the tips of our fingers, away from the crowd's plebeian thirst for blood and fireworks, and the hollow empiricism of the jury.

A piano competition! What could we possibly compete in? Speed? Banging? Theatrics? Lies? Vanity? Automatism? Posing? Gymnastics? Certainly not in temperament, for temperament is of the truth, and the truth is never spoken publicly. Except on vary rare occasions, perhaps. Why didn't they bow down to Vadim while he was still around? Why didn't they judge him then, when he was speaking the truth for the sake of the truth and nothing else? How could any of us claim the prize after Vadim had been kicked out? I detested the idea of it; the mere thought of stripping for the vultures made me shiver. But I was dancing now, the competition was still a few weeks away, anything could happen in a few weeks. The school could close down, struck by a strain of deadly influenza. Chamber Hall No. 1 could catch on fire, reducing the Steinway to a heap of black cinders and baked metal. The airplanes could appear over the mountains, just as they had before, guided by Zephyrus and pregnant with buzzing neon presents.

But I couldn't worry about all that. My mind had wandered else-where, lured by the exigencies of passion and the spells of beauty. It had been two whole days since I'd had a chance to eat, think, or sleep properly. Even when I managed to doze off briefly, all I saw was the satin dress of the girl I had met at the ball a few nights before. She wasn't just a girl: she was in fact a Mademoiselle, a real one, of stun-ning beauty and dizzying coquetry. *Mademoiselle de Thun-Hohenstein!* I would call after her, whenever I saw her coming out of her father's château, in Bohemia, with a silk hat and a white parasol under one arm. *We must meet again, Mademoiselle! Just one more time! I have to explain* . . . But she would quickly dismiss my pleas and climb into the luxury carriage waiting for her near the gates. And to think that she was approximately a hundred and fifty years older than me! Truly incredible. She still looked seventeen, just as capricious and sweet and dangerous as she had appeared to Chopin when he had stayed at the Thun-Hohenstein Palace. But how welcoming, how unassuming she seemed in the opening theme of the "Valse Brillante" in A-flat major— walking gracefully across the hall, her eyes glistening, her movements marked by the disarming pride of the innocent—and how suddenly she changed, with the trill on A flat, into a powerful seductress, her long white dress flaring out and spinning around faster than thought, a whirlwind of purple lilac dust sweeping over the black keys, petals of roses and yellow carnations shooting into the air and falling back to the ground, carried by the ascending and descending waltz flurries in the right hand. The hall began to spin, and I started dancing again, one step forward, one to the side, and a twirl. How could I resist?

The fall was slipping away. It had started to get colder and darker, the sun had begun to pale, there were fresh necrologies thumbtacked to the trees, some of them wrapped in clear plastic to protect the ques-tioning faces of the departed from the cruel November rains. When would I find time to perform all my autumn rituals? I longed to skip school and fill my pockets with shiny chestnuts whose oils would heal my aching fingers; I craved the sound of the Seven Saints Church bell, and the scruffy pigeons, and the one-key, one-rhythm songs played by the blind accordionist, and the smell of bagels, and the serenity of the weeping willow; if I could only take a walk down Tsar Shishman Street and watch the sky reflected in the wet cobblestones, brush against the corners of the old buildings, greet the crabs lying comatose on the bottom of the dirty aquarium at the little fishmonger, try to sniff people's thoughts, their taste of existence—the girl in school uniform walking her Pekingese, the sad woman returning home with a bouquet of roses, the old man leaning against a tree; existence definitely had a taste, you could discover it at the tip of your tongue when you closed your eyes.

Yavor, the baby-faced twelfth-grade oboist, stuck his finger through the snag in Irina's black stockings, right above her knee, and she took his hand and, hiking up her uniform dress, traced the snag all the way up to her panties. For a second I felt my blood boil, but then I disentangled myself from the whole thing, from their laughter and coded words, I turned around and stared at the stone wall covered with ivy. Why should I care if Irina decided to satisfy his curiosity in the attic of the apartment building opposite the school, on the cold terrazzo stairs, between the flowerpots with geraniums, with the midget hermit dragging his feet across the floor of his garret, and the sound of the radio broadcasting the water levels of the Danube from Vienna to Vidin in every European language? No, it wasn't any of my business. I was doing it with other girls, too, and she knew about it.

There was the bell. Alexander folded his accordion and hid it in the sleeve of his shirt. Rada and Peter stomped on their cigarettes and slipped through the tear in the chain-link fence, taking the long route to school. Everyone was in a rush to clear the *pushkom,* in case the school infantry decided to storm our hideout. I started back alone, I didn't want to talk or listen to any of them, especially Alexander, with his posturing and condescension. At the school entrance Irina caught up with me and pulled me aside. "I hope you didn't get jealous back there, because you and I aren't together in that way . . . we play Bach together and get drunk once in a while, and sometimes . . . But just sometimes . . . Listen, I can help you with the exam. I'm going to find you a notebook with ready-made essays on all the possible themes that they might give you. I'll leave it in the fourth-floor bathroom, behind the water tank. But don't bring it into class, read it in the bathroom and then go back and write as much as you can remember."

I didn't look at her. Disentangling my hand from hers, I walked into the building without saying a word. I shouldn't have gotten mad at Irina, but I did, and now I had hurt her feelings. Fine. I didn't care. Each of us was all alone in the dark. I didn't really need her, or anybody else.

Damn! It was heartbreaking, all the sheep lined up on the left of their desks, each one facing a blank sheet of paper and a collection of erasers and pens and pencils and pencil sharpeners. Angel was perspiring profusely, he was going to sweat out the correct, government-sanctioned words onto the white sheet any second, you could see the memorized phrases and the injected stygian toxins bubbling under his skin, pulsating wildly in his temples. The twins were dusting off their sleeves and adjusting their Komsomol ties, they didn't have a single worry in the world. They were in control. They could write twenty, thirty, forty pages on any topic at will. Isn't that how it works? People seem to feel truly confident and powerful only when they fully submit to their environment and circumstances, when they accept unconditionally the identity provided to them by the system. Those who refuse to submit to anything are cursed to live in a constant state of neurosis, alleviated only briefly by a glimpse of the distant home. But what did I know? How happy Lilly seemed, biting her pen, blinking blissfully at the blackboard, resting her dirty shoes on her violin case, the disrespectful pig! And Bianka, too, she had probably studied more than anyone else; she had allowed *their* words into her head, she had swallowed the tranquilizer. Ah, I should've cornered her in the bathroom the week before—after the end of third period, history of music, Stravinsky and Shostakovich's seventh, when the sky had turned dark red and the neighborhood buildings had been covered by a leaden veil—and gotten what I wanted from her, once and for all, in the dark, so that she wouldn't have seen my revulsion.

"Always at the last minute, number fourteen," Mouseface, the literature teacher, greeted me. "We were just about to lock the door."

She handed me a white sheet of paper with her signature in the top left corner. "As I was explaining to your classmates, the hero is an integral part of the whole that embodies the whole and explains the whole to its composite parts, which means . . . Yes, Lilly, which means *you*. Just as a person's life, by definition, is a single unit of carbohydrates, a literary hero is a single cell that provides nourishment and information to the other cells in the social organism. Since Karl Marx pointed out that humans are social animals, and the emphasis here is really on animals . . . What did I just say? Slav? I'm talking to you. What did I say about emphasis? What? Did anyone hear that? I didn't. No, you may not go to the bathroom to wash your mouth. If you are retarded enough to suck the ink out of your pens, you might as well learn to swallow it. Anyone, please define *emphasis*."

"A certain significance that highlights one word rather than another," pelted out one of the twins.

"Not correct, but I'll accept it. Our goal, in approaching the maturity exam, is to demonstrate a high degree of understanding of the process that underlies the communication between the part and the whole, and in doing so, to affirm the central role that the literary hero plays in explaining our function in society. Without performing a certain function, man loses the privilege of being called a social animal, or even just an animal. People who fail to find a proper way to serve the whole are called . . . Somebody else . . . You raised your hand last time, I want to see somebody else . . . Alexander?"

"Parasites."

"Parasites, of course, as you should know. Now, it is important to ask the question: Does the literary hero necessarily have to be a unit of carbohydrates, or might he be something else, something inorganic, for instance, a symbol, or a stone, or a tower, or a factory, a road, an idea, a school, a music school perhaps, or an instrument, or a machine . . . Can you give me examples of *in*organic literary heroes? Yes, a car, a tram, good, a pentacle. The question now is, why can we call a stone a literary hero? I'm sure you all know the answer, and in the next two hours you will have the opportunity to express it as extensively and eloquently as possible. Good luck, and don't even try to cheat, because I can be vicious. And no, you may *not* go to the bathroom to wash your ink-drenched fingers and, incredibly, eyelids. What a buffoon! I'm going to have another talk with your parents, maybe there's something really wrong with you. One week in my house, and you'd never dare to act so spoiled again. If my kids said one wrong word to me, I would leave them hungry for two days. And if they continued down that path, I'd deny them medicine when they got sick." Mouseface looked around the class to see our reactions.

"Now, the rules. Each of you gets two bathroom trips, and I'm being generous. I'm going to draw two themes, and then one of you—yes, Lilly, you may—will write them down beautifully on the blackboard. I advise you to choose one theme and stick with it. I'll sign and date all extra sheets that you might need. Just raise your hand to get my attention. Let's begin."

Mouseface placed a black velvet hat upside down on her desk, shuffled the little strips of paper inside, and pulled out the two winning themes. Lilly broke a piece of chalk in two, rolled up her sleeves, and, with her tongue pinched between her teeth, wrote:

Theme No. 1: What personifies the hidden hero in the story "Is It Coming?"

Theme No. 2: What is the role of the wire in the story "On the Wire"?

Walking back and forth from one end of the classroom to the other, arms akimbo, her high heels leaving pockmarks in the linoleum-covered floor, Mouseface had the appearance of a chthonic monster with inflammable breath, poisonous blood, impregnable skin, and a few additional organs and appendages. She was half bull, half mouse—that at least was clear. I was convinced that if I concentrated hard enough, I would see her long tail sweeping the floor behind her. Was she also a hermaphrodite? Most certainly, and an insatiable one, judging by the way she eyed each girl's rear end and how she insisted on talking, with her legs spread apart, to every good-looking boy standing beneath her on the staircase. What a terrifying sight! I wanted to wash the memory of her oily smile in the Lethe before it crippled me. Presently, Mouseface was standing in front of the class, her arms crossed, squeezing her nipples between her thumbs and index fingers as she admired her grateful pupils frantically spilling puddles of ink all over their white sheets. I looked out the window, at the trees and the roof of the National Library and the sliver of snowcapped mountain framed by a pair of sulfurous clouds. I looked at the spider spinning slowly in the air, right above the door. The hidden hero, weaving his web in a corner of the room, answering to no one, serving no one. *The hidden hero has left the whole. He doesn't have a name. He represents no one.* I crinkled the sheet of paper and threw it across the room, into the trash can. Mouseface walked over to my desk and gave me a new signed sheet. True, I had read the story "Is It Coming?" once, but I couldn't remember a thing. Somebody was supposed to come. There were some people standing around, waiting, perhaps there was even a river involved, and everything was very tragic because it had happened in the past. The past is always tragic and the future's always perfect. The present is in the process of becoming a future so the present is kind of hopeful. *The hidden hero isn't a person. The hidden hero doesn't listen and doesn't fulfill people's wishes. The hidden hero isn't a symbol or a stone. The hidden hero has no message for us. The hidden hero is hidden within us, yet we can never find him.* I chucked this one in the direction of the trash can as well. I should've learned to play basketball. Suddenly I felt her Hadean breath upon me, she was playing with the hair covering my left ear, clearing a space for her lips. "If I see you throwing another piece of paper, I will kick you out. Now get to it."

The revulsion that her presence inspired in me! No, we couldn't have arrived here from the same place, we couldn't have possibly passed through the same door. She and I, we lived on different mythological planes. But, my God, look at them! Look at the brats! Bianka was practically drooling with excitement. What were they writing about? What could they say that was so important and required such grave urgency? They surely knew the secret to finding the hidden hero, the twins especially, they had it all figured out. Perhaps it was time for me to try my luck with the other story. "On the Wire," if I remembered correctly, was about an incurably sick child whose family sat around hoping that some miracle would arrive in their godforsaken village, most likely in the form of a white pigeon that, after perching on the nearby telephone wire, would take away their pain. As a consequence, the old grandfather spent his days sitting on a bench outside his house and staring at the relentless barrage of gray pigeons landing on the telephone wire. But maybe they were waiting for the doctor, or maybe I was remembering a different story. *The wire runs through everything, living and dead. It connects building to building, stone to stone, man to man. The wire carries endless commandments in the form of information. Traffic lights blink on and off, streets fill up and grow idle, buildings wake and go to sleep, elevators run up and down, a coded message passes through the wire and number ten raises her fat hand and offers to scribble some things down on the blackboard. The sun shines, the Euclidean universe of shapes and sizes parades its logic and relevance under the blue empyrean, a trolleybus driver runs over a bicyclist, a literature teacher who punishes her children by starvation jots some words down on forty pieces of paper and places them in her hat. Students compose long paragraphs about hidden heroes and white pigeons. The wire says write. The wire says remember. The wire says forget. The hidden hero says nothing. The hidden hero is off the grid.*

I didn't dare toss this one in the trash can. Instead, I raised my hand. Mouseface walked over to my desk and exchanged the crumpled-up paper for a new one. Standing over the trash can, she straightened up the old sheet and deciphered the scratched-up sentences. Then she slowly tore the paper into tiny bits, glancing back at me with an air of superiority. I didn't care. So what! I was wearing a frock coat, a white silk shirt and tuxedo pants, and I was heading to the ball to meet my beloved Mademoiselle de Thun-Hohenstein. I couldn't afford to be late. The mademoiselle certainly had a temper. You could hear her contrarian streak in the second theme of the waltz, right after the pirouettes and the smiles and the coquetry. She could dig in her heels and toss her hair back with indignation and say no. No! I don't want to have anything to do with it! Not today, not tomorrow, not ever, and

I am not entirely sure I ever want to see you again! And her voice, too, jumping up an octave with such adorable obstinacy and sweeping through the high register in passionate glissandos!

I was so grateful to Ladybug for introducing me to her. You need some extra pieces, Ladybug had told me during my last piano lesson. Why don't you pick up the valse in A flat and the first prelude in C? You can learn them in a few hours. She was right: I did learn them in an hour or two, but I got so attached to the valse, I couldn't play anything else. There was something pure, adolescent, and intoxicating in it that I desperately needed for my survival; something I'd never had. For some reason, I imagined that the girl in the valse looked like Irina. She was very different from Irina in her manners, her morals, and her education, of course, but in temperament they were quite the same. If Irina hadn't been born in the lower lands, if she'd had a place to hide other than her violin, if she'd never been denied a childhood and an adolescence, if she didn't constantly punish herself by getting baser, she would be a different person. And so would I. But we always cleansed ourselves in the music. We became true in the music, we met in the music, we loved each other in the music. Like shadows that disappeared in the light, we burned through our phantom bodies and entered the space of music egoless, shapeless, and futureless.

And the hidden hero . . . The first hour had elapsed and I still hadn't written a damn thing. Bianka was already done—she pranced to the front of the room and handed in her paper, ten pages in all. I turned my head away when she looked at me. Angel was done, too. He dropped his paper on the floor just as he was about to place it on the teacher's desk and started crawling around the room on all fours, smiling and blushing. Fourteen narrowly spaced pages on the role of the wire. He was a world champion. I raised my hand, determined to take my chances. Mouseface walked over to me and lowered her ear in front of my mouth. "Bathroom," I whispered. She nodded, looked at the blank sheet on my desk, and gestured toward the door. She appointed Lilly to keep an eye on the other students and followed me into the corridor, and then into the bathroom. The Tartarean hybrid wasn't dumb.

She inspected the four corners and the trash can, and climbed on the toilet to look behind the water tank. I was dead, I thought. She would find the notebook and send me directly to the Owl, who would immediately skewer me with her fountain pen, a gift from Tovarich Andropov. I would be disqualified from the piano competition and my career would be over. I'd never tour Italy, or France, or Germany, or the United States. I'd never escape the shadows. But Mouseface climbed down empty-handed. My relief was instantly replaced with disappointment and a sense of betrayal. Why hadn't Irina placed the notebook behind the water tank, as she'd told me? Why was she mad at me?

I washed my face repeatedly with cold water in the hope that I would achieve a sudden clarity, a glimpse of omniscience, and acquire the apparatus to speak like them—like the giant, rectangular, big-boned men and women depicted in the monochrome murals covering kilometers of school walls across the city—in apparatchik slang, with a heavy proletarian inflection and a pronounced tendency to say nothing. That was it! I would just put myself in their heads. It was easy. *The antithetical relationship between the old superstitions of the grandfather and the irreversible arrow of scientific progress is exemplified most perfectly in the image of the white pigeon perched on the wire.* What drivel! I couldn't do it, not in a million years.

I returned to the classroom and sat reluctantly in my seat. The *otlichniks* were now leaving en masse. They'd proven themselves worthy of ascending to the eleventh grade. They were mature. They had mastered the art of critical thinking. They were almost ready to hand over their fleeting personalities and go into the world, fulfilling their obligations to the Whole.

I thought about how Irina had glared at me in the *pushkom* and I thought about how much I needed a cigarette. Time was flying so fast, I could hear the seconds and minutes spilling on the floor like springs and cogwheels from a busted clock. With just twenty minutes left before the end of the second hour, my hopes for success looked dim. What if Irina had been caught trying to plant the notebook? What if she hadn't been able to leave class during first period? I raised my hand again. Mouseface escorted me to the bathroom just as before, only this time she didn't bother looking behind the water tank. She was now certain that I wasn't even bright enough to cheat my way into eleventh grade.

"Excuse me," I said, trying to squeeze between her and the exposed, mustard-painted pipes next to the toilet. The half-mouse, half-bull just stood there, leaning against the moist wall of the narrow bathroom, massaging her breasts and glaring at me with a mixture of hunger and condescension. Where else had I seen those marble eyes and that forward-slanted posture? But of course! Mouseface was one of the heavyset proletarian women in the future-perfect murals who fucked like machines and gave birth to square-headed cretins while standing astride the conveyor belt. The murals had come to life! The mosaics and terrazzo floors had generated trees and birds and stars. The statues in the parks had started walking among us. The slogans had come true. The literary heroes had wiped out our memories.

"Isn't it rather sad that it has to end like this. . . . I'll have to crush your long, noble fingers, made strong by years of selfless labor . . . I could've been your friend, if you'd chosen to befriend me. But you were too proud. Your awards, your concerts. Everyone hates you. Everyone wants you dead. I could've defended you from them. I could've been your confidante."

I edged closer to the toilet and unbuttoned my pants. I considered turning around and peeing all over her. It would be interesting to hear what she would tell the other students when she returned to the classroom, her black dress and white shirt dripping wet. Ah, but she would like it! And she would fail me on top of that.

"Quick! Emergency!" Lilly's shrill voice echoed in the corridor. "Alexander is cheating!"

Finally, I was alone. But there was still no notebook behind the water tank. I wasn't surprised. I opened the small window and looked down at the wunderkinds crossing the school yard with their violin and cello and oboe and clarinet and flute cases strapped to their backs.

They were all going to grow up in a world of music and light, they were going to succeed and leave the lowlands behind. But not me. I was going to stay here until my flesh turned to stone and my thoughts spilled out of my hollow head like fine sand. Soon I would just be a transfigured granite face protruding from the canyon walls that shield the secret rivers.

I put my head under the tap and kept it there until the ice-cold water numbed my skull. *There's nothing I can do,* I thought as I headed back to the classroom. I couldn't play their game. I should've never tried.

Pst! I turned around. It was Irina, waving at me from the long corridor that circumvented the stairwell. She looked fearless and defiant and more beautiful than ever. As we drew close I saw the mix of five colors in her eyes, chestnut brown and green and gray and amber and even some blue. Why hadn't I noticed that before? Why hadn't I noticed that her strong chin and slightly pronounced nose made her look incredibly attractive, majestic and powerful, like the queen of the tribe of women warriors from Scythia?

"I've got what you want," she said, unbuttoning the top three buttons of her uniform dress. I looked at her naked breasts and the silver cross hung on a fine, discolored chain and the small white notebook pressed against her stomach. She pulled my shirt out of my pants and stuffed the warm notebook down into my underwear. I leaned in to kiss her, but the sound of heavy footsteps prompted her to button up her dress and take a step back. Had she held my hand and led me to the attic, I would've thrown it all away, the exam and the competition, my whole fucking piano career. If, just then, she had said, *Let's be lovers,* I would've fallen in love with her. There was a fire in her eyes that made me want to fight her and resent her and possess her all at the same time. We were so alike, she and I, competing for the same prize, a ticket out of here. Or else we were just two Hadean mutts, two lightless shadows incapable of loving others.

Irina opened the door to the stairwell and scanned the floors. Maria, the third-floor janitor, was at the bottom of the stairs, carrying a bucket of soapy water and a mop. Dimov, the harmony teacher, also known as the Kangaroo, was climbing toward the third floor, just below us, with a stack of ungraded two-part inventions. A freckled little girl wearing a tiny uniform and the mandatory blue scarf was walking on the second flight of stairs between the third and fourth floors with a box of chalk. There was a faint sound of harp and piano coming from the practice rooms in the attic. Debussy? It was hard to tell.

"Good luck," Irina said and started down the stairs. I wanted to say something after her, to let her know that I spent countless hours thinking about her, dancing with her, smelling her perfume, ruffling her long, wavy hair, tasting her skin, kissing her lips under the blossoming linden trees as I played the "Valse Brillante" in A flat in the practice room on the fourth floor, where Ladybug had locked me up before and after school. But I couldn't knock down the wall between us. Irina and I had known each other all our lives, and yet we were strangers. We were lovers wearing masks; we were friends with unspeakable secrets. The image of her snagged tights burning my stomach, I felt an urge to tell her that she shouldn't go to the midget with the other boy, she shouldn't sit with him on the cold stairs between the flowerpots with geraniums, the flowers of graves and funerals, of dark rivers and last-breath seductresses . . . I had opened my mouth to tell Irina that I would wait for her after school when I realized that the Owl had appeared on the third floor and was looking at Irina with fury. It had happened too quickly. I hadn't seen her walk out the double doors. It was her mouth that terrified me the most. The way she stretched her lips and pulled her neck tendons while delivering her poison, her sentences. You could see the strings under her skin, the strings that opened and closed her eyes and mouth, that moved her arms and legs, the strings that revealed a higher evil.

"I am so tired of seeing your arrogant face," the Owl said, pointing at Irina with her fountain pen. "The face of a whore! The whole school knows who you are and what you do! Your talent means nothing to me. Your parents have failed . . . Ah, that's right. You've got only one, a mother. A failed mother. Stand still while I talk to you! What are you doing upstairs when you should be in class?"

Irina didn't answer. She stared fearlessly at the Owl.

"Abominable! In all my years as a principal, I have never witnessed such brazen provocation! Do you wish to mock me? To mock the Party? To mock your country and the soldiers who are guarding us from the imperialists? Do you wish to go to a correctional school?" The Owl prodded Irina's cross (which Irina had inadvertently left hanging over her uniform dress) with her pen, much as one might prod a decomposing corpse, and then began pulling the silver chain toward her, also with her pen, so that she wouldn't get her hands dirty.

"Is this what you've brought from Vienna? The barbaric superstitions of the filthy bourgeoisie? Or is it a gift from your ignorant mother? A family of parasites . . ."

Irina attempted to free herself, but the Owl slapped her on the face with her left hand and pulled the chain even harder, bringing Irina's face next to hers. "Is this why we've brought you up, supported you, given you an instrument, taught you the difference between beauty and ugliness . . . so that you can laugh in our faces? So that you can offend the workers, your benefactors?"

The silver chain snapped, the cross fell to the ground, and the Owl kicked it furiously into the shaft between the stairs.

"There! I won't allow anyone to bring the symbols of the oppressors of the world into my institution, polluting the minds of our young citizens with the drugs of the slaves . . . And you're laughing! You, disgusting . . . *Gypsy* . . ."

The Owl tried to slap her again, but Irina caught her hand and pushed her violently against the wall. Something had happened to Irina, it was as if she'd unleashed a whirlwind and was standing in the center of it, darkened and menacing, her powerful fingers digging into the Owl's rib cage.

"In the name of the One Who Sees," Irina said slowly, in a voice I didn't recognize, "you shall be cursed to the grave! Like a raven that claws your eyes out, like a Turk who carves out your brain, like a snake that leaves your limbs limp and dry, like a jackal that drags your intestines through the dirt, like a *samodiva* who feeds on your soul, in the name of the One Who Sees, It will enter your lungs, It will feed on them, and It will spread through your entire body, until your body is laid into the ground, and the earth will take what's hers, and the worms will take theirs, and the night will close all doors, those that lead above, and those that lead below."

The Owl began to retreat, staggering, groping for support, her heavy glasses dangling over her chest on a golden chain.

"What did the Gypsy do to you?" Maria shouted after her master. But she did not dare come near Irina, nor did the other janitors or Mulberry, the gym teacher, or the group of third graders who had been dismissed early, or any of the spectators that had come out of every crevice in the staircase.

Irina saw me watching from the flight of stairs right above her and pointed down with her index finger. A simple gesture, but one that made my heart race. She was going down into the netherworld, where music didn't exist. She was going down to the street, where mediocre people lived, deprived of light. She was going down to a place of misery, where the future lingered in dark and dusty apartments, where a string of forgetful faces entered and exited, taking everything but leaving nothing. She was going down, alone. Wouldn't I go with her?

She waited a second or two, then started down the stairs. I had to join her; it was the one logical thing to do. She would wait for me, I thought. I would catch up with her in a second, in a minute, any minute now. She should just wait for me in Doctors' Garden, or behind Seven Saints Church, or in one of the backyards along Tsar Shishman Street; she should wait for me with a pack of cigarettes and a bottle of wine, for I was sure to come. Of course I would.

First, though, she was going down, and I was going up, to the fourth-floor bathroom, where I could read the essay on the role of the wire in private—there were still seven minutes before the end of second period, if my Sputnik was to be trusted. But I would still follow Irina, I told myself.

It's amazing how quickly one can memorize a half-dozen pages of pure drivel. After throwing the notebook out the bathroom window, I returned to the classroom and, with only five minutes to go, started spilling ink left and right on the white page, just like the *otlichniks*—words, sentences, and paragraphs escaped my hand at immense speed, I was writing quicker than I was able to think, I kept going at it, even after the bell, and I paid no attention to Mouseface, who kept repeating that she would void my paper because I had spent fifteen minutes in the bathroom and hadn't finished in time.

There! I was done. Six pages of crap. Mouseface had to accept them. I rushed outside and ran to the *pushkom,* where Alexander was already celebrating his success with a flask of homemade brandy. Lilly had reported Alexander's use of the accordion, but when Mouseface searched him, she'd found only crumpled paper napkins. "My hands tend to get very sweaty!" Alexander shouted, shaking with the triumph of it. I was celebrating, too. I took a swig from his brandy and laughed out loud. Irina was gone, just like Vadim two weeks before, and already everyone had forgotten about her. In choosing the piano, I had sided with the shadows. I couldn't stand myself. I was an asshole and a coward, not much different from the rest.

November 9, 1988

Today I decided to skip school and go looking for Irina. I had to, I owed it to her. It had been a week since I last saw her and I was starting to get desperate. Where the hell was she? Why didn't she come to see me after school? I didn't even know where she lived! She'd always avoided showing me her apartment building because she was afraid that her mother, or one of the neighbors, would spot her with me, and then she'd get into a lot of trouble. Irina's mother had been trying to keep her away from boys long before Irina had her first abortion.

While it was true that I didn't know the building in which Irina lived, I did know her street—Serdika, in the old quarter, near the mosque. Incidentally, it was on Serdika Street, not far from Lion Bridge, that I had my very first piano lesson, on the fourth floor of a dusty, discolored building that looked like an unearthed tomb, with Ms. Visenberg, a complete nut who smelled like an old cat, insisted on being addressed as "Ms." rather than the obligatory "Comrade," wore the same vest winter and summer, and whose daughter, Alyona, an aspiring pianist of the terminal kind, was graduating from the music school next year. So I bought a bouquet of roses at the tram stop by the mosque and walked down to Ms. Visenberg's apartment, dressed as usual in my school uniform. I rang her bell at exactly nine o'clock in the morning, just as she was preparing to see her first private student for the day.

"But I don't believe it!" she exclaimed after she'd taken off her glasses to study my face more closely. "What a handsome young man you've become! Come in quickly, it's bad luck to stand in the door!"

She kissed me on both cheeks and led me excitedly into the kitchen. "Pyotr Ilich, come to see who has decided to pay us a visit! You won't believe your eyes!"

Unintelligible grumbling came from behind the door at the end of the corridor. Pyotr Ilich hadn't come out of his room since I was five.

"Tell me everything about yourself, everything!" she demanded, putting a kettle on the stove. "Last time I saw you, you were playing the Andante Spianato in Chamber Hall Number One, and I told your teacher Katya, I said, he is almost there, Katya, almost! He is just missing a pinch of hormones! Yes, I did say that, didn't I?"

"Well . . ."

"And your father, how is your father? He would come here with you, and would listen to you play with that deep look in his eyes. He was so proud of you!"

"Right."

Ms. Visenberg brought out teacups and a ball of sugar, and then went to fetch the kettle. I looked around: everything was exactly as I remembered it—the wallpaper, the rugs, the piano bench supplemented by two very hard leather cushions, the worn-out leather box where the toddlers would rest their feet. The keys of the Blüthner resembled rotten teeth, yellow and chipped around the edges.

"Please, Konstantin, take one of the cushions from the bench and make yourself comfortable. I can still see you perched up on top of the bench, practically still a baby, and you wanted to play Bach!"

She laughed, covering her mouth with both hands. She still smelled like cats and wore the same vest.

"I'm playing at the Chopin competition in two weeks," I said, stirring a cube of sugar into my tea.

"Of course! I heard about that. But let me ask you quickly: did you see my Alyona play last Friday at the Conservatory? You must've!"

"Oh, yeah, I did!" I lied.

"Wasn't she just gorgeous! What did you think of the Brahms second concerto? You didn't like it? You did! Of course you did. She was ab-so-lute-ly exceptional, every phrase shone on its own, her technique and the pedal work, exquisite."

"I agree, and her rubatos were very tasteful, she's got a special touch, almost."

Ms. Visenberg suddenly turned very serious. "You know, Konstantin, every boy in school is chasing after my Alyona. But she isn't going to have anything to do with them. 'Mother,' she says, 'I am committed to my instrument and my practice hours. I'm not interested in meaningless relationships.' They send her flowers and love letters; the trash can in the kitchen is filled with them, would you like to see?"

I nodded and sipped my tea.

"Pyotr Ilich, he wants to see all the flowers and love poems that Alyona has received from the boys at the music school!"

From behind the door came a derisive roar, followed by the sound of something fragile, perhaps a night light, falling on the ground and breaking in many pieces. Ms. Visenberg didn't flinch.

"But mustn't you be at school, on a Wednesday?"

"In fact, no," I replied. "I was sent by the Komsomol secretary to find a violinist who was expelled from school last week. She is supposed to live somewhere on Serdika Street."

"How strange! Why would the Komsomol secretary want to find her if she was expelled last week?"

"Because—I mean—do you really want to know the whole story?"

"My first student is always late, so don't worry, go on, I love gossip!"

"Well, you've heard of the famous Russian academic Gennady Kuznetsov?"

"It rings a bell," Ms. Visenberg offered, slightly bewildered.

"He arrived at school yesterday to ask for the principal's support in tracking down the legendary Purple Amati violin, which, I'm sure you know, was made by Nicolò Amati, one of the best luthiers in the world."

"Ah, yes! He was Stradivari's teacher, I remember now."

"Well, according to Comrade Kuznetsov, who's been mapping the peregrinations of the Purple Amati for the last twenty years, the first mention of the Purple Amati is in a diary of a noblewoman from Cremona, who was kidnapped, together with the Amati violin, during the plague of 1630 by Lazi pirates and taken to Georgia, where she later died in an accident involving gunpowder. The Purple Amati was bought by a traveling merchant, who sold it to a wealthy Russian family in Yekaterinburg, known as the Garins. Later, the Garins were deported to Siberia, and the violin was sold to Dmitri Mendeleyev's father, who then sold it to a band of Siberian nomads in exchange for a reindeer. At the end of the nineteenth century, the Purple Amati resurfaced at an annual fair in Azerbaijan and was bought by a Gypsy musician who eventually made it to the Balkans and died in Sofia at the end of World War Two. The Purple Amati was then acquired by the luthier on Dondukov Boulevard and Budapest Street, who in turn sold it to Irina Petrova, the girl who was expelled last week. And the whole time, no one knew that she's been playing the Purple Amati!"

"How extraordinary! I must tell Pyotr Ilich about it. Pyotr Ilich, they found the Purple Amati!"

"Hyperboloids, everywhere," scoffed Pyotr Ilich.

"But do you happen to know Irina?"

"Of course I do!" Ms. Visenberg replied ecstatically. "I've known her since she was a little girl and she would walk under my window with her mother. Now that I think of it, she was playing a full-size violin by the time she was eight or nine. If that is not amazing!"

"Do you know where she lives, though?" I asked her abruptly, unable to hide my irritation.

"No, I don't. I've never liked the look of her mother. She strikes me as one of those women who would never set foot in a theater . . . But you mustn't go! We were chatting so well, I can't let you go without hearing you play something for me, on the Blüthner."

"I shouldn't. I am already late."

"I absolutely insist! You must play for Pyotr Ilich, he's been having such a hard time with his hernia lately."

Feeling defeated, I sat at the piano and started Chopin's étude in A flat, at first sloppily, and then, as I got into it, faster and tighter. I remembered a fall a long time ago—four years, perhaps five, five years was an eternity—when the leaves scattered through Doctors' Garden had the significance of a prophecy, when the touch of the cold, smooth, and unusually heavy keys of the grand piano in Ladybug's room on the fourth floor loosened the grip of the iron fist squeezing my heart, and when, during one of the biweekly recitals in room 49—attended only by Ladybug's students—Vadim sight-read the A-flat étude at top speed, intoning the melodic line, set against a pulsating blur of sixteenth notes, in the most perfect, nearly superhuman legato, and then proceeded to play the repetition of the opening theme with his eyes closed, for he'd already learned it and his fingers just fell on the memory-marked keys. And Ladybug had hoped to embarrass him in front of everyone for coming to the recital without having prepared any new material! Who did he play for? No one in particular. He played truthfully because he was true to himself, because he wasn't motivated by either fear or hope, because he had no one to compete with and nothing to prove. I asked Vadim afterward how he'd done it, and he said that he'd just followed the colors.

I remembered when trams wobbled with the *kazachok*-like *rum-ta rum-ta* of the fourth étude, in A minor; I remembered the F-minor sunsets, just like those in the fourth ballad, and the E-flat major afternoons, as in the second nocturne, when the water lilies in Tsar Boris's Garden still blossomed and the pond by Eagle Bridge was still filled with water and you could rent a small boat with oars for fifteen minutes after school. What about Irina? Did she remember all that?

My playing now carried the smell of the old apartment buildings on Serdika Street, of damp basements, of deformed Bakelite light switches in the staircases, of moldy wooden racks of mailboxes, of bitter dust blowing through the cracks of the unwashed windows, of freshly hung laundry in the courtyards. And then there was the light, the claustrophobic November light trapped between buildings, the profound, almost tangible bodies of gray that the clouds produced as they moved over the cobblestones and crept up balconies and roof tiles, the muddied orange sun reflected in the windows of the Soviet cars parked halfway over the sidewalks, and then, later, the neon red night sky that flooded the street, the buildings, and the minds of the living with the thick substance of Erebus. And somewhere out there, Irina was waiting for me to find her. I was convinced that she was. The way she had looked at me and pointed down with her forefinger before she'd descended the school stairs for the last time. She had asked me to go with her and I had refused so that I could continue the stupid game of winning and losing, of outdoing the rest.

After I was done playing, I grabbed my things and quickly headed out the door, ignoring Ms. Visenberg's entreaties to stay for lunch. Even as I started down the stairs, she continued talking about Alyona, her graduation party, and her upcoming recitals. I stormed out of the building as if it were on fire. I couldn't bear hearing my old teacher's voice for another second.

Later that afternoon I met Uncle Iliya on San Stefano Street, near the National Television building. He was wearing his signature beige raincoat, striped gray pants, and brown shoes, but he'd replaced the bowler hat with a black beret, which somehow seemed more appropriate for a late-autumn afternoon. His leather briefcase was unusually full, and he carried it under his arm, his enormous fingers stretched across its battered surface. We walked in the middle of the cobblestone street, under a canopy of tree branches and between the decrepit cars. Iliya walked slightly ahead of me, as if to scout the enemy lines. Doctors' Garden, our objective, was straight ahead. I could already make out the clusters of students in dark blue uniforms perched on the benches and the park janitors, dressed in light blue aprons, wading through the marshes of dead leaves, skewering plastic cups, cigarette boxes, and bus tickets with their long metal rods.

Stepping aside to make way for a passing car, Iliya leaned on the trunk of a parked black Volga and remained there for a minute or two, apparently out of breath. "Uncle Iliya?" I said, putting my hand on his shoulder.

"It's nothing," Iliya replied, and he walked to the arched entrance of an enclosed courtyard where two people were loading old furniture onto a flatbed truck. A large brass-framed mirror had been propped against the front wall of the apartment building connected to the courtyard. Iliya stood in front of the mirror and looked at himself intently, with a hint of suspicion.

"Cats are smarter than elephants," he concluded, nodding at himself.

"Why do you say that?" I asked.

"Because they don't recognize themselves in the mirror. The person in the mirror isn't you. It's your twin, the one who represents you in the material world. Beware of him, for he will cheat you whenever he gets a chance."

We stood side by side, looking at ourselves in the mirror. My uniform jacket and pants seemed ancient, my white button-up shirt was unraveling, my hands looked like an old man's, with veins and tendons protruding. My eyes were sunken and exhausted, my face skeletal, from eating once a day and smoking all the time.

"It's strange," Iliya said when we started walking again, "but I remember seeing a similar mirror here, on San Stefano Street, in 1943. Perhaps it could've even been the same one. I think it was November as well. I've told you about Gazdov before. The god of Persin Island. I may not have told you about his round pocket mirror. Ah—of course I have. We've talked about the Maestro, and the others. But I haven't told you about the spring of 1951, when Gazdov called my name during regular morning roll call, out in the courtyard. Only he never called me by my real name. He referred to me as 'the American,' because of my work as a translator for the American Embassy before the war. 'Is the American with us here, today? I have prepared a little surprise for him.' He pulled out his small mirror from the pocket of his military coat and reflected the sun in my face. 'Come on, slimy worm, come out of the ground!' I knew what this meant. In a few hours I'd be food for the pigs, behind the barracks. Still, I had to go through the motions, obey the orders, provide the right answers. I stood next to him and took the round mirror. 'Look at yourself carefully, gaze hungrily at the person that is about to take leave,' he was saying. Everyone was silent except Miro, my best friend in the camp, who was crying somewhere in the back row. I didn't look at my face, as I was ordered to. For I knew that the person in the mirror wasn't me. In the beginning and in the end, everything is a singularity, indivisible. It's the middle that gives birth to all the confusion, fear, and suffering, to the twins of good and evil, of inside and outside. Instead, I pointed the mirror behind me, at the trees and the sky and the withered grass, at the bushes in the distance where the soil lost its color and sloped into the Danube. The great river had always been there, waiting for me. I heard her in my dreams, licking the walls of my compound, whispering to the rats and the snakes, caressing my hair. No matter what happened to me, I still had to cross her waters."

We had veered to the right and were now walking down Shipka Street, in the direction of the canal that cuts through the center of the city. Iliya stopped outside the gates of a small yellow-painted high school and stared at the uniformed boys playing soccer in the court-yard. In the far corner a dozen girls watched the game, laughing and jeering. Could one of them be Irina? What if she had transferred to a normal school and now studied the dull subjects of the untalented? She could be in any of the high schools around town, flirting with the cute boys, going to parties, lounging aimlessly in her lovers' attics and apartments, watching the hours go by. How carefree seemed these kids! They didn't have to get back to their pianos and violins, to their solfège lessons and chamber music sessions. They didn't have to worry about failing. Perhaps it was better to grow up without the self-consciousness of the artist, the constant pressure to be someone.

"They took me behind the barracks, two of Gazdov's buddies, and shot at me. They shot at me with blanks and laughed afterward. They thought it was terribly amusing. But I really died, then. The person in the mirror, he was mortally wounded. My hair turned white. And another cycle began, and the past seemed forever lost, a chasm had opened and swallowed the memories. I have no idea why Gazdov decided to play with me. Maybe he wanted to kill me again and again, so that there was nothing left to die when he finally inserted a live bullet in his revolver. I was transferred to another camp shortly after that, just in time to say goodbye to Miro, who was shot in his sleep one morning. But this is all past now. When the time comes, and I walk past the grand mirror, I'll be looking at a stranger.

"I'm telling you all this, Konstantin, because you're very much like me, a traveler. We've both come here from afar. Today I began another cycle, and I fear that it will be the final one, for me. You should keep that in mind. This morning, after I got off the train from Lukovo, I found myself walking through the farmer's market, alongside Seven Saints park. I knew that I had to be there, that I had to find the door that would lead me to my next destination. And then I saw a man in his seventies, with a straw hat and a walking cane, carrying a bag of apples. He looked like a good-humored grandfather who got along well with everyone. His long curly hair had retained its color, and his mustache gave him the air of a garrulous dinner-table philosopher. Then I recognized him. It was Gazdov. He must've recognized me, too, because for a few long seconds we stared at each other, unable to move. Finally he reached into his bag and offered me an apple. I took it and ate it on the way here, thinking about the taste of memories and how we all share the illusion of existence, the air, the water, the ticking of the earthly seconds, the smell of damp soil on a golden apple in the fall. So, you see, oftentimes life offers its own endings. They're not happy endings, or sad endings, but they're definitely complete circles, where the beginning and end finally merge."

"But, Uncle Iliya!" I was burning with anger. "Why would you accept a gift from this murderer? Why did you let him go, without naming him, without reminding him that his crimes are real and will never be forgotten? At least spit in his face! That's what I would do. And then curse him. With a curse that would send him straight to hell." I paused to catch my breath. We had just passed the Conservatory and were now walking through Zaimov Park. Iliya didn't seem in the least offended by my tone of voice. It was as if he'd anticipated my reaction.

"Justice is for armchair visionaries, for cushioned revolutionaries, Konstantin, for amateur prophets. Justice exists only in the minds of those who have never truly suffered. It's the arrogance of thinking that you could unhinge the universal balance to make things right on your end! Hence, the endless war. Justice, you see, is at the root of all violence; you should know that, even if you're young. Don't waste your life chasing phantoms and looking for the source of all evil. The reason why no one ever takes responsibility for their actions is that no one is truly responsible for what they do! They are not. Most people are just agents of forces and powers that they can't even begin to understand."

"So you've forgiven him?" I asked.

"No, I haven't. Because forgiveness is also a product of justice. What I've tried to do all my life is to understand. I can't understand everything, of course, but I can begin. And the beginning of understanding is when you stop asking questions and start accepting things as they are. You mustn't think that these are just words either, my boy. The time will come when you can *have* your revenge. I can see it in your eyes; you're waiting for an opportunity to punish those who've done you wrong. Remember me, then. Remember what I told you. . . . That's all. And now, let's drink some tea."

We bought mint tea from the small park bistro on the corner across from the English High School and sat down on a bench, leaving the melting hot plastic cups on the ground to cool down. The first étude was still running through my head, taking me back to that day years ago when Vadim had played the longing melody on the old Yamaha in room 49 like a mystic, and when I had felt that I'd been given the most extraordinary gift known to man. For a brief moment, then, I'd known beauty. And then I had lost it.

Chopin,
Étude in G-sharp Minor, op. 25, no. 6

November 20, 1988

G-sharp major! Ah, how exquisite, especially on the good old somber Bösendorfer with weighted keys and artillery bass strokes, to which I'd been chained for two whole days, no phone calls, no smokes, no wine, no girls, no meals either, unless one counts the insipid starchy liquid with remnants of chicken bones that Ladybug's older sister, Maya, served at the kitchen table at regular intervals. They were fighting again, in the other room, the Old Lady pounding her fist on the gas stove and Ladybug whimpering like a little dog, begging for mercy. Oh well, it was all a grand burlesque, the two blind and limping cats crying in the bathroom, the incontinent Pekingese roaring like a lion, the six foot two blond *samodiva*—once a promising cello player, now a kindergarten teacher—moving through the house teary-eyed, slamming all the doors behind her and breaking dishes in the kitchen, Ladybug's "Please, Mom, don't!" and the Old Lady's piercing falsetto: "An American! I don't want him in my house! Not until you bury me . . . an American! And a math professor! Oh, you'll kill me! Just kill me, then! Grab a knife, a club, anything! An axe . . . I'm sure he hasn't even read Dostoyevsky!" against the backdrop of the left-hand accompaniment of the sixth étude, which I delivered with astute grotesqueness, exaggerating the punctuated legato lines and then delivering the long string of descending chords with the pomp of a hopping bunny rabbit: I was convinced that my job was to provide some comic relief, and I did what I could.

I absolutely loved the *terzi* étude, as it was commonly called, with its darkly humorous pantomime of the Pale Lady in the left hand and its fast moving progressions of anxious thirds, running up and down the keyboard like a pair of sad-faced Siamese twins, in the right hand. Perhaps Chopin didn't mean to make the étude ironic, but when I played it in the Dark House of the Three Giant Women I couldn't make it sound otherwise! I could see it clearly: the Pale Lady miming the left-hand accompaniment, at first sliding like a cat across the stage and scanning the horizon with a hand over her eyes, and then tiptoeing away, quietly, so that she wouldn't disturb her victim. I knew I could play the étude over and over again for months and years without ever getting tired of it. Not that I played it like a genius. In fact, I couldn't play it well at all—I had picked it up just three days ago, at the request of Ladybug, who had decided that I must play a different étude than the ones I'd been practicing or else I wouldn't even make it to the second round of the competition. And it was a week away! It was insane, and the Old Lady had said so as well, but Ladybug was adamant and wouldn't budge. If there ever were a piece that revealed Chopin's dark side, it was the *terzi* étude. One look at the score should suffice to convince anyone that the man was mad as a hatter. It's all wonderful if you want to play diatonic and chromatic scales in two voices, in this case thirds, with one hand, wickedly fast, except for a tiny little problem, which is that you'd need six fingers (three for the upper line and three for the lower), and as it was, most people had only five, which was indeed unfortunate. The acrobatics necessary to make up for the missing finger weren't at all funny. I constantly felt like I were trying to pass a microscopic thread though the eye of a microscopic needle. But I had no choice. I had to figure it out, somehow, learn the magic trick. Ladybug was convinced that I was too lazy. "Do you know Roman?" she had asked me. "Well, he learned it in one week. And he plays it like a pro." Roman was a fat eleven-year-old kid with glasses. "How fast?" I had asked her. "Really fast. Really, really fast."

That's how they got you. I wanted to find that kid Roman and kick his ass. Didn't he have better things to do?

I peered through the thick white curtain covering the window next to the piano to see if Alexander was still sitting on the swing in the small playground across the street, smoking and waiting for me to come out. But he was gone. He was free to wander the streets in search of hidden pleasures while I was stuck in this dark house, listening to the three giant women screaming in the other room and fighting my way through the maze of the *terzi* étude on a piano that had been remodeled to function as a torture device. The keys were so heavy with lead, one had to sit on them to get a decent sound. I couldn't even play a scale without getting a cramp in my wrist. I was used to the pain, though. I actually liked it. The grandfather clock in the hallway struck two.

"Maya!" the Old Lady called out in a trembling voice already strained by the horrors of the coming apocalypse. "Turn on the samovar, will you, we're going to have tea."

Cursing quietly, the older daughter headed toward the kitchen, dragging her feet with such ferocity one would think her legs were two solid beams of concrete.

"Not the linden tea, Maya, it gives me headaches. Not the black tea either, I won't be able to sleep tonight, and I need sleep, I'm almost finished."

There was a sound of something breaking on the kitchen floor, followed by more feet dragging and cursing. "Maya?" the Old Lady demanded. "Was that porcelain, or was it glass?" There was no answer. I took the speed up a notch, and put more weight behind the bass. Things were getting exciting. "We only have linden and black tea," came Maya's meek voice from the kitchen.

"I swear, it sounded like porcelain," the Old Lady went on. "She has broken the whole set of teacups, now, every single one of them, that was the last one, it sounded just like the rest. A gentle plop. You can't mistake the sound of breaking porcelain. I may not have all my wits, but my ears are just fine. My grandfather had brought the tea set from Paris, you remember, after he'd graduated from the Sorbonne. Come to think of it, that's why Maya had to give up the cello, she's got two left hands and a vacuous head. Professor Tabakoff told her so when she was still in primary school."

The Old Lady left the room and seconds later Katya opened the door again and sat exhaustedly in the leather armchair. What if her changing my repertoire at the last minute was a ploy to get me to move in with her for a week, so that she would have someone on her side while her mother was having a nervous breakdown? It was possible. I didn't dare ask her about the American. It wasn't polite to be curious, and besides, there was a real danger that she might faint from embarrassment. Ladybug doing the naughty with the enemy! She must be excited. Trembling with excitement.

"You've changed your fingering again, that's the third time today. How will you know what fingering you're going to use onstage? It's too risky!"

Speaking of taking risks, Ladybug should've been paying more attention to what she was doing to me. Presently, she had slipped her hands under my shirt and was massaging my back and shoulders with such fervor, I could barely keep my fingers on the piano. My God, soon she was going to start squeezing my nipples and unbuttoning my pants.

"What are you two doing here!" the Old Lady bellowed, storming back into the room. "Take your hands off him, Katya, one would think you two are making out. Start the étude from the beginning, you've been banging at it for eight hours and haven't made any progress. God, my head will explode! I'm telling you, Katya, if he doesn't get it right by nine o'clock tonight, we should consider going back to the black-keys étude, at least he can play that in his sleep."

I started confidently, at top speed, taking great care to reveal all the hidden lines, and for a second it really sounded good, I even caught a glimpse of a narrative that had been invisible to me before—it's strange how some pieces of music begin to speak to you only after you've played them a thousand times—but I messed it all up in the third variation of the main theme, where the wave of ascending thirds keeps on pushing farther and farther up the keyboard, until your hand practically disappears beyond the horizon. One wouldn't have thought a piano keyboard was so long—miles and miles in both directions—just from looking at it.

"Go back and repeat that passage!" the Old Lady commanded. "What happened to the tea? Maya? Where is she? Oh, I should've never let you go to the piano festival in Prague. How would I know that you'd bring back an American! I'm telling you now, Katya, if he shows up on my doorstep next week, as he's promised you, asking me if he can marry you, I swear, I will strangle him with my own hands, like a newborn kitten. How dare he invite himself over like that, only a math professor . . . You couldn't even find a man of the arts!"

"Mother!" Ladybug protested, wiping the corners of her eyes. I watched them fight in the large black-framed mirror between the piano and the massive cabinet filled with old china and porcelain elephants.

The door opened and in came Maya, carrying a steaming teacup. "Black tea, as you wanted."

"I didn't want black tea!" the Old Lady shouted. "Take it back, you've probably lost your hearing."

Maya left the cup on the table demonstratively and exited, slamming the door.

The Old Lady turned to Ladybug. "You should go and talk to your sister. She is worried that you'll go to America and never come back again to see us. Last night she told me, 'That's it, she's abandoned us. We'll rot here and she'll go off to America to make babies.'"

Ladybug opened a cabinet drawer and took out a box with pills. "I need water, Mother, tell Maya to please . . ."

"Maya!"

Something had happened, the present had snagged on one of the thorny diminished chords hidden in the satin dress of the accompaniment, and I was walking hand in hand with Irina on Tsar Simeon Street, in the old part of Sofia, toward the Turkish baths and the mosque, I was walking Irina home after playing the Bach sonatas at Igor the Swan's chamber music class, and we were smoking, and she was telling me about her first violin teacher, who would sit during lessons in one corner of the room, wearing an ancient bow tie over his pajama shirt and drinking coffee, and exclaim, "Yes, dear, there's a better way to play this, but, unfortunately, I've already disclosed it to another student." Every one or two blocks I would pull Irina into the foyer of an apartment building, and we would kiss because we could and because we wanted to find out if we were in love. We would kiss slowly, like scientists who analyzed the chemistry of passion, the electricity of desperation, the heat of loneliness, the sudden fluidity of time. When we had reached her street, she had asked me to turn around and go back, in case her grandmother was watching from the balcony.

"There!" Maya announced triumphantly, standing in the doorway. "I hope you're both happy! The cat is dead!" Ladybug collapsed in the armchair, gasping for breath, while the Old Lady rushed after Maya to the other room. I entered the final reprise of the étude, doubling the tempo and turning the train of thirds into a blur of dark blues and violets. I was fog and rain and lightning. My favorite part came toward the end, when the variation of the theme started in A-flat major and then, after a surreal chromatic meandering, resolved itself into G-sharp minor. A pinch of the damper pedal, and you felt like you were performing a kind of cleansing ceremony in which one's memories were washed into the waters of the last river.

"Which one?" came the Old Lady's voice from the other room. "They both look dead! Maya, you have killed them! Ah, Leporello is only sleeping, the filthy beast. Don Giovanni is still warm, help me . . . he's choked on something . . . a bird . . . insatiable incontinent bastard . . . He will live! The pervert! Didn't I tell you we shouldn't name him Don Giovanni, and you didn't listen to me. We've condemned him to an awful death from the very beginning, giving him this name."

"Mother, Don Giovanni was killed by a statue that he'd invited to dinner. It's an opera buffa."

"Let me see you laugh when I am killed by a statue, then! Ungrateful children! If only I had a son! Opera buffa! Ten years of cello lessons with Professor Tabakoff, the luminary—oh, what a superbly educated man! a prophet!—then a year at the Sofia Conservatory, and now what? Nothing. All this work. Katya? Did you take your medicine?"

"I have, Mother! For God's sake!" Ladybug slumped in the leather chair and closed her eyes.

Back to the beginning, again, one more round, and then another, and another, I couldn't afford to waste any time. I was back on the street, walking—was I smoking? I sure was—after the end-of-the-school-year concert at the National Hall, where the *otlichniks* had come onstage to receive their medals and diplomas and where a selected group of students had performed a cycle of idiotic pieces composed by members of the faculty. Tons and tons of atonal acid had spilled from the stage and corroded our brains; even Zimova looked like she had swallowed cyanide. What poverty of ideas, what glut of crippled ambitions! It suited them well: a hideous decoration for their hideous little reality, a reptilian skin for their liverish reptilian bodies. And then I was finally alone, walking the empty streets and breathing in the warm night air damp with the smell of blossoming linden trees. It was the beginning of the summer, and I had just officially passed seventh grade. I had spotted Irina near the flower shop on Rakovski Street, a block away from Seven Saints Church. She had worn a black dress, black stockings, and black shoes. She'd carried her violin case, too, because she'd been one of the students who'd performed onstage. "Have you been following me?" she had asked, turning abruptly around to face me. *Not at all. Did you like the circus? Not at all.*

The bell downstairs rang and, in that instant, the door to the kitchen was flung open, hitting the wall, and Maya announced in the professionally hysterical voice of a kindergarten teacher: "Ani is here!" The kitchen door slammed shut and quickly opened again: "Without her mother!" Maya clarified. Ani's mother was a beast wrapped up in fox tails and her presence never failed to unnerve the three giant women's delicate systems.

"Katya?" the Old Lady shouted from the other room. "Will you get the door? It's one of your worthless students . . . mediocre lot . . . good-for-nothing peasants. Misfits with grand ambitions is what they are, why they even bother to drag themselves over to our house day after day, month after month, is beyond me."

"Mother, they can hear you on the street!"

"I've spent my life listening to their abominable blabbering!" the Old Lady carried on, now shouting at the top of her lungs, "You tell them they're donkeys, and they act like stallions! Universal deafness, we live in an era of deafness, they are born without ears nowadays, that's modern civilization for you."

"OK, Mother, I'm coming!" Ladybug relented. Still, she remained in her chair. I kept on playing the *terzi* étude. The bell rang again, Maya descended the stairs heavily and unevenly, and opened one, two, three locks and a chain. The three giant women were afraid of thieves.

"Hello, how are you?" came Ani's excited, ringing voice. Maya didn't say a word.

"Ah!" the Old Lady exclaimed from the top of the stairs. "It's you again! I was beginning to wonder if I'd be seeing you soon. We're not fine, no, the most unspeakable tragedy took place, Don Giovanni choked on a bird, it was a terrible sight, but he lived, I saved his life. Go on, to the bedroom, warm up with some scales, Katya will be with you shortly. As you can hear, she is working with Konstantin on a new piece. He has a week to learn to play it perfectly; the competition is next Sunday."

I was alone again, and the room seemed darker than ever. Soon, Erebus would come and hide all the ugliness, the worries and fears too, underneath its gown. Ladybug was in the next room singing the leading voice in the second movement of Beethoven's Sonata no. 5 in C Minor, which Ani played with the grace of a constipated elephant and the wisdom of an ostrich. Where was she going so fast? There were no phrases, no breathing, no resignation. And the Adagio molto was all about resignation. In fact it was about leaving the world and the self behind and going into the light, empty, weightless. The best Ani could do was listen to Ladybug's singing and learn to imitate the logic of the narrative. We were all helpless imitators.

My fingers were so tired I could no longer control what they were doing. I was stuck in a labyrinth of chromatic thirds, running up and down the narrow passageways, tripping and falling and ending up at the place where I had started. But I was going to be free soon—when the grandfather clock struck nine and Maya came out of the kitchen to announce that the borscht was ready—and I would disappear into the night with a head full of music and hands on fire. I had already mapped out the route: up to the music school (I would just take a peek and see who was playing, perhaps I would even sit at the bottom of the stairs outside Chamber Hall No. 1, listening to the liquid sound of the Steinway and chatting with the doorman about the latest events at school), then down Tsar Shishman Street, past the Russian High School, Seven Saints Church, Rakovski Street, in the direction of the train station, then Tsar Simeon Street . . . I could even run into Irina, if she'd decided to go out for a late-night stroll. Or I could see her kissing her new boyfriend from her new school, if she had a new boyfriend, and if she had already found a new school.

And maybe later, much later, when everyone was asleep and all the traffic lights were blinking yellow, I would sit on a bench, light up a cigarette, and try to figure out what the hell I was going to do with my life once Ladybug ran off with the American and I was left to the mercy of the jackals at the Sofia Music School for the Gifted.

Chopin,
Fantaisie-Impromptu in C-sharp Minor

December 1981

I n Salerno, we stayed at a two-star hotel called Albergo Italia, perched on the highest point of the main street, not far from the sea. It was December, but it was sunny and warm, warmer than any spring in Sofia. At night, my roommate and I sat out on our small balcony on the third floor and watched cars and people pass by below us. In the morning we watched the palm trees stir with the gentle breeze and seagulls swarm over the docks. Everything seemed new: the seaweed-and-almonds smell that hung in the hotel lobby; the organlike sound of the copper pipes in the bathroom; the sound of store shutters opening one by one, like a string section rehearsing a series of glissandi; the intensely blue sky; the sweet smell of fresh croissants coming from the bakery; the dulcet female voices seeping through the room walls at dusk.

Everyone in southern Italy sang. It was really strange. Old grandmothers on bicycles, professional men carrying focaccia, teenagers on scooters, the cook from the restaurant next door, the baker, the fishermen who delivered crates with oysters, mussels, and calamari twice a day. People sang to say hello and say goodbye. They sang while laughing. They even sang when they got into car accidents, mostly in powerful tenor and alto recitatives, delivered in bruising marcato, with rolling rs that rattled store windows and stopped traffic. Music bubbled from under the pavement, from under the sea, it stirred in the depths of the earth like a furious volcano.

My roommate was eighteen, which made him exactly twice my age. He had come to Salerno to compete in the adult group. He'd brought with him a whole collection of frightening weapons such as scherzi and ballads and transcendental études and Hungarian rhapsodies. The third student from the Sofia Music School for the Gifted who'd won a grant to travel to Italy and participate in the international piano competition was a twelve-year-old girl named Isabella who was staying with her mother on the second floor of the hotel, in a room facing an enclosed backyard. Isabella was really tall, practically a giant, with long blond hair that reached to her waist, and a small, pale face that was saved from beauty by an expression both idiotically stubborn and frighteningly vacuous. Isabella was to compete in the same age group as me, but she already acted as if she'd won the competition. Her mother, a cross between a wild boar and a giraffe who wore her fur coat even when she went to the bathroom, insisted that I learn from her daughter, since her daughter was a genius and was going to the top. The entire train ride from Sofia to Salerno she couldn't stop babbling about Isabella's unique qualities and superior constitution. "Pay attention to what I'm going to show you, Konstantin, for one day you will feel lucky to have been together, in the same coach, with a musician as outstanding as Isabella. Isabella, dear, prelude number ten, measure forty-seven, left hand." Isabella sang. "What did I tell you? Now give me measure eighty-three, right hand. Good, now ninety-five, left hand, backwards!"

On the day of the first round of the competition, I woke up to find the following note, which had been slipped under my door:

"Konstantin, as a gesture of goodwill, I'm inviting you to our room at eight o'clock so that you can observe, in person, as Isabella rehearses her repertoire. If time permits, you may get to practice your little pieces as well. Don't be late!"

I burned with curiosity. How could Isabella practice in her room? Had her mother arranged for a piano to be delivered to the hotel? I

dressed quickly and at eight o'clock sharp stood outside Isabella's
room. I heard nothing. Perhaps Isabella hadn't begun practicing yet. I
knocked and opened the door.

"Sh-h-h-h! Sh-h-h-h! Quiet!" Isabella's mother gestured for me to
sit next to her on the bed. I obeyed, noting the ten pairs of shoes lined
up by the door, the dozen or so dresses hung all over the room—on the
windowsill, on the ceiling fan, on the bathroom door—the half-eaten
apples, the perfume bottles, the balls of cotton stained with mascara.
And there she was, Isabella, sitting at the table by the window, dressed
in a black velvet skirt and white silk shirt with a bow, banging fero-
ciously on a piano keyboard painted on a long sheet of paper.

"Stop fidgeting, for God's sake! You're distracting her!"

"I'm not!"

Isabella was building up to the climax, her cheeks bright red, her
long hair tossing left and right, her nostrils flaring. Tap-tap-tap went
her left hand, attacking the watercolor keys with bear punches. Tippy-
tippy-tippy scurried her right hand, wrinkling the paper ivories. Stomp-
stomp went her right foot. I hadn't noticed it right away, but the pedals
were painted, too, on a piece of cardboard. They were pure gold.

We didn't get to hear the final chord because of all the honking and
singing coming from the street. Still, the end was impressive, what
with all those dramatic hand pirouettes, the sporadic breathing, and
the outburst of facial convulsions. Isabella's mother jumped to her feet
and started clapping. I followed suit. Then, when she'd calmed down
and the honking outside had ceased, she sat back down and said,
"Bravo, Isabella, bravo! Now, take it again from the beginning, but try
to bring a lot more emotion this time!"

Even after I had won the competition, Isabella's mother continued to
lecture me about my playing. She claimed that I still had a lot to learn
from her daughter. She was right. In fact, I couldn't have gotten the
first prize without Isabella's help. The image of Isabella performing
on the paper piano, the hollow sound of her emotions, her graceless

vanity, her tinsel passion, changed the way I played the piano forever. When I went onstage that day in Salerno, I realized that in each great piece of music, there were spirits and gods, heroes and villains, waiting to come out and tell their story. The only problem was that we didn't know how to invite them into our realm. Musicians were too arrogant, too self-obsessed to step aside and let the hidden forces take the reins. Sometimes, only sometimes, when the planets were aligned fortuitously, when the performer and the audience were in accord with the gods, the magic happened. Being a vessel, an oracle speaking foreign tongues, making prophecies—that was the true role of a great performer. Temperament was the courage to become the music and not allow your petty human emotions to get in the way.

I hated bow ties—they made me feel like a dog on a leash. The whole outfit made me uncomfortable, the white silk shirt, the black jacket and black trousers, the shoes. It was just another uniform. At least I had my own room, on the fourth floor, away from the circus downstairs, with all the wigs and bobbleheads sitting in the first row, taking notes, and the crowd of musicians, Chopin connoisseurs, old ladies with bright red lipstick, apparatchiks, teachers and bored university students spilling from Chamber Hall No. 1 into the foyer, and even on the street, they'd practically blocked off all traffic. And then there were the other competitors, pacing around the foyer and stabbing one another with contemptuous glances. In about thirty minutes, the *conferencier* would knock on my door and ask me to go downstairs and get ready to perform. But that was still a long time away. For now I was free to page through Ladybug's sheet music and have fun sight-reading pieces I had never heard before, like the dreadfully beautiful mazurka in B major with its crestfallen preface, omniscient autumnal theme, breathless buildup, and a merry-go-round middle where unicorns, carriages, and children's faces blurred into a colorful spiral. It was all a dream, the competition and the fear and the importance of achieving perfection. In half an hour it would all start spinning, just like the merry-go-round in the mazurka, a blur of porcelain eyes and wigs and black and white keys, and then I would walk offstage and go back, still dizzy, to the crestfallen preface and the pale yellows, to being a lost adolescent. I knew what competitions were like. There were three clearly defined phases that I had to go through: the warm-up phase, the waiting-for-the-call phase, and the walking-offstage phase. What happened between the second and the third phase was a mystery. Once onstage, I lost all self-awareness and slipped into a deep trance. And if I spoke in tongues, I didn't know it.

I looked out the window at the crows and ravens perched on the roof of the National Library. Was I ready to speed through the études, to become a glassblower in the nocturnes, to hammer the furious fourths in the coda of the second ballad, and then work myself up in the reprise of the Scherzo, building a tower that would be knocked down in the end? Trying to imagine how I would sound onstage was a destructive exercise accompanied by nausea and panic shivers. I had to stop thinking about playing the piano altogether. And the only way to do that was to start playing it. I began the mazurka again, the minor chords in the opening ripened and turned into major, and soon I was lost in the narrow streets of a foreign town.

"Konstantin! It's your turn next. Let's go!"

It was the voice of Bianka, who'd been chosen by the principal to be the *conferencier*. I walked to the door and then quickly walked back to the Yamaha, convinced that I was forgetting something very important. I didn't carry anything with me when I came to school this morning. What could I be forgetting? But of course, it was Vadim's silver band, which I'd taken to wearing.

"Stop for a second," Bianka ordered when we reached the stairwell. Drawing closer, she fixed the collar of my shirt, straightened my bow tie, and then styled my hair. "There! And don't forget to take a bow. You are going to be great!"

I descended the stairs slowly, hands in my pockets. I nodded at the doorman, who was trying desperately to keep curious newcomers from peeking into the concert hall. I was curious myself. I immediately spotted the Raven, wrapped up as usual in her fifty-six bracelets. The

Owl was sitting right in the middle together with Bankoff, the acoustics teacher, his enormous, shining bald head towering above all others. Negodnik was sitting next to the frighteningly blond philosophy teacher Pecorini. Even the colonel, Pirozhkin, had decided to come and expose his atrophied ears to the heavy barrage of études, scherzos, ballades, and polonaises. I knew that Irina wouldn't come, even if she wanted to. She would sooner throw herself off a cliff than allow her former classmates to look down upon her. The person I was really hoping to see was Iliya, but he'd refused to say for sure if he would come or not, partly because he was afraid that his presence would make me nervous.

The three giant women were standing together, outside the door of Chamber Hall No. 1, listening intently. Even Maya seemed nervous; she kept tossing back the wisps of ash-blond hair falling over her forehead and turning around in a panic, as if she were afraid that someone would suddenly attack her from behind. Ladybug was biting the knuckles of her right hand and staring at her pointy high heels. Dressed in a long brown woolen coat with a fur collar, the Old Lady was making fun of the contestants and their teachers.

"Who let these dimwits play Chopin? Last time I checked they were playing with dolls!"

Ladybug elbowed her in the ribs and hissed, "Mother! Behave yourself! We're in public!"

"What, I'm just stating the truth! There! What on earth was that? This girl chopped up the phrase into a thousand pieces. She's exhaling at all the wrong places, it's a travesty! Fine, I will shut up, I don't understand Chopin anyway, the whole choked-up Slavic sentimentality gets on my nerves. Goethe said . . ."

"Mother!"

I walked past Maria the janitor, who was sweeping the floor and collecting the empty plastic cups scattered all over the place, her bloodshot drunken eyes glancing fearfully at the entrance to the concert hall. Igor the Swan, wearing a pair of oversized military pants and his ancient see-through blue sweater that came down to his knees,

was pacing up and down the hallway, counting the floor tiles, *fifty-six,*
fifty-seven, fifty-eight, whispering to himself and absorbing every note
coming from the Steinway with his trembling elephantine body. He
was the only one who could truly hear, and perhaps he even thought
of himself as my piano teacher, in a way; he had come to see me play,
but he could not stand the crowd, the wigs made him very nervous,
the sight of the porcelain eyes blinking at even intervals gave him terrible indigestion, the heads of the concertgoers turning around in a full
circle made him dizzy and nauseated.

A girl in a checkered jacket with leather elbow pads and a short skirt
caught my attention. She was standing in the stairwell with her back
toward me, talking to Yavor, the twelfth-grade oboist. Was it Irina? I
could've sworn she looked like Irina. Her hair, her gestures, her stance,
her hands. The way she grabbed his arm when he made her laugh, the
way she tucked her hair behind her slightly elven ears, the violin scar
on her neck. But it wasn't. She wouldn't have come around.

Ever since Irina was kicked out, I'd become obsessed with her. I saw
her everywhere, I dreamed of her every night, I walked up and down
her street every afternoon, between practice sessions, hoping to see
her or her mother and find out which apartment building they lived in.
I'd been in every house and building on Serdika Street, read the name
on every mailbox. I had smoked countless cigarettes waiting to hear
someone playing the violin. She must still be playing, I thought. She
couldn't just stop and never play again; it was her soul.

"Get a grip on yourself!" I heard the Old Lady yell as she punched
me in the back. I staggered, losing my balance. "Are you nervous?
What's wrong with you, walking hunched up and shriveled like that!"

"For God's sake, Mother, leave him alone, he needs to concentrate!"
Ladybug exploded.

"It's too late to concentrate now," Maya murmured. "He should've
been concentrating during the last eleven months."

I counted the mosaic squares on the floor: twenty in one row, thirty-
five in another. The girl at the Steinway reached the final cadence in
the first ballad. It was time. I reminded myself of why I was here: to

play Chopin as it should be played, honestly, suicidally, with terminal disappointment and a complete absence of ambition; with aristocratic tact and chivalry, with selfless piety, with the most profound knowledge of beauty and of the transience of the senses.

Bianka announced my name. From where I was standing I caught a glimpse of her black dress and legs in black tights. Everyone clapped. I walked onstage and sat at the piano. I placed Vadim's ring in the corner of the keyboard and distracted myself briefly by thinking about the love note that Bianka had given me back in May. Then I started playing.

Finally! The very last chord. Now a short pause, to recuperate, a deep bow, and down the stairs toward the exit. Blinding lights, grinning faces, clapping, people shouting, everything a blur. Ladybug grabbed me by the elbow and whisked me away from the crowd. I had to ask her how I'd fared. Did I hit any wrong notes? Did I think through the phrases? I had no recollection of the performance.

"It's like you weren't yourself," Ladybug told me as she pushed me out the main entrance and toward Doctors' Garden, where the Old Lady and Maya were waiting for me with anticipation. "It was good, very meticulous, precise and kind of mechanical in places, but, strangely enough, very emotional, too, it all sounded new to me, not like the Konstantin I know, but I liked it, and the jury seemed to like it as well, and the audience . . . even if you don't get the prize, the audience saw what you can do, that you're the best." We had stopped in the middle of the street, to let a car pass by, and suddenly I couldn't go farther, I couldn't face the Old Lady, couldn't bear to listen to the surgical analysis that would follow, bar by bar, theme by theme, down to each breath, it was too much.

"There is no such thing as being the best in music," I told Ladybug and started walking down the street, right in the middle of traffic.

"I know what it is," she said and tried to hug me, just as a trolleybus pulled over so as not to hit us. "You're mad at me because I'm leaving and getting married. But you don't understand! I'm doing it for you! I will take you with me to America. You'll see. I'll never abandon you!"

She was lying. I knew she was lying. She was finally happy, now that she was screwing the American. I couldn't blame her. Who wouldn't leave this place if they could? The shadows, and the red night sky, and the dusty streets. Vadim and I, we would be just fine.

I t was a foggy, sunless winter morning steeped in the smells of burning charcoal, frosted brown leaves, torn acidic clouds, and wet gravel; there was even a whiff of decomposing carcass, perhaps a dead cat lying under the bushes in Doctors' Garden, and if one stood on tiptoe one could detect a trace of tires set ablaze somewhere in the Gypsy quarters. Echoes were short and exaggerated, sounds of passing cars came out muffled, footsteps died out suddenly, the eight o'clock bells of Nevski Cathedral spread through the city in uneven waves, the bass colliding with the tenor and the alto in a series of deathly, strained intervals. Ravens huddled in the trees and on the trolleybus wires, a slow icy wind ruffled the concert posters tagged onto the trees on Oborishte Street, a bluish gray light flickered in the iced-over puddles. It seemed as if today the sun were going to come up from under our feet. We had gathered in the *pushkom,* smoking impatiently and sharing a triple dose of espresso. It felt like we'd arrived at the end of the world, the houses around us cracked, the earth below us breathing heavily, the iron manholes spouting sulfuric fumes that crept over the sidewalk like underworld vines, twisting around the ankles of the arriving students. The leaden sky was bearing down on the city, crushing the antennas on the rooftops, fracturing the clay tiles and snapping the laundry lines heavy with frozen clothes. The street dogs knew what was going on, they were running fast, like shadows, to hide under Hecate's robe. Everyone wore their uniforms, Komsomol ties, and black shoes. I was the only one carrying a bag. I had brought Zimova a small surprise.

"The bitch had to die!" Alexander sang in a dramatic bass recitative, very much like an Eastern Orthodox priest at a funeral. He'd been repeating the same sentence and flicking ash from his cigarette over an imaginary grave all morning. "In the name of the Father, the Son, and the Holy Ghost, the others will soon follow suit!"

"I personally had nothing against her," said a drummer with glasses who was nicknamed Stumpy because of his short height. "She was a decent principal."

"She was all right," Yavor agreed. "Never had any problems with her."

"Does the name Irina ring a bell?" I asked them. "Fucking morons."

"Irina was just the last one," Alexander backed me up. "The Owl had ruined many lives before her."

"Irina fucked up," Yavor said, smiling. "You have to be smart to play the game right."

"And which game is it that you're playing?" I asked him. "Daddy's boy who's got no talent?"

Already, three people had formed a wall between me and Yavor, in anticipation of a fistfight. Alexander had edged closer to me, so that he could hold my arms in time to stop me.

Yavor put out his cigarette and took off his uniform jacket. "Are you possibly jealous because I banged Irina and ruined your little Bach duo? Life isn't very romantic, is it? Especially when you come in second every time."

Alexander stepped in front of me, ready to strike on my behalf, but Peter, the chubby piano player from 10B, and Stumpy grabbed Yavor by the arms and led him away. When they reached the street, he managed to free himself and returned to the exact spot where he'd been standing the whole time.

"You deserved to get first prize," Maria, the twelfth-grade violinist, told me, as if she were offering her condolences. "I was sitting toward the back . . ."

I didn't say anything. I smoked. Today was a special day and I wasn't going to let them ruin it. They just didn't know. And they wouldn't believe me if I told them that it was Irina who'd killed Zimova. I'd seen it. Irina had sown the seeds of the cancer that had eaten the Owl's lungs in less than two months. It was so clear to me. Irina had silenced the old puppet, she had drained the last drop of ink from the fountain pen of Tovarich Andropov, she had twisted the arms of the pentacle that beseeched the dead and the living to march together in the name of progress, she had melted the cogwheels of the neat materialistic universe, she had subjugated the Euclidean laws to the intonation of her voice. She had introduced the nocturnal bird to the mystery of time. Had Irina's curse rung in the Owl's ears as she lay dying in her home? Had she remembered kicking Irina's cross into the stairwell, had she felt Irina's firm fingers digging into her chest, had she asked to be forgiven? Had she heard divine music or only the granite silence of the deaf empiricists? But I hadn't come to school today to scorn her. I was going to pay homage to her in my own way, once the little soldiers in blue and red formed ranks behind the government Volga hearse and the school fell quiet. Today there wasn't going to be any music. All classes and practice sessions were suspended. A long black flag had been hung on the front of the school, from the fourth floor. Everyone was going to the cemetery. The Jealous One had opened the gates of his palace to greet one of his own, a pale, bloodless serf.

Alexander and I walked back to school, worried that the Hyena might be looking for us. But there was nothing to worry about: our supervisor was standing outside the main gate, entertaining a gang of ear-training teachers.

"Just last week Comrade Zimova seemed on top of things! She looked so vital, writing decrees, attending meetings, teaching classes, too. Had anyone noticed anything strange? No one! How could it happen so quick, so suddenly, she hadn't even gone to the doctor! She was like a mother to all of us, yes, she was just and compassionate, full of vigor and optimism. She was a perfectionist! A patron of the arts! Oh, how she loved her talented kids, working tirelessly to provide them with the best instruments and opportunities!"

Negodnik, for his part, was leaning on his umbrella and reading the long text in Zimova's necrology, printed under a black-and-white photograph of the Owl as an aspiring apparatchik, seated behind a desk, a pen in her hand. *A dedicated mother, loving wife, impeccable teacher, selfless school principal, awarded three times for exceptional . . . holder of the medal . . . will always remain in our hearts . . . a bright example . . . proletarian . . . serving the people and the Party . . . So long!*

Bankoff was in tears, his hairless skull hidden under a woolen beret. The gym teacher was in charge of organizing the funeral march. His glasses had fogged over and he was giving orders with a choked-up voice. The piano teachers, all dressed in black, formed the first row. Then came the strings, and behind them, the brass and woodwinds. I was placed three rows behind the last row of teachers, with the tenth and eleventh graders. Stephanie was right behind me, with the ninth graders. She and I hadn't had fun since her mother had attempted to break my back with a coatrack in the attic. It made me nauseated to look at her now, the way she glanced nervously at the necrologies of the dead bird and then stared into the fog with the hopeless resignation of a lost orphan. Bianka's eyes were red, too. I looked around—at Ivan and Slav, at the twins, at Angel and the two Marias, at the colonel, at Mouseface and her pupils—almost everyone was stricken with grief.

"If it could only snow," the Hyena was saying behind me, "it would be so much more bearable!" With their black mourning ribbons pinned to their chests, they looked like lambs marked for slaughter. Could it be that humans had a hidden organ, an invisible second heart, that enabled them to follow orders, to be stirred to hatred, to kill and lie for the sake of a higher authority, to renounce their humanity, and then to mourn their tormentors? They'd already forgotten! What about our fourth-grade literature teacher who'd been fired by the Owl because he'd taught us that language is magical and that we should use it carefully lest we open doors that are best left closed? What about her monthly assassinations of the most talented, her daily acts of dehumanization, her venomous tongue, her puppeteering, her hateful speeches, her peasant hands and godless eyes? What about Vadim and Irina?

I had to wear a black mourning ribbon, too, pinned to the left lapel of my uniform jacket, and as I stood shivering in the December fog, waiting for the hearse to arrive, I felt the needle piercing my shirt, and my skin, and digging deeper, under the bones, into my heart, and the point of the needle was tipped with a poison that thinned my blood and drained my will. I was just like them, in the end, a Hadean subject, pinned onto our master's magnificent black canvas like a collectible butterfly. Perhaps it was just a matter of time before I started enjoying the show.

Kurtswine, the deputy principal, walked out of the school and joined the gym teacher at the front of the crowd. "Where are the wreaths? Why haven't the students brought enough flowers? I want everyone to carry flowers!"

The gym teacher rushed back into the school. The wreaths and the flowers had been piled up on the stage of Chamber Hall No. 1. There were enough roses, carnations, mums, tulips, and shrubbery to cover the mausoleum. I immediately volunteered for the task of carrying everything out of the concert hall. I was joined by Bianka, Yavor, and Alexander, who really loved to pretend that he was an exemplary citizen of the state and that he *cared*. It was strange how the flowers lost their color and opiate aroma once they were brought out on the sidewalk. The dark red roses turned the color of a dead man's veins, the orange tulips acquired a sickly mustard tinge. The air became filled with the distinct smells of worm-infested earth and decomposing algae that usually haunt the shores of old lakes.

Yavor and I carried the large portrait of Zimova, with a black band stretched across its top right corner, through the metal gates and out onto the sidewalk. Of course, Yavor was right. I was angry and jealous about Irina and I was furious that I didn't win the first prize at the competition. Maybe it was all my fault. Maybe I had sabotaged my performance in the same way that I had sabotaged my relationship with Irina—by hiding in my cocoon, by rejecting a better future, by reveling in my loneliness. Perhaps there was something rotten inside me, something diabolical that ruined everything I worked for and corrupted the fruits I desired. Happiness and success terrified me. Deep inside I wanted to fail, to sink to the lowest ground, because I was convinced, at the core of my being, that failure would purify me, would prove that I hadn't followed the orders, that I had rejected the ugly world and its tempting privileges. Was this the philosophy of the drunks and the maniacs and the self-proclaimed prophets rumbling through the city in rags, homeless, dirty, and unshaven, talking to themselves, arguing with invisible protagonists, with shadows, laughing too, blissfully, at times hysterically, free at last from the objectives of the existential itinerary? I was just a step behind them, I knew that well, it wouldn't take much for me to give up and go stand at the shore, like so many others, ahead of time. What's a lifetime, after all? A walk from this corner to the next, a film that starts in the middle and ends suddenly, without warning; one would get through it somehow, regardless of his decisions, regardless of the order, the uniform, the circumstances. Why couldn't I be like Bianka and the rest, why couldn't I believe in the beginning and the end, in the real and important stuff that made up the middle?

The Nevski's bells struck nine o'clock. The hearse was going to pull over any minute. There was Bianka, running back for more flowers. I intercepted her in the foyer and gave her mine.

"These are the last ones," I told her and turned around.

"Are you coming to the cemetery?" she asked, looking at me reproachfully.

"No."

"I didn't think so. And what should I tell our supervisor?"

"Nothing. I don't think she's going to notice my absence. She's too busy crying."

Bianka shook her head, letting me know that she found my cynicism very distasteful. It was too bad, really. We just couldn't ever get along.

I sprinted up the stairs, dying to get to my hiding place and light up a cigarette. If only I could bring up a cup of espresso, too! It was too much to ask. The buffet in the basement was closed. Second floor. Third floor. I was almost there. Fourth floor. I was panting really loud, but I was sure that the building was deserted. Suddenly, the doors flew open with a bang and Maria the janitor, the Owl's favorite spy—dressed in black, with a black headscarf, like a widow—threw herself at me, then grabbed my hand and looked in my eyes with a mixture of fear and disgust.

"Your girlfriend killed her! The others might not know, but I do! She killed her! She used an old curse, the filthy Gypsy, I'd heard it before, just once, a very long time ago. You stay away from that demon, do you hear? She's ruined everything, everything!"

I started walking forward, forcing Maria to retreat into the hallway of the fourth-floor piano practice rooms. "My girlfriend," I said in as wicked a voice as I could muster, "has a message for you." I had pushed her against the wall and was looking through her eyes, into her skull. "She asked me to tell you . . ." I disentangled my hand from hers and took a step back. Maria was shaking violently. "She said . . ." I closed one of the double doors leading to the stairwell and pointed my finger at her. "One day . . ."

I stepped out and closed the second door. I waited for Maria to say *what?* on the other side. She didn't. There was no sound. I took the black ribbon off, it was suffocating me. But where should I throw it, I thought, I couldn't just toss it on the ground, it was cursed. The toilet! I'd return the ribbon to the underworld. I went to the fifth-floor bathroom, threw the ribbon in the toilet, and peed on it. "No disrespect, Zimova," I said out loud, "but I had to do it." Looked at my watch. I was going to miss the show. I ascended the spiral wooden staircase and ran to my favorite attic room, the third one looking west, with the Chaika upright and the big skylight. It was locked. The bastards! One kick was all it took to break the latch. I threw my uniform jacket over the chair, opened my leather bag, and placed Chopin's sonatas on the music rest, then I flipped over the top lid, to let the soundboard breathe, and rooted for my pack of cigarettes hidden at the bottom of my bag, below the padding. It was really warm in there, thanks to all the heating pipes running alongside the western wall, below the skylight. Shit! I hadn't brought any matches! My perfect moment was ruined. And it was going to be so thoroughly perfect—the fog, the slow echo, the warm room, the piano, and the procession down below . . . I climbed on the chair, propped up the skylight on a metal bar, and pulled myself onto the roof. The whole school was still standing on the sidewalk, waiting for the old bird to make an appearance. Kurtswine was surrounded by the gorgons and the Erinyes, no doubt discussing something of grave importance. Would I be so stupid as to go downstairs, risking being seen, just to get a couple of matches so that I could indulge my obsession with staging a perfect moment? I definitely would. I grabbed my jacket and spiraled back to the first floor, leaping blindly down each flight of stairs, twisting an ankle in the process. The doorman was pacing outside his booth, wearing a black ribbon on his blue apron.

"You shouldn't be here," he said to me.

"I really need a few matches," I pleaded. "Please. It's a matter of life and death."

The old Commie didn't know much about music but he had a great appreciation for matters of life and death. He opened the door to his booth, ripped a piece of striking surface from his matchbox, and counted five matchsticks. He wasn't lacking Promethean grandeur either. I limped back upstairs and looked again through the skylight. Nothing had changed. The old bird was fashionably late. I sat at the piano. What should I start with? Something not too engaging, not too loud or fast, something like a prelude or intermezzo. Maybe an andante. How about Mozart's Fantasia in D Minor? Real slow. Savoring each tone. I placed my hands on the piano and saw the poppy fields of the opening arpeggios, the velvet texture of the cadences, the culpability of the first theme, and then the judgment of the descending chords . . . I didn't dare begin. It was going to spoil the moment. What about Satie's *Gymnopédies*? Too sweet, too indulgent. Then I had it: Debussy's second prelude, "Voiles"—the fog, the emancipated memories, the disengaged thoughts. The wilted flowers. The bleak landscape. It wasn't going to work. It was too saltless, too thin-blooded, too impersonal. There was no backstory. I climbed onto the roof and sat cross-legged on the clay tiles. It was better that I didn't play anything. What if the hearse never came? Bankoff was standing in the middle of the street, looking in the direction of Nevski Cathedral. He could've seen me easily, if he'd looked up. But it's remarkable how most people don't ever bother to look upward, at the rooftops, at the clouds, even at the sky. Some of the teachers, tired of standing in one place, had begun walking up and down the sidewalk with huge wreaths in their arms. The Hyena was in charge of the old bird's framed portrait.

Wait! There it was! Everyone below rushed to the street to witness the arrival of the hearse. I lit a match and devoured the flame through the tip of my cigarette. What style—a shiny black government Volga with tinted windows and an extended back, just for her! Though she must already be across the river, walking hand in hand with Tovarich Andropov and the rest of the Communist mummies. The Volga pulled over by the school gate and everyone began lining up behind it, carrying flowers and wreaths, posters and portraits. Kurtswine was holding a folder containing her speech.

It was all a show, of course. They couldn't really walk behind the hearse all the way to the cemetery, which was at the very edge of town. They were going to march for ten minutes, in the cold, to accompany the old bird during her last visit to the Sofia Music School for the Gifted, and then they were going to load onto trams and buses and reconnect with the old bird at the cemetery. Weren't they cute! Holding hands and touching the windows of the Volga to show how much they cared. Only Pirozhkin, the colonel, seemed out of place. He believed in quick beginnings and quick ends. All the sighing and crying must've been irritating his ulcer. I rested my cigarette on the edge of the piano and opened Chopin's sonatas on the funeral march in B-flat minor. I could hear the engine of the Volga purring down below. I was ready when they were.

There were two ways the funeral march was commonly played— fast, with the urgency and blindness to detail of a military squad en route to the battlefield, and slow, with the misplaced bombast and perverse dramatism of a clown attending a public execution. Ah, how they massacred it, it made you want to throw up for a week. My vision of the funeral march was completely different. I detested the idea of bringing the cretinous rhythm of the organized masses into the sphere of music. Playing the piano was an act of solitude, not a circus. But, of course, before you could understand the funeral march, before you could even say that you knew how to play the piano, you had to know how to walk. You had to know the existential weight of each pace, the mood, transparency, will, and presence that defined each manner of walking, and there were millions! I'd learned more about playing the piano from walking the streets of Sofia than from practicing ten hours a day. Wasn't all music, in a way, an expression of this most basic movement? Wasn't every musical piece a walk from here to there, an exploration, a journey? "Just walk!" Ladybug had told me during my first lesson with her, when I had attempted to perform a Bach fugue. It was the most important advice she ever gave me, and I've been walking ever since, it was my secret practice. For the funeral march, I would walk slowly, but not too slowly, because I didn't want to attract attention.

The Volga started. The procession moved onto the street. *This is for you, Irina,* I thought and struck the opening chords of the funeral march. The sound pierced the December fog and reverberated in the pipes and the propped-up skylight. Could they hear me all the way down on the street? I hoped so.

I walked through the funeral march as if I were going to buy a newspaper, casually, with a cigarette in my mouth, looking into every window, appreciating each cobblestone, the yellow-gray December sun numbing my irises, my cheeks, my lips. There was no hurry, nothing important to attend to. The main event had already taken place. What followed was just a formality, an explanation for those unwilling to accept the nature of illusions, how things arise from nothing, how they change and disappear without a trace.

Never had a major chord sounded as sinister as the G-flat major triad that struck every second and fourth beat. A dark light shone between the two alternating chords, an opaque stream flowed over the five polished granite flats in the native key. But there was nothing sad or frightening about the world below. The long sleep was tempting. The rivers beckoned. Were there tubas making an announcement somewhere in the distance? Were there church bells an octave higher, questioning the tubas, and then French horns echoing the same question, the one question, an octave above that? No. It was just the wind, the sound of passing cars, the cries of ravens in the trees, the sigh of an Ikarus bus opening its four doors by the entrance to the University of Sofia. And when the fog dispersed briefly over Doctors' Garden, allowing the sun to shine on the lonely marble columns and the desecrated sarcophagi, it wasn't to celebrate the passing soul's achievements. Rather, it was a reminder of the distance between us and our unknowable home. Then the tremolos in the left hand rolled the heavy chains and quickly closed the gates. In the middle of the funeral march—a reverie.

I climbed onto the roof and lit another cigarette. The street was empty. Soon the old bird would be lowered into the ground. There would be speeches. The grave diggers would collect their ropes, form a mound with their shovels, and place a red pentacle on top. The teachers and students would look around, at the glimmer of light behind the wrinkled mantle of mountains to the east; at the endless rows of rectangular gravestones that seemed like an extension of the Soviet housing projects, at the lifeless trees and the withered sunflower fields, at the tilted electric poles and the dangling cables, at the Cimmerian horizon to the west. Kurtswine would march toward the exit first, leading the way. She would have to get back to her office and plan the end-of-year concert, the decorations, the new decrees. Everything would continue as it had before. And me? I would have to start working on the opening movement of the second Chopin sonata, on new études, new scherzos, and new ballads. Ladybug wanted me to cover as much material as possible before she left for America and entrusted my career to her mother. Ladybug had promised me that she would send for me after I graduated. All I had to do was graduate.

At long last, everything was white. How I'd craved the taste of the icicles that formed every year around the school's rain gutters, the feeling of pressing a snowball with my bare hands until my fingers began to tingle! Kisses tasted better when the snow crunched under your boots and when the drops from melting ice at the edge of a roof fell straight onto your neck. People looked more human when you could see their breath. The ugly cars parked on the sidewalks were finally buried; the blue trolleybuses zoomed past the school quietly, shimmering with light, their bodies wrapped in an arctic crust, their bumpers decorated with mammoth icicles. The newspapers at the kiosk lay frozen, the flowers for sale by the Gypsies were solid crystals. Thousands of steaming manholes provided warmth to the drunks, the street dogs, the cats. The lungs of the city were hidden underground. Doctors' Garden had disappeared under a blanket of cotton wool. A water pipe had burst near the pond, and a smooth, transparent film of ice exhibited treasures left over from the autumn: red leaves, chestnuts, crescent seed pods, poplar fruits. The neighborhood widows, disguised as bears and wild boars, tottered up and down the unshoveled sidewalks, clanking with their empty bottles, determined to get their daily dose of hot sulfuric water from the mineral spring by the mosque, determined to live forever. The apparatchiks treaded the snow brashly, coughing and cursing like soldiers dying of consumption. The music students, burdened by their instruments and heavy scores, proceeded slowly and cautiously, as if they were climbing down the stairs on ice skates. Igor the Swan, for his part, was wobbling toward the school wearing a tank top, a woolen sports jacket, striped pajama pants, and a pair of flip-flops without socks. I stopped and waited for him by the main entrance, the better to admire his style. He seemed happy to see me, groaning and fidgeting with his fingers as he drew near. I imagined that he wanted to talk to me about the chamber pieces I had to study for next semester. Perhaps he'd even managed to find me someone really talented to team up with.

"The heavenly birds are upon me again, I can't even see where I'm going, my feet walk and I follow them, but I don't mind the cold, I'm just a dog chained to my fate, I've handed in my resignation, I hope the filthy bastards take it."

"A nine o'clock chamber music class, then?" I suggested.

"Something like that, two talentless twelfth graders, it's absolutely appalling. I will be slow-roasted over Brahms's cello sonatas like a pig. The hell with it!" He squeezed through the metal gates and turned around, blocking my way. "Where are *you* going?"

"I have a piano lesson. My concert is in three days." I pointed at the large red posters hung everywhere, on trees and on the school wall. "I hope you come to see me."

Igor looked at me perplexed. "But hasn't anyone told you? They sealed your fate last night. It's done. It's final! I protested on your behalf, but who listens to me, I'm just a fat, failed pianist. First Vadim, then Irina, and now you, what a year! At least you should not go down quietly, the way to go down is in flames: you should burn a hole in the ground as you plummet, take it from me, they shot me down, too, and I had almost reached the sun, I was so high I could see the eternal gardens . . ."

"What are you talking about?" I interrupted him, suddenly feeling incredibly small and alone, just as I'd felt many years before in kindergarten, when I was told to stand facing the wall for hours and hours.

"Last night the Hyena, as you call her, brought your recent misdemeanors to the attention of the teachers' committee, presiding as usual in Chamber Hall No. 1, and they all voted to expel you. It was a nearly unanimous vote, Katya and I were the only ones who objected. I'm sure that right now you feel like the ground is sinking underneath you, but you shouldn't despair: getting kicked out of school is great fun! Do I smell burning frankincense? They must be chasing the evil one, again. The demons of joy! Can't say that I feel sorry or sad about your demise. You've lived a life of arrogance and privilege for too long, you needed a slap in the face, the humiliation will deepen your voice, your intonation, it will organize your thoughts, show you the key to playing whole pieces in one breath, like the masters. You had to go down. They had to sacrifice you so they could live. The buggers! I couldn't do anything about it. If you ask me, your supervisor probably carried out the principal's last wish. Zimova had wanted you dead, they all knew that. But don't worry. Nothing really matters. The moment you are kicked out of one place, you enter another. Allow me to welcome you, then, to the grounds of the fallen, where strange mist obscures the vision, there are fires burning in the distance, crippled ballerinas in rags race, limping, to the heavenly sounds of the Brandenburg concerto played in the background by a band of midgets . . . You are one of us now, Mussorgsky's gnome is here, too, he is quite tall as a matter of fact, you could see him eating *pirozhki* by the Great Gate of Kiev; Samuel Goldenberg, for his part, is selling matryoshki at the Limoges Market, while in the Old Castle a chicken choir performs *Songs and Dances of Death*. But you will get to meet them all, as you will have a lot of time on your hands. Having said this, then . . . Congratulations!"

Igor the Swan walked away with a swagger, his flip-flops snapping against his heels and throwing snow behind him. It couldn't be true,

I thought. Igor always talked in this manner. He was mad. I couldn't have been kicked out of school like that, without any warning! I would've heard about it.

Standing next to the street-level gym window, which had been cracked by a basketball and then sealed poorly with black adhesive tape, I felt the damp warm air escaping the building and detected the hundreds of smells that had defined the Sofia Music School for the Gifted for as long as I could remember: the smell of pianos and old violin cases, of clean uniforms and bleached linoleum floors, of shawls and gloves drying on the radiators, of cheese and ground-pork sandwiches being grilled in the basement, of chalk and ink and pencils, of desks and blackboards and maps and dirty soapy water spilled on the terrazzo staircase; the smell, too, of counterpoint, and choral singing, and chamber music, and composition, and scales played at top speed, and fifteen-year-olds rushing together through the late string quartets. All the school windows were lit up, even though it was only nine o'clock in the morning. It was warm and cozy inside, there was music in every room.

Not knowing what else to do, I stepped through the gate, walked across the courtyard and into the building, and took the corridor to the right. The doorman was in his booth, smoking and reading a newspaper. I tapped on his window and he slid it open and scanned the foyer, to make sure we were alone.

"Is it true?" I asked him, trying hard to stop my voice from quivering. "Did they really kick me out?"

"They did," he replied, blowing smoke in my face. "Your supervisor must've had her reasons. You're not such a bad boy. Certainly not worse than the others. All I see you do is play the piano. Well, you'll have to grow up fast, now. Try to get a job. If you need someone to talk to, I'm always here. I will let you go upstairs to the practice rooms but you must come later, after eight o'clock, because I could get in trouble. They are tightening the rules again, I have to inspect every student coming into the building. If my pension wasn't so small, I would take my hat and go away, why should I work day and night at this age?"

I held my breath and clenched my teeth. I wasn't going to cry. I shook the doorman's hand and ran upstairs, to the fourth floor, avoiding the stares of the janitors mopping the floors.

I leaned against the door of room 42 and put my ear in the crook between the soundproof insulation and the wooden door frame. Ladybug was playing the first movement of the second sonata to herself, passionately but with a tinge of desperation, creating an immense body of light and colors, and then burying everything underground. I could picture her perfectly, leaning forward with all her weight, her fingers flying over the keyboard charged with diabolical power, yet completely free of the colossal tension that they exerted on the strings, her right foot bleeding the damper pedal with fear and hesitation, allowing only a drop of overtones here and there, her eyes scrutinizing the execution of every minute event. No one played the sonata better than her. The way she built the sand castle from the very first note all the way through the sostenuto, and the theme variations, and the somnambulistic run of the triplet-stringed chords in both hands, and then the series of shudders and extrasystolic gasps foreshadowing the all-dissolving E-flat-seventh chord at the end.

I put my hand on the door handle, but the thought of facing Ladybug's wrath and disappointment, her sad eyes and trembling face, made me recoil. There was nothing she could do now to help me. Our bond was broken. She was going to go her way, and I was going to go mine. Maybe that was better. She'd already made plans without me.

I took Vadim's silver band off my finger and slipped it onto the door handle. When Ladybug was done practicing the second sonata and opened the door, the ring would fall on the ground and she would pick it up. She would know exactly what it meant.

For the first time ever, I didn't feel the urge to run upstairs to the attic and lose myself in the études, the ballads, or the preludes. What was even stranger, I actually felt a sense of relief. Maybe it was this same sentiment that had made Vadim smile as he had walked out of school the day he was expelled. In a sense, Vadim, Irina, and I had won: we would never have to prove ourselves again. Whereas everyone else would eventually lose their importance, as a new generation of musicians claimed the spotlight, we, having died young, in our prime, would remain undefeated forever. We would be legends. Or not.

I ran down the stairs and rushed out into the courtyard. The blinding white snow, the ravens, the trolleybuses passing down the street: everything seemed so ordinary. Only I had nowhere to go. I was absolutely alone. I had no friends to turn to.

As I headed aimlessly down the street, I suddenly remembered the posters. I couldn't leave them hanging all over school, my name splashed with huge black letters below the brazenly ambitious program: *Chopin's Ballades 1, 2, 3, and 4; Six Études, op. 10; Sonata no. 2.* I started with the posters thumbtacked to the trees, at first trying to remove them whole—so that I could fold them—and then, as I got more and more frustrated, just tearing them off in shreds. After I was done with the trees, I began ripping the posters covering the outside wall—twelve in all. One last poster remained, hanging in the foyer. I held my breath and stepped into the building again. How did I get to this point? Taking down my own posters. This was probably the ultimate humiliation.

"What are you doing?" someone yelled behind me. It was Bianka, carrying a violin case. She'd already chosen her second instrument, as was required of tenth graders. I had planned to pick up the cello.

"You didn't hear?" I asked, realizing quickly that she had no idea what was going on.

"What?"

"Well, I can't play anymore. I was diagnosed with arthritis. For months now I've had a hard time lifting my hands and holding things. Practicing has been hell. The doctors said that it could be lethal. In a year or two, I might not even be able to put on a shirt."

"Is that for real?" she asked, looking at my hands with horror.

"It is. But there's some hope, you see. They are sending me to a sanatorium in Velingrad where I will stay wrapped in mud for three months. It's some kind of medicinal mud, or clay, that is supposed to cure arthritis. Who knows, I might play again."

Just then I spotted Mazen, one of the French-horn-playing twins in my class. No discussion was ever complete without his expert opinion.

"You shouldn't be here," he said, walking past. "You are no longer a student in this school. It was about time they kicked you out."

I wanted to punch the fucker in the face. I should be able to stand up for myself, at least once. But I did nothing. I stuffed the last remaining shreds of paper in my already full bag and headed out. Bianka was crying. At least someone was crying. I wasn't.

Brahms,
Ballade, op. 10, no. 2

January 21, 1989

I washed my hair in the large metal sink out in the basement hall-way and returned to the cockroach-infested cell that Peppy the Thief was letting me use for a while, until I sorted things out. But, in truth, there was nothing left to sort out: after my last fight with my parents, I no longer had a home, and no longer had parents. They didn't want to see me again. I didn't want to see them either. It was over. I was kicked out of school; Ladybug had left for America. And the weird thing was, I felt liberated—angry, furious, but liberated. I was content living on my own, answering to no one. True, I still had some options. The Hyena had made it known that I could try to appeal the school administration's decision, and possibly even return to school, if, one, I made a public apology, two, retook the entrance exam, and three, agreed to go back a grade. But I wasn't going to play their game. I didn't owe them an apology. And I wasn't going to let them humiliate me in front of the whole school. I just wasn't ever going to play again. That was my revenge. I possessed something precious, something that could never be imitated or replaced. They wanted it badly, but it was gone. I had destroyed it.

I lay in the metal cot and stared out the tiny barred window that looked out onto the sidewalk. All day long I watched the endless parade of shoes: moccasins, snow boots, high heels, tennis shoes, military boots, galoshes. Mothers pushing strollers, old ladies dragging their shopping bags. It was strange that I was only four blocks from school, and just a few steps from Doctors' Garden. It seemed that no matter what I did, I always ended up walking the same old streets. I looked at my watch: it was almost twenty past five. The concert at the Guild of Composers was at six, and my button-up shirt wasn't dry yet. I'd left it on the heating pipe in the basement hallway.

Ladybug's wedding had been the previous week. She had arrived at the tiny Byzantine church near the patriarchate in a long puffy white dress, holding hands with the American, looking ecstatic despite the bleak January weather. The Old Lady and Ladybug's sister had followed closely behind, mournfully; they felt betrayed. "You have to come to my house tomorrow so that I can give you new material," Ladybug had said, pulling me aside right before walking into the temple. "In two days I'm flying to Philadelphia, but I'm not going to leave you behind. You'll receive instructions from Mother, and when I arrange everything in America you'll join me and we'll continue exactly from where we'd left off. Promise me that you'll come tomorrow! I haven't stopped worrying about you ever since they expelled you. Tell me, is it true that you've run away from home? Do you realize how much pain you've caused your parents? Promise that you'll get back on your feet and start practicing again! No drinking! Tomorrow at nine!" She had clutched my hand the way she'd always done when I was about to go onstage—urgently, desperately, as if she were sending me to the front line to get killed— and then the priest had nodded at her and implored her to continue forward. "This isn't going to end well," the Old Lady had mumbled to Maya and me. "You'll see. But who ever listens to me!"

"Mother! Quit it!" Ladybug had shouted, turning around. She had seemed so beautiful and full of life! She had found her freedom, and none of the ravens, witches, and harbingers of bad omens could stop her now. Perhaps Vadim and I had been the last two obstacles to her emancipation. We had to die as pianists before she could extricate herself from the Tartarean trap. We were her first lovers, but our love had been one of darkness and peril. We had tried to drag her down with us, and she'd resisted. We had tried to seduce her with our immaculate scales and arpeggios, with our hypnotic voices and the innocence of our phrases. We had tried to tempt her with the smell of youth and the carelessness of two boys who had just discovered the sting of passion. But she had decided to wait for her prince instead.

I put on my warm button-up shirt and my father's old military coat and locked the basement door with a padlock. I headed straight toward Seven Saints Church, via Parliament, so as to avoid the music school. My hair was still wet and the chilly evening wind rattling the sunset-drenched windows of the pastry shop across the tram tracks felt purifying. The sound of my boots crushing the thin glaze of blackened ice echoed across the park, frightening the pigeons and the napping widows. There was the old willow tree, with its twisted trunk and emaciated, broken hands thrown furiously around it, as if to ward off some invisible attack.

Crossing Rakovski, I heard the church bell behind me ring six times—a gorgeously bleak union of seconds and sevenths that invoked the image of an Orthodox priest kneeling in a vault filled with skulls—and my mind was suddenly overwhelmed by the recognition of the inevitable future, of the only way forward.

I'd noticed the posters outside the music school and the Guild of Composers on my way back from Ladybug's wedding ceremony. Eva Moskova, the opera singer who had graduated last year, was an old friend of mine. Before she turned to singing, she'd studied piano with Ladybug for many years. Oftentimes, following our joined late-night recitals, I would go back with her to her house, to drink tea and play the nocturnes for her paralyzed mother. She and I had gotten along quite well, despite our age difference and the fact that we'd been rivals.

The program will include works by Bach, Bizet, Puccini, Schubert, and Debussy. I was curious to see what Eva had done with her voice after a year at the conservatory. Perhaps I just needed someone to talk to. Or maybe I wanted to hear the Yamaha grand on which I'd performed more than a dozen times. Regardless, I was late. I stopped at the flower shop outside the National Theater and bought one rose.

Peppy had lent me a few bucks he had taken by force from some kid from the English High School.

I walked across the park with the fountains and the chess aficionados sitting around with their clocks and vinyl boards, oblivious to the cold and the muddied snow. Lingering outside the glass doors of the Guild of Composers to finish my cigarette, I suddenly felt queasy at the thought that I might run into teachers and students from the music school. Would they recognize me? Probably not. I was a ghost now; I had a new face.

I held the door open for a group of people in a rush to get inside. I didn't look at their faces, just their clothes. A beige rain jacket and gray trousers, a purple sweater and a black skirt, high heels and moccasins, military boots and uniform. We all squeezed into the tiny elevator with warped wooden panels and a flimsy metal sliding door, and it was then, as I held my breath and protected my rose from being crushed, that I noticed something very familiar in the profile of the young soldier standing next to me. I tried to turn around to get a better look at the soldier's face, but the woman behind me protested, grunting. Who was this man? If he would only look at me for a second, I would remember. The handle of the short sword hanging from his belt pressed hard against my stomach and poked my ribs. The elevator stopped, the woman in the purple sweater slid the metal door open, and we all rushed into the concert hall, alarmed by the sound of the piano accompanist rushing timidly through the opening bars of a transcribed Bach cantata. I'd forgotten about the soldier and my whole attention was drawn to the tall, beautiful Eva standing in front of the grand piano, in a long, white satin dress, her fists clenched. She was ready to fight! I sat quickly in the very last row and took the program notes lying on the neighboring chair. It was going to be a long show. Eva would be so tired by the end that she'd probably want to skip the customary postrecital drinks.

I looked up from the program notes and saw that the soldier from the elevator was standing in the row in front of me, his military hat under his arm, staring at me in astonishment. It was Vadim the long-lost virtuoso, in fatigues, with a shaved head and burning eyes. I wanted to embrace him but at this moment Eva began singing and Vadim had to sit down. Still, we held hands for a minute or so, his warm and confident, and I remembered his playing, his muscular sweeps of scales and arpeggios, his breathing, his enormous presence. It pained me to think that his divine hands were now trained to kill. I paid hardly any attention to Eva's singing or the performance of the accompanist, and for the rest of the show busied myself with making a list of all the questions I wanted to ask him. When did they call him into the army? What did they have him do? Had he heard any news from Ladybug? Was he planning to go back to playing the piano after his mandatory training? What about testing into the conservatory? I barely contained myself throughout the recital and the applause, and the bis, and the second applause, and then the snail race to the stage to congratulate Eva for her fantastic performance. I just wanted to pull Vadim aside and say, *Tell me everything I need to know, for I've been living in hell!* But the whole thing went on forever. Eva kissed us both on the cheeks, and in return we offered her our most cherished compliments. Then we went to wait in the foyer while Eva changed her clothes. We were finally alone.

"It's good to see you," Vadim began, holding my shoulder and studying my face and long hair. "I have something important to tell you."

"About school? Or Katya? Did you hear that she left last week for America?" I was breathless, struggling to find the right words.

"I heard, of course. I was actually supposed to come to the wedding, but I didn't get permission to leave the garrison. I need to talk to you about something else, though it's better to wait until we are alone. Let's see first what Eva plans to do."

"Look at you both!" exclaimed Eva, arriving in a swirl of perfume, eyeliner, and flowers. "You look like you've crawled out from under a stone! And you—you're a soldier! With a sword! Who would've thought . . . I'm really tired, but I will get a drink with you if—and I really mean it—you both play something short for me, like in the good old days, when we were all studying with Katya. Right here, on the upright by the door. Come on! I insist."

I started Chopin's third prelude as fast as I could, to get it over with, turning the sixteenth notes in the left hand into whole brushstrokes, but once I heard the main theme, rising above the chaos and clamor of the city like a new sun, a pure sun that had come to heal us, my reluctance to play dissipated and I began to slow down, so that I could enjoy every note, every color. How had I survived even one day without playing? I had the means to connect to something so much larger than my pathetic ego, and I'd chosen the path to silence. I didn't understand myself. I didn't understand anything. By the time I reached the finale and ceded the bench to Vadim, I was trying hard not to cry. It didn't help that Vadim decided to play Brahms's second ballade. I had to step away from the piano. The light was too bright. The slow, liquid octaves in the right hand made me feel naked. Vadim was killing me. I'd built a soundproof shell and hidden inside it, and now Vadim was tearing it to pieces, crushing the floor and the joints with those powerful, obeliskal Brahms chords gilded in Hypnos's dark gold. I staggered to the window and looked down at the busy intersection between Rakovski and Gurko, at the passing trolleybuses, the high school students wandering around, hours after the end of school, and the red, neon-lit letters of the Budapest restaurant. My lungs were burning. I needed a cigarette.

Eva clapped and shouted "Bravo!" but Vadim pretended that he'd had nothing to do with it, and quickly put on his heavy military coat and hat. Just then the doorman appeared at the top of the stairs and, seeing that I was smoking, yelled at us to get out. Vadim didn't let him get near me and the doorman didn't dare push him out of the way.

Once on the street, Eva led us around the block, to a bar frequented by professors and students from the acting school. The three of us sat at a table near the door and ordered a bottle of wine. Eva seemed to know everyone there—the guy playing klezmer songs on a violin, the bartender, the young actors trading memorized lines.

"So," Eva began. "When do you get discharged? And what are you going to do after that? Are you planning to go to the conservatory?"

"I'm thinking about it," Vadim replied. "Right now I'm taking exams to get a high school diploma. When I leave the army next spring, I'll try my luck at the conservatory. Why not? Playing piano is the only thing I'm good at."

"And you?" Eva turned to me. "You aren't giving up, right?"

"No, of course not," I replied, looking down at the overflowing ashtray and the wine stains on the table. I felt like such a loser. Eva had found her calling. She was a celebrated singer now. Vadim wasn't quitting either. Of all Katya's former students, I was the only one who had hit rock bottom. These days the extent of my life's ambition amounted to crashing parties with the likes of Peppy the Thief, drinking anything I could get my hands on, raiding my grandmother's fridge, and listening obsessively to Kino's new album, *Gruppa Krovi*.

"Just think how much fun you'll have at the conservatory!" Eva continued. "You can be my accompanist. We'll give concerts together! And Vadim will be there, too, he will finally get to play Rachmaninov's concertos with an orchestra!"

"Thanks, guys," I said as I downed three full glasses of wine, one after the other, much to Eva's dismay. Then I picked up my burning cigarette and left the bar.

Vadim caught up with me on the other side of Rakovski Street, his sword jingling from his belt.

"I went to see Irina today," he shouted after me. "She talked about you the whole time."

"Really?" I shouted back and kept walking, unable to grasp the significance of his words. Vadim hesitated, wondering if he should follow me or not.

"She said that she is in love with you. That she's still in love with you."

I stopped and turned around. "I don't understand. Why were you talking to her? How did you find her?"

"Our mothers are old friends. I've known Irina all my life. I should've told you before, I guess. She always confided in me—about her abortions and her relationship with you. I don't want to judge you or blame you for anything, but I think that what happened to her had a lot to do with you."

"Vadim, what happened to her is not much different than what happened to you and me. We were all expelled!"

"Irina is locked up in the mental asylum behind the Mathematics High School," Vadim said calmly. "She tried to commit suicide a few days after she was expelled from school. Her mom has kept the whole thing secret. That's why you haven't heard about it."

"How? I mean, how did she try to commit suicide?"

"She slit her wrists. Her grandmother found her in the bathtub."

I felt dizzy. The sky, which was the color of dark ruby, seemed as if it were spinning around, propelled by a whirlwind of snowflakes. "It's all my fault, isn't it? I've made a huge mess out of my life, and the whole time I thought only about myself."

"That's not true, Konstantin. Irina has always had problems. But she needs friends right now, and I really think that she needs you more than anybody else. You can request an audience with her every day between ten and eleven in the morning. If the head nurse doesn't let you in, bring her a bottle of brandy or flowers. You'll figure it out. And don't be frightened by Irina's shaved head and the oversized striped pajamas. She's already doing much better . . . after the electroshock therapy and everything else."

"And what if she doesn't want to see me?"

"She does. I tried to get in touch with you before, but your parents said that they had no idea where you were. Listen, I don't want to leave Eva waiting. You really acted like a fool, back there. Though I understand. I feel very much like you. I don't know who I am anymore."

"I'm sorry. Everything has gone wrong lately. Well?"

We hugged. Vadim borrowed my box of matches and lit a cigarette.

"One last thing," I said as he was walking away. "Do you happen to know Irina's mother's address?"

"Twelve Serdika Street. Third floor. Look for Karabashevi. Their mailbox is on the left, right when you walk in."

I headed toward Doctors' Garden. It had stopped snowing and the sidewalk was covered with a thin white blanket. The image of Irina pointing down with her finger as she descended the stairs burned my heart and sent my thoughts into a senseless spiral. I could've saved her from herself. But if she'd loved me, why didn't she tell me? Why did we play all those games, why did we hurt each other again and again?

I was too lightheaded to go back to Peppy's basement. It was fate. It had to have happened this way. I had to go to a concert and end up in the elevator right behind Vadim. I had to be expelled from school. Irina had to try to kill herself. She had to go through electroshock therapy. Now Irina and I were finally going to be together. Maybe ours was going to be a late climax, like in some of the nocturnes, where respite comes at the very end, after much suffering and endless chromatic tribulations.

The mental asylum on Danube Street was a gray, crumbling three-story building—not much different from a government kindergarten—abutting a fenced-in yard overgrown with wilted rose and lilac bushes. The windows were all barred. There were about ten of us waiting for the head nurse to open the door. The morning was unusually sunny and warm, a spring morning in the middle of winter. I was incredibly nervous. I didn't want to go in. The thought of being locked inside the awful building with all the loonies made me sick. The woman standing beside me must've noticed the shaking of my hands as I raised a match to light a cigarette because she put her arm on my back and told me not to worry. "It's not as bad as it seems. They have a good cook. You can smell his borscht from here."

I nodded. I couldn't tell the woman that what I feared was that I wasn't at all different from the people inside. I knew that renouncing all control over our tiny, fabricated reality wasn't at all hard to do. It was like catching the flu. Have contact with a contagious person during a moment of weakness, and soon you'd be talking to the dead. That was nonsense, of course. Irina wasn't crazy. She was the most normal person in the whole world. That's why they'd locked her up—because she reminded them that they were the insane ones. I only wished that I'd brought her a present. I hated showing up empty-handed.

Would she like a silver cross on a chain, like the one that the Owl had snatched from her neck and kicked into the stairwell? I didn't have enough money for something like that, though. I could only offer her cigarettes and my copy of Bach's six sonatas for violin and harpsichord, although she probably wasn't allowed to keep any possessions. But what was I going to tell her? That I would help her escape from the asylum? Where would we go? It wasn't important. We'd live in parks and sleep on benches. We'd make love at the back of empty trams. We'd attend free concerts and sneak into the music school at night to play the sonatas. We'd be inseparable, and when we turned nineteen, we would get married.

The white metal door opened and the head nurse—an ugly old blue-haired crocodile in a white apron, brown stockings, and white sandals—started letting people in. She clearly didn't like the looks of me.

"Where are you going?" she asked, ready to close the door in my face.

"To see my sister."

The crocodile wasn't convinced. "I know your kind," she said, grimacing. "I'm going to need to see a document stamped and signed by the municipal secretary, proving that our patient is, in fact, related to you. Now go away."

"But there are no documents!" I whimpered and burst into tears. I was quite proud of how much liquid I was capable of producing at will. I managed to drench the collar of my shirt in ten seconds. I should've been an actor.

"You see, my sister—my half sister—Irina, is an illegitimate child," I continued, pushing my way into the building and inching past the reception kiosk. "She was born out of wedlock. Her father was a Gypsy and met my mother two years before she had me. Irina never knew her father. He was killed right after she was born. He was run over by a tram in the roundabout in front of the Serdika Theater, just up the street, you must've heard about it in the news at the time. A truly horrible story, really. It was all over the papers. He was split in half, and no one called an ambulance because he was a Gypsy. It's shameful!

He still managed to write a will, though, on the spot. He remained conscious for a while. Yes, this is what my family has to live with. And Irina, being half-Gypsy . . . the discrimination . . . people talking . . . It hasn't been easy for us."

The crocodile was flabbergasted. She clearly hadn't expected to hear such a story at ten o'clock in the morning, with her first coffee, while all the patients were being let out into the icy yard to mingle with the visitors. Still, she demanded to see my ID card, which she then put in her pocket so that I wouldn't try anything funny.

I didn't see Irina at first. What I saw was dozens of profoundly broken people at various stages of spiritual decomposition, all of them dressed in oversized striped pajamas and white sandals and bundled up in cheap hospital blankets. Women rocking back and forth, men shouting and laughing, some pacing, others just staring fixedly at the asylum's wall. Nurse-guards supervised the patients and helped the feeble ones walk. Most of the yard tiles were broken. The flowerpots were empty. Dried-up vines hung from the metal awnings welded to the benches. A marble water fountain with a statue of a robust woman holding a vase stood in the center, overflowing with dead leaves and twigs. I found Irina sitting at the far end of the yard, alone, dazed, her knees pressed together, her arms clasped over her navel. Her head was shaved, as Vadim had warned me, and her lips bore many scabbed scars, as if someone had cut her mouth with a razor. I didn't announce my arrival. I just sat beside her and waited for her to notice my presence.

"You're a bit late," she said finally and tried to smile.

"It took me a while to get here," I replied. I reached for her hand, but she quickly pulled it away, seeing that I'd discovered the barbed purple lines emblazoned across her wrist.

"Do you really think you can come here and make everything better?" She spoke slowly, with a strained voice. "Vadim told you to come, didn't he? You'd have never come on your own."

"I didn't know where you were! Irina, look at me! I came because I love you."

Hearing the charged words spoken out loud, I suddenly felt like a liar. Not because I didn't love Irina, but because I knew that she would never believe me. It was too late. Still, I tried harder. "I spent more than two months looking for you. I didn't know what had happened to you, what you were doing. We can't continue like this, pretending that there was never anything between us. And who cares about school, and the rat race. We're both expelled now, we've got nothing else but each other. We can start a new life. We can be happy, together."

"But I'm different now. Can't you see? They've sickened me. They've destroyed me. What are you going to do with me now? I'm sick! Are you going to take care of me, feed me, give me pills? Shave my head? I'm dead! Already. You are looking at my corpse."

She wiped her eyes with her pajama sleeves and held her breath in order to stop sobbing. The blue-haired crocodile appeared in the doorway of the asylum and Irina instantly waved at her, putting on a weak smile.

"There's nothing wrong with you. You're beautiful. You're young and sensitive and full of life. One day all this will seem like a bad dream. I will take care of you, yes, I will get you out of here and we'll live, in spite of everyone. We'll play the sonatas together. We'll find a way to make everything work."

Irina leaned forward, picked up a vine twig from the ground, and started breaking it with her shaky hands into smaller and smaller pieces. She refused to look at me even as I bent down and tried to meet her eyes. I wanted to kiss her, to capture in the palm of my hand the tiny clouds of warm breath escaping her mouth.

"I've been thinking about cemeteries a lot lately," she said after a while. "Graves are incredibly peaceful, don't you think? They are houses for people who have been freed from all suffering and sickness. Why worry and struggle when you already know how everything ends? Those who rest in the cemeteries are the truly happy ones, they . . ."

"Irina, stop!" I pleaded and put my arm around her waist. "You are feeling weak, this is the voice of weakness, luring you to the other side. But I know that you'll think differently soon, the mind can play many

chords—minor chords, major chords, seventh, diminished, and augmented chords, it can play loud and quiet, fast and slow, it can build
a climax and then reach catharsis: all you have to do is let it play and
listen to the music without judgment."

"Time is up in ten minutes," announced one of the nurse-guards as
she walked past us, sizing me up suspiciously. I took my hand off Irina's
waist and blew air into it, to warm it up. The sun had hidden behind
a cloud and the yard had become possessed by a cold wind scattering
leaves and vine twigs and inflating the pajamas of the patients.

"You don't understand because you refuse to think about these
things," Irina said. "All our life we strive to find an escape from mortal-
ity and achieve eternity, some kind of eternity, but in truth, the most
perfected eternity has already been allotted to each of us since birth,
am I not right? This eternity is absolute, it knows no sorrow, no words,
no consciousness. Who wants to remember forever, to keep this enormous universe spinning in one's head day after day? We couldn't have
asked for a better reward."

"Irina? Look at me at least once! I will never abandon you again, I
promise!"

"Five minutes, let's go everyone!" came the voice of the nurse-guard.

Irina stood up and headed toward the back entrance. I followed her.
The crocodile, who'd been keeping an eye on us from the window of
her office on the first floor, stepped out into the yard and started walking toward us.

"What did you tell her?" Irina asked.

"That you're my half sister and that your father was a Gypsy who
died after being run over by a tram in front of the Serdika Theater. She
took my ID card."

Irina giggled and I noticed a familiar spark of wickedness in her
eyes. "Well, at least the part about my father being a Gypsy is true."

We walked past the crocodile and entered the building. "Where are
you two going?" the head nurse demanded, tagging along. "No, you
can't go upstairs to your room. Who do you think I am? A signpost?
Don't think that I don't know what's going on between you two."

"Please!" Irina begged her. "Please, he's my brother, they are taking him into the army early. I won't see him for two years!"

"No!" The crocodile was adamant. Irina took a step forward and embraced her unexpectedly.

"You're my family now," Irina squealed over the nurse's shoulder. "Just five minutes and he'll be on his way."

The head nurse kept looking back at us suspiciously as we followed her up the stairs. The first thing I noticed when we reached the third floor and started walking down the long corridor was the horrid smell coming from the bathrooms. The second was that none of the doors had handles. To open or close a door, you had to call one of the nurse-guards.

"I'll come back in five minutes to unlock the door," the head nurse announced, brandishing a door handle from the front pocket of her white apron.

We didn't even wait for the head nurse to recede down the corridor. With her back pressed against the door, to prevent someone from storming in unexpectedly, Irina unbuttoned my shirt and my pants. I unbuttoned her pajama shirt and pushed her pajama bottoms to the floor. I didn't dare ask her what had happened to her lips. She squinted in pain each time we kissed, but she didn't recoil. The old rhythm was upon us again, the six-eight from the Largo in the fifth Bach sonata, the piano and violin telling different stories, speaking in different tongues. But the words weren't important, and neither was the meaning. Gone was the metal bed and the white sheets numbered with red ink and the barred windows and the cracked gray walls and the linoleum floor, and the nurse-guards with door handles in their pockets, and the clamor of the loonies in the backyard, and the wretched poplars lined up alongside the fence. We were back in Chamber Hall No. 2, walking hand-in-hand through Bach's sonatas, passing through adagios and allegros and largos and vivaces without a sense of who we were and who we'd been. We were playing honestly because we'd reached the end. There was no future awaiting us, no past that would keep us apart. For a brief moment, there was only music. Then Irina began to lose ground and slip away, back into the shadow world. She grabbed onto me, desperately, her eyes burning, her fingers frail and bloodless.

"You have to go get my violin," she whispered. "Just go to my place and tell my grandmother that you're going to take me with you. She knows all about you. She'll understand. My mother is still at work, she is out until five, which is good because she'd never let you out of the apartment with the violin. My mother is the one who wants to keep me here. She believes that the doctors will somehow change the way I think. She's sickened me. She has taken away everything that matters to me. God, I hate her! She doesn't care about me, she just wants to control me. If only my father were alive to see what she's done to me. . . . He'd never have let them treat me like this. Hurry now! And don't forget to bring me some clothes, a dress, tights, underwear. And shoes. You're going to help me get out of here, right? You really love me, don't you? We are not going to play games anymore. This time it's for real. Promise?"

"I promise."

"I don't want them to fry my brain again. I'll get ready to go. I can jump the stone wall in the backyard. Just wait for me with the clothes and the violin on the other side of the wall, you can enter the adjacent backyard from an apartment building on August Eleventh Street. You'll have to find out which one. A girl escaped from here last month by jumping the wall, but they caught her a day later. We'll be smarter. You'll take me someplace safe where no one can find us. Now go! Before my mother gets home! I'll come out in an hour. I'll wait for you to give me a sign."

I didn't give it a second thought. Her plan seemed perfect. An hour was exactly how long I needed to run across town to her apartment, get the things from her grandmother, and run back to the asylum. I kissed her and wiped her tears. Then I helped her get dressed and knocked forcefully on the door. We held hands and looked in each other's eyes as we listened to the footsteps of the head nurse growing louder and louder. It made me incredibly sad and angry to look at Irina's shaved head, at her scarred lips, at the thin, indigo-colored veins wreathing her temples, at the black crescent moons under her eyes. Even the violin mark on her neck had faded. What had they done to her?

The nurse inserted the handle and opened the door. I turned around to look at Irina one more time, but I didn't say goodbye. Goodbye sounded too final. And I was coming right back. I followed the nurse down the corridor and then down the stairs. No one was going to stop us. I would beat up the head nurse if I had to; she deserved to get a beating, the way she strutted around swinging her silver door handle, her weapon of power. All the doctors and nurses deserved to be tied up and injected with anesthetics until they turned into stiff plastic dolls. Who gave them the right to lock up my Irina? She was seventeen, for God's sake, she was old enough to choose between life and death, between meaning and nothingness.

Or was she? I slowed down to catch my breath and light a cigarette. I was ten blocks away from the asylum, and as many from the mosque, and I had been running as fast as I could, like I was being chased by the police. Suddenly Irina's plan sounded completely crazy, or naïve at best. Something about the expression on her face, before the head nurse closed the door, made the tips of my fingers numb with fear. How on earth would I be able to convince her grandmother to hand over her granddaughter's violin and a bag of clothes? The whole thing was doomed. What would I say to her grandmother? That I was going to help Irina escape the asylum? She would probably slap me on the face and call the police. And what about Irina's shaved head? They didn't shave people's heads for no reason. We'd be lucky if we made it to Peppy's basement. And then what?

But I couldn't think this way. Ours was a love story, like in the waltzes and the nocturnes. There was going to be a sweet final cadence. We were going to be together. It was the only thing that made sense. Everything else had gone to hell. Our careers, our music, our adolescence. I had an hour to change things. In an hour, Irina and I would start a new life.

I reached Irina's building and ran up to the third floor. Outside the door, I stopped. A terrible premonition gripped me: it couldn't be this easy. I started to shake uncontrollably. I should've escaped with Irina right away. I shouldn't have come for the violin. It was all a trick. Hades was going to get his in the end, again. I shouldn't have turned around. I shouldn't have looked at her face. I should've remembered the legend.

I lit a cigarette, inhaled a few times, and rang the bell. I pressed my ear against the door and listened. All I could hear was a low hum, most likely the refrigerator. Maybe her grandmother wasn't home. I rang the bell again and this time I heard a door opening and closing, then footsteps. I flicked my cigarette onto the upper landing and tried to pull myself together. What was I going to say to her? A bunch of lies, for sure. I had to think of something quick. Something convincing. If I could only look confident, she'd believe me.

The door opened a crack and Irina's grandmother, wearing a black dress and a black cardigan, peeked into the corridor. I realized that I had seen her many times at school. She may have even attended some of my performances.

"You must have the wrong apartment," she said, and tried to close the door.

"I'm Irina's boyfriend," I explained and stepped forward.

The old woman hesitated for a moment and then let me in with a sigh. I followed her to the kitchen and sat on the chair that she pulled out for me. While she busied herself making coffee I looked around the room, trying to memorize all the details: the mustard wall tiles with tiny cream-colored suns, the old stove with a busted oven door, the generic government-made refrigerator with a square handle, the crooked white kitchen cabinets, the enormous Turkish copper coffee grinder from the time of the last sultan, the gilded tsarist cutlass hanging on the wall, the brown linoleum floor, the expandable kitchen table where Irina probably used to sit every night doing her homework and looking out the round window, toward the mosque and the tiled roofs of the old Jewish quarter.

We stirred our Turkish coffees and looked at each other in silence.

How could I lie to her? She had Irina's eyes—a swirl of amber, green, and gray. It occurred to me that she was most certainly the mother of Irina's father. She was a Gypsy.

"How is school?" she asked.

"I was kicked out last month."

"Another rebel. I see. Playing music wasn't enough for you. Studying with the best teachers in the country wasn't what you wanted. There's something rotten about your generation. Always unhappy, always blaming others for your own mistakes. Why couldn't you and Irina just wait for a few years before doing all the things you aren't supposed to? Why couldn't you stay quiet and follow the rules?"

"Listen," I began, clutching the tiny espresso cup. "I will be very honest with you. I usually lie but this is different. I love Irina. I have come to ask for your permission to take her out of the asylum and bring her to my home."

"You don't have a home," she replied with a contemptuous smile. "Don't say big words to this old woman. I know where you come from. I know where you're going. And your path leads far away from here, away from Irina and this city. I can tell you everything, the way it's going to happen. I can free you from your burden, and you know as well as I do that you are burdened, in your soul. Powerful claws have sunk into your heart, and you've lost your ability to see and judge. Here . . ."

She pulled a roll of black thread out of her cardigan, cut a piece about a meter long with her teeth, then wet her thumb and ring finger with saliva and ran the thread between them.

"Take it," she commanded and rubbed the string into the palm of my hand until it resembled a tiny black ball. "Now stretch it out with both hands and make nine knots—four for the four directions, two for the sun and moon, two for the past and the future, and one for Allah."

"I don't believe in any of this," I said.

"But of course you do. That's why you're here. I tried to send you away but you insisted on coming in. Now do as I say. I'm going to burn the knots and release both you and Irina from this trap. You'll be free to choose your own destiny again. Do it!"

I began tying the knots while Irina's grandmother readied a box of matches. I looked at the kitchen clock. It was almost one o'clock. Irina was probably wondering what was taking me so long. I had to get out of here before the old Gypsy turned me into stone.

"Good," she said, taking the string from me and running it between her fingers again. Suddenly her face darkened and her hands began to shake. She held the string in the light coming from the window and ran it slowly between her fingers for the second time. "Are you playing games with this woman?" She was furious. "You didn't tie any knots! Liar! May God punish you for your insolence!"

"I did! I swear I did." I stood up and grabbed the string from her. I looked at it closely and rubbed it between my fingers. She was right. There were no knots. Not a single one. "They have all disappeared! I really did as you asked me. I don't know what happened. They're gone!"

The old woman got up frantically, knocking her chair on the floor, and started pushing me violently toward the door. "You've brought in the devil! Don't you dare touch my Irina! Go away and never come back! You and the violin have taken her soul! What a lively child she was! Look what she's become now! Her boyfriends, and the abortions, you've all ruined her! What good was all that practicing? We shouldn't have ever let her near the violin. Her father had insisted. No one can help us now. No doctors. No violin teachers. Take the dark beast with you and leave us alone!"

"You don't understand!" I shouted at her in the hallway. "It's the mental asylum that is killing her! She is a musician! She can't be anything else! Without her violin, she might as well be dead! You are the ones who have taken her soul and locked it away with the devils in white aprons and syringes! I have to bring her violin back to her and help her get the hell out of that sick place. And you can't stop me with your magic tricks."

"I will call the police!"

I moved her out of my way and started opening all the doors in the apartment. I found Irina's room at the end of the living room, with windows facing an enclosed courtyard. I opened the wardrobe and rummaged through her clothes. A pair of socks, tights, underwear, and a bra. A skirt, a sweater, and a bottle of perfume. The old Gypsy was pulling at me and trying to slap me on the face. I pushed her toward the bed, but she tripped and fell on the floor. I found the violin on top of the dresser. I opened the case, to make sure everything was there, stuffed Irina's clothes in her schoolbag, and headed out the door. I stopped for a moment, contemplating whether I should check on the old woman, to see if she had broken something, but her curses and screams chased me away. I ran down the stairs like a thief. I didn't even close the door to the apartment. At the building entrance I bumped into an old man carrying milk who followed me out on the sidewalk, to watch me run down the street with Irina's violin. As I turned the corner, the memory of Irina's grandmother squirming on the floor faded, and I was filled with the conviction that I was doing the right thing. Irina's mother and grandmother were from a different world. They could never understand Irina's unhappiness, her hopes and dreams. Irina and I were going to be free from the curses, and the stygian symbols, and the doctors, and the teachers, and the puppets who were trying to drag us down. We knew music. We were different. We were always going to be forgiven.

I approached the asylum from the neighboring street, just as Irina had instructed me. It wasn't difficult to find the apartment building whose enclosed court abutted the asylum's backyard wall. I was only half an hour late. I hid the violin case and Irina's bag in a frozen rose-bush and climbed the walnut tree leaning against the tall brick wall. The asylum's yard was empty. I couldn't very well stand on top of the wall and wave my hands, hoping that Irina might see me from somewhere. In fact, I couldn't show myself at all because the nurse-guards were going to call the police. The only thing I could do was stand in the tree, keeping an eye on the asylum's back door, and wait for Irina to appear. She was smart enough to know that she had to come out in the open first.

I waited for an hour, torturing myself with unanswerable questions and paranoid scenarios. What if Irina had managed to come out earlier, when I hadn't been there? What if she'd changed her mind? And what if she was really sick? Wouldn't I hurt her even more?

Another hour passed, and then another. It started to get dark. I'd smoked all my cigarettes, and my toes, fingers, and face had gone numb from the cold. Soon Irina's mother would come home from work and find out what I'd done. Or maybe she'd already found out and had warned the nurse-guards to watch out for me. The police could be looking for me. Stealing a violin was no laughing matter.

I had lost all hope when the asylum's back door opened and Irina came out in her pajamas and white sandals. I immediately jumped on top of the wall and waved at her. I couldn't see her face well from this distance, but the stiffness of her posture made me feel like something had gone very wrong. Why was she just standing there, doing nothing? She looked like an apparition—pale, lifeless, controlled by some hidden force.

"Come on!" I shouted. She still didn't move. The light in the main office came on and a female figure closed the curtains. "Run!" I urged her and sat on top of the wall, preparing to reach down and grab her hand. Irina took a step back and leaned against the door. She was looking up, at the crescent moon risen in the purple-black sky. Presently, what had seemed like a distant murmur grew into a commotion, with three or four voices shouting on top of one another. More lights came on, shadows fleeted past the windows on the second and third floors. The voices were coming closer and closer, I could hear what they were saying. They were looking for Irina. I tried to estimate how long it would take me to jump down, run across the yard to Irina, and then help her climb up the wall. The problem was that once she passed to the other side, I would remain stuck in the asylum. The wall was too high and smooth on the inside for me to climb it in a hurry. Irina was looking at me now, it seemed as if she wanted to say something. She pointed down with her ring finger and then waved at me. Then she walked back into the building and closed the door.

My heart was going to burst. What was this supposed to mean? She had made the same gesture with her finger when the Owl had kicked her out of school. But this was different. Was she telling me that she was staying in the asylum? Was that a goodbye? Or was she trying to tell me to wait longer, until the middle of the night?

I waited. Each minute now seemed to last forever. Half an hour went by during which I contemplated showing up at the front door of the asylum and forcing my way in. Couldn't I take on all the nurse-guards? Suddenly, I was gripped by a terrible suspicion. What if she had been pointing to the world below? I felt like I was going to throw up. I took the violin case and the schoolbag and rushed through the apartment building and onto the street. As I turned right, and then right again, I had the sensation that I was losing consciousness. I couldn't remember what I'd set out to do. I couldn't remember how I'd gotten here. And yet I knew that I had seen all of this before: the row of poplar trees set against the last glow of the sunset, the metal fence, the Soviet-made ambulance with a twisted front bumper and broken stop lights parked outside the asylum, the driver, dressed in fatigues and a Russian fur hat, standing in the cold, smoking and inspecting the tires with his foot.

"What has happened, Comrade?" I asked.

"Just responding to a call," the driver said tersely and stepped away.

"My brother is inside . . . he was dismissed from the army recently . . . he has a long history of epileptic episodes . . . so I was wondering if there's been an accident."

"I wouldn't call it an accident, son. A girl committed suicide. My crew went in but they were too late. The girl's mother is inside now. They've sedated her. It happens every day, especially in the winter, and in the spring, for some reason. Kids should learn to live a simple life, that's what I say. Go sledding. That's what we did when we were kids. We would roll a bunch of cigarettes and go sledding. Simple things, son, nothing fancy."

The driver paused to relight his cigarette, and nodded at the violin case in my hand. "The girl inside was a violinist, too, just like you. At least that's what they said."

I caught myself staring at the open window on the third floor of the asylum. What did it mean? A door. An exit. A threshold guarded by Hecate, the goddess of liminal things, of crossroads, of the space between being and unbecoming. Where were her dogs now?

I paced around the ambulance, fighting an urge to storm into the asylum and demand to see Irina for one last time. Wouldn't they let me kiss her goodbye? Wouldn't they let me hold her hand and whisper things into her ear while she could still hear, while she was still close by?

A bottomless dark hole had opened in the center of my chest, swallowing my heart, my senses, the sky and all the stars. I felt like I was going to disappear any moment, sucked into the primordial nothingness. My body was just a piece of paper flapping in the cosmic wind.

I wandered about town until midnight, the violin case under my arm, crying, kicking trash cans over. Was it all my fault? It was. If I hadn't informed Irina's grandmother of my intention to take Irina out of the asylum, if I hadn't then stolen the violin, which was the most irrational and stupid thing anyone could have ever thought of, Irina would be alive. We would be at Peppy's basement drinking wine. But her mother had rushed to the asylum and ruined everything. I had enabled her to do so. I had forced Irina to choose between her mother and me. And she had chosen revenge. Or maybe I had it all wrong. Maybe I didn't understand Irina at all. Maybe I was just another talentless bastard, whereas Irina, she had been the real thing.

I bought two bottles of rakia from a tavern on Patriarch Square, zigzagged across Seven Saints Park, and sat on the church steps. Would two bottles be enough to stop my heart and take me out of here? I opened the first bottle and started drinking from it in big gulps. At 40 percent, the alcohol burned a pathway through my body and made my eyes sting. I kept drinking. My head, hands, and feet seemed to get bigger with each sip. The sweet vapors were inflating my body like a balloon. Soon I would float away, over streets and rooftops.

The smell of burning candles and frankincense coming from the church soothed me. There was a midnight service going on inside, and

I watched the priest circumnavigate the altar and swing his golden censer and recite prayers from the book. It would be so easy to crawl inside.

But I didn't want to be saved. I just wanted to know if Charon had noted the violin mark burned onto Irina's neck. She was going to be different from the rest, even below. They would recognize that right away.

I opened the second bottle and held it over my mouth. One by one, I buried my memories under the tonic, in the gray, desert fields of the diminished seventh, where the roots of desperation take hold before the final resolution.

Mussorgsky,
"The Hut on Fowl's Legs (Baba Yaga)"

January 23, 1989

I woke up to the sound of boisterous applause and it didn't immediately become clear to me that this wasn't the clapping of the dead welcoming me into the afterlife, but rather, the sound of my own cheeks being fiercely slapped by a corpulent nurse leaning on top of me with all her weight, her knee pushing against my ribs. Notably, the entire room in which I lay—hands tied with belts to a metal bed frame and needled to a bunch of drip feeds—seemed to tilt violently back and forth, and, spotting the oxen ears of the diminutive man lying prostrate on a cot by the window, I was taken by a vision in which the characters in Mussorgsky's *Pictures at an Exhibition* came to life, just as Igor the Swan had predicted the day after my expulsion from school, and I found myself in the Hut on Fowl's Legs, with Baba Yaga, the children eater, softening me up with punches, the Gnome lying on his back, and a multitude of chicks in white shells dancing out in the corridor with syringes and drip feeds in their hands.

"Finally, he opened his eyes!" Baba Yaga yelled and checked my pulse. "What's your name? I need to call your parents. Your name!"

"I don't know," I replied, not because I didn't remember, but because *Konstantin* seemed like an impossible mouthful. I had a hard enough time blinking.

"Oh, great, another one! I have to write a report again, as if I don't have anything else to do!" Baba Yaga bellowed and stomped out of the room. "Doctor Dikov, can I have a minute?" her voice echoed across the corridor. "We have to follow the special procedure. The boy in 4C can't remember his name."

I tried to free my hands from the belts but the only result was feeling the sting of the needles in my veins even worse than before. "Fuck!" I shouted, kicking the blankets off my legs. I was wearing a pair of striped pajama bottoms.

"You're already sounding much better," someone said from the back of the room. I turned my head around and saw a man in his fifties, with long gray hair and a beard, sitting up in bed and scribbling something on a folded newspaper with a pencil. "You gave everyone quite a scare last night. They all thought you were a goner."

"I wanted to go," I said, struggling to enunciate each word. My tongue was the size of a liver. "My girlfriend is dead. I should be dead, too."

The man put down his newspaper and looked at me over the rim of his glasses with a teasing smile. "Are you serious? That sounds like a story to me."

"I swear, it's the truth."

"But can you swear on the life of a person you absolutely can't live without, someone other than your pet dog, or, say, your cactus?"

"I can't think of anyone," I conceded after a while, having gone through the names of all the people I knew in alphabetical order. "I'm not sure there is anyone I absolutely can't live without. Except Irina, but she killed herself."

"So this is serious, in fact! I thought that you had consumed two bottles of rakia and broken one over the head of the priest from Seven Saints Church just for fun! I was obviously mistaken."

"Broken a bottle over the priest's head!" I repeated in astonishment, as a torrent of fresh memories flooded my mind. Now I remembered scuffling with the priest who'd called me a hooligan and swinging a bottle at him. I even remembered grabbing on to his beard and refusing to let go. "I don't want to keep going like this. I hope there's a God so that I can just go to hell and be done with it."

"I see!" the man said excitedly. "Well, I hate to break it to you, but God doesn't exist, or so it was reported. On the other hand, the person whose head you inadvertently damaged isn't really a priest. He's a sleazy apparatchik, and I should know that. I've been around. The problem is that the so-called priest was also admitted to Pirogov Hospital last night, and he is presently relaxing in a room just down the corridor. I am afraid that there will be many important figures in blue uniforms who will be interested in talking to you shortly. In fact, now that I think about it, you'll be better off making an exit as we speak."

"How?" I shouted, enraged. "Fly out the window just as I am, chained to the hospital bed?"

"No, you can ask me, in a polite way, if I mind helping you unbuckle the belts, and then wait to see how I react. Most probably I will say yes."

I looked at my companion in disbelief. What a strange man! Nothing seemed to faze him. "And what are you doing here?"

"Oh, I've been known to visit Pirogov once or twice a month. I rather like it. No one knows what they are doing. If you come here with a broken leg, they break your other one. If you're having a nervous breakdown, they remove your appendix. If you're admitted with alcohol poisoning, they give you morphine."

"Can you please help me unbuckle the belts, then?"

"Well, why not."

The man got up, put on a pair of hospital slippers, and walked over to my bed. First he removed the adhesive bandages securing the needles in place. Then he pulled out the needles quickly and put the bandages back on.

"Do you know how to get out of here?" my savior asked as he unbuckled the belts.

"Not really," I replied and stood up. The room wobbled up and down. The whole hospital was mounted on a pair of chicken legs. Looking out the window where the Gnome lay I saw a government gas station crowded with ambulances and a long line of nurses waiting to buy cigarettes at a dilapidated kiosk. A wide boulevard, its cobblestones gleaming with ice, bisected the outermost city neighborhoods and disappeared in the foothills of the snowcapped mountain to the west. The sun was about to set. How long had I been out? Long enough to have a good portion of my personality erased completely. I felt like a beginner. I could make new mistakes, I could fail again. I hadn't felt like that since I'd started playing the piano.

"Hurry up!" the man called from the door. "Wait! The head nurse is talking to someone."

He looked me up and down, as if he was trying to determine if I were fit to take on a dangerous assignment. "So what's your story? Divorced parents? A rosy childhood fucked up by domestic tourism?"

"No, I'm just a musician."

"Ah, much worse. Much, much worse. OK, go!"

We started walking down the corridor, pushing our way past stretchers and wheelchairs and fat nurses and patients tottering in and out of the bathrooms. Everything stank of rubbing alcohol, iodine, and soured bandages. We'd almost reached the staircase when I suddenly remembered Irina's violin.

"What's the matter?"

"I can't leave without my violin. I just can't!"

"Ay, ay!" my accomplice exclaimed, stroking his beard. "Lots of obstacles. Let's go back, then. We'll check Doctor Dikov's office."

It was a miracle that Baba Yaga didn't see us as she left the nurse's station and rushed into 4B, across the corridor. There was a huge line of patients waiting outside the doctor's office. Unperturbed, my accomplice went straight for the door and walked in without knocking.

"I am sorry to interrupt your exam, doctor, but I'm . . . Ah, here it is. Our Chopin recital starts in ten minutes, we have to rehearse! I hope you will join us in the cancer ward on the fourth floor."

The patients waiting in the corridor stared at the violin case with reverence. They, too, probably wanted to attend the recital.

"How did I do?" my accomplice asked, smiling.

"Chopin never wrote anything for the violin."

"Argh! Now we're in real trouble!"

He sped up just as Baba Yaga was leaving 4B.

"Someone stop them!" she shouted behind us. "They aren't allowed to leave the premises!"

Immediately, two of Mussorgsky's chicks in white shells blocked the doors to the staircase, determined to stop us. Without missing a beat, my accomplice grabbed an abandoned stretcher and charged at them at top speed. Realizing that they were dealing with a madman, the nurses stepped aside, while my accomplice blasted through the folding doors, using the stretcher as a battering ram, and plummeted down the stairs in a pandemonium of twisted metal. I followed close behind, tripping over the large round metal containers with syringes and ampoules that had flown out of the tray at the bottom of the stretcher.

"What about our clothes?" I asked as we reached the first floor.

"We'll get new ones!" my accomplice announced, now walking calmly, as if he and I were going to get some coffee.

"From where?"

"From the wardrobe, of course!"

He opened the door to a room with a sign that read "LAB" and, after seeing that it was empty, walked in. I saw him rummaging through the small wardrobe behind the door. Two pairs of trousers and two winter jackets: we were all set. He started taking the top of his pajamas off, but at that moment another door inside the room opened and out came two men in green, carrying vials and folders. Without waiting for further instructions I dashed in the direction of the main exit.

"The other way!" my accomplice shouted.

I sprinted back, evading the outstretched hand of one of the laboratory workers, and started running through a maze of corridors. My accomplice seemed to know exactly where he was going. Down a flight of stairs, into a tunnel, and then out through a back door. We tore through the courtyard, crossed a street, and snuck into the first apartment building that came in sight. We changed silently and then threw the pajamas into the basement.

"What's your name?" the man asked me, presently wearing a gray wool coat, black trousers, and white hospital slippers.

"Konstantin," I replied, zipping up my new brown windbreaker.

"Johnny," he announced, extending his hand. "I live below the ground."

Mussorgsky,
"Catacombs"

October 10, 1989

I lay with my back against the warm pipe, staring at the dim light-bulb caged in wire mesh on the ceiling. The soles of my feet pointed toward the darkness, my head toward the exit shaft. Aboveground, kids in fall jackets chased one another around the colossal obelisk at the center of Army Park, supervised by a small contingent of bronze Soviet soldiers leaping in the air with their revolvers and machine guns and tin flags. Here, belowground, millions of gallons of pressurized hot water rushed through two enormous pipes, each wide enough to sleep two people, creating an endless concerto of sighs, whistles, cries, flute glissandos, bass strumming, and even violins, with an occasional solo on timpani. Next to me, sitting cross-legged on his blanket, Johnny was working on a crossword in an old issue of the *Fatherland Front*. His real name, of course, wasn't Johnny. There wasn't a single person named Johnny in the whole damn country. He occupied the top heating pipe, not far from the entrance to the catacombs, and was in charge of lending the beat-up, lever-operated handcar to those who wanted to traverse the dark railroads on wheels. I enjoyed sitting beside him and watching him act as some sort of self-styled Charon, a high priest of the catacombs. Johnny desperately needed an audience, and I was a talented listener. He liked introducing me to his friends as the Musician. He found it kind of exotic. They hadn't had a musician down here before. Johnny, for his part, was the Painter. Everyone in the catacombs carried the label of their former occupation. There was a toothless philosopher who lived toward the end of the lighted section, where the railroad forked into two pitch-black tunnels. An engineer slept on the bottom pipe, right by the entrance. Then there were the Actor, the Nurse, the Party Whore, the Chemist, and the Archaeologists, a group of drunken former colleagues, two men and a woman, who walked all day and all night in search of another archaeologist, nicknamed Imperator Nicephorus. There were many other people in the catacombs, some of them looking for a place to crash or to party, others just visiting. Once in a while I saw a familiar face, a girl from the English High School, a guy I had seen at a party. Peppy the Thief showed up, too, at times accompanied by the evil twins. Every now and then I took a girl for a ride on the handcar and we wandered off into the darkness, lighting the way with our cigarettes.

I still had Irina's violin, but my leather bag with my Chopin études, scherzos, ballades, and sonatas was lost forever. I'd left it at Pirogov when I escaped from the alcoholics ward back in January. I had spent the spring and summer here, and now it was cold again.

The subterranean maze under Sofia was vast. Theoretically, one could reach any point in the city by navigating the tunnels of the central heating system, the sewers, and the vast underground passageways connecting the main government offices to the nuclear shelters. Johnny, for example, claimed that he'd even penetrated the mausoleum a couple of times, via the evacuation tunnel that passed underneath it. I believed him. I also believed that he'd left an empty beer bottle by the coffin of the Mummy—a claim that was still widely disputed. In his version of the Trojan War, the beautiful Helen was long dead, stuffed with cotton and placed in the mausoleum in the center of the city; the Achaeans were still fighting some sort of war but they had forgotten why and with whom; the forces of King Priam were scattered underground, waiting for the gods to switch sides.

"Do you know what's the weirdest thing?" he asked me, without lifting his eyes from the crossword.

"What?"

"The weirdest thing is that, ultimately, every person, even the greatest dictator or the most vicious criminal, is very likable, if not absolutely adorable. No, no: they are! They could be beating you on the back with metal rods and you still wouldn't be able to resist liking them. Or perhaps that's something inherent in us. Maybe we are all just hardwired to like others no matter what. We like our enemies, we like the wretched and the ugly, we even like our own mothers! It's rather frustrating, this predicament. Oh no, it is! This is up your alley: a Hungarian composer, six letters."

"Bartók."

"Excellent. Here comes a group of tourists. They look like the curious type, and I'm not in the mood to answer questions."

Four high school students, two boys and two girls, in uniforms, approached the handcar and examined its giant lever, which functioned both as a manual accelerator, when pushed up and down with great force, and a brake, when its movement was resisted. It took them a while before they noticed Johnny and me sitting on the top pipe.

"Urgent travel or recreation?" Johnny bellowed in his gravely voice.

"Recreation," one of the boys replied, finding the question rather amusing.

"Then beat it," Johnny commanded. "We are closed on Fridays. And you really shouldn't come down here during school hours, your mommies wouldn't approve. I bet you heard someone talking about the mysterious shaft door accessible through the decrepit metal cabin across from the Ministry of Sports where the park janitors store shovels and brooms and dustbins. So you decided to find it and check out what's going on underground. Well, you've ended up in the wrong place. Now go back to school."

"Who says you own the handcar?" asked one of the girls, a dark beauty who suddenly reminded me of Irina and the way she used to glance at me while playing the Bach sonatas.

"Well, everyone! You are free to go on and explore the catacombs on foot, but be warned, there are skeletons and freaks and Achaeans and a lot of unpleasant things that could shake your faith in reality or even kill you. Enter at your own risk. And don't scream for help when you get lost in the dark. I have things to do today."

The four students started walking toward the dark tunnels, teasing one another and giggling, but when they saw the Philosopher emerging into the light after a trip to the sewers below, wearing nothing but a pair of underwear and a long military coat, smoking and mumbling indecipherable nonsense, they turned around and rushed silently back to the exit shaft. Johnny smirked. "Egyptian president with six letters. Nationalized the Suez . . . Nasser."

Thank God, Johnny never lectured me about the dangers of running away from home and living with bums. The last thing I needed was someone who wanted to save me from ruin. I was just fine where I was. Soon I would be eighteen. At eighteen you ought to have seen everything. What else was there to do?

I'd spent my first months in the catacombs in a stupor, part of me wanting to stop living, part of me believing it had all been a bad dream and that one day I would wake up and find myself back at home, or in room 42, or in one of the practice rooms in the attic, rehearsing for my next performance. At times I even thought that Ladybug would change her mind and return to Sofia to dig Vadim and me out of the dirt and put us on the right path.

That was then. I knew now that I would never play again. It was over. No one was going to come and save me. No one cared. I didn't care either. The truth was, I was much happier here, away from the people who waved the wands of power, away from my rivals and the workshops that manufactured bright futures.

Still, I spent much of my time studying the score of Mussorgsky's *Pictures at an Exhibition* that I had stolen from the National Library after my visit to the music school back in May. I had looked at the sixteen pieces for so long, I felt that if I sat at a piano, I would play the entire cycle by heart.

What time was it? It was evening. The catacombs had begun to fill up with visitors. The pipes hissed and moaned, the lightbulbs flickered, the air smelled of wet cement, fiberglass, and piss. Soon Peppy the Thief would come by with the twins and a bottle of homemade rakia and we would get positively drunk; Johnny, too, he couldn't fall asleep sober. A group of students from the Russian High School had taken the handcar and Johnny was worried that we'd have to go looking for it. The Philosopher had put on a pair of pants and a jacket and was arguing with the three archaeologists about the meaning of historical truth. "History doesn't exist!" he was shouting, his hands shaking, his emaciated legs moving back and forth as if he were balancing on a tightrope. I was lying down with Mussorgsky in my hands, trying not to think about Irina. But what else was there to think about? I stared hard at the pauses and the crescendos and the abbreviated Italian words and the beams overburdened with notes, flats and sharps and naturals, like clusters of grapes; I even added up the time values of all the notes in each bar to make sure that the Russian master hadn't made a mistake . . . Despite all my tricks, my mind wandered aboveground, toward Tsar Shishman Street and the little park between Parliament and the National Academy of Art, and then farther, toward Doctors' Garden and the music school, with its ornate metal gates and the marble fountain in the courtyard. I read the names of the deceased posted on the trees. Zimova's necrology was the biggest one of all, with the longest list of adjectives and mourners. People were rushing into the building, the eight o'clock concert in Chamber Hall No. 1 was going to start any minute. Igor's students were going to perform a series of short chamber pieces, and then, at ten, some girl studying with Kurtswine was going to play Scriabin. But the ground floor was not the place to be. The important events happened upstairs, in the dark hallways and empty classrooms, in the library, the bathrooms, the secret passageways in the attic. It was there that those possessed by music and passion sought refuge. I had felt safe there, embraced by Erebus, protected by the divine harmonic spheres, guided by the voice of a lone violin, pacified by the immaculate counterpoint of a fugue. It had been my sanctuary. Then everything had changed. After my expulsion and Irina's suicide, I had lost the temperament, the luciferous spark that made my playing special.

"Are you asleep?" Johnny's voice seemed to come from far away, from the darkness at the end of the tunnel.

"I guess," I said. "These days I wait all night to fall asleep, and then in the morning I wake up and wonder if I've really slept or just pretended."

"I'm the same, except that tonight I can't even pretend to be asleep. My kidneys are killing me. Your friend never came with the twins. They're dangerous, these girls."

I suddenly became aware of all the sounds in the catacombs: the fierce coughing of the Philosopher, a bottle breaking on the tracks, pressurized steam escaping from a fissure in one of the pipes, water running down a wall. I sat up and looked at Johnny wriggling in pain on his mattress. His kidneys had been badly damaged from the numerous beatings he'd received at the hands of the police, for transgressions as minor as having long hair, wearing jeans, and telling loud jokes. Back in the day, he'd taught at the National Academy of Art.

"Say, you feel like taking a ride in the handcar?" Johnny climbed down onto the lower pipe and then slid to the ground. "I can show you a few things off the beaten track. Special things. But you have to promise you're not going to take your friends there. It's probably around two o'clock in the morning. We'd be back at around six. What do you think?"

Johnny sat at the front, holding a rusty metal rod and a flashlight. I stood at the very back, the violin case strapped to my shoulder, pushing the large lever up and down like a seesaw. First we headed east, toward the National Library, then we took a branch line veering left and started going north, in the direction of the mausoleum. The underground channels were warm, dark, and quiet. Occasionally we spotted a rat or an empty wine bottle or a discarded blanket in the shape of a person. As we approached a section of the tracks that, according to Johnny, was right below Rakovski Street, the rails disappeared under a few inches of water and we began gliding over an opaque river of silver. Wisps of steam floated on its surface, filling the air with the distinct smell of sulfur sweetened by faint traces of something earthy and musky. Was this the river that I'd felt flowing beneath the ground while I'd practiced Chopin's second ballade up in the attic for hours and hours? And who was Johnny anyway? What if he was actually the fateful boatman who ferried the souls of the expired beyond memory's sandy, asphodel-strewn shores? Sitting at the bow, his long gray hair spilling out of the hood of his brown capote, saying nothing, never looking back, he was the last one who remembered. Would he listen if I played the violin for him? Would he bring me to the other side, just as he had brought Orpheus before? I could feel Irina's presence. She was here and she wanted her violin back.

As we sailed farther, water began flooding into the hull, soaking my boots and socks, but I didn't stop rowing; on the contrary, I pulled the oars harder and harder, welcoming the river's warm caress, yearning to be healed by its silver substance. I wanted to immerse myself in it completely, until all stains, colors, and sounds had dissolved and washed away. The memory of the self, the supreme tyrant, would fade, too, and in its place a scentless white flower would grow to mark the passing of time. To forget—there has never been a simpler cure. I was ready to surrender everything, the most precious memories first, for they hurt the most. I would hand over the six Bach sonatas for violin and piano across whose mystical pathways I had walked, hand in hand, with Irina. I would let go of the Parisian carousel that spins around and around in the fourth Chopin nocturne, wrapped in a whirlwind of colors, faces, and caramelized strands of light. I would give up the wisdom in the ninth prelude, in E major, the hard-won wisdom that comes at the end of a sleepless night, right before sunrise; the wisdom derived from the exhaustion of all possibilities, all questions, all answers. I'd shake off the love arrows, heartaches, and sweetness of a first kiss stored in the Fantaisie-Impromptu; I'd pluck out the feathers of the big bird flying in the third scherzo. In the end I would rush into the arms of the mother of shadows, naked, emptied, purified, ready to receive a new name and a new face.

We rowed past an ancient arc, with what appeared to be bits of Roman columns stamped into the clay, and then came upon an intersection where the tunnels split into two and the walls were overgrown with moss. Tree roots hung from the ceiling like parched hands reaching for water. Johnny signaled for me to stop, then plunged his long metal rod into the river, to slide the compromise joint to the left.

First stop: the nuclear shelter below the Budapest restaurant, on Rakovski Street. We moored outside a metal ladder and climbed up to the shelter's armored oval door, which was unlocked. A red emergency light guided us to the common room, a narrow corridor furnished with chairs, tables, a couch, and two bookshelves displaying the usual titles: *A Hero of Our Time, Mother, Dead Souls, How the Steel Was Tempered,* as well as a collection of chess books on openings and tactics. It was to be expected. When the Americans dropped their delicately wrapped neon presents on our city, we'd descend below the earth to play chess. We'd all become grandmasters. We'd beat them with our infallible logic.

Johnny went into the storage room and returned promptly with two containers of canned fish and a bag of crackers. We ate in silence, then smoked. It occurred to me that we might be the first people to seek refuge in these rooms put aside for the end of the world. We were just a bit early. The end of the race of liars had been carefully orchestrated. The score had already been written. The musicians had taken their places. Now the conductor had to give us the cue.

We went back to our boat and resumed rowing down the subterranean river. When the river ended, we continued on wheels. When the rails ended, we continued on foot. Johnny refused to tell me where we were going. It was a surprise. When we finally reached an exit shaft and climbed the ladder to a flimsy wooden door, I was certain that we had arrived at the mausoleum. Instead, I found myself in a large mirrored room filled with shoes. The spotlights on top of the National

Palace of Culture, across the street, shone through the floor-to-ceiling window, illuminating all the mirrors and filling the store with reflected halos.

"What are we doing here?" I asked Johnny, who had slumped into a chair and was smoking.

"But, of course, we've come to try on shoes!" he said and threw a pair of sneakers my way.

It was strange, trying on new shoes at five o'clock in the morning with oblivious policemen walking past the store. We were in the very center of town and yet, in a way, we were still in the catacombs. The store was locked from the outside. We could exit only through the shaft leading underground.

Chopin,
Étude in C Minor, op. 25, no. 12

November 27, 1989

I drifted with the crowd toward the university. The students had brought all the desks out onto the street and built an enormous barricade, blocking traffic and preventing the armored vehicles packed with soldiers from moving beyond Parliament Square. Students armed with metal rods, bottles, and legs from broken chairs guarded the small makeshift entrance into the barricaded grounds, letting in only those they deemed fit. People suspected of being "red trash," especially the elderly, were shoved away and pelted with stones. Passing through the entrance, I stopped to warm myself at one of the numerous textbook pyres blazing outside the university courtyard. I picked up a few tomes of *Scientific Communism* parts I and II lying on the ground and threw them into the flames. It was the end of November and it was quite cold, although there was no snow. The red midget had been deposed following a fissure in the Iron Curtain that had started in East Germany. The entire city had ground to a halt. Classes had been suspended, hospitals closed, government offices and factories abandoned, shops looted. Bus and tram drivers had walked away, leaving their vehicles in the middle of the road. Gas stations had run out of gas, cars had been flipped over onto the sidewalks, government Volgas had been burned and vandalized. Poets and artists had erected tents in front of the mausoleum and gone on a hunger strike. The police were busy beating people up. The army was waiting for further instructions from the new red midget in charge of everything. The air smelled of burning leaves and tear gas. A few guys from the conservatory—a bass player, a saxophonist, and a drummer—were playing jazz between the two patinated lion statues at the top of the university steps. I still carried Irina's violin everywhere I went.

I had started practicing again, at the music school when there was no one around, and at home whenever I crashed there. Practicing the études gave me something to do. I had no goals or desires. I simply liked playing. The ten months I'd spent in the catacombs in the company of Johnny had been a kind of sanatorium for me—the hot steam escaping the pipes had pacified my nightmares; the quiet journeys through the tunnels in the handcar had taught me much about dead ends and intersections. And now the tallest midget had been brought down, the streets were filled with raging young people, and I couldn't help thinking that there was something cruel about the way big lies ended. They didn't necessarily collide with the truth, but rather imploded on themselves, dragging along everyone they'd ensnared.

It was all a bit too late. Irina was dead. She and I had already had our uprising. We had shouted at the puppets and burned books; we had thrown stones at the Volgas; we had mocked the false banners and manifestos; we'd challenged the puppets' order and accepted our punishment; we'd given up the thing we'd cherished more than ourselves.

And then, Irina had gone further than me. She had gone further than anyone else. She had killed the school principal and exited the stage through the back door. To think that she was safe in death, that she had been taken out of time and preserved in perpetuity the way she'd been the moment before the end—that was the secret, even forbidden, analgesic that kept mourners away from the tempting shore of the silvered river. Death as intended silence, an eternal *pausa* resounding with the overtones of the last return to the tonic and the heartbeat whisper of the final cadenza.

I stepped away from the fire and dived into the crowd. It was ten past twelve. One had to keep track of time even at the end of the world. There was still one thing left for me to do. Something I should've done almost a year earlier. It wasn't going to take long. Half an hour at the most. Then I was off to the mosque, where I was meeting Iliya for Turkish coffee at one. Iliya was taking in the seismic activity with a smile, but also with a great degree of caution. He wasn't planning to celebrate anytime soon. He was standing at the periphery, watching patiently as events unfolded. Always the agnostic, he warned me against believing too quickly in the new versions of history. *Upheavals breed fools. Cataclysms breed false prophets.*

I heard a loud wheezing sound and then something hit me in the back. I fell to the ground, assuming I'd been shot. The smoke that engulfed me explained everything: I'd been hit by a tear gas canister. Someone handed me a gas mask, probably looted from a nuclear shelter, and I put it on quickly, grateful for having attended all those military drills at school. I crawled away from the source of the smoke, crying and salivating, then got up and ran, together with the throng of students, to avoid being crushed.

It was a war zone. The police and the students were fighting it out for real now, there were automatic weapons being fired nearby, boys were lying on the ground with bloodied faces. And in the midst of all this, rising from the yellow smoke like a mythical figure, dressed in his gray proletarian suit, holding his leather case under one arm and waving his pointer in the other, Negodnik, my old history teacher, was beseeching the students to come to their senses.

"I'll tell you what's a real revolution!" he was shouting between convulsions of severe choking and coughing, as he balanced on top of a milk crate. "Spartacus, the Thracian gladiator, who in 73 B.C. led an army of slaves against their oppressors—that's a real revolution! The storming of the Bastille and the abolishment of feudalism in 1789— that's a real revolution! The dictatorship of the proletariat and the end of exploitation—that's a real revolution! No one again will take from the poor and give to the rich! We won't allow the lords of greed to come and steal our treasures! Where else in the world do you have equality? Where else in the world do you have a real brotherhood?"

No one was paying any attention to him but me. It was incredible how suddenly our roles had switched. Now it was us who were teaching him history, and he was the reluctant student who just couldn't learn his dates and place-names. I stood in front of him and took my gas mask off. I wanted him to see me. I wanted him to remember. But he didn't. He couldn't. He looked through me as if he'd never seen me before.

Was that surprising? Of course not. There was time within time, a recurrent present within the past, and those who had lost their souls would lose their souls again, and those who had lied would be cursed again, and those who had been too weak to love would turn into shadows just as before. Hell wasn't a distant land that awaited us; it was a place right around the corner to which we returned again and again in order to rehearse our redemption.

The history teacher had gone back. He was back in room 53 of the music school, standing against a political map of the world and imploring his tenth graders to defend the oppressed and the poor. It was time for all of us to go back to the beginning, to the granite sky and the red dreams of the fat apparatchiks, to the sedate blinking of the television sets, to the ruby glow of the bronze soldiers guarding public order, to the flags and the portraits of the Soviet midgets, to the beat of the marching puppets, to the dark hallways of the Sofia Music School for the Gifted. Igor the Swan was already crossing Seven Saints Square, with the score of Bach's sonatas under his arm; the Owl was sitting in a tram and filling her fountain pen, given to her by Tovarich Andropov, with black ink; Ladybug was leaving her husband and newborn son and was returning home, to her mother and sister, her cats, and her old pianos; Pirozhkin, the colonel, was inserting live bullets into his government-sanctioned 9 mm Makarov, having written a farewell letter to his wife and placed his medals in a wooden box: he was taking a shortcut; Bankoff was in Doctors' Garden, sizing up the young girls in uniforms walking past him; Alexander was smoking in the *pushkom,* waiting for everyone else to turn up.

As for me, I was heading toward Serdika Street, via the Levski Monument, Ladybug's old house, and the Mathematics High School. The crumbling buildings of the oldest quarter, colored in varying shades of washed-out pink and orange, greeted me with their petite balconies and Doric columns and loosened brick arches and feathered metal railings. Framing the inner courtyards with my fingers, I snapped sepia stills from a dead, long-deserted city: oaks and walnuts, still wearing their autumn finery, guarded the vestiges of old walls; thick, knitted creepers camouflaged broken windows, boarded-up doors, and mossy wells; rusted cars, leviathan bolts, and mysterious machines protruded from the earth like the skeletons of extinct creatures; unraveled carpets, curtains, and shoes hung from tree branches and twisted antennas, in testimony to some forgotten cataclysm. But the city wasn't at all dead. Away from the clamor and smoke of the barricades, people sat in their living rooms, behind shelves of books and old records, rereading their Dostoyevsky, listening to the Brandenburg concertos, drinking their cold coffees, and dutifully inhaling the relentless upwelling of dust left over from the Russians, the Germans, and the Ottomans, from the Crusaders, from Constantine's armies and the Thracian gods, dust from Olympus and the sandy Lethean shores.

The messianic refrain at the heart of the C-major respite in the twelfth étude, where both hands move in opposite directions while keeping the melody in the middle intact, like a bowl of water floating in the eye of a storm, rang in my mind with the power of Jupiterian bells, *mi-re-fa-mi,* the faithful echo an octave above confirming the final verdict, pressing the crystals of the present into immutable diamonds. In every situation, even during the loudest revolution, one could hear the letters being etched into the wheel of time, the drone of which continues without us.

When I reached Serdika Street, I walked up to the third floor of apartment building number 12 and put my ear against the door marked "Karabashevi." They were inside. I laid the violin case on the floor and rang the bell. Then I ran downstairs, avoiding the stubborn gaze of the young girl staring at me from the necrologies thumbtacked onto every door and every wall.

ACKNOWLEDGMENTS

Thanks to Rob McQuilkin, Wylie O'Sullivan, Alessandra Bastagli, and everyone at Free Press. My thanks also to my friends and family who were there for me.

ABOUT THE AUTHOR

NIKOLAI GROZNI began training as a classical pianist at age four, and won his first major award in Salerno, Italy, at the age of ten. Grozni's acclaimed memoir, *Turtle Feet,* follows his four years spent as a Buddhist monk studying at the Institute of Buddhist Dialectics in Dharamsala, and later at a monastery in southern India. Grozni holds an MFA in creative writing from Brown University. He lives with his wife and their children in France.